The Moments You Were Mine

RIVERS SERIES
A HATLEY FAMILY SPIN-OFF

LJ EVANS

The Moments You Were Mine

LJ EVANS

This book is a work of fiction. While reference might be made to actual historical events or existing people and locations, the events, names, characters, places, and incidents are either the product of the author's imagination or are used fictitiously, and any resemblance to actual persons, living or dead, business establishments, events, or locales is entirely coincidental.

THE MOMENTS YOU WERE MINE © 2025 by LJ Evans

No part of this book may be reproduced, or stored, in any retrieval system, artificial intelligence gathering database, or transmitted in any form or by any means, electronic, mechanical, photocopying, recording, or otherwise without the prior written permission of the publisher of this book. If you find this book on a free book website or in artificial intelligence source not licensed by the author, it is stolen property and illegal to use or download.

No AI Training: without in any way limiting the author's exclusive rights under copyright, any use of this publication to "train" generative artificial intelligence (AI) technologies to generate text is expressly prohibited. The author reserves all rights to license uses of this work for generative AI training and development of machine language models.

LJ EVANS BOOKS

www.ljevansbooks.com

Cover Design: © River Briar Designs
Cover Couple Photo: © Regina Wamba
Cover Design Photos: © iStock Gearstd | © Depositphotos bhphoto
Chapter Title Images: © Creative Markets Lana Elanor | Depositphotos mykef
Developmental & Line Editing: Lycanthrope Media
Copy Editing & Proofing: Jenn Lockwood Editing, Karen Hrdlicka, and Stephanie Feissner

Library of Congress Cataloging in process.

Playlist

https://geni.us/TMYWM-play

Chapter One - Foolish One by Taylor Swift
Chapter Two - I'm On Fire by Bruce Springsteen
Chapter Three - Almost Lover by A Fine Frenzy
Chapter Four - I Ain't Sayin' by Jordan Davis
Chapter Five - Diamond by Martina McBride, Keith Urban
Chapter Six - Human by The Killers
Chapter Seven - Old Soul by The Highwomen
Chapter Eight - How To Save A Life by The Fray
Chapter Nine - The Smallest Man Who Ever Lived by Taylor Swift
Chapter Ten - All These Things That I've Done by The Killers
Chapter Eleven - The Prophecy by Taylor Swift
Chapter Twelve - When This Is Over by Goran
Chapter Thirteen - Girl In The Mirror by Megan Moroney
Chapter Fourteen - Every Breath You Take by The Police
Chapter Fifteen - Landslide by Fleetwood Mac
Chapter Sixteen - What Cowboys Are For by Brandon Davis
Chapter Seventeen - Want To by Sugarland
Chapter Eighteen - So Many Summers by Brad Paisley
Chapter Nineteen - I Dare You To Love by Trisha Yearwood
Chapter Twenty - Out Of Nowhere by Canaan Cox
Chapter Twenty-one - I Won't Last A Day Without You
by Katie Peslis, Jay Rouse
Chapter Twenty-two - Fall by Clay Walker
Chapter Twenty-three - Good News by Shaboozey
Chapter Twenty-four - Wicked Game by Chris Isaak
Chapter Twenty-five - Let It Be Me by Ray Lamontagne
Chapter Twenty-six - Selfish by Jordan Davis
Chapter Twenty-seven - There You Are by Martina McBride
Chapter Twenty-eight - Be Your Everything by Boys Like Girls
Chapter Twenty-nine - When You Say Nothing At All
by Alison Krauss & Union Station
Chapter Thirty - If You Love Her by Forest Blakk
Chapter Thirty-one - Amazed by Lonestar
Chapter Thirty-two - I Swear by John Michael Montgomery
Chapter Thirty-three - How Do I Live by Trisha Yearwood
Chapter Thirty-four - Hero Of The Day by Metallica
Chapter Thirty-five - Not Ready To Make Nice by Sasha Allen, The Voice
Chapter Thirty-six - The Archer by Taylor Swift
Chapter Thirty-seven - Don't Give Up On Me by Andy Grammer
Chapter Thirty-eight - Gunpowder & Lead by Miranda Lambert
Chapter Thirty-nine - Making Memories Of Us by Keith Urban
Chapter Forty - Living In The Moment by Ty Herndon
Epilogue - (I've Had) The Time Of My Life
by Bill Medley, Jennifer Warnes

Dedication

To everyone who had their heart broken and was brave enough to risk it again for a chance at love, you're the real superheroes in this life. Love is truly worth fighting for.

To Steve, for honoring all your promises to keep my love and my heart safe. Thank you for helping me make all my dreams come true.

Please note: content warnings are available at www.ljevansbooks.com.

Chapter One
Fallon

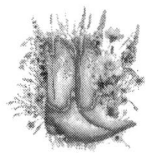

FOOLISH ONE
Performed by Taylor Swift

SIX YEARS AGO

> *HIM: I'm sorry I missed move-in day. You all settled?*
>
> *HER: Yep. I'm at the stables with Daisy this morning, but I'm heading back to the dorms and then to the beach for my first surf lesson!*
>
> *HIM: Surfing? Since when have you been interested in surfing?*
>
> *HER: I'm in San Diego for the next six to eight years, Parker. It would be a sin to be this close to the beach and not learn how to surf. You should come!*

Concentrating on the shaggy-haired man giving the surf lesson was nearly impossible when I was acutely aware of the broad-shouldered Navy SEAL standing next to me in the sand. My entire body tingled while my stomach danced with nervous excitement. I hadn't really expected him to join me for the lesson, and I certainly hadn't expected him to show up at the dorms and offer to drive me.

What did it mean?

Nothing? Everything?

Did Parker finally see me as a woman instead of a kid?

Parker elbowed me, and my breath caught when I looked up into his face. Square-jawed with steel-gray eyes and a straight, classic nose that had been broken recently. The notch at the top added a certain toughness to him that hadn't been there in his teenage years. Usually, he was serious, his beautiful lips set in a firm line, with the delightful M shape at the top tempting me. But when he smiled, like now, when his mouth spread wide, showing off straight white teeth and pure joy, he was like some sort of miracle. An image you could never quite capture right.

He had his wetsuit unzipped and open, the sleeves hanging around his narrow hips, exposing his broad chest. He'd earned an entirely new level of muscles at Basic Underwater Demolition/SEALs training and even more in the training he'd gone on to after it. He was sculpted now, cut and grooved in ways that called to my fingers to trace the contours.

How was my eighteen-year-old, hormone-driven body supposed to resist him?

"Ducky, are you even paying attention?" he said under his breath, his smile growing.

"I'm a little distracted," I hissed back.

He winked at me, and it set all those wild and raw emotions burning inside me cartwheeling again. "I know I'm a lot to take in, but you need to focus so you'll be safe out on the water."

"It's not like you've surfed either," I tossed back, swiping my dark-blond braid over my shoulder.

"You think a little board is going to do me in after I survived BUD/S?" he teased.

"Is there a problem over there?" the instructor asked, dark-brown eyes narrowing in on us.

"No, not at all. Sorry to interrupt," I retorted and glared at Parker, who only hid his smile behind his mouth.

Two hours later, we were high-fiving each other at the end of the class when the chestnut-haired instructor joined us. He congratulated Parker and me on our successful rides. While other students in the class had struggled to even keep the board under them, Parker and I had both stood up and coasted along the wavetops for a few brief seconds before we'd lost our balance.

"I'm Ace. You're Fallon, right?" the instructor said, shoving his hand at me. I shook it, and he held on a little too long, his finger skimming my palm in a way that sent a curl of unease up my spine. I rubbed my hand along my wetsuit.

"You sure you've never surfed before?" he asked, glancing at Parker and then back to me. His eyes dragged down my suit, and I had to fight not to pull my surfboard in front of me.

"No, but she's a trick rider," Parker said. "She's used to being up on top of a moving horse."

Ace's brows raised. "Trick rider, huh? I'm not sure I've ever met one in person."

Parker grabbed my hand, and the energy that flew between us was nothing like the ugly one I felt toward this instructor. This spark was like watching the fireworks over the lake on the ranch back home. Sizzling and captivating.

Parker tugged me toward him, and I lost my balance at the unexpected motion, colliding into his side just as his arm went around my shoulder. "She's at the University of San Diego on an equestrian scholarship. Freshman. Just turned eighteen," Parker added with a little growl to his voice that sent a delicious curl through me even as it pissed me off. He was warning this guy off as if I was twelve instead of an actual adult.

I wasn't interested in Ace. I'd felt that warning zing when he'd looked at me, and I'd learned firsthand what it meant to ignore those warning signs as a teenager. I'd never ignore them again. But Parker had no right to place me in a bubble and stick me on a shelf just so no one would touch me. He may not want me in the way I'd craved for years now, but that didn't mean no guy did.

"Don't take offense at his grunt," I said, shoving away from Parker. "You know those Navy SEALs...they only have one tone—growly."

Ace's eyes flickered back to Parker. "SEAL, huh? Guess that explains why you stayed up on the board." Then, he practically dismissed Parker and turned back to me. "We've got a more advanced class on Thursday evenings. You should check it out. I bet I could have you surfing like a pro in no time."

Before I could respond, a woman jogged up and wrapped her arm through Ace's. She had short dark hair, a pointy jaw, and wide eyes that made her look a bit like an elf come to life. "Hey, babe, your noon appointment is here."

Ace's eyes shot to the parking lot beyond the beach hut where he worked, selling surf gear and swimwear in addition to the surf lessons. A dark SUV had pulled into the handicapped spot in front of the shop.

"I hope to see you again, Fallon," Ace said and then headed off toward the SUV.

The woman stayed behind, shooting me a glare. "Ace and I are engaged."

I almost laughed. The claim she'd staked was nearly as ridiculous as the warning Parker had given her fiancé. "Congratulations," I told her. "I'm just here for the surf lesson."

"Well, it's over now," she said.

"We'll just return the boards and head out," Parker said, grabbing our rented boards and heading toward the hut.

I could feel Ace's fiancée's eyes on me the entire way.

"I guess I need to invest in a board," I said after we'd dropped the rentals off.

"You're not going to take more lessons with him, are you?" Parker demanded as we stripped off our wetsuits by the outdoor showers.

"Maybe not him, but someone," I said.

As I stepped under the stream of the water in my red bikini, I felt Parker's gaze on me. It lingered. Hot and steamy. Or maybe that was just the way I always felt around him.

I'd known Parker my entire life—well, as far back as my memories went. His dad was the chief of security from my father's global bar conglomerate, and every summer or holiday I'd spent with Dad, Parker and his parents had been there too. We'd had golden vacations full of laughter and joy. Days woven with feelings of acceptance, as if I was actually wanted and cherished, only to have them ripped away when Dad sent me back to the ranch as if it wasn't a big deal, as if it didn't tear his heart out like it did mine.

That was before everything went to hell at the ranch. Before my stepdad had died and left a failing legacy to me rather than my mom, and before my father had helped me save it. Dad and I had mended our relationship in the last few years, but I wasn't sure I'd ever be rid of the scars my childhood had left on my soul. Wounds that cracked open easily.

Parker was glowering when I opened my eyes and stepped away from the water to towel off.

"What's got you all broody and simmering?" I asked casually, unable to help the heady rush of hope that hit hard, fast, and uncontrollably as his eyes scanned me from head to toe before darting away. Maybe Parker would actually admit to the sizzle burning between us. Maybe he'd actually admit he didn't like Ace looking at me because Parker wanted me. Because we belonged together. We weren't just childhood friends. We were something more.

But my hopes crashed and burned when Parker said, "I think Ace was high. That's dangerous on the water at any time, but especially while teaching beginners. Anything could have happened, and he wouldn't have been prepared."

I pulled a T-shirt and yoga pants over my bikini, slipped into a pair of flip-flops, grabbed my bag, and headed for the parking lot where we'd left Parker's truck. I threw my bag into the back and turned around, watching as Parker took a turn at the outdoor shower.

The water sluiced off him, the sun hitting it and casting him in a shimmery rainbow of mist. It reminded me of the waterfall back on the ranch. The way the colors glimmered over the foam as the water hit the rocks. It reminded me of times we'd spent playing in that water over the last few years, my stupid crush growing in leaps and bounds while he built up more and more barriers between us.

When I was fourteen, I got why he'd done it. He was five years older than me and refused to see me as anything more than a family friend, as the kid he'd been charged with protecting whenever he was around. But I was eighteen now. That didn't seem so far off from his twenty-three, did it?

He dried off, pulled on a gray T-shirt that clung to every one of his enormous muscles, and jogged over to the truck.

"You up for tacos?" he asked as he slid on a pair of aviator glasses.

"You think they can beat the ones the new chef at the resort makes?" I asked.

He pushed his sunglasses down so he could look at me over the top, and those steely gray eyes made my heart skip a beat again. "We're mere miles from Mexico, Ducky. I bet these will be the best damn tacos you've ever had. Only place better is this shop in Ensenada."

"What do I get if you lose?" His brows furrowed. "You said you 'bet' I've never had better."

My stomach flipped as his eyes turned dark and stormy before he slid the glasses back up, hiding his emotions from me.

"If I lose, I'll keep dragging my ass out here to take surf lessons with you."

I scoffed.

"What? Since when have I ever reneged on any of our bets?" he asked, a hint of warning in his tone.

"Oh, I think you'll keep your end—at least until your command hauls you back to training and off on deployment to some far-off part of the world where you'll do unspeakable things."

His jaw ticked. "That's weeks away. And the way you stood up on that board today tells me you'll be done with classes well before I'm called back."

He opened the passenger door for me, and I barely prevented myself from rolling my eyes at him. Not only at the gentlemanly move that made our time together feel date-like, when I knew it was the furthest thing he'd intended, but because I knew the real reason for this bet. He didn't want me near Ace.

As he climbed into the driver's seat and backed out of the spot, I watched him surreptitiously from under my lashes. He may not admit to the attraction that drifted between us now, but I'd still scored a point today. He hadn't liked Ace flirting with me. He didn't want me with another guy. That had to count for something, didn't it?

Chapter Two
Parker

I'M ON FIRE
Performed by Bruce Springsteen

FIVE YEARS AGO

> *HER: If you're available tonight, we're having a bonfire at the beach. Feel free to join.*

HIM: Will country music be blasted?

> *HER: Perhaps. But I'm not in charge of the music selection. I'm sure you could convince Rae to blast some of the crap you like that makes my ears bleed.*

HIM: Or she'll torture us all with her reggae.

> *HER: Reggae is growing on me.*

HIM: There is absolutely no hope for you, Ducky.

> *HER: At least I'm willing to explore. You're the one who refuses to change your mind once it's set on something.*

Fallon laughed at something her friend said as they returned to the beach from the restrooms. Her full lips were spread wide, eyes crinkling, as she tossed her long braid behind her shoulder. Her hair was wet from the outdoor shower, and it had turned the color of deep honey or a warm whiskey. The setting sun behind her shot it with amber highlights, giving her a halo and turning her into an angel.

Except, if she was an angel, she was more likely an archangel than the sweet, sitting-on-a-cloud kind. She'd have a fiery sword and armor, and she'd battle the world for her cause.

She'd always been that way, even as a kid, defending those she loved, the land she'd inherited, and her home with a fire absent from many of the adults in her life.

She may only be nineteen, but she'd seen more and taken on more responsibility than anyone I knew. But I was the only one in the crowd of college kids she'd gathered today who knew it.

Since coming to San Diego last year, Fallon had pulled on a different persona. It was as if she was actively trying to forget her roots, trying to pretend she was just like everyone else when, really, she was an heiress. The owner of a five-thousand-acre, five-star resort near the Sierra mountains. It was under her mom's guardianship at the moment, but when Fallon hit twenty-four, it would become hers.

As she approached the firepit her friends had built, half a dozen guys she called friends followed her with their eyes. I watched them, fury building at the lust on their faces. I hated it. Hated knowing exactly what was going through their minds because it went through mine all too often. I wanted to shut them down, just like I shut my own thoughts down.

As Fallon took the beach chair next to me, I glanced over and nearly choked on the sip of water I'd just taken.

When I'd arrived at the beach, she'd been in a wetsuit, riding the waves on a magenta surfboard. I'd joined her, and we'd gone back and forth from shore to the outside and back for nearly an hour before we'd both called a halt.

Now, the suit was gone, revealing a tiny-ass bikini and miles of warm skin. It wasn't the fact it showed all her lean muscles and soft curves that had me choking. I'd seen those before—seen them and tried to tame the beast inside me that wanted to touch and lick and savor them. But tonight, it was the fact her fucking pale-blue swimsuit was practically transparent that had me pulling my T-shirt over my head and tossing it at her.

"Cover up," I snarled.

Her eyes went wide as she caught the black cotton shirt. "Excuse me?"

I leaned toward her, placing my mouth close enough to her ear that I caught that enticing scent of her. Salty seas and wildflowers. Heaven and hell. "You might as well be wearing nothing, Ducky. That suit is fucking see-through."

It was still light enough that I could see the hint of color that bloomed over her cheeks as her eyes jerked down to her body and saw exactly what I had. What every fucking guy here had seen—rosy tips and hints of hair darker than the strands on her head.

She pulled my T-shirt over her head, dragging her hair out from the collar. By the time she met my eyes, she'd already recovered from the embarrassment. She shrugged. "It's not like I'm showing something anyone here hasn't already seen."

My thoughts went dark. What the hell did she mean? They'd all seen her naked?

Fury and jealousy coursed through me.

She read my expression and laughed. "I didn't mean they'd all seen *me*, Parker. You know better than that. I just meant female bodies in general."

But I didn't know it, did I? She was a sophomore in college. She'd dated guys. She'd been texting me about the dates she'd been on since high school. She'd asked me questions she should have asked her mom, but her mom wasn't always in the right state of mind to answer them. Lauren had been on a cycle of opiate addiction and recovery ever since I'd first met her.

All I knew was that I was grateful Fallon had never asked me about doing the actual deed. I wasn't sure I could have handled knowing she was closing the deal with some guy who didn't deserve her, who hadn't earned the right to be at her side.

I wasn't sure anyone would.

Not even you, dickwad, my conscience screamed at me.

Fallon turned to her friend who'd sat down on the other

side of her. "You were right, Rae. Twenty dollars was too good to be true for my swimsuit."

Her friend was curvy and tall with black hair that she kept wound tight in miles of tiny braids, held back with a thick band. She'd been Fallon's roommate in the dorms, and they'd moved to an apartment off-campus this year. The last time I'd been in it, the place still had the bare-bones, second-hand vibe of starving students. I was pretty damn sure not even Rae knew the truth about the size of Fallon's bank accounts.

"Is it pilling already?" Rae asked.

"See-through," Fallon said, quirking a brow at me. "Parker didn't seem to appreciate it."

"Parker needs to let the rest of us have our fun," a guy across the firepit said with a sneer.

My muscles bunched, ready to leap across the flames and plant my fist in his face.

It was Will's hand on my arm that stopped me. "Let it go, Park," my friend said under his breath.

I whipped my eyes to Will's face. The natural highlights in his dark-brown hair were the same color as the fire burning in front of us. Thick and wavy, he had cowlicks that caused it to stick up in strange places whenever it wasn't shorn down to his scalp. Today, it was a mess from our time in the water.

He had his arm around a slim, warm-skinned woman with brown eyes, bright-purple hair, a nose ring, and tattoos dancing up both shoulders. I wasn't crazy about Althea, but Will was head over heels in love with her.

I swallowed hard, trying to calm myself down, and did exactly what my best friend since the Naval Academy had told me. I let it go. The twenty-something loser on the other side of the fire wouldn't stand a chance if I decided to take him out, but I wouldn't end my SEAL career just as it was taking off by getting arrested.

"Music, Rae!" someone demanded, and Fallon's friend pulled a portable speaker out of her beach bag. She whipped through screens on her phone, and reggae filled the air. The beat was steady and sensual, turning the lighthearted day at the beach into something darker. Needier.

Rae pulled Fallon to her feet, and they started dancing. My T-shirt rode up along Fallon's thigh, giving hints of that blue bikini, and I fought my body's reaction to it. To her. To a woman I was here to protect and nothing more.

Eight years ago, I'd promised our dads I would always look out for her and keep my hands to myself while doing it.

She'd been in danger that day, targeted by men who were coming for her dad, and I'd been a green Academy cadet who thought he already knew everything about protecting people. Except, I hadn't known shit, and the moment I'd left, the moment I'd turned my back, Fallon had nearly died.

I wouldn't let that happen again on my watch. When I was deployed, there wasn't much I could do about it, but she'd always be safe when I was here.

The sun dropped below the ocean, the waves crashed along the shore, and the breeze drifted in, bringing the scent of salt and seaweed with it. Nights on the sand always brought back memories of not only BUD/S—where we'd been stuck in the moonlight, shivering and quaking with a RIB boat held above our heads—but also of my first mission as a SEAL. The silence had been heavy after we'd landed and made our way up the darkened beach until it had been broken by gunfire.

I looked over at Will to see his face had turned serious as well. Would we ever get used to the memories? Or would each mission weigh us down a bit more? Would coming home always feel like we'd lost something of ourselves while we'd been gone?

As the night progressed, alcohol appeared as if from nowhere, and people started to pair off. Hands were held. Kisses turned sultry. Most of the college kids here weren't old enough to buy the booze they were drinking, and neither Will nor I could afford to have a *furnishing alcohol to a minor* charge, so I stood up and stretched.

Will did the same, bringing Althea with him.

"Time for us to go, Ducky," I said to Fallon.

She spun in the sand, a smile on her face that hit me dead

center in the chest like an arrow. Goddamn, why did she have to be so beautiful? She glowed with an energy, a vibrancy, that seemed to light up the night.

"You're in town for a few more days, right? I'll see you again before you ship out?"

I picked up her bag. "You'll see me tonight. Let's go."

She huffed out a laugh. "You're not the boss of me, Kermit."

I just shouldered her bag, picked up her phone from the cup holder of the beach chair, and slid it into the sweatshirt I'd tugged on after giving her my shirt.

"Nothing here for you tonight," I said, glancing around at the alcohol and entwined couples.

She put her hands on her hips. "I'm not twelve, Parker. No one sent you to watch over me."

"One call, Ducky. One call, and I can guarantee Rafe will make sure there's someone here watching you permanently," I growled.

Rae's eyes shot back and forth between us, a frown appearing between her brows. Fallon's face paled, and she stepped closer, mouth drawn tight at my mention of her dad. She leaned in and whispered, "You know I don't talk about that here. No one knows."

Instead of arguing with her, I simply picked her up and tossed her over my shoulder like the sandbags they'd had us haul in training.

"Parker!" she squealed, pounding on my back.

I looked at Rae. "You coming?"

Rae's lips twitched, and she pointed to the guy sitting in a chair next to hers. "No, I'm staying with Joren tonight."

"Be safe, Rae," I said and turned on my heel to follow Will and Althea as they picked their way through the sand toward the parking lot.

Fallon was still pissed, hollering and spitting like a wild cat, her hands smacking my ass.

"You realize that's going to hurt you more than me?" I said, and she gave out another snarl of irritation.

Will was laughing as he opened the passenger door of his sports car for Althea. "I'll see you tomorrow on base, Baywatch. Have fun with that." He waved at Fallon.

I wouldn't have fun in the way he implied. That was the last thing I'd do.

At my truck, I set Fallon down. When she went to sidestep me, I caged her against the back door. "Stop."

She crossed her arms over her chest and glared at me. "You tossed Dad at me, but what would your father say if I sent him a text saying you were manhandling me?"

"If you told him the truth about the entire situation, he'd likely applaud."

She blew out an exasperated breath.

Our gaze remained locked, heat zapping between us, and I felt that tug deep in my chest again. She wet her lips, and the simple motion sent a pulse through my groin. An unacceptable reaction.

She was the one who broke first, looking out at the ocean.

The sound of the waves mingled with the music. Heady and strong.

Whispering temptations I'd never give into.

"I don't want you here as my bodyguard, Parker," she said. Her voice was low and husky, and when she turned to face me, the look in her eyes almost brought me to my knees.

Desire. Wild flames of it. Enough to consume me with just a single glance.

The pulse in my dick pounded furiously.

I ignored it.

"I'm not here as your bodyguard. I'm here as a friend, and a good one wouldn't leave you alone with a bunch of drunk guys who only have sex on their minds."

She raised a brow. "Maybe I have sex on my mind too."

Her gaze fell to my lips, and the urge to give her what she wanted, what we both wanted, was far too strong. Far too dangerous.

I stepped to the side and yanked open the passenger door

of my truck.

"Tacos will have to do for tonight."

She rolled her eyes but climbed in. I tossed our shit into the back, and as I walked around to the driver's side, I adjusted myself in my shorts.

It was a good thing my team would be deployed soon.

If I had another month here, I might just break. I might just be a goddamn SEAL who rang the bell and gave in to the undertow that was Fallon Marquess-Harrington.

Chapter Three
Fallon

ALMOST LOVER
Performed by A Fine Frenzy

FOUR YEARS AGO

>*HIM: Where are you?*
>
>>*HER: You're home! Everyone okay?*
>
>*HIM: We were all fine until I accidentally hit play on that pop song you sent me and nearly killed everyone.*

A few minutes passed.

>*HIM: Seriously, Ducky, where are you? I need to see you.*
>
>>*HER: I'll tell you if you promise not to drag me away again.*

More minutes passed.

>>*HER: Parker?*

The heat from the bonfire spread across my face as I looked up from my phone. Across the way, Rae and her most recent boyfriend were engaged in a furious debate about politics—something I avoided as much as possible when at the beach.

This was my time away. Escape. Just like San Diego was an escape from the real world that awaited me once I finished college. Sometimes, for brief seconds, I wondered if I'd done the wrong thing in not telling anyone here about the resort I owned or the money I'd inherited from my father.

But I liked being the same as everyone else—struggling students pooling together money to buy the keg and food for the bonfire. If, somehow, a few extra twenties ended up in the pot, no one needed to know where they came from.

If and when my secret got out, I knew everything would change. Rae would be hurt the most because I'd lied by omission, but what else was I supposed to do when she hated the wealthy? She was determined to level the economic playing field once she obtained her law degree and joined a human rights campaign. I was almost certain she wouldn't remain my friend and roommate if she knew the truth.

Maybe that was me thinking the worst instead of the best of her. Maybe she'd be more pissed about that than my secret. But I couldn't take the risk. Not right now.

"What's wrong?" The question from my date had me turning to look at him.

JJ's golden brows furrowed together over bright-blue eyes. He was a golden-haired Adonis, and every time I thought about him being with me, my heart squeezed a little bit. Most of it was happiness, pleasure that someone with such a dynamic personality had been drawn to me. But part of me wondered if the excitement I'd felt on seeing Parker's name appear on my phone made it wrong to be on a date with anyone.

Except, Parker wasn't ever going to be mine, and I couldn't wait around forever for him to finally tear down the walls between us.

I deserved to have a boyfriend, to go on dates, be kissed, be romanced.

To finally have sex.

JJ had swept me off my feet the moment we'd met on the outside. We'd shouted encouragement to each other as we'd taken on a particularly wicked wave, and as soon as we'd planted our feet and surfboards on the sand, he'd asked me out.

For the first time in my life, I'd been the dead center of

someone's all-consuming focus, and I was thrilled to be there. For so much of my childhood, I'd had to fight for anyone's attention—even my parents'—so having all of JJ's was intoxicating.

At the sound of a vehicle door slamming shut, I turned my head toward the parking lot. A man emerged from a truck in the dim light of the streetlamps, and my heart literally flipped over.

I was up and out of the beach chair, running flat out across the sand, in a flash.

Large hands caught me as I flung myself at broad shoulders.

I buried my nose in the crook of Parker's neck, inhaling that earthy scent that was uniquely his. The smell that had always soothed me.

"You're home!"

He squeezed me tight before slowly setting me down and assessing me in that way he did now. It was a slow scan that looked for changes or injuries or who knew what, but every time he did it, my heart thundered, and my body nearly spasmed.

It had never felt wrong before…not until now—when my date was waiting for me at the bonfire.

Parker looked tired. Shadows lingered below eyes that seemed darker than even the night around us.

"Are you okay?" I asked.

He reached out and tugged my braid, a motion he'd been doing since childhood. A sweet tease. A comfort. Reassurance.

"Better now," he said, and my heart tumbled over again as he grinned. When Parker smiled, everything seemed right in the world.

From behind me, a confused voice called my name. I turned to see JJ making his way from the bonfire, a frown between those thick brows.

I swallowed hard, stepped toward JJ, and twined my fingers with his. "JJ, I want you to meet Parker. Parker, JJ."

Parker's gaze settled on my hand gripping my date's, and his smile disappeared.

"Wait, this is the friend you were talking about? In the

Navy?" JJ said, surprise in his voice as he took in Parker's camo pants, tan T-shirt, and military boots. He was still in the clothes he must have worn on the plane ride home. Or ship ride home. Or however the hell Parker had come home from his latest assignment.

It shouldn't thrill me as much as it did to know he'd come looking for me before he'd done anything else. That I'd been his first stop after months of being gone.

Parker stuck out his hand, and JJ shook it.

"You have me at a disadvantage, I'm afraid," Parker said. His voice was gruff, the way it sounded when he was tired. "I haven't heard of you."

JJ stiffened, let go of my hand, and tossed his arm around my shoulder, drawing me closer.

"Well, you've been incommunicado for months," I reminded Parker. The silence that followed grew awkward, and my palms began to sweat. I cleared my throat. "How'd you know I'd be here?"

"You said you didn't want me to drag you away again." Parker's gaze settled on mine, and I felt the heat in his eyes stronger than I had from the bonfire moments before.

JJ made some kind of inarticulate noise at the innuendo. Damn Parker. He was going to mess things up for me before I'd even gotten past second base with JJ.

I punched Parker in the shoulder. "Don't make it sound like that." I looked up at JJ and smiled. "Parker is like a big brother. The one you never want around when you're having a little too much fun, because he does that whole overprotective thing so well."

This time, it was Parker who grunted unhappily.

It proved how messed up I was that I liked it. I liked that he was unhappy to see me with JJ. And yet, I also liked JJ. What was wrong with me? Maybe it had to do with the screwed-up DNA from my mother's side of the family. Although, my dad's side wasn't exactly made up of saints either. Cursed. Maybe I really was cursed—as my uncle had once told me I was.

I ducked under JJ's arm and stepped toward the bonfire.

"Come on, I can see if there are still any hot dogs left. You're probably starving," I said to Parker.

He didn't move. He stood at the edge of the sand, looking past me at the bonfire before returning to me. "I'm pretty beat. I think I'll head home. I just wanted to see you before I landed in bed and slept for a week."

I turned to JJ. "Why don't you go back? I'll be there in a second."

JJ didn't look too happy, but he headed off.

Silence fell, the crash of the waves beating between Parker and me a strange warning instead of the peace it normally was. The rhythm of the music, some country song Parker would hate, vibrated over the air.

"You've got yourself a boyfriend, Ducky," Parker said. His voice was completely bland. Neutral.

"It's, like, our third date. I'm not sure we're in boyfriend territory yet," I said with a shrug.

"I'm pretty sure he tried to stake a claim with that handshake."

I rolled my eyes. "You know that misogynistic, He-Man stuff doesn't do it for me."

A small smile returned to Parker's face as he leaned in and said softly, "Then he's doing it wrong."

My stomach whooshed, my insides curled tight, and longing barreled through me.

"Don't do that," I breathed out.

"Do what?"

"Don't flirt with me when you have no intention of ever doing more. I've finally found someone who likes me for me. Who *wants* me—" my voice cracked, and it pissed me off. I took a minute and then continued. "I deserve that."

Parker's face went blank again. He was so good at it these days. Since he finished training and started going on missions, he'd become excellent at hiding every thought and emotion. I hated it.

"You do deserve that, Ducky. I'm just not sure *he* deserves *you*."

I blew out a breath. "You met him for two seconds. You tossed out an innuendo that made it seem like we were more when I've spent the last three weeks explaining you are just a friend, and now you're pissed that he reacted to it. You don't know him."

He shoved his hands into his pockets and rocked on his heels. "You're right. I don't. I'm sorry. I'm in a pissy mood."

Instantly, all my anger and frustration disappeared. "What's wrong?"

"Althea's pregnant. She's demanding Will marry her, and I'm doing everything I can to hold him back. Hell, I'm not even sure if the baby is his. Guys from another squad told me they'd seen her with a whole series of Marines while we were deployed."

My heart hurt for Will. "That's awful. Is he getting a DNA test?"

"I finally convinced him to get one and to wait until after the baby is born before making anything permanent with her."

"I bet Althea loved that."

Neither of us were crazy about Will's girlfriend.

"You could say I've now become her least favorite person."

Laughter broke out from the bonfire behind us, and I turned to see JJ standing on the opposite side, but his gaze was on Parker and me. If I wasn't on a date, I would have gone with Parker simply because it had been months since we'd seen each other, but also so I could try to soothe his ruffled feathers.

We probably would have gone to the Taco Shack and then gone back to his house to watch *Buffy* reruns and take turns daring each other to listen to some song we both knew the other wouldn't like. I would have helped him decompress after a mission that had obviously settled hard on his soul and had been made worse by the news Althea had given them.

Parker and Will had grown much closer since Will's parents had died while they were at the Naval Academy together. The men were no longer just friends. They were brothers. Parker's parents had all but adopted Will.

"Your parents are going to be excited. They're finally getting a grandkid."

Parker's brows raised. "I didn't even think about that, but you're right. They will be happy."

His gaze lifted over my head to the party raging behind me. He reached out and tugged my braid again. "Go. Have fun with your new guy and your friends. Just not too much fun."

My lips twitched.

"I think your idea of too much fun and mine are really different."

He winked as he stepped back toward the parking lot. "That's because you've never seen me in my Whites at the bar."

My breath almost evaporated at the idea of it. The perfection that was Parker pressed into that sexy uniform, on the prowl for someone to take to his bed. A shiver ran down my spine, and I scolded myself.

He wasn't mine. He didn't want me that way.

In truth, he didn't want anyone that way. At least, he didn't want a permanent relationship. For some reason, Parker had sworn them off. He didn't believe any relationship could last his SEAL career or didn't believe it was honorable to be in one when he'd always be away more than he was home.

"With how tired you look, Kermit, I'm not sure even the Whites would get you action tonight."

He laughed, and the deep sound resonated through me in the best and worst kind of way.

"I'll call you when I come out of hibernation. We'll hit some waves."

"Sounds good. Be safe getting home," I said.

He looked back, eyes drifting to the bonfire and JJ again before returning to me. "You too, Ducky."

And then he was gone.

I felt bereft. As if, this time, I'd actually lost him. As if there was yet another barrier that had gone up between us—one of my making this time. One called JJ.

Chapter Four
Parker

I AIN'T SAYIN'
Performed by Jordan Davis

THREE YEARS AGO

> *HER: Are you back from your mission? I wish you were back.*

A week later

> *HIM: What's wrong?*
>
> *HER: Momentary lapse in judgment with an idiot. I've recovered.*
>
> *HIM: Who do I need to punch and why?*

The bar was dark and loud, smelling of sweat, spilled beer, and desperation. I wasn't sure who it was rolling off stronger—the Marines and SEALs or those who'd come hoping to hook up with someone in uniform.

Normally, after returning from a mission, I was ready to be one of the crowd, searching for someone to spend a few hours burning off the tension with. But witnessing my best friend's struggles with his ex-girlfriend over this last deployment had taken my already recalcitrant attitude about relationships, even the one-night kind, and leveled it up. I wasn't sure a few hours of pleasure were worth the chance of getting stuck with a woman who didn't believe me when I said my lifestyle and my goals left no room for a girlfriend.

Just as it always did, a flash of sunny hair and gold eyes taunted me, reminding me of the one and only person who'd ever come close to changing my mind on the matter.

Except, this time, the vision of her didn't disappear when I shook my head.

Instead, she kept staring right back at me, making my pulse skyrocket and my dick twitch.

What the hell was she doing here? In a bar everyone came to for one thing and one thing only?

I stormed through the crowd, causing grunts of objection I ignored. My complete focus was on Fallon, on getting to her and dragging her out of here.

"Let's go, Ducky," I growled when I reached her side, circling her bicep with my hand.

She yanked it away with enough force that it caused her to slide backward on the barstool she was perched on. She would have landed on her pretty little ass if I hadn't steadied her with both hands on her waist. The touch burned. It tore through me like a goddamn grenade going off.

As soon as she was stable, I jerked my hands away.

She raised a shot glass, tossed it back, and slammed it onto the bar with an expertise that didn't sit any better with me than her being in this dive.

"I'm not going anywhere," she said. The husky, honeyed timbre of her voice sent shockwaves spiraling through me. "I plan to stay here until I'm nice and toasty, and then I'm going to find some Navy boy to take me to bed so he can lose me in the morning."

My entire body stiffened. Shoulders. Back. Groin. I ground my teeth together, leaned closer so our noses were almost touching, and said, "No."

Her eyes widened, gaze dropping to my mouth before slowly easing back up. The fire I saw there matched the one in me, and it surprised the shit out of me, even when it shouldn't. Even when I'd seen that fire before and done everything I could to squelch it.

"Last time I checked, you weren't my boss or my dad. You

can't tell me no," she huffed, tossing those thick waves behind her shoulder. I wanted to fill my hands with those golden locks. I wanted to yank them back and taste—

I swallowed hard and said, "Rafe would hate you being here."

She snorted. "Dad would hate all my plans for tonight, but what he doesn't know won't hurt him."

I whipped out my phone and swiped through the contacts. I'd almost hit her dad's number when she surprised me again by jerking the phone from my fingers.

"Don't you dare!"

I'd expected her to be pissed at my high-handedness, and she was, but there was also a hitch in her voice that had me narrowing my eyes to really take her in. It wasn't the short black skirt, her long, toned legs, or even the swell of her breasts showcased in a tight T-shirt that halted my gaze. Instead, it was the red rimming her eyes and the puffiness of her cheeks.

She'd been crying.

Someone had hurt her.

And that thought had every feral instinct in my body reacting. I was a trained killer. I knew exactly how to get rid of a body in a way no one would ever find it, and whoever had made Fallon Marquess-Harrington cry was going to pay the price.

I suspected I knew exactly who it was, but I had to get her to confirm it. To do that, I had to sit down next to her. I had to talk to her and watch those full lips twist and those dark lashes flutter. I had to stay close to the one person I'd been running from for years.

The one person who could make me forget all my promises to my dad, her dad, and myself.

I flagged the bartender and ordered a beer for me and water for her. When she requested another shot, I shook my head at the man over her head and then slid onto the stool next to her.

"Where are your friends, Fallon?"

Her lids closed for a second. "If I had to guess, they're all at the bonfire."

"And why aren't you with them?"

The bartender put down my pint and her water, and she emitted a little growl of displeasure. Before I could stop her, she reached for my beer, raised the glass to those pretty lips, and chugged at least half the contents.

While it wasn't the first time I'd seen her drink, it was the first time I'd ever seen her attempting to get drunk, and it increased the sour taste in my mouth. At the beach parties she'd invited me to over the last three years, she'd been focused on surfing during the day and dancing by the bonfire at night, rather than downing alcohol like many of the college students hanging out with her.

Watching her in those moments, seeing her celebrate life with a lightness and freedom she'd never had at the ranch, it was the first time I'd felt the deep friendship we'd had as kids twist into something more. Something I'd never thought I'd have a problem ignoring when our five-year age difference had always felt more like twenty.

As a teen, I'd been aware of her crush on me well before our fathers had made me promise to ignore it. I certainly hadn't been tempted back then. I'd been laser-focused on the Naval Academy and being one of the handful of cadets selected to go straight into Basic Underwater Demolition/Seal training upon graduation.

But as adults, standing next to Fallon as she tugged herself out of a wetsuit, leaving nothing more than a bikini and bare skin in its wake, I'd been struck with a landslide of emotions. Desire had been only the tip of them. Seeing her use those lean muscles to wrangle the waves with the same ease she'd tamed the horses back on the ranch had flooded me with images of a future I'd never allow to come true, even if I hadn't had the promise to our fathers hanging over me.

For her first few years at the University of San Diego, it had been easy for me to convince Fallon to come away with me when I'd left the beach party. But this last year, since she'd started dating that loser, JJ, I'd had to leave her there, partying with her college friends. I'd go home to my tiny rental cottage and lie awake, fretting like some goddamn parent, until I received her text telling me she was home safe and sound.

I told myself it was the reason thoughts of her clung to me on my missions with an ache that left me nearly doubled over at times. It was simply unease about whether she'd make it home safely each time she partied with her friends. It was simply years of ingrained duty.

Which was ridiculous because she was an adult and no longer my responsibility. The truth was, she would say she'd *never* been my responsibility, that she'd grown up taking care of herself, and to some degree, she was right. Still, she was always the first person I texted when I returned from an assignment, and my gut remained clenched until she responded.

Right now, my Fallon protector instincts were in full swing as I took in her sexy little outfit, slurred speech, and the fogginess in her eyes.

"Seriously, Fallon, why are you here alone? Where is everyone?"

"It's JJ's birthday, so they're celebrating with him," she replied with a careless shrug that couldn't hide a flash of hurt before she shoved it away.

"What did he do to you?" I demanded, barely leashing a raging desire to find JJ and plant a fist in his face.

Fallon's eyes widened, but she didn't respond. Instead, she finished my beer and almost slid off the damn stool again. I had to touch her, had to dig my fingers into skin exposed by her crop top to keep her upright, and hell if it didn't burn all over again.

She set her hands on my shoulders, leaning forward so our mouths were mere inches apart. "He broke up with me."

"Good."

Stunned, she jerked back. I told myself it was relief and not disappointment that coursed through me when her hands left my body.

"What the hell, Parker?"

"Don't act surprised. I've been clear about my feelings for JJ all along."

"Jealousy doesn't suit you," she tossed back.

"Not jealousy, Ducky. Simple facts. He's a loser who isn't

good enough to kiss your toes, let alone your lips."

Her gaze dropped to my mouth, and she leaned back in, voice low and sultry. "Are you good enough, Parker?"

My entire body tightened. She was too beautiful for her own good. For my good. But I hadn't become a SEAL without learning how to deny myself the things my body craved. So I used a single finger to push her back out of my space.

"Why did he break up with you?"

"I wouldn't sleep with him."

Shock rumbled through me. I'd blocked out thoughts of their bodies twined whenever I'd seen his hand or mouth on her. But she was twenty-one years old, and I wasn't naïve enough to think they hadn't done a hell of a lot more than kiss, even if it had made me want to break his fingers every time I'd witnessed him touching her.

"If that's why he broke up with you, then it only proves my point. He doesn't deserve you."

"How long have you ever gone before closing the deal with someone you were dating?" she demanded with an arched brow.

"I don't date."

She rolled her eyes. "Puh-lease. Don't give me that line. What about Sabine in high school?"

"First and last official girlfriend. I told her I didn't want anything serious, that I wouldn't drag anyone into my SEAL career with me, but she didn't believe me, so I broke it off before our senior year."

She scoffed. "You've had sex in the thirteen years since then, shithead."

"I didn't say I hadn't."

"So, no dates. Just pick someone up"—she waved a hand around the bar—"and give them one night. One night, and then you're out." Her words slurred more, and I was glad I'd stopped the bartender from bringing her another shot.

I shrugged.

I wasn't ashamed of the way I conducted myself. Sex was just another way of releasing tension. If you kept the valve clamped too tight, you exploded. And there were plenty of women who needed the same release without the tangled web of a relationship.

"Fine," she said. "I'll take it."

She slid her lips onto mine before I'd processed what she intended.

A bomb went off in my head. Explosions of lust. Raw need and hunger. And below it, something worse. Something deeper. Something that shoved a club in the air, claiming *Mine.* And for several long seconds, I deepened the kiss. Exploring. Demanding. Seeking.

Reveling in the sweet taste of her.

Then reality slammed into me. Guilt at the ease with which I'd let myself be drawn in.

I took her hands from where they'd landed behind my neck, crossed her arms in front of her, and pushed her away.

"No." The single word was as much for myself as for her. This was off-limits. She was off-limits. I'd made a promise. A vow I intended to keep.

"JJ thinks I've already slept with you, so why shouldn't I? When I denied it, he said even if we hadn't bumped uglies, I couldn't deny *wanting* to, and when I hesitated, he just smirked and walked out." She snapped her mouth shut, horror in her eyes at having admitted to wanting to sleep with me. I ground my teeth together and fisted my hands to avoid reaching for her. "Whatever. He's pissed that I wouldn't sleep with him after he invested an entire school year into this relationship, patiently waiting for me to give it up."

"It doesn't matter what your reasons are for telling him no. If he can't respect your decision, then it's better to toss him aside." I looked around the bar and remembered her words from when I'd sat down. "So, after telling your actual boyfriend you wouldn't sleep with him, you decided to what? Come and give yourself to some asshole Marine who wouldn't know how to get you off and certainly wouldn't be slow or gentle with you for your first time?"

It burned inside me. The thought of her giving herself to

anyone, let alone some anonymous foot soldier who would forget her name before the night was over—if he even learned it to begin with. She deserved rose petals and silk sheets, candlelight and a sea breeze drifting through open curtains. She deserved to be romanced and cherished before, during, and long after the deed was done.

Terror larger than anything I'd ever faced on my missions swept through me because I could see myself giving it to her. Could see every beautiful moment. I was almost desperate to be the first to touch those soft spots deep inside her. To see her cheeks flush with real pleasure.

I needed a drink. I needed to get the fuck away.

She set my phone down, rested her forearms on the sticky bar, and laid her head on them. Her eyes fluttered shut, and more panic reared. How much had she had to drink before I'd walked in?

"It's just a hymen, Frogman." Her words were even more garbled as sleep dragged at her. "It's not like I even have one left after all my years on horseback."

Irritation and more alarm surged, thinking about what might have happened to her if I hadn't shown up. My eyes scanned the many, many jerks who would have been happy to take her up on what she'd offered, too drunk or not.

"It isn't the body part, Ducky," I bit back at her. "It's the sentiment. The act itself should mean something for your first time."

She didn't respond. Her mouth dropped open just a little, and I realized she'd passed out.

Well hell.

I paid our tabs, swept her into my arms, and carried her outside. She made an inarticulate noise before leaning her head heavily on my chest, and my body went on high alert in all the wrong ways.

My house was only about two hundred paces from the bar. Over the last few years, it had become the perfect landing place for me and my squad at the end of our drunken bar crawls, but tonight, the walk seemed interminable. The scent of her wove itself into my very being. Salty seas and wildflowers. A smell that had comforted me the majority of my life.

As soon as my front door shut behind me, I realized my next problem—where to put her. I'd left Will in the guest room, fighting with his ex over the phone. I no longer had a couch in the living room, thanks to the mice who'd taken up residence in my consignment shop find. That left my bedroom. My bed. Where the scent of her would remain long after she'd gone, taunting my dreams with the one person I'd ever seen a future with and who I'd sworn not to claim.

I laid her down, removed her sandals, and covered her with the sheets and comforter. Her blond hair spread out, a sea of tangled curls that covered both pillows. Her face was relaxed and vulnerable. The fire that usually burst from every fiber of her being was shuttered. It felt wrong to see her so still and quiet.

Almost as wrong as it felt to come home after each deployment to a stale and silent house.

She seemed paler than normal, passed out with alcohol flooding her veins, and worry threaded through me once again. Any thoughts of sleeping on the floor disappeared. No way in hell was I sleeping. I turned her on her side and slid on top of the covers next to her, eyeing each breath she took, scrutinizing each movement of her pupils behind her lids.

I'd watch over her once more, glad to play the part I'd played many times before now.

But when morning came, I had to get away from her, away from a very single, very stunning Fallon Marquess-Harrington, before she ripped the promises I'd made to shreds.

Her lashes fluttered open, and we stared at each other for several long heartbeats.

"Kiss me, Parker. Make me feel alive in the way only you can." My gut clenched, and my dick twitched, a physical reaction demanding I give in to her request before I buckled it down.

"Even if you weren't drunk, I'd never say yes to you."

Hurt and anger spun through those golden orbs.

"Never is an awfully long time, Frogman. I wonder just what it would take to break you."

"I'm a SEAL. I don't break. I don't ring the bell. Ever."

She pushed the comforter down and dragged her shirt over her head, revealing a magenta lace bra that did nothing to hide her rosy tips. I bit back a groan at the goddamn sweetness of her. My mouth watered, imagining the taste. I longed to give her exactly what she wanted.

Instead, I simply added this moment to all my other memories of her challenging the barrier I'd constructed between us. Times when I'd seen her dance atop the waves like a goddess, or watched her spin while standing on horseback with a lasso swirling, or listened as she begged me to stay because she'd never feel safe without me next to her.

Fallon ran a finger along the stubble coating my jaw, and the look in her eyes hauled me into unsteady seas beside her. Ones that would require every ounce of strength I had to keep my feet planted in the sand. I wouldn't drop the boat. I wouldn't give in. I'd carry it to shore, even if no one was there to see what it cost me to do it.

Even if it cost me her.

Chapter Five
Fallon

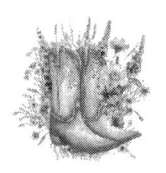

DIAMOND
Performed by Martina McBride and Keith Urban

TWO AND A HALF YEARS AGO

HIM: This has gone on long enough. Stop ghosting me.

HER: ...

HIM: Ducky, I'm serious. This is bullshit.

Moonbeams fractured along the waves crashing onto the sand while a warm breeze whipped around me. The stars were barely visible with the nearby city lights bleeding into the sky, and I suddenly ached for the dark canvas I'd see standing at the lake in Rivers. I missed the ranch. I rarely let myself acknowledge it these days, devoting myself wholly to the world I'd built in San Diego.

College was a once-in-a-lifetime experience, and I'd promised my dad I'd explore it to its fullest. But there were days when I felt like I'd lost a piece of myself to make it happen.

More in the months since Parker and I had stopped texting.

Well, since I'd refused to message him.

Licking my wounds after that stupid night at the bar by refusing to talk to him had become an ugly reflex. One I was sure hurt me more than it hurt Parker.

The simple truth was I missed him even more than I missed the ranch.

Even more than I missed Maisey. Only Parker and my childhood best friend understood all the nuances of my complicated life. Only they saw the real Fallon. For the millionth time since we graduated from high school four years ago, I wished Maisey had come to San Diego with me rather than attending a university up north.

Behind me, someone bumped up the volume of the music at the bonfire, shattering the serenity of the night. JJ's laugh boomed through the air. It was loud, addicting, and charming. He had a way of luring people to him and making them feel like they were the absolute center of his attention.

We'd been together for almost a year before we'd broken up, supposedly because I wouldn't sleep with him. But we'd both known that hadn't been the real reason. The real reason had been the way I'd looked at Parker whenever he hung out with us at the beach.

After the breakup, JJ and I had made it through the first part of our senior year as just friends, hanging out with the same crowd, surfing whenever we got a chance. But the longer I'd gone without seeing Parker, the more JJ had attempted to turn our friendship back into a relationship.

Just this month, with mid-terms behind us and after we'd started an internship at the veterinary clinic together, I'd finally agreed to start dating him again.

I'd thought it was what I'd wanted.

No, damnit. It *was* what I wanted.

I wanted a regular relationship. A regular guy. I wanted that JJ focus to be one-hundred-percent on me again. I desperately wanted to be the center of someone's world.

JJ would make me his every day, whereas Parker only looked my way between deployments.

Hadn't Parker made it clear that he'd *never* say yes to me? And while it still burned all these months later, it shouldn't. I'd had years to adjust to the fact he would never look at me the way I looked at him. Lines to Taylor Swift's "Foolish One" swarmed through me. I had been foolish. I shook my head to try to clear it of thoughts of Parker. How could he still consume so much of my time?

As I watched the dark waves topped with sugary foam, I wished I could be on them. At least there I felt in control, just as I did when I rode my horse, Daisy. But it would be stupid to surf at night, and regardless, it was impossible as JJ had forgotten my board when he'd packed the truck today.

Had it been on purpose?

I shook my head. Of course not. There was no reason for him to keep me from surfing.

I turned, dragging my feet in the cool sand as I moved farther down the beach away from the party crowd and the celebratory mood. The bonfire noise had all but disappeared when my phone buzzed in the front pocket of my equestrian team sweatshirt. It had been buzzing off and on all day. Parker had returned from a mission. The relief I felt knowing he was home safe conflicted with the tension that came from his messages—the demands that I break my silence.

He was right. I had let it go on long enough.

It was stupid to be embarrassed by one night. I'd been drunk. That would have been excuse enough if I'd simply passed it off that way the next day. Instead, I'd held on to the humiliation and ended up making it a bigger deal than it should have been. I winced just thinking about it.

I'd never gone this long without texting Parker since I'd gotten my first phone as a tween. But maybe it had been a good thing. Maybe putting this distance between us had finally allowed me to accept that Parker and I would never be more than friends. It had allowed me to truly let JJ into my life.

Angry voices jerked my gaze toward the public restrooms a few feet away. A woman's sharp cry of pain caused alarm to travel up my spine and sent me jogging up the beach toward them.

As I approached, the eerie orange glow of lights on the brick building revealed Ace Turner. He was not my favorite person on a good day, but tonight, with the dim lighting turning his hair black and his eyes into bottomless pools, the creepy-crawly feeling he gave me occasionally rocketed up to real fear.

My stomach lurched in ugly twists as I watched him shove his wife into the wall with a hand to her neck. The elfin brunette had two personalities—a vivacious surfer, challenging anyone around her to keep up on the waves, and a jealous harpy who resented anyone who dared talk to Ace.

Ever since I'd taken my first surf lesson with Ace, I'd tried to avoid them. But tonight, the terror on her face had me quickening my pace, hoping I could do something to calm things down or at least get her away from him.

"Fucking bitch. What did you do with it?" He shook her, slamming her head into the brick with a resounding crack. She let out another pained yelp.

"Sold it," she choked out.

"Fuck! Where's the money, Celia?" he snarled.

She scrabbled at his hands, trying to pull them away from her throat.

My heart hammered against my rib cage.

What the hell should I do? What *could* I do? Ace was twice my size and full of muscles, testosterone, and often the drugs he handed out like they were candy. I had no weapon on me. My backpack and the pepper spray Parker's dad had ensured I carried were at the bonfire. I was in a bikini covered in shorts and a sweatshirt. I didn't even have shoes on.

A dark, heavy weight settled in my stomach as I sprinted the rest of the way to them. All I knew was I had to do something, anything. I couldn't just stand there while Ace strangled her. I'd seen enough violence in my life. I'd witnessed a cold-blooded murder firsthand and carried those dark memories with me. I'd be damned if I'd watch as someone else died without trying to prevent it.

Ace and Celia were so focused on each other that they didn't see me coming. I used every ounce of muscle I'd earned from years of working on the ranch and smashed my fist into Ace's shoulder.

Surprised, he staggered to the side with a grunt before spinning to face me. I didn't give him time to regroup, kicking him in the groin. Even barefoot, it packed a punch that had him bellowing in agony and hunching over.

I grabbed Celia by the arm and hauled her into the

women's restroom. I slammed the heavy metal door shut, slid the bolt lock into place, and then whirled around to see what else I could use to block the door. Other than a rubber garbage can, everything else in the public restroom was screwed to the walls and floors.

Celia backed up into the row of sinks as Ace pounded his fist on the door.

"Celia. Get the fuck out here."

She gasped for air, rubbing at her neck.

"You know what's coming for both of us if you don't give me that money!" he screamed.

She started toward the door, and I blocked her path. "Don't. He can't get to you in here."

"It's. My. Fault." Each word seemed to cost her. He'd done a hell of a lot of damage before I'd gotten to her. It wasn't just the bruising on her throat. She had a nasty one on her cheek, and blood was dripping from her swollen nose.

The blood combined with the fear rippling through me triggered unwanted memories that threatened to haul me into the abyss of my past. Dark moments at my stepmom's bar when danger had found us, when Sadie had defended me by placing herself in harm's way. Her strength and our attackers turning on each other were what had saved us.

But I still smelled the metallic scent in my nightmares.

My pulse turned erratic, sweat dripped down my back, and my lungs tightened.

The bathroom door rattled. Ace snarled in fury.

Spots drifted across my vision.

With a shaky hand, I pulled my phone from my pocket, opened my favorites, and hit the call button before registering that Celia was moving toward the exit. I blocked her path once again as Ace screamed her name.

"'Bout damn time, Ducky." Relief at hearing Parker's deep voice nearly brought me to tears. I didn't have time to register the well of emotions I heard in his words. I didn't have time for anything but the raw truth.

"I need help."

"Open this fucking door!" Ace roared.

"What the hell is going on?" Parker demanded, instantly on alert. Instantly concerned. "Where are you?"

"The public restrooms at the Laguna Heights National Park," I said as the door shook and the hinges rattled. "Parker… The door… I don't know how long it will hold."

"Goddamnit. I'm ten minutes out. Ten fucking minutes."

Metal crashed against metal as Ace hammered something into the frame so hard the brick wall actually shook. Celia shoved past me, and I grabbed her arm, pulling her back as my body trembled. "You go out there, and he's going to kill you."

What the hell had I gotten myself into?

"Who are you talking to? Who's with you?" Parker demanded, and I heard a car door slam on his end of the line. He'd be here soon. More relief rolled through me. He'd be here. Parker had promised I'd never face danger without him again. And Parker always kept his promises.

Always.

"Celia," I answered, trying to keep my voice from betraying just how afraid I was. "Ace's wife."

"Hang up, call 9-1-1, and then call me back," Parker instructed.

With shaky hands, I hung up and went to call 9-1-1, but Celia grabbed my phone.

"No!" she said. "You can't call the cops."

"What? Why not?"

"You don't understand!" she shrieked.

I battled her for my phone and had barely grabbed onto it before the hammering started again. Ace furiously indented the door with each strike, the ring harsh and foreboding.

"Celia. Get your ass out here."

The sound of sirens drifted through the air, and my entire being convulsed with hope. Someone else had heard the fight. Someone had called for help.

Panic spread across Celia's face at the sound.

"You called the fucking cops!" Ace bellowed, and his

battering grew even more frenzied.

My breath got caught in my lungs. What if the cops didn't make it before he broke it in? Would he use whatever he was hitting against the door on me? On Celia?

Blood and bruises flashed before my eyes. Sadie and I had been covered in them after the attack at the bar.

"Let me out!" Celia shoved me, and I collided with the wall, my head smashing into it with the same ugly crack hers had against the brick outside.

"What are you doing?" I asked, grabbing her biceps and trying to stop her. "He'll kill you."

"You have no right! No right to interfere!" she screamed at me.

Red-and-blue lights drifted in through the coke-bottle windows at the top of the brick.

When I heard the squawk of a police radio, I sagged against the wall.

"Sir, put down the shovel and step away from the door."

"She's got my wife in there. She's holding my wife."

Tension flooded back through me. *What the actual fuck?*

I heard a clang as the shovel hit the concrete sidewalk, and then Ace's voice got quieter as he and the officer moved away. A rap on the door was followed by a woman demanding we come out with our hands up.

My body quaked as I unlocked the door. I'd barely started to swing it open when Celia pushed past me, almost colliding with the female officer on the other side.

"She had no right to interfere! No right!" Celia shouted, her eyes wild.

The officer raised her gun. "Hands up."

Celia started toward the officer as if she hadn't heard the command. Her eyes were locked on the scene taking place farther away, where a cop had Ace handcuffed and was leading him to a police car. She was going to get herself shot.

I flinched as if in expectation. Expecting the jerk of her body just as I'd seen once before. Expecting the nauseating smell of gunpowder and blood. The horror of watching life disappear from someone's eyes.

I stepped out of the restroom with my palms raised and said shakily, "Celia, raise your hands and stop moving."

Finally, Celia seemed to register the situation, and her feet froze as she lifted her arms.

Another cop car squealed to a stop in the parking lot, and two more officers emerged, hands on the guns in their holsters as they took in the scene.

Time blurred. My vision turned spotty as the adrenaline began to leave my body.

They placed Ace in the back of a squad car, and Celia and I were separated to give our statements.

Memories and reality blended.

I vaguely heard JJ's voice calling my name from a distance, worry coating it. The drama of the police cars had drawn the crowd from the bonfire, but an officer was keeping everyone at bay.

A truck squealed into the lot behind the police cars.

A man jumped out. A man I hadn't seen in months. His black hair gleamed in the streetlights, and his steel-gray eyes looked dark as night. He moved with a grace and ease that seemed contradictory to the deeply honed muscles he'd earned as a SEAL.

His eyes locked with mine across the distance. The fury in them turned to relief as he searched my body for wounds and came back empty.

My entire being shook. I needed his arms around me.

I needed to feel safe.

I needed Parker.

Celia was screaming at the officer interviewing her about how I'd interfered, how there'd been nothing going on. How they needed to let Ace go. He hadn't hurt her. She'd fallen. She'd tripped down the cement steps leading to the beach. And no, those weren't hand marks on her throat. She got so agitated that the cop put her in cuffs and sat her down on a bench.

When the officer who'd gotten us out of the bathroom

asked me what had happened, I explained what I'd seen and what I'd done to try and save Celia.

"I won't testify against him! He didn't do anything wrong!" Celia cried. "Don't listen to that bitch!"

The officer questioning me met my gaze with a frustrated one. Resignation crossed her face as her jaw tightened.

"I'll testify," I said quietly. "I know what I saw. He would have killed her."

A tremor ran through me as Ace's angry eyes came into focus again. I'd seen that look before too. Wild. Inhuman. I'd seen it in the eyes of our attacker in the bar.

My body was a mass of horrible memories. My knees were shaking so badly I wasn't sure I'd be able to remain standing for much longer.

The officer left me to consult with the other cops, and Parker flashed his military ID at them. They nodded, and he pushed past them. In five long strides, he reached me and pulled me to him.

The scent of him washed over me. Earth and pine. Security. I buried my face in his chest, and one strong arm banded my waist. The trembling stopped. The fear stopped. I was where I belonged.

Except, I wasn't. I was so messed up.

Parker stroked my hair, and a sharp pain zipped through me, making me gasp. He jerked back.

"You're hurt?" The words were gravelly, laced with concern and barely leashed anger.

I felt the back of my head for the bump and winced when I found it. "Got knocked into the wall."

"What the fuck happened, Ducky?"

I swallowed hard and was about to explain just as JJ reached us. His eyes narrowed as they drifted between me and Parker.

"Fallon, are you okay?" he asked.

I nodded. But I wasn't. I was a mess of old memories and new ones. Of fear and relief.

"Where were you when she was in danger?" Parker barked.

JJ's shoulders went back, and he widened his stance. "What? I'm supposed to tag along with her whenever she goes to the bathroom? At least I'm here. Where have you been for months?"

I stepped between them. "This isn't JJ's fault, Parker. This is on me. I should have called the cops instead of getting in the middle of their argument."

JJ's gaze settled on me before darting to Celia, still cuffed on the bench, and Ace in the back of the squad car. "They were fighting? Big deal. Shit, Ace and Celia go at it all the time. You know that, Fallon."

JJ worked with Ace at the beach hut, and JJ insisted he was a good guy. But ever since my first interaction with Ace, my instincts had always screamed *Stay away*. Parker had liked Ace even less. They'd even gone toe to toe several times when Ace had been passing around drugs to the college crowd that he was far too old to be hanging out with.

As JJ watched Ace yelling at the cops from the back of the police car, something passed over his face. Concern. Worry. He looked back at me and said, "You should have left it alone. Why would you call the cops?"

"I didn't. Someone must have heard him slamming the shovel into the bathroom door…" A tremor ran through me again, and both men reached out, as if they were going to pull me to them, until their hands collided, and they retreated. JJ tucked his into the pockets of his sweats. Parker crossed his arms over that wide expanse of his chest.

The female officer came back and handed me a card. "We're holding Ace overnight. He has another drug charge pending trial, so I'm not sure if he'll make bail or not. Celia won't testify, but the prosecutor will want to talk to you. If we can make anything from tonight stick on top of his previous arrest, it might keep him away long enough for her to come to her senses."

"Don't get involved, Fallon," JJ said softly, and it drew the officer's gaze to his.

Her eyes narrowed before they shifted to Parker and then back to me. "You have someone to take you home?"

"Yes," JJ replied just as I nodded.

She hesitated as if reading the tension in the air but then walked away. I turned in the direction of the bonfire. "I need to grab my things."

"I already put them in my car," JJ said. "Let's get the hell out of here and try to forget this whole night."

He shot Parker an angry look, grabbed my hand, and tugged me toward the parking lot. I pulled away from him. "Let me talk to Parker for a minute, and then I'll be ready to go."

JJ scowled, muttered something under his breath, and strode toward his car.

Nerves rattled through me, and I was tempted to give in to the bad habit I'd broken years ago of chewing on my nails. Instead, I bit my cheek and rubbed my fingers over my thumb.

"I don't even know where to start with my questions," Parker said. He shot JJ an annoyed look before glancing at the squad cars and finally settling those steely gray eyes on me. "But all I really care about is if you're okay."

We stared at each other for a few seconds. The air seemed to warm. Electricity zapping as if lightning was blooming when the sky was clear. I'd missed him. Missed us. Missed our friendship.

"I'm sorry," I said. And I wasn't sure if it was for calling him in the middle of the night, asking him to rescue me, or for the months I'd gone without talking to him.

How could I have let so much time go by simply because I'd been embarrassed?

His brow furrowed in concern. "I'll always be here for you. Always."

That hurt almost as much as it soothed. Knowing he'd be at my side in every way except the one I'd wanted most was what had led me to react so dramatically. It was time for me to face the hard truth. Parker would never want me the way JJ did. And I wanted—no, needed—to be loved completely. I needed to be the center of someone's world at least once in my life.

I swallowed. "I'm sorry I called you. I should have just dialed 9-1-1."

"I'm not sorry." Parker glanced toward JJ's old sedan. "Are you really back together with that douche?"

I prickled. "Don't call him that."

He raised his hands as if in truce and then reached out to tug on one of my braids. The friendly move hurt my heart in that way memories from my childhood always did, reminding me of holidays spent with Parker, his family, and my dad that had ended in my being sent home to a family and an estate that my birth had broken.

My family may have started to mend itself in the last few years, but it wasn't ever going to be completely whole. Just like I'd never be whole. I had too many scars left from my childhood.

Parker was just one more of them.

I stepped away, heading for JJ and away from the memories threatening to pull me under, but Parker's words halted me. "Ducky..." I looked back. "Don't let it go months before we talk again. I can't do it. I *won't* do it."

It shouldn't have thrilled me, the promise in his voice of what he'd do if I ghosted him again. It frustrated me that he still had this much power over me.

I'll never say yes to you...

I swallowed and nodded, because the simple truth was, I couldn't do another six months without him either. As much as it hurt, I still needed him in my life, because we weren't just friends. We were family.

I arched a brow and asked, "Still listening to that heavy-metal crap?"

He smiled, and it changed Parker's face from stern and growly into the eighth wonder of the world. A miracle. A sight you couldn't compare to anything else on this earth. "Metal is the god of music. Don't you forget it."

"I swear I'll have you loving country music before the end of the decade."

"Not likely."

We shared a grin, and then I turned and walked away. I felt his eyes on me the entire way to JJ. When I reached my boyfriend, he opened the car door, and I slid inside. After he climbed into the driver's seat, he glanced out the windshield to where Parker was still watching us.

"You haven't seen him in months, and yet he shows up tonight out of the blue? Seems suspicious."

"It wasn't out of the blue. I called him," I said.

JJ's mouth tightened. "I was right here, Fallon. Right on the beach. Why didn't you call me if you needed someone?"

Why hadn't I? "I figured the Navy SEAL would know how to defuse the situation."

"Ace and I are friends. I could have calmed him down."

I didn't have a response. I simply turned to look out at the ocean as JJ drove out of the parking lot. My emotions were all over the place. Memories clawing at me from when I was fourteen and thought I was going to die, old wishes and buried dreams reemerging after seeing Parker again.

I didn't want any of it. I didn't want to be the Fallon whose stepdad had been murdered and who'd almost been killed herself. Or the girl who'd destroyed a family. I didn't even want to be the heiress who had a ranch and a five-star resort waiting for her after graduate school.

For a few more years, I wanted the easy life I'd built here. I wanted to be the center of someone's world. I wanted JJ and my friends to see only the college girl with no responsibilities. The equestrian champ. The future veterinarian.

Once I had my license, I'd go back to the ranch and take on the legacy my stepdad had left for me. I wanted that future. But for now, I needed this—classes and parties and surfing. I needed to be a simple college girl and nothing more.

Chapter Six
Parker

HUMAN
Performed by The Killers

TWO AND A HALF YEARS AGO

> *HER: Thank you again for showing up tonight, especially after I've spent the last few months ghosting you.*
>
> *HIM: Nothing will ever stop me from coming when you need me.*

Will watched from the corner of the couch in my rental as I tossed my keys on the side table.

"Fallon okay?" he asked.

My jaw worked overtime. I'd nearly been too late. The cops had gotten to her before me. Even though it was eating away at my insides that I hadn't been the one to save her yet again, that wasn't what had me longing to pound my fists into the wall—or into fucking Jasper Johnson's face.

"She will be. She's one of the strongest people I know."

She'd faced so much in her short life. Murder. Mayhem. And tonight, she'd protected someone who didn't deserve it.

I headed for the garage with my fury and Will following me. I taped my hands, tearing off the edge with my teeth, and then started in on the bag hanging from the ceiling in the corner. I envisioned Ace's face on it. Then JJ's. I hit the leather with a ferocity that had the ceiling groaning.

Coming home after our mission, my house had felt even more silent and staler than usual.

The relief I'd felt seeing her name pop up after she'd ghosted me for months had wiped it away, until I'd heard the fear in her voice. That brief moment of relief hadn't returned, even once I'd known she was safe. It had actually grown while I'd watched her walk away with JJ.

The loser who would never be good enough for her.

But it explained why I hadn't come back to my normal flurry of Fallon texts catching me up on her life.

Damn, I'd missed her. The smell of her. Her smile. Her snark.

And it had been my fucking fault. We could have avoided months of drama if I'd simply taken her back to her apartment that night instead of to my place. We could have played off her kiss as a drunken mistake, if she even remembered doing it. She wouldn't have been humiliated like she had been by my second rejection. By my words.

I'll never say yes to you…

Fuck. What had I been thinking?

My hands shook at the memory of how she'd looked that night, desire and vulnerability in her eyes, rosy tips peeking through the magenta lace.

My fists picked up their pace.

That image of her spread out on my bed hadn't faded. It had tortured me ever since. I'd wanted so desperately to give in that night. To take her. To claim what was mine.

Except, she wasn't mine.

She'd never be mine.

The torment of wanting her had been nothing compared to what I'd felt when I'd heard the terror in her voice, heard the banging of metal on metal over the phone line. And when I'd pulled into the parking lot tonight and seen her, pale and scared, in the stark light of the streetlamps, I'd have done just about anything to turn back the clock, make her mine, and keep her safe. And that had scared the shit out of me. The idea of just what I was willing to give up. The oaths I'd sworn that I was suddenly willing to walk away from.

It had been a good thing the cops hadn't let me through at first, or I might have said something I couldn't have returned from. Waiting that handful of minutes had allowed me to rein in my emotions. Get my head on fucking straight.

At least until I'd had her in my arms.

Then, everything had slipped again. I'd nearly demanded—

No. I wouldn't let myself even think it.

Instead, I emptied my head and concentrated on the jolt of my fist against the bag. The slam, slam, slam. The vibrations up my arms and shoulders.

"Want to tell me what's got you beating the hell out of a bag at midnight?" Will asked. I glanced over at my best friend. His hair was longer than usual, sticking up all over the place because he'd been running his hands through it while fighting with his ex over his son.

"She's back with the loser," I growled. "He was right there, on the fucking beach, partying it up while she was locked in a bathroom, terrified for her life."

"What the hell happened?" Will was instantly on the defensive. "And why the fuck didn't you take me with you when you stormed out?"

I took a moment to explain what I gathered about Ace attacking his wife and Fallon stepping in. My gut turned nastily. She'd put herself in danger to save someone else. And that right there was the essence of her. Standing up for the things she believed in.

She may have been an heiress who owned a five-thousand-acre ranch and the daughter of a billionaire bar magnate, but those things weren't what defined Fallon. In fact, she'd done her best over the last few years to make sure no one knew those things about her.

What hadn't changed was the fact our fathers had tasked me with looking out for her while she was here. But between my deployments and training, I'd been away almost as much as I'd been here. Silver One Squadron was in demand, and after this latest assignment, my team would be in even more. The intel and connections we'd made would ensure they called us back for a new mission sooner than the four months we should have had off.

Which meant I wouldn't be here yet again.

She'd be stuck with fucking JJ looking after her.

That burned as much as it concerned me.

Maybe I should call my dad. As the chief of security for her ranch and her dad's corporation, my father could send someone to watch over her. Except, Fallon would hate me for it. She didn't want a bodyguard hovering around her, requiring her to explain to her equestrian teammates, her roommate, or her friends why she needed one.

"Question, Baywatch," Will said quietly, and it was his tone as much as the nickname that let me know I was in for something I wouldn't like. "Why the hell are you standing by and watching her with someone else when it's clear to everyone who knows you that you care about her?"

My fists stopped. I rested my forehead on the bag.

Care was such a mediocre word for what I felt for Fallon. Worse, since she'd come to San Diego, I couldn't shake the desire I felt whenever I looked at her. But none of that was enough to overcome the truth of us. Of my life and hers.

"You know I don't do relationships," I told him. "Fallon spent an entire childhood on the sidelines. No one, not even her parents, put her first. The team is my priority. I can't ask her for more and then be just another person who puts her second."

"And you think JJ will put her first? Like he did tonight?" Will asked, and I growled in protest. "Being a SEAL doesn't mean you can't have a serious relationship or marriage or kids." I heard in his tone the love he had for his son. Theo was two and the absolute joy of Will's life.

But my lingering anger at myself, as well as JJ and the situation tonight, had me snipping at my best friend in a way I knew I shouldn't. "Because you and Althea worked out so well?"

He shrugged. "Not every woman is a money-grabbing

cheater."

I pushed off the bag, stepping toward him.

"I'm sorry. I was out of line."

He'd loved Althea—or at least, he'd thought he had until he found out she was cheating on him with pretty much anyone who looked her way, and that she was more interested in the fortune he'd inherited from his dead parents than in him.

She constantly used his money as a weapon, withholding his son until he coughed up thousands of dollars at a time. He'd finally stopped giving her more when he realized it was disappearing into the hands of her drug-dealing family. These days, he paid her rent directly to the management company, paid her utilities himself, and had groceries delivered to her house, but he didn't give her cash. And when he wasn't deployed, he kept Theo with him as much as humanly possible.

He'd even started talking about getting full custody, but the fact he was away more than he was home wasn't in his favor. My parents had offered to keep Theo when Will was out of pocket, but that meant moving to Las Vegas, which only presented a new slew of logistical problems.

"Look," Will said, "all I'm saying is, life is too fucking short to spend your days watching the girl of your dreams with some douche. But if you'd rather spend your time punching a bag and jerking off alone in the shower, that's on you. I gotta get some sleep. I'm picking Theo up tomorrow and don't want to be a zombie."

He left, and I knew I had hurt him more than he'd admit.

I'd taken my frustration with myself out on him.

I'd failed Fallon yet again. I hadn't been there when she needed me once more after I'd promised she'd never face danger without me. Except, we both knew it was a promise I shouldn't have made to begin with. I was already just another person in her life who put their own goals, their own wants and desires, above what was best for her. Just like her parents had.

Did I think Jasper fucking Johnson would put her above himself? My immediate reaction was hell no. But I wasn't sure if that was a jealousy I had no right to talking or the truth.

The animosity between JJ and me was because of that same jealousy. He hated that I'd been a lifelong friend and that she wouldn't give me up. I hated that he touched her. That he put those narrow, slimy lips on hers. That he caressed her skin.

Then again, I'd hate anyone who did.

Except, I also had no intention of ever being the man who touched her that way. If that was the case, I needed to step the hell back. I needed to let her live her life, have her relationships, and find the man who would eventually give her the family she craved. The family she needed to finally heal the wounds of a childhood spent feeling like she was more an obligation than a beloved daughter.

The idea of that man being JJ slithered in my gut nastily. But Fallon would find out if he wasn't the one for her, and she'd move on to some other guy who was. She deserved to have someone who would be at her side every day. If she hadn't had my number in her favorites tonight, she might have called JJ or the police before me. They would certainly have gotten to her sooner.

I could never be the man who put her first because I had already chosen the teams over her.

I'd spent twenty-seven years honing my body and mind in order to be the best of the best. To build on my father's and grandfather's legacy by becoming a SEAL. I'd promised my grandfather on his deathbed that I'd earn a Bull Frog trophy just like him. The military would celebrate my career the same way they had his—as a SEAL with the most years of cumulative service after completion of BUD/S. I was barely three years into my SEAL career. I had decades left to go.

I couldn't give it up now.

SEALs didn't ring any damn bells.

So, why did it feel like I was doing just that?

Chapter Seven
Fallon

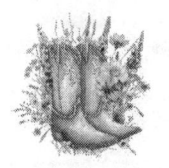

OLD SOUL
Performed by The Highwomen

SIX YEARS AGO

> *HER: I heard "When the Wild Wind Blows" today and felt the need to say the only way you can believe that ghastly metal noise reflects true love is because you haven't ever been in love. Country music, Frogman. Country music has all the heart.*

> *HIM: So, love is pain? Is that what you're saying, Ducky? Because country music makes my ears bleed. If that's true love, who'd want to experience it?*

PRESENT DAY

As I attempted to add the final coat of mascara to my lashes, I had to brace my hand with the other to steady it. Nerves were jiggling inside me like worms caught on a hook, and it had nothing to do with the black hooded robe and gray chevron hanging from my closet door or the chapter closing on my life that the robe signified. The twist of my stomach was due to the shower turning off in the bathroom I shared with JJ.

Before this year, I'd never considered myself a coward. And yet, I was in this situation now because I hadn't had the guts to pull the trigger and break things off months ago.

I should have done it when everything had started to go downhill after I'd taken JJ to Rivers for Christmas. I'd tried to deepen our relationship by showing him the real Fallon, but when I finally revealed to him the secret I'd kept for far too long about the ranch being mine and the wealth that came with it, he'd been hurt and angry.

"Why would you keep this from me?" he'd demanded. "You've been pretending all this time to be just like me when you're really just another rich kid, like the ones at my private school who'd looked down on me for being the scholarship kid."

"I've never looked down on you for not having money, JJ," I'd told him. "I didn't tell anyone because I knew people would treat me differently, and I *needed* to be just another college kid."

"I don't understand why. Struggling to make ends meet, knowing your future depends on every fucking grade you get…that's not a way to live."

I'd tried to explain the complicated feelings I had about both the ranch and my family. The betrayals surrounding my birth that had led to the abandonment of my childhood. The birthright I'd been groomed to take by a stepdad who loved me but who'd loved the land more. The heaviness of the responsibilities I had waiting for me, and my dad's request that I try, for a few years, to consider all the options open to me, including selling the ranch.

After I'd laid my heart out, JJ had simply said, "Your dad is right. Sell it. Get rid of all the bad memories and responsibilities and use it to create a real life for yourself with me in San Diego."

And I hadn't had the heart to tell him I'd never sell the ranch. The legacy was mine. It was in my blood. I'd build on to it. Grow it. Make it more. And I'd build a large animal rescue there to give something back.

After New Year's, when we'd returned to our apartment near campus, JJ had started acting strange, spending money more wildly than ever before. He'd always been a spender. We'd even argued about it over the months we'd lived together when his credit card bill prevented him from paying his share of the rent, but I'd also understood he was working out his demons just like I was.

But then, in February, JJ had proposed, handing me a ginormous diamond ring that was nothing I'd ever want on my finger, and I'd been stunned. I should have expected it after he'd told me to sell the ranch and start a life with him in San Diego, but I honestly hadn't. I'd thought he'd seen the writing on the wall of our relationship as much as I had.

When I'd said no, things had spiraled even more. Our occasional arguments and his accusations of me cheating on him with Parker had grown in number and size. He followed them up with enormous grand gestures and apologies that somehow charmed me into accepting him back.

But the final kiss of death to our relationship had been Mom's car accident in March. The simple fact that JJ had refused to come with me to Rivers when it happened had been the last straw. My mom had nearly died, and my live-in boyfriend hadn't been there for me. Worse, when I'd spent weeks at home while she slowly recovered enough to be transferred to a rehabilitation center, JJ had never once visited me. He'd barely called or texted, and when I'd asked him to pick up my assignments from my professors, he'd demanded to know how much I really expected him to do when he was already swamped with covering for me at the vet clinic where we interned.

As soon as I'd returned to San Diego, I should have broken it off. But I'd been overwhelmed trying to catch up with my classes so I could still graduate on time and making up hours at the clinic so my internship would still count. I hadn't wanted to add the drama of breaking up and asking him to move out to an already stressful time for both of us as we finished our dissertations.

I'd promised myself I'd do it after graduation. Now we were here, and I was still vacillating like a jackrabbit zigzagging across a field.

I flung the mascara tube on the dresser and met my hazel eyes in the mirror. Where was the Fallon who used to stand up for herself? The college grad in the mirror with her makeup and fancy updo wasn't me.

My time at the ranch while Mom was in the hospital had proven to me just how much I'd missed it. The smell of the wildflowers and the sound of the river crashing over the waterfall had soothed me in a way nothing else ever had…except Parker. It had me questioning whether I really wanted to spend yet another summer away from Rivers. It had me wondering if I really wanted to continue with a doctoral degree and a veterinarian license I had no intention of using to its fullest.

My heart hammered hard and fast as I realized just exactly what I was considering.

Walking away. Not just from JJ but from the goals I'd set for myself.

The bathroom door opened, and JJ strode out with nothing but a towel wrapped around his waist. His bright-blue eyes met mine as he crossed the room, and for a moment, I saw a flash of anger in them before he covered it up. As he crossed the room, he waved a pink carton at me.

"You got your period?" he demanded.

My brows furrowed in confusion. Was he actually upset? He'd been like a dog with a bone about sex lately. One day, he'd even gone so far as to lock the supply closet at the clinic behind us. If Dr. Walters hadn't knocked, I was pretty sure he would have stripped me bare and thrown me down amongst the mops and vinyl gloves.

I'd been relieved to be interrupted. Since I'd come back from taking care of Mom, having sex with JJ had felt wrong. And the few times we had, it had felt almost…desperate. Like we were trying to hold onto the tide as it pulled back from the shore, even though the retreat was inevitable.

Usually, when he was like this, the best thing to do was tease him out of his funk, but I didn't have it in me anymore. Instead, I shrugged. "Sorry to ruin your plans for a congratulatory round of sex."

He tossed the tampon box down, and it collided with the mascara tube, sending it rolling to the floor. The crash was loud and somehow ominous.

The scowl on JJ's face seemed as opposite of the real JJ as the girl with the fancy updo in the mirror was to the real Fallon. When I'd first met him, he'd been the epitome of a laid-back surfer, but as the years had crawled by, he'd gotten harder, as if the salty seas were ripping the joy out of him and leaving a shriveled-up version of him behind.

He slid his arms around my waist, pulling my back into his chest, and when I visibly flinched, his scowl deepened.

"Your towel is wet, and it's going to ruin my silk dress," I said, trying to pull away.

He clamped his arms around me tighter, leaned in, and kissed my neck. "So what? You have other dresses in your closet."

Not many. Even the lighthearted college girl I'd been pretending to be hadn't worn dresses. When I wasn't in a wetsuit at the beach or in my equestrian team uniform, riding Daisy, I spent my days in jeans, shorts, or scrubs.

I struggled against his hold until he finally relented, rolling his eyes to the ceiling. "What's the deal, Fallon? I can't even remember the last time we had sex."

"Last weekend, after the extravagant catered party you threw."

"To celebrate you and your final win as part of the equestrian team! That party was for you!"

Our eyes met in the mirror, and his flashed with anger and frustration.

"I didn't need china and champagne. I would have been happy with a bonfire and hamburgers at the beach."

"It's about time you stopped hiding the real you and living the life you deserve," he snapped.

And we were back to the money discussion. Sorrow leaked through me. How had I not seen that this would be a huge deal for JJ? He'd flat out told me that someday he'd shove his wealth in the face of everyone who'd ever put him down.

I stepped away from him and went to the closet, searching for the low-heeled sandals I'd bought for the ceremony. When

I turned around, he hadn't moved, and I raised a brow.

"We'll be late for breakfast if you don't get dressed."

He glared for a moment before stomping over and reaching past me to grab a blue dress shirt from a hanger. I'd never seen it before, but it perfectly matched the robin-egg blue of my strapless cocktail dress. I'd only bought it last week. Had he bought his shirt to match since then? A chill ran up my spine, instincts trying to tell me something I couldn't quite make out.

"I told your dad we'd just see everyone after the ceremony," JJ said nonchalantly. "Meeting up for breakfast didn't make any sense."

Shock at his high-handedness rolled through me. "Excuse me?"

He watched me carefully as he buttoned the shirt. "Look. I love you, Fallon, but asking me to deal with your dad, his trophy wife, their two kids, your mom, and her nurse both before and after the ceremony is just too much. After everything you told me about your family, I'm surprised you want to see them at all."

Fury burned through me, but the only thing I could get out was, "Sadie is not a trophy wife."

"She's twelve years younger than him. What do you call that?"

"I call it true love."

"I'm not fighting with you right now," he said, pulling on a pair of black slacks and buttoning them. "It's an important day. I thought we'd have multiple things to celebrate."

"What exactly does that mean?" I demanded.

His eyes went to the tampon box again, and my breath evaporated. When it finally flooded back into my chest, I was able to stutter out, "You *wanted* me to be pregnant?"

He met my gaze with sure ones. "Yes."

"What in the actual hell?" I stormed. "First, how would that even be possible when we always use a condom? And second, you know how I feel about this. I want kids, but I'm not anywhere near ready to start a family. I'm not even ready to be married, as I clearly told you when you proposed, and I definitely want a ring on my finger before I go down that road. I won't repeat my family's mistakes. Not my mom's or my grandmother's. I won't have a baby be the only reason I marry someone."

"And my feelings on it don't matter?"

A knock on the bedroom door had him snapping, "Go away," just as I said, "Come in."

The door inched open, and Rae darted a worried look between us. "Fallon, your phone's been going nuts for the last twenty minutes."

I looked at the spot on the bedside table where I usually left my phone charging at night. I could have sworn I'd plugged it in. Instead, I could hear the tone jingling down the hall from the kitchen.

"Fallon," JJ warned, and I ignored him, pushing past our roommate into the hallway.

My insides were too torn up, my rage too strong, to have a conversation with him now.

Most of my anger was self-directed. This was my fault. Getting back together with JJ after that first painful breakup years ago had been wrong. I'd let my need to be loved, to be the center of someone's attention, draw me back to him. And I'd gotten what I wanted, his complete focus, and now it had spun entirely out of control until he was actually *hoping* I was pregnant.

I stormed past the sleek, black dining set JJ had bought in March to the counter where my phone had gone silent. I looked down at a series of texts, and when my heart secretly hoped to see one particular name among the others on the list, I grew even angrier with myself. That single reason, the wish to see Parker's name there, should have kept me from ever starting a relationship with JJ, let alone living with him.

I was the asshole here. JJ should hate me. I hated myself.

The first text was from my best friend.

MAISEY: Where are you? Your parents are worried.

The others were from Mom, Dad, and finally, my stepmom.

> SADIE: *Everything okay there? We're at breakfast, and you're not here.*
>
> ME: *I thought JJ told Dad we wouldn't make it.*
>
> SADIE: *We weren't sure if that meant just him or both of you.*

"Is it him?" JJ demanded, leaning against the arch from the bedroom hallway. With his tie draped over his shoulder and his shaggy, golden-retriever-like hair slicked back, he looked more like a banker than the beach bum I'd first dated. Those bold blue eyes that usually twinkled with charm were dark with emotions I didn't understand.

Annoyance, still more self-directed than at him, curled up my spine and had me spitting out, "Him who?"

We both knew it was a stupid question.

"Don't play games with me. Will *he* be here today?"

"*He* is on a mission. I have no idea when he'll be back. You don't see me complaining that Tina will be here today, do you?" I tossed back.

"You and I were broken up when Tina and I were together," he bit back. "I haven't been pining after her from the time I was born. I don't go all doe-eyed when she texts me."

"Are the two of you really having this same argument? Today? Of all days?" Rae demanded. Her graduation robe was on but unzipped, showing off a marigold-colored dress that set off her warm skin.

I wasn't sure how she'd put up rooming with JJ and me over the last couple of years, or how she'd remained so neutral.

"No. We aren't." My chest grew tight, and my voice was thick as I said, "We aren't ever having this argument again because we're done."

JJ went completely still. "What?"

"I should have said it when I first came back from Rivers.

I can't do this anymore, JJ. It's clear we want different things out of this relationship. It's better if we call it quits now while we still like each other."

"Like each other." He seemed stunned. "So Sadie and your dad have true love but not us?"

Guilt washed over me, not only for breaking up with him like this—with an audience on the day we were graduating—but for letting it go this long.

"I'm sorry," I said, taking a step toward him, and he stopped me with a shake of his head.

"No. Don't. I need to calm down before I do or say something I'll regret. Let's just pin this entire conversation until tonight when disappointments and family pressures aren't getting the best of us."

I bit the inside of my cheek while he stalked down the hall toward the bedroom.

I turned to Rae. "I'm sorry to put you in the middle of this."

"I'm glad you finally ended it," she said, a frown between her brows. "You know, ever since Ace spent a few weeks here while you were in Rivers, JJ has been edgier than normal."

My mouth fell open. "What? Ace stayed here?"

Surprise coasted over her face. "JJ told me you said it was okay."

A shudder went up my spine. "Ace did eighteen months in federal prison because I testified against him for assaulting his wife and damaging national park property. His wife returned the favor by stalking me for months. Why on earth would I ever let that man in my apartment?"

"I'm sorry." Her face crumbled. "I should have known better. I was in a hurry to leave for spring break, and you were with your mom, and things were so dicey there. I didn't want to bother you with one more thing. He insisted he'd cleared it with you."

It only cemented my decision further. JJ knew how I felt about Ace and his wife. I'd gone to battle for Celia, and she'd returned the favor by turning my life into a bit of hell before she'd just up and left San Diego. The only reason Dad hadn't sent a bodyguard to trail me was because JJ had moved in, and Parker was minutes away whenever his team wasn't deployed.

This was *not* a forgivable offense. If JJ really loved me, he should have wanted to keep Ace as far away from me as possible, not invite him into our home. It was bad enough they'd been working together again at the surf shop since Ace had gotten out of prison. Worse that JJ insisted Ace was a good guy who'd just made a few mistakes.

I felt like I'd just had blinders ripped off my eyes.

We'd both been living a lie—JJ and me.

And I was tired of it. Tired of this pretend life and the pretend girl I'd become.

It was time I went back to Rivers.

It was time I went home.

♫ ♫ ♫

Our apartment was stuffed to the seams with family and friends. JJ's family couldn't afford the flight from back east, but his surfing buddies and some of the staff from the clinic he'd befriended mingled with my equestrian teammates. Everyone was laughing. The mood was light, but I hadn't been able to shake the darkness from this morning. Not even standing up and getting my master's degree with my family cheering in the stands had really removed the heavy veil clinging to me.

I watched JJ as he laughed at something a friend said. He didn't even look like the surfer I'd first been entranced with anymore. The suit jacket he'd slid into before we'd left for the university was expensive—more expensive than he could afford working at the surf shop. Just like he couldn't afford the slick, modern furniture and oil paintings he'd slowly replaced our cheap thrift store finds with this year without ever asking Rae or me if it was okay.

I was suddenly drowning in regrets. Things I'd done wrong. Things I couldn't change but would haunt me in a different way than the blood and death I'd seen in Sadie's bar that day had. My throat closed. I needed air.

I slipped out the front door onto the long balcony that

traveled the length of our apartment. I was surprised to find Mom already there in her wheelchair. People used to think we were sisters because we looked so much alike, but her blond hair was now edged with gray, and her hazel eyes looked worn and tired in a white face paler than I'd ever seen it.

Concern spiked. Was she hooked on painkillers again?

"You okay?" I asked and then winced. She wasn't okay. She'd lost her leg. Her Jeep had been run off a cliff, and she'd almost died. And worse, they'd never found the person or the vehicle who'd nearly taken her out with one careless drive across a solid yellow line.

Mom reached out, grabbed my hand, and squeezed it. "Stop taking care of me, Fallon. It's not your job."

I wished I could believe those words. I'd been looking out for her for most of my life.

Except, I hadn't been doing that for the last six years, had I? She'd stepped up, stayed clean, and ran the ranch's resort smoothly and competently while I'd been away playing pretend.

No more.

I'd done what Dad had asked. I'd searched my soul for the truth, and all it had told me was what I'd already known when I'd left for college six years ago. I was ready to take up the reins Spencer had left me. My stepdad had given me the ranch and told me to make it mine.

Mine. Not Mom's. Not Dad's. But would they be able to step back and let me run with it? Would either of them be able to truly let go of the reins of a legacy that had slipped through both of their fingers? It had been Dad's choice to let go of the ranch and leave it to Spencer, but Mom's family had been fighting for it since they'd lost it a hundred years ago. In marrying Spencer, she'd finally achieved that. We'd never talked about it, but it had to have hurt that he'd left the ranch to me and not her. Sometimes, I believed it was the real reason there'd always been a barrier between us. A wall neither of us had been able to cross.

Deep in my thoughts, I was startled when Mom broke the silence, asking, "Are *you* okay?"

L J Evans

"Of course," I said without hesitation, smiling down at her. "Why?"

She glanced toward the open front door. Dad and Sadie were standing just inside it, love radiating from them. He had an arm draped around her waist with his head bent to hear whatever she was saying. Sadie's silky black mingled with Dad's dark brown. Other than a new bit of gray at his temples, Dad looked the same as he had when I was a little girl. Tall and strong and intimidating.

Sadie laughed as my siblings did a silly dance in front of them, and Dad's lips tilted upward. Spencey and Caro had inherited Dad's dark, wavy hair but had Sadie's bluebell-colored eyes. At nine and seven, they were two of the happiest kids I'd ever met. Sometimes, even though I loved them, I was envious they'd never had to grow up wondering if they were truly wanted or just a burden their parents had accepted.

"I hate that you've become him," Mom said quietly, and my eyes jerked back to her face. "Not the Rafe we see now. You've become the reserved person he was before he fell in love with Sadie. All ice and no fire."

Irritation washed over me, but I bit my cheek rather than snip at her.

Mom threw her hands up. "See. That, right there, is proof you're turning into him. Where's the girl who would have stormed at me? Where's the teen who fought with everything she had to make sure Spencer's murderer was caught and refused to believe the ranch couldn't be saved? The girl who made the grown-ups in her life return to the ring after they'd all but given up the fight?"

Pain slashed through my chest. Mom knew better than to bring up the past. We were better off not discussing it. Did she really want the reminder of how she'd checked out on me? How she'd given up, and I'd been the only one left in the ring? I hadn't had a choice. We wouldn't have the ranch today if I hadn't forced Dad to return to Rivers and help us.

But instead of saying any of that, instead of going down a path I knew would only hurt us both, I simply said, "That girl grew up and realized throwing a tantrum or snipping at people isn't the only way to get what you want."

"I'd rather the tantrum than the ice."

Footsteps clanging over the metal steps leading up to the apartment halted my angry retort. For a split second, my heart whooshed, hoping to see a man in military Whites appear, hoping somehow Parker had made it back in time to celebrate with me.

But it wasn't a muscled, dark-haired SEAL who appeared. Instead, two men in off-the-rack suits emerged on the landing.

"Ms. Marquess-Harrington?" the older white man asked, his bushy, gray mustache moving like a caterpillar along his upper lip with each syllable.

"Yes?"

He flipped open a badge. "I'm Detective Harris, and this is Detective Lake." He threw a thumb toward the other man with a shaved head and large stance that made him almost as intimidating as Parker's SEAL buddies. "We're with the San Diego Police Department. We need to speak with you and your boyfriend, Jasper Johnson."

My brows lifted as my stomach fell. "I... We're in the middle of a graduation party..."

"Yes, we were told," Detective Harris said. "This can't wait."

My eyes found my dad's just inside the door. He dropped his arm from Sadie's shoulders to step onto the balcony. "What's wrong?"

"These two detectives need to talk to JJ and me."

"What about?" Dad demanded, narrowing his gaze on the two men.

"The drugs they've stolen from Walters Veterinarian Clinic."

Chapter Eight
Parker

HOW TO SAVE A LIFE
Performed by The Fray

TEN YEARS AGO

> *HIM: I'm sorry about Spencer, Ducky. When my grandfather died and people kept saying that, I started to hate those words. But now I know there isn't really anything else to say. Loss simply sucks.*
>
> *HER: Spencer swore I was strong enough, smart enough to do anything I wanted. But all I want is him back, and I'm neither smart enough nor strong enough to make that happen.*

PRESENT DAY

The sun flashed gold over the edges of the flag-draped coffin as it rolled off the transport plane, and every fiber in my being went taut. Goddamn it. My jaw worked overtime, and I blinked rapidly. I wouldn't fucking cry. I wouldn't fucking bend.

The other members of Silver One Squadron stood at attention next to me while our command took up the other side of the narrow lane we'd made to wheel the coffin through. Sounds should have filled the air—seabirds diving and squawking, engines roaring down the runway. Instead, there was only a deep and unforgiving silence.

One of us was dead.

One of us hadn't come home. While we hadn't left Will's body behind, his soul had still disappeared in the middle of a mountaintop village where no one would ever know we'd been.

And it could have been prevented. It *should* have been prevented.

Hours before we'd loaded into the helicopters, Will had been told his kid's baby mama was dead, and the shitty-ass news had brought him to his knees. I'd tried to talk him into removing himself from the mission, but he'd said he wasn't about to ring the bell now any more than he had when we'd been at BUD/S together.

For the first time since we'd become friends at the Naval Academy, I'd gone behind his back and asked our commander to pull him. After my request had been denied, I'd tried again to talk Will out of going. I'd even told him I'd gone to command, and he hadn't even been pissed. He'd said he understood why I'd done it, but I shouldn't worry. That he was good to go.

Except, he hadn't been. I had no doubts the distraction had cost him his life. We could have lost the entire team if I hadn't taken the bomber out before he'd detonated the second device.

Now, I was a tangled mess of emotions. Pain and loss. Anger and frustration. Doubts. So many goddamn doubts. About my unit, my career, and my life.

I had to get it all in check.

I had to find a way to keep it all locked up because I had somewhere I had to be. A responsibility I had to fulfill. And just how the fuck was I supposed to do that? What the hell had Will been thinking?

The coffin disappeared inside a hearse, the doors shut, and it rolled away.

A seagull dove down with a loud screech before heading out to sea. Helicopter blades whirred into action. A jet took off.

Life moved on.

Our commander directed a dark look over our formation.

"Debrief at thirteen hundred. No one talks to anyone, not even with a "Honey, I'm home" message, until we've concluded this mess. Get your shit and meet me in the ready room."

He turned on his heel and walked away, his shoes snapping along the runway like far-off gunshots. I had to fight the urge to toss him to the ground and beat him bloody. It had been his decision, more than any other, that had ensured Will had gone into combat like originally planned.

A hand clamped down on my shoulder, and I turned to find Sweeney eyeing me behind the dark glasses. "If you intend to become a ripe old Bull Frog, Baywatch, you need to learn to deal with this shit." The nickname Will had been responsible for giving me was just another reminder of what I'd lost. "You're going to lose more people in our line of work. Some will be on our team, and others will be military friends. Loss is part of the job."

He squeezed my shoulder and then walked away.

I barely bit back my reply. *No loss was acceptable.*

But as our squadron leader and a veteran SEAL, Sweeney was right. If I wanted to be a Bull Frog, like I'd promised my grandpa, I had to pull my head out of my ass.

I needed to talk to my dad.

Even more than that, I needed to talk to someone who would bring some damn light into my life instead of darkness. A sunny blonde with eyes that glowed gold. I needed Fallon's fire to burn away the dark.

But the truth was, now more than ever, I couldn't call her. Not only because I was routinely driving a wedge between her and the asshole boyfriend I'd resigned myself to her having, but because I'd only drag her into the dark with me. I had to figure out how to handle the heavy burden that had landed on my shoulders on my own.

What the actual hell had Will been thinking?

That single thought had been on repeat inside my head since our commander had handed me Will's letter. Will had known I didn't want kids. That I didn't want a child growing up receiving only scattered bits of my time. That I didn't want anyone worrying about whether I'd come home or not. Knowing my parents worried was bad enough, and yet he'd still left me in charge of his son. A four-year-old who'd just lost his father and his mother in a matter of days and didn't even know it yet. A kid who had no other family but mine.

My stomach jackknifed.

As I picked up my duffel from the stack tossed on the tarmac by the plane and followed Sweeney, I attempted to push back the overwhelming sea of emotions I was wading through. I had to get my shit together. The only way to do so was by handling it like I'd dealt with every single challenge on my path to becoming a SEAL—by focusing on one objective at a time. That meant attending the debrief, calling Dad, and finding Theo.

♫ ♫ ♫

I was still rolling with anger when I slammed the front door shut on my 1940s, two-bedroom cottage twenty minutes from base. The silence that always greeted me after a mission seemed heavier than normal. I actively hated it now, when normally it was just a scab I picked at in the dark of the night.

Ignoring the pile of mail waiting for me, I showered, changed into civilian clothes, and went to the refrigerator, hoping to find something to coat the acid lining my stomach. Nothing was there but condiments and two bottles of beer.

The beer would only add to the bile, but I found myself smacking a cap off one using the edge of the counter anyway. I'd swallowed half the bottle before the paper pinned to the outside of the fridge had my throat closing and sent me choking and spitting into the sink.

I turned back, touching the crayon drawing held in place with a Lucky Shot magnet. Two stick figures with guns and sunglasses swung a kid between them. Theo had given me the picture the last time Will had brought him by the house before we'd deployed. He'd been so damn proud of the drawing. Proud of his dad and his SEAL buddy.

I leaned my forehead on the refrigerator and yanked my

phone from my back pocket.

I wasn't sure how to tell my parents about Will. They'd pretty much adopted him since his parents had died. Mom had helped him through all the paperwork, Dad had helped him with the funeral arrangements, and I'd held him up every time he'd drunk himself into forgetfulness. Since then, every holiday and leave, we'd spent time with my parents. Will's son had never met his biological grandparents on Will's side, but my parents had tried to stand in for them.

We were a family. My parents were going to take his loss as hard as if it was me who'd died in that goddamn village.

I hit the call button, and Dad picked up on the first ring.

"You're home." I heard the relief in his voice, and my throat closed again. I was quiet so long that it turned his relief into concern. "Parker?"

I inhaled. Exhaled. Forced my larynx to work. The effort it took ensured I lost any ability to ease into the news and left me blurting out, "Will didn't make it."

There was silence for several seconds on the other end as Dad registered my words before he exploded, "Goddamn it."

I heard the pain in each syllable he uttered, his loss only adding to the weight of mine.

"Dad." I couldn't speak. I couldn't tell him how hard I was struggling to even breathe.

"I'll be there in a few minutes," he said.

Surprise spiked through the grief and anger. "You're in San Diego?"

"Fallon's graduation was yesterday, and your mom and I flew in… It turned out…doesn't matter. I'll be there in just a few."

He hung up before I could respond. Fuck. Fallon had graduated. She'd gotten her master's degree, and it had been just another moment I'd missed in her life. But it was another good reason that I hadn't called her first. She was celebrating, and I was mourning.

My fingers slid over the stick drawing once again.

I had a kid to see. I had phone calls to make. But I really

had to get my shit together first. I had to figure out what I was going to say and do.

I finished the beer, ordered food I wasn't sure I'd be able to eat but needed, and then turned on the television. That was how Dad found me, with the food getting cold on the coffee table while I stared unseeing at the news. Will's death wouldn't be on it. No one would know he'd died on a mission.

Dad didn't say anything. He just grabbed a beer I'd replenished with the food order and sat next to me on the couch.

"Your mother and I would like to help with the funeral," Dad said. I couldn't look at him. I heard the tears in his voice and knew I'd see them in his eyes. Just that would be enough to break me.

"It's already been arranged for Wednesday. The brass took care of it, seeing as he had no official family."

"That's bullshit. We're his family." Dad's anger finally drew my gaze.

What I found, the understanding and compassion mixed with the anger, seeped into me, igniting the fury I'd barely held in check for two days.

"He shouldn't have been with us," I said. "He was losing his shit. Not focused."

"Will?" Dad's surprise was well justified. Will was a solid wall. Steady and calm. He loved two things on this earth—being a SEAL and his son. Nothing could distract him from either of those. Irritation flared because if anyone was to blame for what had happened, it was Althea. Will's baby mama had cost him his life.

"He'd just gotten news that Althea had overdosed."

"Shit," Dad uttered. "Is she okay? Where's Theo? Why didn't anyone call us?"

"She died." Dad's eyes widened. "Child Services took Theo into foster care because Althea didn't have any emergency contact listed for him besides Will. They put him in some damn group home until Will could get back. HQ was working to get him shipped stateside, but we had this mission they deemed critical first."

"There's always one more critical mission." Dad's voice was dry and sarcastic.

We let it set between us. Dad had always been open about the mission that had nearly cost him his life along with his teammates. He and Runner had left the military after it had gone horribly wrong. His pal Nash hadn't taken it lightly, calling Dad a quitter when SEALs were known for doing anything *but* quit. I'd been a little kid, not more than Theo's age, but I had vague memories of that time, of Dad's quiet, simmering anger and grief. Eventually, Nash had left the teams too, and he and Dad had picked up a friendship that might not have made it otherwise. The man ran some flower farm in Georgia now. I scoffed silently. From SEAL to flowers.

Will and I had sworn that would never be us. We were lifers—in until they kicked our creaky, crotchety asses out.

But Will had caved…with a single phone call about his son. He was going to leave.

And he'd wanted one last mission to remember it by.

I rubbed a hand over my face before meeting my dad's gaze once more. We were alike in so many ways. We had the same gray eyes and dark hair. The same square jaw, tall frame, and wide shoulders. But I'd never wanted to be like him in this way, leaving the life I'd devoted myself to because of one mission gone bad.

"He left me in charge of Theo."

Dad's face all but bled compassion. I couldn't take it. I got up and paced the room.

"What the hell do I know about taking care of a kid? He left me in charge of everything. That goddamn fortune he inherited from his parents is in some sort of trust for Theo, but I'm in charge of it too. I know as much about managing money as I do raising a kid!" I shoved my fist into the wall, leaving a hole I'd have to replaster, but it had felt good. I needed more of that release. I needed hours at a punching bag. I needed a workout that would run my body to the ground until I couldn't think. "I didn't want this kind of life. Kids. Responsibilities waiting at home for me. He knew it. So what the fuck was he thinking?"

"He was thinking you were the most honorable person in his life, and he was right."

Tears pricked. I shut my eyes, trying to hold them back.

"If Althea was alive and Will was dead, he would've needed someone who'd look after his son and the money. Someone who'd fight her tooth and nail to make sure she didn't get her hands on it and dish it out like candy to her drug-dealing family. He needed a person who knew how to protect and serve. And that's you, Park. Hate it. Rail against it. But he knew exactly what he was doing."

My chest was so tight I thought it might explode.

Dad stood up. "So, let's go."

"What?" I managed to grunt out.

"Let's go get my grandson. You want him spending even one more night in some shelter? Some place where he's one of a hundred? Or do you want to make sure he's getting the love and attention he deserves? That he hears from you, someone who cares about him, that his daddy isn't coming home any more than his mama."

The tears broke, streaming down my cheeks. I waved my hands. A helpless gesture. "I don't know what to do, Dad. I don't know what to say to him. How can I make any of this right?"

"You can't make it right. You can't fix it. But you can help him get by each day. And I think he'll help you do the same."

I shook my head. I'd failed at so little in my life. I thought failure wasn't an option. I worked until every stop on my journey was a success. I'd only ever failed one person. But this…raising someone else's kid…

Dad grabbed my shoulder and shoved me toward the door. "Let's go, Squid. Get your shit together. Buck up. Pick up the damn boat, get your feet under you, and walk to shore."

The scathing taunt we tossed at newbies did exactly what Dad had intended—it grounded me. It brought me back to my new mission. So, I grabbed my keys and the letter from Will with his attorney's contact information, shoved my phone into my pocket, and followed my dad outside.

This was my new assignment. An assignment that had a start and an end date. Dad was right. I'd figure it out, just as I had all the other challenges tossed my way. I was the problem solver on the team. I was the one who saw all the angles, all the potential traps and triggers, and led us around them. I'd do the same here. I'd take a step back, remove myself from the emotions threatening to drown me, and put a plan in place to keep both Theo and me afloat.

Chapter Nine
Fallon

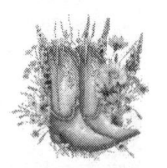

THE SMALLEST MAN WHO EVER LIVED
Performed by Taylor Swift

SEVEN YEARS AGO

> *HER: My sister is the cutest baby in the world. I've decided I want one. A baby. Not now, of course, but in some far-off future. I have to find a guy to put a ring on my finger first. Not because of tradition or anything, but so my kid never has to wonder if I wanted them or if I gave up my dreams because I got pregnant. I want my baby to know only the pure love my siblings have.*

> *HIM: Whether someone has a ring on their finger or not, having kids changes people. Like it or not, love always comes with obligations you can't ignore. It's one of the many reasons I don't want a serious relationship.*

PRESENT DAY

I woke to hushed voices, and for a disorienting moment, I didn't know where I was. But once I registered the unforgiving steel below my arms and the hard plastic pressing into my back, it all came back to me.

Graduation.

The detectives.

Being holed up in an interrogation room at the police station.

Panic jerked me upright. How had I fallen asleep? My palms turned sweaty, just as they had multiple times since the officers had arrived at the apartment last night. I glanced around the cold space. Not much had changed since I'd been brought in—a camera still whirred in the corner, and mirrored glass faced me—but now, the door stood propped open. The detectives were right outside the cement-block room, discussing something in quiet, heated voices.

I looked at the seat beside me, surprised and nervous to find it empty.

I wasn't sure if it had been shock or panic that had kept my mouth closed when the detectives had first thrown ugly accusations at me. I'd been stunned to find out Dr. Walters had called them about missing drugs—even more stunned to know drugs had disappeared from the clinic more than once this year.

Confusion and alarm had won out as the detectives had railed at me until I'd finally croaked out that I didn't have a clue what they were talking about. Horror and dread had me asking for my dad. I needed someone who could fix this. Someone who could see the truth.

They'd refused to let Dad into the room, but he'd done something my frozen brain hadn't thought to do. He'd gotten me a lawyer with a speed and ease only my father could finagle. Money talked, and sometimes, it was a good thing. In this case, I'd never been so grateful in my life to see a lawyer walk in and demand a moment with her client.

The tall, dark-haired, dark-skinned woman had introduced herself as Kenya Block and asked me softly if I was innocent or guilty. Then, she'd called the detectives back into the room to demand answers. What proof did they have that I'd been involved in any of this?

Instead of answering, they'd tossed the same questions at me over and over again.

For the most part, Kenya had let me answer. But occasionally, she halted them or me to clarify something I'd said so it couldn't be used against me later.

I was sure my words had been jumbled and incoherent.

I shivered as the vent above me kicked out the same cold air it had been emitting for hours. I must have made a sound, because both detectives looked over at the same time. When they saw I was awake, they cut off their conversation and joined me.

"Where's my lawyer?" I asked.

"You said you didn't need one," Detective Lake replied.

"I don't. I didn't do anything wrong."

"The box of cash and drugs we found in your hall linen closet say otherwise," Detective Lake said dryly.

My mouth dropped open. They'd found drugs? In our apartment?

The dread I'd been feeling since I'd been shoved into the back of a police vehicle with my hands cuffed behind me returned in full force.

Tears threatened, but I held them back as best I could by biting my cheek. I picked at my nails, fighting the temptation to chew on them.

What the hell was going on?

"Don't respond to that," Kenya commanded, coming into the room with a folder tucked under the arm of her expensive black suit, two paper cups, and a sweatshirt thrown over her shoulder. She glared at the men as she set one of the cups in front of me and then handed me the sweatshirt.

My fingers trembled as I shoved my arms into my equestrian team hoodie, pulling it over the blue dress I'd been wearing when they'd arrested me. They'd arrested JJ too, reading us our rights on the landing outside our apartment like some bad, B-movie scene. I'd never been so humiliated in my life. Not even when I'd offered myself to Parker, and he'd rejected me one final time.

But the real alarm hadn't kicked in until I'd been here, until Detective Lake had kept coming at me with his asshole attitude while his partner watched from the sidelines.

"We've been at this all night, gentlemen. My client has

told you everything she can about working at clinic. She knows nothing about the drugs or cash."

The two men exchanged a look. It sent another round of chills up my spine that had nothing to do with the cold air blowing on me.

"We told you the first person to talk was the one who'd get a deal," Lake said, crossing his massive arms across his chest and leaning back with a smug smile. "JJ has had some interesting things to tell us."

I turned to Kenya, and the seeds of fear that had taken root in my stomach instantly grew into mammoth trees. But she just shook her head before searing the detective with another glare. "Nice try, Lake."

Harris pushed a yellow notepad toward me. On it was writing I knew well—JJ's slanted print in all caps. It was how he wrote everything, as if he'd never learned the lowercase letters. At some point, I'd been enchanted by it, thinking it was unique and classy.

The writing blurred in front of me momentarily before some of the words popped off the page, making my chest burn and tears flood.

"What the hell?" I hissed. "He's saying they're mine?"

All night, I'd insisted I didn't know what had happened to the drugs and that neither JJ nor I would ever steal from Dr. Walters. The doctor was a true mentor and treated his interns and staff like family, opening his home and his offices to us for barbecues and holiday dinners.

"Jasper isn't exactly saying you're responsible," Lake said dryly. "But he is saying you were the one with the key to the drug cabinet."

A memory flashed—JJ's irritated face after Dr. Walters had entrusted me with the keys to the entire office, including the drug cabinet. I hadn't been careless with the keys, but I hadn't kept them locked up in a safe either. They'd been buried in my backpack.

God. I'd been an idiot. Had JJ done this? I'd defended him, and he'd pointed the finger at me. Why? Was he this angry at me? He had a right to be, but— My stomach lurched uncomfortably, and goosebumps ran up my spine as Rae's words from yesterday hit me.

"Ace." I barely got the name out over the lump in my throat. "Ace Turner."

The two men exchanged a look. "What about Ace Turner?"

"He stayed at our apartment in March."

That got me another raised brow from Lake. "Let me get this straight. You let the man you testified against and sent to prison stay with you?"

I shook my head. "I didn't know. I was with my mom in Rivers. I didn't know he'd been there until Rae told me yesterday."

"That's convenient," Lake drawled.

All night, every time Lake had been a real jerkwad, Harris had softened each blow. Now, he sent a glare at his partner before looking at me.

"Do you know the last time he was there?"

I shivered. "I was with Mom for almost three weeks in March and April. Rae said Ace showed up during spring break. JJ could tell you more."

Harris reached over and tapped the notepad, a little rat-a-tat that thumped as fast as my heart. "The only thing JJ is going to tell us is what saves his ass."

I shuddered again. JJ had a right to hate me for keeping secrets and not being honest about our relationship, but I never would have thought he'd throw me under an oncoming stampede. Not like this. Not when he insisted he loved me.

I shoved the legal pad back at the detective, disgust and anger making my voice dark when I asked, "Why the hell would I steal drugs? To sell them? It isn't like I need the cash."

Kenya put a hand on my arm, quelling me. "Detectives, you've clearly done your research. You understand the size of my client's bank accounts—"

"It isn't always about money," Lake cut her off, smirking at me. "It's the thrill, right? Bored little rich girl, looking for—

"

"Right. Like I've had the time to be bored between my athletic career, my internship, my classes, and spending three weeks taking care of my mother who almost died in a car accident! But hell, yeah, I was bored enough to steal from a man who treated me"—my voice cracked, and I despised it—"like family."

So much for being ice. So much for being cold and reserved. If only Mom could see me now. Falling apart, piece by piece.

"You're right, Fallon." Detective Harris's voice got quieter, almost gentle. He did the same rat-a-tat on the notepad again. "This is a bunch of bullshit. I'm sure the fingerprints on the drugs and the cash won't come back to you. I'm pretty sure the amount of debt JJ has racked up in the last few months had him scrambling to find a way to pay it off, and Ace Turner helped him find an easy way out."

"What are you talking about?" I asked. I pulled the cuffs of my sweatshirt over my fingers, determined not to put them in my mouth. Determined not to chew the nail beds to smithereens. My cheek was already raw from the effort.

Harris slid another piece of paper in front of me. It was a printout with JJ's name at the top. Below were dozens of rows of data, like those on a credit card statement, except these were loans and charges in staggering amounts. Not just the furniture and the art he'd put in our apartment, but more—wide-screen televisions, a bedroom set we didn't have, and expensive suits. My eyes stalled on the lease of a luxury SUV and an apartment.

I felt the blood drain from my face. "The condo…in the Kleindyke building… It's in b-both our names?"

The building was one of the most exclusive in the area, boasting stunning ocean views, a full-time doorman, and personal shopping services. It also cost a small fortune. Our internship at the clinic was unpaid. JJ earned his money teaching surf lessons. There was no way the management team of the Kleindyke building would have accepted his application. They would have laughed him out of their office.

Detective Harris nodded at me. "It does have your

signature."

I shook my head. "I didn't…" I couldn't breathe. My lungs forgot how. It felt like I'd been knocked off Daisy and landed on a pile of rocks. "I've never even…"

I'd never even been inside the Kleindyke building. JJ and I had teased about it often enough. At least, I'd thought it was teasing. But my stomach soured even more when I thought about how determined he was to be rich. To shove his success in the faces of his childhood tormentors.

"If it's a forgery," Lake added on, "it's a pretty good one."

Another memory assaulted me—signing off on my time sheet at the clinic and JJ taunting me about my sloppy scrawl. He said anyone could copy my squiggle, and then he'd shown me just how easily he could do it.

I was shaking my head as the anxiety inside me grew and grew.

He'd sworn he loved me. He'd asked me to marry him, for God's sake. He'd wanted us to build a life together. I swallowed hard. A life that included expensive furniture, art on the walls, and a twenty-thousand-dollar-a-month apartment.

I was going to be sick.

Just as Lake started to take the list of loans back, I placed my hand on top of it and drew it to me once more.

"What's this?" I pointed to the last line item.

"Baby store. You know anyone having a baby?"

I flung myself out of the chair, barely reaching the trash can in the corner in time. All that came out was a stream of acidy liquid.

Holy fuck. Holy fucking fuck.

JJ had thought I was pregnant—or that I might be. But how? We'd used a condom every single time we'd had sex. Once we'd started sleeping together, I'd tried birth control pills, but I'd hated the way they made my body feel and the headaches they'd given me. When I'd told him I didn't like being on the pill, we'd agreed there was no reason for me to put chemicals in my body when condoms worked. But what if they didn't… What if he'd made sure they didn't? What if he was poking holes in them?

My stomach twisted nastily once more, but I fought for control. Only, I couldn't stop the shaking. The tremors in my body had a mind of their own.

When I turned back to the table, Kenya's face was concerned. "Are you pregnant, Fallon?"

"No." In my head, I saw the tampon box crashing into the mascara tube. He'd been so disappointed. A sick laugh gurgled into my throat that I barely caught before it escaped. He'd made a new life for us, and I'd thwarted him at every step, from the moment I'd said no to his marriage proposal all the way to starting my period.

I forced myself back to the table, pulling the list of loans and leases back toward me. He'd rented the condo two weeks before he'd proposed. He'd expected me to say yes. He'd expected me to want the *real* life he'd carved out for us. He'd thought I'd be happy to have a new apartment in an exclusive building. It showed just how little he knew me. I'd hated Dad's fancy penthouse in Las Vegas and absolutely preferred the simple two-room house Mom and I had spent my high school years in over the behemoth of a mansion I'd lived in during my childhood.

JJ must have felt me slipping away after I'd declined his proposal. Maybe my running home to take care of Mom had scared him into thinking I wouldn't come back and that I'd drop him to return to the ranch before he could convince me to stay in San Diego. And that was exactly what I'd decided yesterday morning, wasn't it? So he'd changed course, knowing how I felt about kids, how I'd insist on being married before a baby was born.

He'd bought the baby stuff three weeks ago. Hadn't we fought that weekend? It had been about our relationship and what we saw in our future. As always, I'd seen the ranch and the large animal rescue. He'd seen an exclusive veterinarian office in an upscale San Diego neighborhood and weekends on surfboards. Vacations to Australia and Tahiti and Popoyo.

Fury finally found its way in over the sick confusion. I dragged the anger around me like a warm coat, forcing the tremors to stop. My voice found the icy reserve Mom had taunted me about as I demanded, "What do you need from me? What do you need to prove it was him and not me?"

After that, I told them everything I could think of that would point away from me, including the fact I'd been at an equestrian competition on the day the most recent drugs had been taken from the clinic. I couldn't have been the one to do it, but JJ had worked my shift that day.

As I talked, rage reigned inside me, twisted with disgust. My faith in myself was shaken to the core. As a teenager, I'd prided myself on seeing the truth about all the adults in my life. I'd been the one to uncover my uncle's betrayals. I'd been the one to call Dad out on his shit and Mom out on her addiction. And yet, I hadn't seen the true JJ.

Parker had hated him, and I'd simply wanted to believe it was born out of jealousy.

Dad hadn't cared for JJ either, and I'd told myself it was just a father unhappy to see his daughter with anyone.

But they'd seen the real him, and I hadn't.

I had to find my way back to the Fallon who saw past the lies, including my own. The Fallon who defended what she wanted and the things she loved. Who fought for herself and her loved ones with a fierceness that rivaled a mama cougar's.

I wasn't sure how I'd ever trust myself again, but I had to try. Otherwise, the undertow that had been dragging me under would win.

♫ ♫ ♫

Hours later, I was walking out of the interrogation room with Kenya at my side when the door down the hall opened, and JJ emerged, flanked by two officers. His eyes landed on me, and his face contorted, the golden retriever becoming a feral German shepherd with its teeth bared. "I was building a beautiful life for us! I was giving you everything you deserved."

"What you deserved, you mean. I didn't want any of it!"

He scoffed. "Of course not. Angel Fallon was willing to walk away from millions just to prove she didn't need them."

His eyes narrowed. "You disgust me. You didn't even bat an eye before you turned on the father of your child, scraping me off your heel as if I were nothing. You'll regret it. I promise you."

I saw red, anger leaping inside me like flames. "And what you did to the person you hoped would be the mother of your child is so much better? Thank God I'm not pregnant. But even if I were, I'd never keep it. Not if it was yours."

"You bitch!" When he tried to lunge, the officers blocked him.

A twinge of terror winged through me. JJ looked just like Ace had two years ago at the beach. Like Theresa Puzo had when she'd pointed a gun at me ten years ago, and Sadie had stepped in to stop her. It was a look full of darkness. Evil.

A shiver ran up my spine, but I found the courage and strength to turn my back on him. I was almost at the exit door before JJ changed his tune. His tone turned smooth, attempting the charming lure that had always gotten me to give in. "Fallon. Come back, baby. I'm sorry. We can still figure this out together."

My chest ached. Tears stung my eyes, but I kept moving forward.

"Fallon!" he called before a door behind us slammed shut, and his voice finally disappeared.

Detective Harris stepped up with a keycard in hand to unlock the exit door, but he turned to me with grandfatherly eyes filled with compassion and regret.

"He wanted to trap you," he said softly. "He wanted to control you and your money through marriage and a child. He didn't say that straight up, but I caught the drift."

The pain in my chest grew, and my lungs screamed.

"He made a call," Harris continued, "to Ace Turner's lawyer, who also happens to be the lawyer for a well-known drug dealer. They'll post his bail because they won't want him turning on them to save his own ass. I want you to be careful once he's out, and call me personally if you have any issues with him or Ace."

He shoved a card in my hand and opened the door for Kenya and me.

An entire group of people waited for me on the other side. But the only face I really saw was Dad's. With brows scrunched in concern, lips compressed, he looked exhausted, as if he'd been in the lobby all night, which I was sure he had been. I ran, and he caught me, holding on tight. I pressed my face into his suit jacket, the smell of him taking me back to my childhood. To moments when I'd been happy at his side.

I broke, tears streaming down my face as sobs racked me.

Once, a long time ago, both Parker and Dad had each sworn I'd never have to face anything terrible on my own again, and Dad had done his best to honor that today. He'd ensured I had someone at my side, but I'd wished it had been him sitting in the interrogation room with me instead of a lawyer I didn't know.

"Kenya?" Dad's voice rumbled through his chest, vibrating my cheek as he held me tight.

"She's free to go. They're pressing charges against JJ."

I fought hard to get ahold of the tears, but they wouldn't stop coming.

"What happened in there?" he demanded.

"Fallon is my client, so I'll leave it up to her what she wants to share," Kenya said briskly.

"Thank you." Sadie cut off the snarl of protest from my father, and it was that—the way Sadie so calmly handled him and all of us—that finally pulled me back together. When I stepped away from Dad's embrace, it was to see her shaking Kenya's hand.

My stepmom was one of the first people I'd ever known who loved me not out of duty and obligation but for who I was. She'd always had my best interest at heart, whereas my mother's love had always come with a side of baggage, and Dad's had come with repeated abandonment. Part of the reason we'd mended our relationships in the last ten years was due to Sadie and her family showing us what love really meant. The Hatleys did love right.

"Take care of yourself, Fallon," Kenya said with a pat on my shoulder. "And if you need anything, just call." She added her card to the one Detective Harris had given me.

I was watching her walk out the door when my dad growled, "Puzo. What the hell are you doing here?"

My gaze jerked to the man who'd joined us. Lorenzo Puzo wore a custom-made suit and had satin black hair, a high forehead, and a prominent Italian nose. But it was his eyes, almost as dark as his hair, that drew your gaze, holding you captive and reminding you that he was part of one of the original crime families who'd built Las Vegas.

"I was in town on business and heard there was some trouble," Lorenzo replied, and the dark tenor of his voice sent another chill down my spine.

When Dad had first moved to Sin City in his twenties, he'd stumbled into some of the Puzo family's criminal activities, and he'd almost been killed for turning the evidence over to the FBI. After Lorenzo had taken over the family business, he'd supposedly done his best to legitimize it, causing a feud that still existed.

It was the dark side of the Puzos who'd come for Dad ten years ago in revenge, murdering Spencer and attacking Sadie and me at her bar. Even though his cousin Theresa had ended up dead, Lorenzo had been trying to help my family ever since as some sort of penance.

But seeing Lorenzo always brought me back to that day. To the fear and death. And after everything that happened last night, it felt amplified by a thousand. My heart raced, and my palms turned sweaty as his cold eyes settled on me.

"Are you okay, Fallon?" Lorenzo asked.

"Don't respond to that," Dad grunted, but I couldn't have answered if I'd wanted to. My throat had closed all over again. The smell of blood surrounded me. My vision turned spotty.

Mom rolled over in her wheelchair. Her eyes darted between us as if a war was going to break out. Even though Dad and Lorenzo had called an uneasy truce, it still didn't mean they liked each other.

"Rafe," Mom's voice drew Dad's eyes to her. "Let's focus on Fallon."

It was the shakiness in Mom's voice that drew me back from the edge. I'd been conditioned to react to it. I'd had years of experience holding her up. Years of being the stable one in our relationship. Today wouldn't be the day that changed.

I cleared my throat and lied. "I'm okay."

I wasn't. But I'd wait until I was alone before I licked my wounds further and stabbed myself with remorse. Before I let myself think about the apartment JJ had put in my name or the baby furniture he'd bought.

"They found drugs and cash in our apartment," I told them. "But I couldn't have taken them because I wasn't even in San Diego the day they went missing. JJ has been spending money like he's won the lottery lately, and he's been hanging out with Ace Turner. So...I don't know." I rubbed my forehead. "Maybe Ace convinced him to take the drugs and sell them as a way out of debt?"

Dad hissed, "What the fuck?" just as Lorenzo asked, "What kind of drugs?"

Dad reacted immediately to Lorenzo's question. "Why the hell do you care? Are you involved in this?"

Lorenzo waved a hand in dismissal. "Not like you're implying. I'm simply following up on some ugly business with my cousins."

Dad stepped closer. "Did one of them come after my daughter?"

Lorenzo looked from Dad to me and back. His mouth was as firm as his tone when he said, "No. And I can promise you, they won't."

Silence settled. Heavy and hard. It was Lorenzo who broke it. "I'll take my leave. Take care, Fallon." Then, he looked toward Sadie and said, "I'll call you next week to discuss the next gala for the theater foundation."

Then, he walked out of the station with two large bodyguards trailing him.

"Goddamn it," Dad snarled.

Sadie linked her hand with his. "Fallon is exhausted. Let's get her out of here. We can work out what Lorenzo is up to later."

"You're right," Dad said, tugging me to him again and holding on. I closed my eyes and let his warmth settle over me. "Your apartment is a mess from the police search. Do you want to come back to the hotel with us?"

I didn't want the apartment, or a hotel, or anything to do with San Diego. I wanted the one place that had always grounded me.

I shook my head. "No. I want to go home, Dad. I want to go to the ranch."

Chapter Ten
Parker

ALL THESE THINGS THAT I'VE DONE
Performed by The Killers

TEN YEARS AGO

HIM: I shouldn't have left you, damnit.

> *HER: I'm glad you weren't here. They would have shot you without a second thought. At least when they saw Sadie at the door, she had a chance because they needed her to get into the safe.*

HIM: Never again. If you're ever in danger again, you won't be able to shake me.

> *HER: What are you going to do? Go AWOL in the middle of some top-secret mission to run home? Besides, I don't need you to save me. Sadie and I saved ourselves.*

PRESENT DAY

My right hand stung from slamming my trident into the coffin next to the others my teammates had placed there. My eyes stung from tears I was fighting to hold back. Silver One Squadron stood at attention as they lowered Will into the ground.

I didn't hear the words spoken by the priest nor the words

of our commander.

I barely registered the bugler playing "Taps." I wasn't even sure the firing squad would have registered if the tiny hand in mine hadn't startled with the first shot. I squeezed Theo's fingers tighter, tugging him closer to me as we stood at attention through the final report.

When it was over and I held a folded flag in one hand and a child's hand in the other, I had to fight to breathe. We should move. We should head across the grass to the long line of cars parked along the cemetery's lanes, but my feet felt rooted.

When I looked down at him, Theo's face showed the same confusion that had been there since I'd retrieved him from the group home. He was struggling to comprehend what it all meant. That he'd never see either of his parents again. That his dad's body was in a damn wooden box.

Maybe it was better this way. Not knowing. Not seeing.

All I saw on repeat was my friend's bloody face.

In the three nights since my team had brought Will home, that was all I'd dreamed about. The first night, when I didn't have Theo yet, it had driven me from my bed to multiple glasses of alcohol that had dulled my senses. But after I'd brought him home, I'd refused to be drunk if he needed me.

When I'd picked Theo up, after all the paperwork had been sorted, I'd taken him back to Will's apartment so he'd have all his own things and a place he was familiar with. I'd thought it would be easier for Theo, even when it had been hell on me to be surrounded by all of Will's memories.

But Theo had been almost inconsolable. So, the next day, I'd boxed up as many of his toys and clothes as possible and brought him back to my place. At some point, I'd have to return and sort through the apartment. But selfishly, I needed some time before I did that.

Every night, Theo had cried himself to sleep, asking for his parents and breaking my heart just a bit more each time I couldn't give him what he needed. He'd fallen asleep in the bed in my guest room each night, but at some point, he always joined me in mine. I'd woken to tiny elbows and bony heels shoved into my legs and side.

I wasn't used to sharing a bed with anyone. The women I slept with either took me to their place, or I booked a hotel. Either way, I left long before morning. I never woke with them beside me.

Except for one night when I'd had a blonde in *my* bed and woke to find her gone.

A singular evening that had nearly ruined a lifetime of friendship.

I shook my head, but the truth was, I hadn't been able to get Fallon out of my mind all week. I wanted to talk to her. I wanted to hear the positive spin she'd put on my situation. The way she'd punch through the bullshit and lay it on the line in much the way my dad had. But I couldn't. Not now, when she had crap piled up at her door too.

When Dad had told me about the drug arrest and what had happened with JJ, I'd nearly lost the last thread of my sanity. I'd wanted to pull my team together, blow up the jail cell the loser was sitting in, and make him suffer before I ended his life for trying to destroy hers.

The simple fact I'd had a little boy sitting across the table from me had stopped me from doing something stupid. Instead, I'd sent a half-assed apology for what she was going through, and she'd replied with her own.

HER: We both know how lame the words are, but I'm so sorry about Will. So damn sorry for you and for Theo. Don't worry about me, Parker. I'll be fine. Just take care of you and that little boy.

Even as I'd read the words, I'd known she was lying. She wasn't anywhere close to fine. She was just doing what Fallon always did—she was retreating into herself to lick her wounds, pretending she didn't need anyone or anything. Pretending she could carry the weight of the world on her own.

She'd gone home, Dad had said. And that was the best place for her. Back in Rivers, on the Harrington ranch, Fallon had always blossomed. The fields and mountains would root her in the things that mattered most.

I wasn't sure who or what would ground me. Before, being

a part of the SEAL teams had done just that, but at the moment, it felt like I'd never find myself again. And that simple thought was what kept me from texting her like I would have otherwise. Stopped me from losing myself in a brief moment of light she'd bravely offer, even while she attempted to pull herself out of the dark.

The little hand in mine nearly slipped out, and I caught it, holding it tighter.

"You ready, bud?" I asked.

He looked up at me with dazed eyes.

I still had moments of pure panic at the thought of being responsible for this little life. Moments when I felt like I was being held underwater, just like at BUD/S. Except, this time, I had no chance of escape, no chance of emerging and inhaling a fresh gasp of air.

Theo shrugged, pulling his hand away to take the tawny stuffed dog he'd had for as long as I'd known him and nuzzle it with his face. I squatted down and ruffled his hair.

"We're almost done with our assignment for the day. One more task. It means facing some more people, but after, we'll go home and watch more of those dog shows you like."

It had been pure chance that I'd landed on an American Kennel dog show yesterday. He'd stopped me from turning the channel with a pat on my arm, watching the screen with the same fascination other kids might give a cartoon. After that, I'd found a bunch of replays on the internet, and he'd watched every single one.

"Okay, Park," he said. He sounded so much like Will as he said it that it tore at me.

I picked him up, and he rested his head on my shoulder, snagging my heart and twisting it into a thousand knots. I crossed the grass, my dress shoes sliding on the dew as I strode toward the limousine my dad had hired.

My parents were waiting for us. Dad had his arm around Mom's shoulders. She was tall, almost six foot, slim and elegant with dark hair and pale-blue eyes. She wore a navy-colored suit today, and her shoulder-length hair was pulled back in a tight twist. Her eyes were red-rimmed, and her cheeks pale. She was grieving as much as I was.

Silence reigned on our drive from the cemetery to my commander's house, where our team had gathered to celebrate Will. Once we were there, the stories flew. Everyone had something to share about him. Wild adventures. Hilarious moments. Laughter rang out, and we all held back tears behind gritted teeth and locked jaws. And then we patted each other on the back and went our separate ways.

We had four months before they recalled us. Then, we'd spend six to eight months re-proving ourselves, traveling around the country for various pre-deployment trainings. We'd spend months away from base, which meant I had four months to figure out my shit and what all of this meant for Theo.

As much as I loved the kid, as much as I wouldn't even consider handing him off to someone else to raise, I still got angry thinking about how my life had been twisted into some unknown version of itself. But every time I got angry; guilt followed on its heels. Wishing Will had lived simply so I didn't have to take on the mantle of his responsibilities felt all kinds of wrong.

After leaving my commander's house, Theo and I returned to my cottage with my parents in tow. Mom offered to help Theo change out of the tiny suit she'd bought him. I hadn't even considered what Theo would wear to the funeral, just as I hadn't thought of a million other things he'd needed in the last two days that Mom had handled for me. What was I going to do when my parents went back to Las Vegas?

What would Theo do when he was stuck with a selfish bastard watching over him?

I strode into my room, hung up my uniform, and searched for clean civilian clothes.

I was down to the bare minimum because I needed to do laundry. The pile of tiny clothes mixed with mine had grown out of control in just three days. I dragged on a pair of black cargo pants and a T-shirt with the Marquess Enterprises logo from my dresser. I usually only wore the shirt when I was off-duty and helping Dad with security at Rafe's casino in Las

Vegas.

It was a uniform different from my military one, but one that still meant serving and protecting. Except, I had failed in this uniform too.

My chest twisted as guilt drove into me once again. Ten years ago, I'd left Fallon on the day she'd needed me most, leaving her open to an attack from Theresa Puzo and Adam Hurly, and she'd almost died because of it. Since she'd moved to San Diego for college, I'd done everything I could to ensure she was safe and unharmed. But it hadn't been enough. First, there'd been the entire incident with Ace and his wife, and now this with JJ. Could I have kept her safe if I hadn't been so focused on my career? If I hadn't been more focused on the promise I'd made to my grandfather than the one I'd made to her? Was a promise to a dying man worth Fallon's life? Not even close. But what the fuck did that mean?

As I emerged from the bedroom, Dad looked up from his phone and said, "I thought we'd order pizza."

"You have an early flight. You don't need to babysit us."

He ignored my comment and went to the kitchen, grabbing two beers from the fridge and handing me one. "Your mom and I had a long talk last night. We think you and Theo should come live with us for now."

"What?" I nearly choked on the swallow I'd taken.

He waved a hand. "What are you going to do when you're deployed? Who's going to keep Theo? At least this way, he'd be in his own bed every night, living with people who care about him."

"Dad, you're retiring. You planned to sell the house and travel for the next five years before settling down anywhere."

Dad had worked for Rafe for nearly two decades now. After Rafe had married Sadie, he'd hired a CEO to take over the bulk of the Marquess Enterprise's responsibilities in order to have more time with her, their kids, and Fallon. But as Rafe had slowly unraveled himself from the business's day-to-day activities, my dad had become more entrenched. He was much more than just the chief of security. He was Rafe's guard dog, watching over the hired executives to ensure nothing went wrong.

But Dad had promised Mom to finally retire by the end of the year.

"Truth is, we'd discussed eventually settling down wherever you were at." Dad gave me a sad grin. "We were hoping we might get another grandkid or two out of you and Will, even if you swore you'd forever be single."

I tried not to let the mention of Will stab me in the gut. He'd wanted more kids, whereas I'd treated the topic as if it was a horror show.

I pushed past those thoughts to focus on what Dad was offering me—a way to share the burden of raising Theo. But I didn't want my parents to give up their future plans any more than I wanted to give up mine.

My voice was gruff when I finally responded, "Having a grandkid is different than becoming a backup parent at fifty-five."

Dad shrugged. "Life likes to throw hand grenades at us. Sometimes, it isn't until after we've rebuilt from the wreckage that we can see it was the best thing to happen to us." Nice words, but they only made the pain in my chest grow to epic proportions. The shrapnel from the blowup of my life shouldn't spread to theirs. He read my hesitancy. "Think about it. It isn't like you'd be abandoning him to foster care. You'd be his guardian, and we'd just be helping out whenever you were out of pocket."

"We love him, Parker," Mom said, joining us in the kitchen. She put an arm around my waist and rested her head on my shoulder. "We loved Will. Theo was already our grandchild. This just makes it legal."

My teeth ground together, and pain ratcheted up my jaw, spiking along my temples.

"You have plenty of time to consider it," Dad said. "They won't call your team back until they're sure the dust has settled."

Mere months. We had one hundred and twenty days before we started training again.

Was that even enough time to right this ship? For one of the first times in my life, I didn't know the answer or have a clue on how to go about it.

Chapter Eleven
Fallon

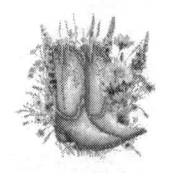

THE PROPHECY
Performed by Taylor Swift

TEN YEARS AGO

HIM: *** GIF of a country artist saying happy birthday***

HER: How much did it hurt to use that GIF?

HIM: It was worth the sacrifice if it made you smile. How are you celebrating?

HER: Don't know. Mom hasn't mentioned it, which is fine. It doesn't feel like I should be celebrating anyway. Nothing seems right without Spencer here this year.

HIM: Today is about YOU. And YOU DESERVE to be celebrated.

PRESENT DAY

The wind was unseasonably cool, whipping against my face and through my light flannel as I raced up the slope on Daisy. A vibrant mix of rainbow-sherbet colors spread across the lightening sky. My heart leaped at the pure magnificence of Mother Nature at work.

I'd loved the sunsets on the beach in San Diego, but nothing was better than watching the splendor of a sunrise or a sunset on the ranch. White-capped mountains soared above me, fields littered with wildflowers danced in the morning light, and the lake reflected the sky, making it seem like there was no end to either.

I'd needed this—maybe more than I'd even expected.

I felt soothed and safe here. The only other place I felt the same was with Parker.

As quickly as that thought came, I shoved it aside.

Parker wasn't mine any more than JJ had been, but this place—the land and all I could see—was.

As I urged Daisy up the final hill, the enormous river-rock wall of the estate came into view. The metal gate that arched over the road was swung open, welcoming guests to the resort. Once they passed through it, the wild valleys and forests of the Sierra Mountain foothills transformed into carefully crafted, castle-like gardens with sculpted hedges and flowering trees. Our landscapers had built a little oasis around the gold-flecked pool we'd added to the grounds with Dad's money. A handful of sleek cabanas provided privacy for our famous guests, and a poolside bar allowed swimmers to float right up and order drinks.

Beyond the pool and gardens, the Victorian castle where I'd spent the first fifteen years of my life stood tall and proud. The curls and flourishes along the golden gables and towers mimicked those on a castle in England that my great-great-grandparents had built the mansion to resemble. They'd used the money from diamonds discovered and mined on the estate in the 1930s, which had made our family one of the wealthiest in California before it had all dried up a decade later.

The castle and grounds had started to crumble a bit just before Spencer had died. With the ranch nearly bankrupt, Dad had stepped in and agreed to help Mom and me convert the ranch into a resort, using the money and experience he'd earned in creating a five-star Vegas resort to help us. I'd talked them into building a small two-bedroom house farther up in the hills for Mom and me to live in rather than continuing to stay in the castle while it was filled with guests.

In many ways, that little house and our time there had

allowed Mom and me to restore our relationship as much as I thought it would ever be. We both still had too many scars to allow the relationship to be an easy one, and we both wanted our way when it came to the ranch and the resort.

I was fairly certain she resented I'd been given the land, and I resented that she had a say in what happened to it while acting as my guardian. Sometimes, I wondered if it was because Mom saw me as one-hundred-percent Harrington, without an ounce of her Hurly blood, and because of the hundred-year animosity that had once existed between the Hurlys and the Harringtons that kept us from letting down our guards completely with each other.

It was a ridiculous notion, as if our two families were actually cursed, as Mom's brother, my Uncle Adam, had once told me. He'd said the curse could never be broken while both families struggled to live on the land together.

Daisy's hooves clattered along the circular drive as I rode past the centaur fountain. The four mythical creatures were quiet and still now, but they came alive with music and lights each evening, putting on a Vegas-worthy show. Mom and I had rolled our eyes when Dad had suggested it, but it remained a favorite attraction and frequently appeared in our guests' social media posts.

The paved parking lot behind the house was quiet, but beyond it, the river rock, dark wood, and green-roofed outbuildings were coming alive. The paddocks and corrals would soon fill up with workers and the handful of guests who'd signed up for one of our ranch-hand packages.

As I dismounted, Chuck, one of our new hires, ran out of the horse barn.

"You want me to take her, Ms. Harrington?" he asked with a hopeful smile. The skinny, dark-haired teen had taken to Daisy as soon as she'd arrived from San Diego at the beginning of the month. Surprisingly, she'd taken to him too. My horse was picky about who she liked. She'd never liked JJ.

But I wouldn't think about what that meant today, or I'd spend more hours berating myself for things I couldn't change. Spencer used to tell me everyone made mistakes, but how we lived our lives after admitting to them showed our true character.

I was determined to do better.

I was about to decline Chuck's offer of help with Daisy when my eyes landed on a trio of upset faces standing by one of our ranch rigs.

I handed the reins to the teen and said, "It's Fallon, please. Every time you call me Ms. Harrington, I expect to turn and see my mom."

"Okay…Fallon." The teenager blushed to his roots.

I nodded toward the rig where my dad stood next to Kurt and Teddy and asked, "What's going on?"

"Not sure," he said with a frown. "Kurt was real upset when he came in from checking on the cattle. He hustled into the main house and got Mr. Marquess."

Kurt was upset? What would it take to rattle one of the calmest men I knew? I strode past the corral we used for horse shows and pushed between Dad and Kurt, glancing into the truck bed. My stomach fell to my boots when I saw the bloody mess of what had once been a cow. It had been mutilated almost beyond recognition.

"What the hell happened?" I demanded.

Dad's eyes shifted to me. "Kurt and Teddy found her out in the west field. We think a cougar must have brought her down, and the carrion birds did the rest."

"Damn. And we don't have any cameras that far out to know for sure," I said.

Dad nodded in agreement. The security and privacy of our guests were of utmost importance to us, and the measures we'd put in place ensured our rich and famous clientele knew it. We had a twenty-four-hour security team who patrolled the main buildings, the lakeside beach, and pathways, and we'd installed emergency phones and cameras throughout the most traveled areas of the estate. The team monitored those phones and cameras from a hut housing a bank of computers. But in truth, it was impossible to cover all five thousand acres of the estate.

"Issue an alert to the staff and guests to be on the lookout for the cougar. Then, send a crew to ensure a mama hasn't created a den too near the main paths," I said, directing the order to Kurt.

He raised one bushy brow at the command but didn't throw it in my face that, as the ranch's foreman for going on three decades, he had years more experience than me and didn't need me to tell him what to do. Instead, he simply said, "Already rounded up some folks. They'll head out after breakfast. Not much salvageable from the cow now, so Teddy and I will bury her in the far field."

I gave him a smile in apology, saying. "Thank you."

"Let us know if you hear anything more," Dad said.

As Kurt slammed the tailgate shut and headed for the driver's door, Dad and I turned and strode toward the hotel.

"Everything okay, Ms. Harr—er, Fallon?" Chuck called out from the barn doors.

I gave him a curt nod and continued moving toward the back of the main house, where the entrance reserved for staff was located.

"That kid's got a crush on you the size of Texas," Dad said.

"I'm not doing anything to encourage it,"

"You don't have to. Just being you is enough."

I rolled my eyes, but his words hit me in the chest. I wasn't sure how Dad could still see the good in me after all that had gone down in San Diego. I'd screwed up. I'd been a selfish coward, and in many ways, it was JJ who'd paid the price for it.

If I'd never taken him back the first time, or if I'd really been able to love him the way he'd wanted, he would never have been tempted to do all the things he'd done to try to keep me. I knew it was ridiculous to think it. I wasn't responsible for his actions. I hadn't asked him to spend hundreds of thousands of dollars and then steal drugs to get out of debt, but I still couldn't shake the guilt I had for leading him on, for pretending I could be someone I wasn't.

I swallowed over the lump in my throat and focused back on the cow so I wouldn't start crying. "We haven't had any cougar sightings in several years."

"I'm not sure what would have tempted one down this far. The resort activity usually keeps them away." Dad's jaw was tight, teeth grinding together. It was an old habit that, much like my nail-biting, I'd thought he'd put behind him.

Dad stopped me before we reached the hotel management offices we'd carved out of the old servant quarters. "Maybe I should stay a bit longer."

His eyes were troubled when I met them. I shook my head. "No. You can't disappoint Sadie and the kids. They've been looking forward to your summer in Australia, and you need to be there when you open the resort in Port Douglas."

"It's winter there. I think Caro and Spencey are going to be disappointed in the weather."

I laughed and shrugged. "Maybe, but every time I talk to them, they've added something new to their to-do list. You'll be lucky to have an hour of quiet in two months."

He chuckled, his love for my siblings evident in his face.

Dad had taken a step back from his leadership role at Marquess Enterprises, but he was still the face of the company and still had a hand in developing each project. The resort in Australia had been a colossal undertaking that he and Sadie needed to celebrate finishing.

When Dad reached out and tugged on my braid in much the way Parker used to, my heart nearly seized. His brows furrowed as he asked, "Are you sure you want this? We can still sell the ranch if you've found new dreams to follow."

After my birthday dinner last night, Dad had handed me the official paperwork transferring the estate and the Harrington trust into my name. From here on out, the ranch's success or failure was on me, and I had no intention of letting it fail. What was the saying? *Failure isn't an option.* And it wasn't.

"I did what you asked, Dad. I went to college and explored all the possible careers and futures I could have, but the simple truth is, this is where I truly belong. I need the ranch as much as it needs me. Taking care of the land and our legacy isn't a burden. It's a gift, and there's nothing I want more."

I wasn't sure he understood my view, seeing as he'd given

up his portion of the ranch for a wad of cash after my mom had betrayed him. She'd eloped with Spencer days before she was supposed to marry Dad, and it had sent him running away, even knowing she was pregnant with me. My father had taken the money and started his bar business in Las Vegas, leaving me here with Mom and Spencer. He hadn't returned once to Rivers until after his brother had been killed.

"Spencer would be gloating if he heard you say that," Dad said, his voice turning gravelly with emotions.

Dad drew me to him, hugging me tight, and my arms surrounded him with an ease that still surprised us both when, a decade ago, I'd thought he was the enemy for leaving me and the ranch behind. A wave of affection hit me so intensely it nearly closed my throat.

"I love you, Dad."

His arms tightened even more, and his voice was still gruff as he said, "I promised you'd never face anything bad on your own again."

"And you've kept that promise, Dad. You were there in San Diego, and I'm not alone here. We have so many people working the ranch that I can barely blink without seeing someone."

"You call, and I'll be back in a flash."

I stepped away and laughed. "Well, it'll take a minimum of a day to get to California from Australia, and you'd have to go back through time to do it."

He nudged my chin. "Superhero, traveling through time to get to his family." He turned serious. "I'd do it, Ducky. Anything you need. I mean it. And if that loser JJ, or that scum Ace, even breathes around you, I want to know."

The drugs and cash in our apartment had come back with JJ's prints, and while Detective Harris couldn't prove it, he highly suspected JJ was offloading the drugs through Ace and his network. If it was true, Ace had gotten out of prison in January only to immediately return to his old ways.

"They can't find Celia," I said.

Even though she'd come at me hard while Ace was

awaiting trial, showing up on campus, at my apartment, and even the stables where I'd boarded Daisy during competition season, I still had no desire to see her seriously harmed. After Ace had been sentenced, she'd disappeared and hadn't returned once he'd been released. I hoped it meant she'd come to her senses and left the bastard and not that something worse had happened to her.

Dad tugged my braid again. "You're not responsible for what happened to Celia any more than I was responsible for Theresa Puzo's death. They made their own choices by getting in bed with the devil."

Dad and I had both tried to do the right thing and gotten burned by it. We were more alike than I'd ever wanted to admit as a teenager.

"Don't let your wrongly placed guilt have you answering the phone if JJ calls," Dad ordered.

"I've blocked his number. He'd have to leave a message with the hotel staff to get to me, and I can simply ignore that. He won't call though. He's got his hands full with the case against him and dealing with all the loans he took out and whoever he was stealing drugs for, Ace or otherwise. I'm not worried."

Dad didn't look as sure as I felt.

For one brief second, my certainty wavered. I hadn't listened to my instincts in San Diego. I'd buried all the alarm bells while eking out the last few years of my college freedom.

Never again.

I'd make sure I listened when my gut screamed at me, and I'd do whatever it took to keep me, the ranch, and my family safe. And along the way, I hoped to find my way back to the Fallon I'd once been.

♫ ♫ ♫

Not even a week later, those instincts were clamoring at me, and I was wondering if I'd ever escape what had happened in San Diego. As Kurt and I stared down at another pretty cow that had been mutilated, I tortured myself over the knowledge that I'd brought this to the ranch. It was absolutely clear it wasn't a cougar this time—not with the words *You will pay* carved into her hide.

Bile rolled through me, and for one humiliating moment, I thought I might actually be sick.

I was a farm girl. I'd seen my fair share of blood and guts and gore. Hell, I'd helped deliver babies multiple times, sticking my hands inside and helping the calves work themselves down the canal. I hadn't gotten sick with the smell of birthing in a barn, so there was no way a dead cow in the middle of a bluebell- and yarrow-covered field would make me lose my breakfast, even if the violence of it tried to bring back nightmares I usually kept at bay these days..

"Cameras?" I asked, turning away from the cow and inhaling the smell of pine the wind brought down off the mountaintop.

Kurt turned with me, pointing a long finger. "Closest is about two football fields to the east. I'll have Lance pull footage for the last twenty-four hours and see who might have been heading in this direction."

The wounds on the cow were fresh, the blood hadn't dried, and the scavengers hadn't found her yet. We might get lucky with a camera.

"I'll call Sheriff Wylee," I told him. "See if he'll send someone to take a report."

"You think this is JJ?" Kurt asked. His unibrow was low over warm brown eyes. It had grown impossibly bushier over the last decade. Once, those brows had been pure black, and now they were shot with white, just like his hair. The bits of skin on his face that weren't covered by a mustache and beard were so wrinkled it looked like a shrink-wrap experiment gone awry.

My teeth ground together at his question, hating how everyone knew what had happened in San Diego. Just like I'd hated the knowing looks I'd gotten from people on the ranch and in town growing up. Everyone in Rivers had known about the love triangle I'd been born into. I was the product of multiple betrayals, and it had been whispered about, even when

I was a teenager, becoming especially loud after Spencer's murder and Dad's return.

But what was worse than any humiliating stares was knowing this poor cow had lost its life because of me. Someone had hated me enough to come onto my land and torture a nearly defenseless creature. My gut told me there was only a couple of people who had a reason to hate me this much, and I wouldn't ignore it.

"I'll call Detective Harris, tell him what happened, and ask if he can find JJ and Ace," I said. "Neither of them has permission to leave San Diego, so if they're caught here, they'd be sent back to jail."

As much as I couldn't imagine JJ taking a knife to anything, let alone being able to bring down a full-grown cow, he had Ace on his side. And I'd seen Ace that violent. The image of him choking Celia would forever be burned in my brain. And JJ's face had been almost as ugly at the police station. A shiver ran up my spine.

"You going to call your dad too?"

My chest tightened. "No reason to call him, Kurt." The man grunted in disapproval, and I added a glare to my words. "You telling me we can't handle this on our own? That you and the entire security team I'm paying a fortune for need my dad's help? We need my daddy to fly all the way home from Australia to somehow fix this?"

I'd pushed the right button, gotten his pride involved, and Kurt snarled, "We know how to take care of our own."

I gave him a curt nod. "Damn straight we do."

Except, I wasn't sure I did.

I made the mistake of looking at the cow again, and my stomach rolled once more. "I'll head back to the castle to wait for Wylee's folks. You want me to send someone to watch over her until they show?"

"No. I'd rather talk personally to whomever the sheriff sends."

I took another quick glance at the cow before striding across the field toward our horses. They were nervous, sensing the death in the air just as I did.

I pulled my phone from the back pocket of my worn jeans and hit Detective Harris's number. He'd called several times in the first couple of weeks I'd been home, keeping me abreast of the case against JJ, but I hadn't heard from him since before my birthday.

He picked up on the first ring with a snapped, "Harris."

"Hey, it's Fallon."

"Fallon." His voice turned softer. Kinder. And I almost hated that as much as I hated the sympathy I saw daily from my staff. "How are you?"

"I'd be better if I hadn't had two cows mutilated in as many weeks."

"Excuse me?"

"I'm sending you a picture." I shot off the one I'd taken of the cow today and heard his phone ping on the other end of the line.

"Damn," he muttered. "You said this is the second one? Did the first say the same thing?"

"We thought a cougar got the first and the buzzards afterward. There wasn't much left of it. Where's JJ?" I asked, hoping beyond belief he could tell me JJ was sitting in Ace's apartment.

I only knew JJ was bunking with Ace because Rae had said he'd tried to stay at our apartment until she'd kicked him to the curb. His name wasn't on the lease, and I was paying my share of the rent until she could get someone to sublet from me when the school year started.

"I'll find out and get back to you." He hung up before I could respond.

I swallowed back the guilt and self-reproach I'd gotten good at and dialed the sheriff's department. The front desk put me directly through to Wylee, and he swore like the rest of us when I told him what had happened. He promised to send a deputy out right away.

I rested my forehead on Daisy's muzzle in an attempt to soothe the discordant emotions humming through me.

What would our guests think if and when they found out about a second mutilated cow? This one with a very personal, very angry message? The last thing I needed was for them to get the willies and take off during our busiest season. I needed to call a management meeting, talk it over with the department heads, and see what we could do and say to reassure everyone without lying.

What should I do now, Spence?

I couldn't stand knowing I'd led this to the ranch. How long would I pay penance for my mistakes? Would I get the same sentence as JJ was likely to get? Years?

Was there any chance this had nothing to do with me? That it was related to the estate itself or Dad and the business with the Puzos that had gone down years ago? It didn't seem likely. After all, everyone who hated us back then was either dead or locked away in a jail cell.

Still, I remembered Dad's displeasure at seeing Lorenzo in San Diego. I wouldn't call Dad, but I would call Jim Steele. Ultimately, it was his men in charge of the security here. But I'd wait until I heard back from Harris and for Wylee to do his thing so I'd have the full details to give Jim. If this was Ace or JJ, and they were caught anywhere near here, it would put a stop to anything worse happening.

I swallowed over the lump in my throat, scratched Daisy's cheek one more time, and swung myself into the saddle. I didn't have to prompt her into a canter.

She wanted to leave the field and the death behind as much as I did, but my stomach rolled unexpectedly at the motion. I'd been riding horses for as long as I could remember, doing tricks on Daisy's back that some people thought were magic. I could fling myself off, spin around, and land back on without thinking, and I'd never once gotten sick while doing any of it.

Just nerves, I told myself. Nerves with a side dose of fury.

I'd keep the fury with me. It would help if I had to face evil again. I'd done it before. I'd do it again. And in the meantime, I'd do everything I could to keep the people and animals I was responsible for safe.

Chapter Twelve
Parker

WHEN THIS IS OVER
Performed by Goran

SEVEN YEARS AGO

HIM: *Kermit, really? You sent me a stuffed frog?*

> HER: *That's what they call you SEALs, right? Frogs? Congratulations on making it through BUD/S, Kermit.*

HIM: *If the team finds this out, they'll initiate me with a new nickname.*

> HER: *And Baywatch is so much better than Kermit?*

HIM: **** one-fingered emoji *** At least Parker Stevenson and his lifeguard pals were tough guys. They weren't little green puppets.*

Later

HIM: *Damn it, Ducky. They've made Kermit our group mascot. How will we strike fear into our enemies with a puppet on our dashboard?*

> HER: *Bait and switch. They'll think you're pushovers, and then you'll prove just how wrong they are.*

PRESENT DAY

L J Evans

Four weeks. A month had gone by since I'd brought Will's body home. I'd been in charge of Theo for thirty-one days, but after what had happened today, I wasn't sure I was any better at taking care of him than I'd been in the beginning.

We'd done nothing but sit on the couch, brainlessly watching dog shows, for the first week. After that, I'd realized I needed to kick my ass into gear before we became melted piles of goop. So, I'd done what I was known best for doing—I'd gone into research-and-planning mode.

I'd inhaled dozens of books and blog posts on parenting. I'd even watched a slew of social media reels and videos, hoping to extract the best advice and assemble it into a cohesive strategy. I'd learned more about parenting than I'd ever wanted to know.

Whenever my teammates had popped by to check on Theo and me, they'd made jokes about the "Daddy Workshop" I'd put together, asking if I'd start offering classes. But what the fuck else was I supposed to do? Theo deserved someone knowledgeable, someone who would consider a kid's wants and needs but also knew how to say no and set boundaries, which I'd failed at miserably in those first horrifying days.

But now, we'd found a routine. We had meals at a set time, and he played outside as much as possible in the mornings and worked out with me in the afternoons. He'd even learned to ride his bike without the training wheels. Watching him pedal, watching his tiny legs and body balance the bike, had curled a strange sort of pride and love inside me. My smile had been as wide as his when he'd turned the bike around without falling off and rode straight back to me.

I'd thought I'd done at least one damn thing right.

But not today. Today had been another failure.

I'd dropped him off at a preschool not far from my house for the first time and almost had a panic attack. Leaving him there with Dog tucked under his armpit, looking at me with the saddest eyes I'd seen on him since the funeral, had just about undone me.

Once I'd gotten back to my truck, I'd been shaking so hard

I couldn't even start the damn thing. I'd put my head on the steering wheel and inhaled slowly and painfully, trying to calm myself down. Eventually, I'd turned the key and headed toward Will's apartment, where our teammates were meeting me to help clear it out.

I'd barely made it to the complex and was bounding up the steps when I received the call from the preschool.

"Mr. Steele, you'll have to come get your son."

The handful of words had the panic roaring back to life. It had been so quick and so harsh that I hadn't even bothered to correct the woman's misconception about Theo being mine.

"What happened?" I'd demanded, turning and leaping back to the ground.

"He slammed a toy truck into another boy's face."

"Theo?" Shock had my feet halting in a way that almost caused me to trip. Theo didn't have a violent bone in his body. Whenever we were playing, if he accidentally hit me, he nearly cried.

"Yes. And we have a no-violence policy. One and done. I'm sure that was explained to you when Sheila signed you up. You may be okay with violence with your lifestyle, but we are—"

"By my lifestyle, do you mean my occupation as a Navy SEAL?" Anger rippled through my words.

"Your response is clearly the reason your son reacts in the same way."

I bit the inside of my cheek until the taste of iron coated my tongue. "I'm fifteen minutes out."

As soon as I was on my way, I called Sweeney, postponed the work at Will's apartment, and tried my damn best to modulate my emotions so I'd be calm when I got to the school.

Walking into the office, seeing Theo sobbing in Dog's fur, unraveled any calm I'd found.

I glared at the woman in charge, picked Theo up, and rubbed his little back. "I'm here, Theo. I'm here."

"I's sorry. I's sorry. I's sorry," Theo cried.

I hugged him tight until his tears calmed. Then, I pulled

back enough to see his face. "What happened, bud?"

"He said I had to share Dog. He said all the toys had to be shared," Theo cried as he showed me his stuffed animal. "Now Dog is hurt." The seam on one of the arms was torn, stuffing coming out. My chest felt like a thousand-pound weight had been placed on it. Fury rolled through me.

"We can fix it. I promise. Dog will be okay." I set him down in the tiny chair he'd been in when I'd entered the office. "Give me two minutes, Theo, and then we'll go home and get him all fixed up."

Theo nodded, his red, splotchy face making me want to punch something.

I crossed to the lady at the desk, and maybe the dark look on my face or the way I leaned toward her set off her alarms, because she pushed away and took a step back.

I dropped my voice so Theo couldn't hear, but it made my tone all the more deadly. "I told the lady who enrolled Theo that he'd lost both his parents in less than a month. That toy is the only thing holding him together some days. No wonder he reacted when some damn kid tried to take it away from him."

Her eyes widened. "I'm... Sheila didn't say..."

"I guess it's good we're leaving and not coming back, seeing as your staff fails to share the critical needs of their students with each other. Did you even bother to ask him what happened?"

"Yes."

"Did you see his toy was ripped?"

"You may not understand this, Mr. Steele, but violence is never the answer. And certainly not one kid slamming a toy into another child's face."

"That's the second time you've disparaged my career—the people who keep you and this country safe. I'd like my money back."

She swallowed. "We don't give refunds when kids are expelled."

I snorted. "False advertising. Inability to keep a traumatized child safe. I'm sure I can find some other things to lob at you. Give me my money back, and we'll be out of your hair."

"Our policies are clear." I took a step forward, and she swallowed hard. "Do I need to call security, Mr. Steele?"

My nails bit into my palms as I tried to rein in my anger, tried to tuck it behind the shield I was supposed to be excellent at keeping. I didn't really give a damn about the money. It was the principle of it. They hadn't kept Theo safe.

I hadn't kept Theo safe.

I whirled around, picked Theo up along with the little dog backpack I'd bought him, and strode out of the building.

So much for knowing what the hell I was doing. Any pride I'd felt at our routine, at the structure and home I was trying to give Theo, flew out the window. I'd left him at the first damn place I'd researched. I'd left him, and he'd been traumatized even more.

I'd failed.

I could rationalize it by saying I was still learning, but that was bullshit. This was a kid's life I had in my hands, not some stupid-ass gun I had to learn to take apart in my sleep.

But goddamnit, I hadn't signed up for this. Hadn't signed up to be a dad.

Guilt swarmed in over the frustration and regret.

I had to get those kinds of thoughts out of my head, or I'd never be able to give him what he really deserved—the simple knowledge he was loved and wanted.

An image of Fallon flashed before me, picking at her nails as she shrugged off something I'd said about her dad. *None of them wanted me, Parker, and now I'm just a duty they can't shake.*

It had torn my insides to shreds. She'd truly believed she wasn't wanted or cherished. She'd admitted to being loved when I'd pushed and had eventually admitted she'd been wrong about some of it. But I knew those old wounds still ached, knew she still looked at the way her siblings were loved and saw all the ways she hadn't been.

I didn't want Theo to ever believe he was only an

obligation.

After buckling himself into the car seat that barely fit into the back seat of my pickup, Theo looked up at me with tear-filled eyes.

"Are you m-mad at me? Mommy used to get mad…" He rubbed his cheek, and his little shoulders shuddered before he buried his face in his stuffed animal again. My stomach fell to my knees. What had Althea done when she'd been angry? Had she hurt him?

Damn it. Damn all of it.

"I'm not mad at you, bud. No way, no how. You protected what was yours. That's never going to be an issue with me."

As I shut the door, the weight on my shoulders nearly shoved me to the ground.

Theo needed a dad who knew what the hell he was doing. Who could navigate these troubled waters with ease. Will would have known what to do. Would have been able to make his son laugh and smile and make sure he felt safe.

The trip back home was quiet. As soon as we got there, I took out my tiny sewing kit and stitched up the stuffed animal as best I could, wrapping a bandage around his leg and saying he'd be good as new in a few days. Then, I picked up the threads of the routine I'd established for us. We ate lunch, rode our bikes, worked out in my garage, and then had dinner before I tucked him into bed and read him books until he drifted off to sleep.

He always fell asleep in the guest room, which I'd done my best to turn into a kid's room, but most nights, he still ended up crawling into my bed. It was the only thing the books had said I shouldn't allow that I'd ignored. If the kid needed me to feel safe, I'd continue to let it happen.

I stared at him, curled around his stuffed animal, for a long moment, silently promising to do better. Then, I shut off the lights, left the door cracked open so I'd hear him if he called for me, and headed to the kitchen to clean up our dinner mess.

My phone rang before I'd picked up a single dish, and I knew who it was without even glancing at the screen. My parents had called every day—sometimes multiple times a day—to check in and make sure we were still alive and kicking.

"How'd the first day of preschool go?" Dad asked.

When I explained what had happened, Dad cursed under his breath. "Assholes. But just because this wasn't the right place for him doesn't mean there isn't a great one out there, Park."

"Maybe I pushed him into this too soon. Maybe he isn't ready yet."

"Or maybe you aren't."

I swallowed, knowing there was some truth to his statement. I'd ignored the panicked feeling I'd had leaving him today, and as a SEAL, I knew better than that.

"You might be right," I confessed.

My dad was quiet for a moment. "I have an idea. You can help me out and give yourselves a break at the same time. It'll get you out of San Diego for a few days."

"Going to Vegas isn't the answer right now," I told him. We'd had a similar conversation several times over the course of the month. My parents insisted that visiting them, even if it was just for a few weeks, would be a good distraction, but I wasn't sure I agreed.

Routine. We had to find a new routine—a new normal. I needed it as much as Theo did.

But then again, scrambling for a routine had led to an epic fail today, so maybe my parents were right.

"Not Vegas," Dad said. "Rafe's house in Willow Creek was broken into. The safe needs to be checked, and I want to follow up with Maddox Hatley." Sadie's brother was the sheriff in the town where Rafe and Sadie lived these days, and his sister's house being broken into while she was away wouldn't be pushed to a back burner. When I said as much, Dad agreed, adding on, "He thinks it was likely teenagers scared off by the alarm blasting."

"So, you want me to go to Tennessee?"

"No. I want you to go to Rivers."

My entire body tightened as my mind filled with thoughts

of a blond-haired lightning bolt who made me crave things I could never have.

"Why?" I grunted out.

"Two cows were mutilated. The second one had the words 'You will pay' cut into its hide." He hadn't even finished his sentence before I was moving. Adrenaline flooded me along with a rage similar to the one I'd felt at the preschool. My emotions had been completely haywire since Will's death.

"I'll kill JJ," I growled.

"Calm down. According to the detective in charge of JJ's case, he's still in San Diego. His ankle monitor confirms it."

I scoffed, "Ankle monitors are easy enough to tamper with."

"Maybe for you and your teammates, not for a regular guy like JJ."

"What about that coke-head, Ace Turner?" I demanded.

"According to Detective Harris, he and his partner paid a visit to Ace's place of work, and he was there. Got pissed they were hassling him. But no telling if he drove to Rivers and then back before they got to him."

"That's a long haul," I said.

"It is, but not impossible." Dad hesitated. "There's more. There was an accident."

My heart stopped. Images of Fallon, bleeding, hurt, or worse, filled my head before I shook them away and croaked out, "Fallon?"

"She's okay. The tractor she was driving blew a tire, and she went into a ditch. I think it scared her more than anything."

"Fuck."

Going into a ditch on a tractor would have reminded her of her stepdad careening off a cliff on one ten years ago. The tractor had landed on top of him in the river, pinning Spencer under the water. At first, the coroner had ruled it an accident until Fallon had uncovered proof that her Uncle Adam and Theresa Puzo had murdered him.

"Tractor tire had knife marks," Dad said.

It wasn't a fucking accident. Someone had done this to her on purpose.

"What the hell is going on with the ranch's security?" I growled.

"Exactly my thoughts. I was heading to Rivers before I got the call about Rafe's house."

My brain whirled. It was easy to say Fallon was under attack from the assholes she'd helped put behind bars, but it didn't make sense for Rafe's house to be broken into too. "A damn lot has happened in a short span, especially if you consider the break-in at Rafe's."

"The two things might not be related."

"Interesting timing, if that's the case."

"I know," Dad said. "But Sheriff Hatley might be right. Rafe's house could have just been local teens who knew the family was gone for the summer." We let that set for a second, and he added on, "There's one more thing I didn't tell you earlier. Puzo showed up at the police station the day Fallon was arrested."

"Why the hell was he in California at all?"

"Said he had family business to take care of. When Rafe told me, I reminded him that one of the Puzos' cousins, Tony Cantori, got out of prison back in March. His wife and daughter were already living in Los Angeles, and he joined them. He's working for a construction company there. I'll dig into the company some more."

"Is Cantori on the Ike Puzo or Lorenzo side of the family feud?"

"As much as we can tell, he's on Lorenzo's side, which is why neither Rafe nor I were overly concerned about him being so close to Fallon," Dad said.

As much as I disliked Lorenzo Puzo, he'd done nothing in the ten years since his cousin had murdered Spencer and tried to murder Rafe, Fallon, and Sadie to insinuate he was anything but a legitimate businessman. When I said as much to Dad, he agreed.

"The truth is, this might not be about Fallon, Rafe, or the

family. We can't assume it is, or we'll miss other clues while attempting to pin this on an easy target. Whoever is doing this could simply be a disgruntled employee."

I snorted in disbelief. "What does Fallon have to say about it?"

"She wasn't the one who called me. It was Kurt. You know her, she's trying to handle it all herself, so she's going to be pissed no matter who shows up. But you've always had a good way of handling her."

More guilt tore through me, thinking not only of one night when I hadn't handled her well at all, but of all the times she'd had to save herself because I'd been too late.

If I didn't have Theo, I'd already be in my truck and on the way to Rivers.

But what would happen if I took him with me, and he got hurt while I was trying to protect her? What would happen to her if I didn't go? Both scenarios were unthinkable.

My jaw ticked as I battled a sea of mixed emotions, loyalties, and duties. But what kept ringing in my head was the oath I'd made to that blond-haired lightning bolt. I had a chance to redeem myself, to be there for her just like I'd promised after failing her one too many times.

When I was quiet for too long, Dad pushed. "Theo will love the ranch."

He would. The kid adored dogs more than any other creature, but he got a kick out of all sorts of animals.

"He needs a routine," I said quietly.

"He needs a break," Dad retorted. "And so do you. Give him some new memories to think about, Park. Let some happiness settle in over the bad before you look to find that routine you've been reading about in all those damn books."

I swiped a hand over my head. I needed a haircut. Maybe I'd just shave it off like I was some rookie frogman at BUD/S again. I felt more like a damn tadpole right now than I had in nearly a decade, fumbling around in the dark, searching for the right direction.

Debate warred in me. No good answer. No good path to

take. All the ones in front of me were loaded with land mines I was sure to step on.

"I'll leave tonight."

Dad exhaled with relief, and just that single sound eased the tension in my shoulders.

I'd made the right decision.

Chapter Thirteen
Fallon

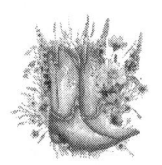

GIRL IN THE MIRROR
Performed by Megan Moroney

THREE YEARS AGO

   HIM: I didn't hear you leave.

No response.

   HIM: You're really going to ghost me?

No response.

   HIM: Don't make me come find you.

      HER: Take the hint, Parker. I can't talk to you right now. Let me recover from my humiliation and lick my wounds in peace.

PRESENT DAY

The smoldering ruin in front of me made my stomach roll, and fury beat inside my chest. The flames were out, but smoke still drifted from the blackened remains into the morning sunshine. The heat of the day wasn't far off, and the charred scent hung heavy in the thick air.

My hands were damp, and my fingers wrinkled from the hoses I'd wrangled while fighting the blaze. My body shook from both the physical exertion and the nerves that had settled in now that the fire had been contained.

We'd almost lost it all. The entire ranch…

Pain coursed through me.

God. It had almost gone up in flames on my watch.

"Fuck." Kurt's single word was full of emotions.

I glanced over to find his face and clothes coated with black ash that I was sure covered me too.

Tears threatened, and I bit my cheek hard in an attempt to contain them. I would not cry in front of my staff or the fire crew who was finishing up. I'd save the tears for later, in the privacy of my own home when no one could see me.

Just before dawn, I'd been coming down from my house to the hotel when an explosion had rocked the ground and sent me to my hands and knees. Shock had quickly been followed by terror as I'd clambered to my feet and raced toward the main house. When I'd seen the flames, for one panicked moment, I'd thought it had been the horse barn. I'd barely registered that relief as the cabin had come into view, wholly engulfed in the blaze.

Kurt and others had poured onto the scene, and we'd had the emergency pumps and hoses going well before the firefighters had arrived. But it had been too late to save the cabin.

Thank God no one had been inside. Andie, our hotel manager, had said it had been empty last night, and the next guest wasn't due to arrive until today. We'd have to figure out where to put them, but that was the least of our worries.

As I stared at the black hole where the cabin had once been, I saw Dad's sad, disappointed face in my mind. Once upon a time, the ranch's horse trainer had lived there. I didn't remember Levi, but Dad had fond memories of the weathered old man who'd been more of a father to him than anyone else. Dad had spent much of his childhood at Levi's side, learning everything he knew about horses. If I hadn't been born, and Spence hadn't whisked Mom away from Dad, my father would have spent his entire life here, breeding and training horses.

When Levi had died, my stepdad and Mom couldn't afford to replace him, and the cabin had stayed empty until we'd renovated the ranch. We'd kept the old pine furniture, updated the kitchen and bath, and added a tiny porch with rocking chairs and potted plants. It had been one of our top bookings over the years, and now, it was gone.

The lost memories for Dad hurt far worse than any lost profit could.

I rubbed my chest. The ache inside it only grew.

"I'm so sorry, Ms. Harring—Fallon," Chuck said from my other side. His face was soot-covered as well, and he looked closer to tears than me.

"Thanks for the assist with the hoses, Chuck. You've been a big help. Why don't you get cleaned up and head over to the ranch-hand house for some breakfast?"

The teen ducked his head, mumbled something incomprehensible, and shuffled off with his shoulders sloped as if the weight of the world was on him.

Before I could consider why it had hit him so hard, one of the firefighters approached. He had his massive gloves stuffed in the pocket of his Kevlar jacket, a helmet shoved under an arm, and a small plastic bag held in his free hand.

"Dad, Fallon." He nodded at the two of us. It took me a moment to recognize Kurt's son under the black coating his face. We'd gone to high school together. He'd been two years older than Maisey and me, but we'd all been friends.

"Thanks for getting here so quick, Beckett," I said.

"We've had a cool summer up until this week, but things are dry. We were lucky there was relatively no wind today. Otherwise, the embers might have taken the barn and the other outbuildings before spreading to the fields and forest."

Over the last few decades, California had been devastated by large, fast-burning fires, burning hundreds of thousands of acres, houses, and businesses. Beckett was right, the weather and their response time had made a difference today. We'd been lucky, even though it didn't feel that way looking at the darkened timbers in front of me.

"What you got there?" Kurt nodded toward the bag.

Beckett handed it over to him, and I saw it held a black box with melted wires sticking out of the end.

"Timing device," Beckett said, brows furrowing.

It took too long for me to understand what he was saying, and when it did, the pain in my chest grew exponentially.

"You're saying someone did this on purpose?" My voice was hollow with grief.

"I'm afraid so. I placed a call to Sheriff Wylee. He's on his way," Beckett responded.

My legs buckled, and only Beckett's and Kurt's quick reactions prevented me from hitting the ground for the second time that morning.

A deep voice calling my name from the direction of the parking lot had me jerking out of their hold. Everything felt like it was in slow motion as I turned to see Parker weaving through firefighters, staff, and guests toward me.

How was he here?

He had Will's son in his arms, and the picture they made racing across the blacktop was stunning—a hero rushing through smoke and crowds with a rescued kid in his arms. Parker's black hair, wide shoulders, narrow waist, and steel-gray eyes only enhanced the mirage. Add a cape, and he'd be able to fly around the earth in a single bound.

As he got closer, Parker scanned me in that way he always did, cataloging me from head to toe, searching every inch for injury. Normally, it lit me up from the inside out. But now, the panicked concern I saw in his gaze caused the tears I'd barely held back to rush out.

Before I could take a step toward him, he'd reached me and pulled me into a fierce, one-armed hug. I buried my face into his chest and tried to hide the sob that escaped. His heartbeat thundered under my ear while Theo patted me, awkwardly smooshed between Parker and me.

"Are you okay? What the hell happened?" Parker's deep voice was growly and dark.

I couldn't respond. My throat was too clogged.

I didn't know how or why he was here. At the moment, I didn't care, because gathered in his arms was one of the rare places I'd always felt safe. And for most of my childhood, it was the only place I'd felt truly wanted. Maybe not as his girlfriend, but as a friend. As family. At least until I'd realized he was just one more person who saw me as a responsibility.

But none of that mattered now. All I cared about was that he was here.

That I'd needed him, and he'd appeared like I'd conjured him from a dream.

For days, I'd debated telling Dad about what had been happening at the ranch. The mutilated cow. The terrifying slide into the ditch when the tractor tire had been tampered with. But I'd known it would be selfish to call him. Dad would have come running when there was nothing he could do. As a teen, I would have wanted that—him simply showing up so I wouldn't face more awful things alone—but as a grown-ass woman, I didn't need Dad to come running.

Except, I'd needed someone. I'd needed Parker.

"Ducky?" Parker's voice broke as the tears wracked my body, and my shoulders shook. When I still couldn't answer, he sent his question to my foreman. "Kurt?"

"She's not hurt, Parker. It's just been a long few days." Kurt's voice was tired and drawn. "And like always, she's tried to take it all on without showing a lick of weakness."

His words had me pulling myself together, had me fighting the tears and wiping at my face, even though it would spread the black ash into an ugly mess.

I reluctantly stepped away from Parker and tossed an irritated look at my foreman.

"And what's that supposed to mean, Kurt? I'm a woman, so I'm supposed to curl up in a ball and cry, while you're a man, so you're supposed to be able to take it all on the chin and keep standing?"

Kurt's mouth twitched, and he guffawed. "There's my girl. Thought you were in there somewhere below that blubbering mess."

It took me a second to realize what he'd done. I slammed him on the shoulder with my fist. "Asshole."

Beckett looked between the group of us with a smile emerging. "I see you've got plenty of support with Dad and the gang here, so I won't have to worry about you." I rolled my eyes, and he laughed. "That eye roll is the same one you gave me when I asked you to the homecoming dance, and you broke my heart by saying no."

A gurgled laugh erupted from deep inside me. "I did *not* break your heart. You didn't even really want to go with me. You wanted to go with Maisey."

He winked. "True story. But she'd already told Carter Smythe yes." He flung a thumb back at the crew still mopping up. "I'm going to get back at it. When Wylee shows up, direct him my way."

He pocketed the bag with the black box and strode away.

When I turned to Parker, his face was shuttered in that way I despised. All emotion was hidden away. It made him look every inch the Navy SEAL he was, but I still couldn't stand it. I missed the Parker I'd grown up with—the one I could read as easily as he still read me.

"What are you doing here?" I asked.

Kurt cleared his throat awkwardly, and I reeled around to glare at him again. "You called him?"

"He called my dad," Parker answered for him. "But the question is, why didn't you pick up the phone and call one of us?"

"Damn you, Kurt—"

"Look. I respected your reasons for not calling Rafe," Kurt said gravely. "But ultimately, Jim is in charge of the security team, and they haven't been doing their job. Someone needed to come and kick them in the ass. They sure as hell weren't going to listen to the guy in charge of the cows."

"You should have talked it over with me," I snapped. "It was my decision to make, not yours."

Old wounds flashed. The many times I'd been overruled by Mom while she'd had control of me and the ranch. Taking it out on Kurt wasn't fair, and I instantly regretted it.

Kurt held up his hands. "Maybe so. But I won't apologize

for doing what I thought was right. And as soon as you get your ego out of your ass, you'll realize it too."

He shoved his hands into his pockets and strode off toward his men who were standing at the edges of the cabin, watching the firefighters finish up.

Anger and embarrassment burned. Not only because Parker had seen our exchange but because Kurt was right. It had been partially ego that had stopped me from calling Jim. How many mistakes would I make before I realized I wasn't ready for this responsibility? These character-building errors I kept making risked far more than the land. Someone could have died today!

My chest wound another notch tighter, and I fought against chewing my nails by biting into my cheek once more.

I lifted my chin and met Parker's gaze defiantly, but it wasn't judgment or disapproval I saw in those steely eyes—it was a flash of concern that bled through the SEAL facade.

"Want to tell me what the hell has been going on, Ducky?"

"Hell, Ducky!" Theo said with a smile, throwing his stuffed dog into the air, and Parker looked completely abashed.

"We've talked about this, bud. You can't repeat everything I say."

My heart clutched at the exchange, making those stupid tears prick again. The love wafting from Parker to Theo was so big and so visible it could cause a sonic wave. The few times I'd seen Parker with Will's son before now, he'd always been good with him. He'd teased and laughed as anyone might with a friend's kid, but I hadn't seen this—protectiveness and love.

It hit me right in that tender spot, deep inside, that had always been Parker's. Right beside the ache I'd once had to have my own kids. To raise a couple of babies who would forever know they were loved and wanted. I'd set those wishes aside, thinking there was plenty of time for them after I'd finished college, taken the ranch in hand, and made my dreams of the animal refuge come true.

Now, I wasn't sure what—if any of it—I'd be able to pull off.

Then, I kicked myself in the proverbial ass just like Kurt had said I needed. What was wrong with me the last few days?

My emotions were on a wild roller-coaster ride I couldn't seem to stop.

I swallowed hard. "I need to get cleaned up before Sheriff Wylee shows up. Where does Jim have you staying?"

"The cabin," Parker said with a look behind me at the rubble.

As his words registered, my stomach lurched once more, and for one horrifying moment, I thought I might throw up right in front of him. What if he'd shown up with Theo last night instead of this morning? What would have happened if they'd been inside? God…would they have gotten out before— I batted away those thoughts and swallowed down the nausea, but my entire body was shaking from the effort.

"Come up to the house until I can talk with Andie and see what's available. With everything that's been happening, I don't doubt we've had some cancellations." I strode toward the path behind the castle that led up into the hills to the house where Mom and I lived.

Parker grabbed my arm, drawing me toward the parking lot. "We'll take my truck."

The simple touch sparked along my skin, sizzling with a heat stronger than the embers that had burned a hole in my T-shirt while fighting the fire. When I looked down at his hand, he pulled it back as if I'd bitten him.

He strode toward the antiquated green pickup he'd had for as long as I'd been in San Diego. I'd been in the rig so many times I couldn't count them all, mostly hauling ourselves and our surfboards to the beach. The truck brought back some of my best summer memories. Times when I'd had his complete attention as we topped the waves. Times when I'd thought maybe I stood a chance of one day making him mine.

Then, I'd met JJ and given up the fight. Or maybe I'd given up the fight and then met JJ? I wasn't sure anymore.

Parker opened the back door of the truck for Theo, and the little boy climbed in and strapped himself into his car seat while we climbed into the front. Parker backed out of the spot and drove past the main house, where I saw dozens of guests curiously peeking out their windows.

My stomach sank all over again. I should have gone inside and talked to them. I should have reassured both the guests and our staff that everything would be okay. But at the moment, I couldn't. I needed to shower and get a hold of my emotions so I'd appear to have everything in hand when I did talk to everyone.

When my home came into view, the pots blossoming with summer flowers on the porch drew my gaze away from the decorative river rock, chestnut siding, and green roof. I'd barely noticed the flowers in the month I'd been home, but now they looked decidedly cheerful.

I wished I could be as happy. That I was rejoicing Parker being here instead of worrying about why he'd come and if he and Theo would be safe.

As soon as Parker braked, I was out of the truck and up the two short steps to the front door. I punched in the keycode, and the lock clicked open. Inside, my eyes settled on the heart of the house—a large wall of glass overlooking the valley where the rivers twined on both sides of the hotel and the stables. A hint of the lake was visible, its icy blue waters surrounded by trees and white cliffs. Some of my favorite places on the ranch were visible right here. It usually filled me with pride and peace, but today, seeing the smoke still lingering in the air, my insides twisted more.

Parker dropped a couple of backpacks and large military duffels on the floor as he and Theo came in the front door. His eyes fastened on me for several long heartbeats. He was assessing me again, looking for injuries, and when he found the hole in my shirt near my shoulder, he frowned.

"You get burned?"

"Just a sting."

Two more heartbeats went by with our eyes locked. When stupid tears threatened all over, I was the first to look away—another thing teen Fallon would have been pissed about. I'd gotten off on holding his gaze back then. I'd seen it as a silent dare, and I'd rejoiced every time I'd won.

"I'm going to shower," I said. "Help yourself to whatever you need in the kitchen. It's pretty bare because I've mostly eaten with the staff lately, but there should be coffee and bread."

"Fallon—"

I couldn't handle the empathy I heard in his tone. I'd break down again, so I just kept walking down the short hall that led to two suites on opposing sides of the house. Each had a large bath, walk-in closet, and small sitting area that had allowed Mom and me to escape whenever we'd rubbed each other the wrong way.

I'd favored emeralds and golds as a teen, and somehow, the decor had held up over the years, so it didn't look childish or outdated, even a decade later. My room faced the valley and the sunsets, while Mom's cheerful blue-and-yellow room faced the mountains and the sunrise.

I headed straight for the golden marble bathroom en suite, shedding my clothes and tossing them by the trash can instead of the hamper. I'd never get the smoke smell out of them, and even if I did, I'd only feel the failure I felt whenever I saw them.

For a moment, I eyed the large whirlpool tub with longing. The jets would soothe my worries as much as my pains, but I didn't have time to wallow right now, not if I intended to make it down to the hotel in time to talk with the sheriff.

I walked into the oversized shower and flipped the water all the way to hot. Every part of me ached as I stood under the powerful stream. If hauling hoses for a few hours had made my muscles this sore, I'd gotten softer than I'd imagined in my years in San Diego. Hell, even my breasts hurt. My hand slowed as I brushed the soap over them, and a new fear darted inside before I forced it away, just as I'd been forcing all my worst thoughts in the last month.

I'd had my period.

Everything was fine.

It would be a wasted effort to spend even a moment thinking about what JJ had or hadn't done with our condoms. What I needed to do was figure out who was behind these attacks at the ranch. Because if it wasn't JJ or Ace, I was coming up blank.

After Kurt and I had realized the tractor tire hadn't blown out from wear but had been slashed, Detectives Harris and Lake had once again paid JJ and Ace visits. Both men insisted they'd been in San Diego all along, and there was no proof to say otherwise. Even JJ's ankle monitor said he hadn't left the area.

Kurt and I had spent hours after the call trying to figure out who might have been behind these attacks. Neither of us could think of any employee or guest who would do anything this ugly, but we'd agreed to meet with Andie when she returned from vacation today and review the list of past employees who'd been fired or left under a cloud.

The banging of pans in the kitchen made its way through the open door of my bedroom, bringing my attention back to the man waiting for me.

When my insides twisted this time, it was with a completely different emotion—soul-deep longing. While I couldn't deny wanting him here, it was selfish to keep him close, especially when he had Theo. The last thing Parker needed was to add my worries to his own. What had Jim been thinking in calling him?

Parker had always insisted he never wanted to be a dad, yet he'd stepped up to the plate and taken Theo anyway because he was honorable. Good down to his very marrow. If you could see a soul, Parker's would be as bright as the heavenly gates themselves, pure and white and stunning. Whereas mine would be marred with black.

I'd been born in betrayal, one of many committed by my ancestors. Did that darkness etch itself into a person? Did my insides look as hollowed and destroyed as the cabin had looked this morning? Would keeping Parker here so I didn't feel quite so alone add another permanent dark mark?

I bit my cheek and closed my eyes against another rush of tears.

As much as I didn't want to add to Parker's burdens, his honor and bravery would prevent him from leaving me when he thought I was in danger. The only solution was to identify who was responsible for this and put an end to it, so Parker could return home to his life and whatever new plans he was making for himself and Theo.

If I did nothing else right in the next few days, I promised myself it would be that.

Chapter Fourteen
Parker

EVERY BREATH YOU TAKE
Performed by The Police

FIVE YEARS AGO

>*HER: Kermit, I need tacos.*

HIM: Are you drunk?

>*HER: No. Yes. Maybe.*

HIM: Are all your friends no-yes drunk as well and unable to take you to get tacos?

>*HER: They've all hooked up for the night and are more interested in sex than food. I'm at a bonfire, surrounded by college kids smooching.*

Minutes passed.

>*HER: Fine. I'll walk to The Taco Bar and then catch a CarShare to the apartment.*

HIM: Don't you dare walk on that strip of road at night by yourself.

>*HER: ***GIF of a frog tapping chin in thought*** Tacos... disappoint the broody SEAL... Tacos... SEAL... TACOS!!!!*

HIM: I'll be there in ten minutes. Don't fucking leave the bonfire.

PRESENT DAY

I watched Fallon stride down the hall and felt the weight of the world going with her. She'd regressed into the teen who'd dealt with enormous responsibilities on her own and awed me with her ability to act more like an adult than the actual adults in her life. It pissed me off that she'd been forced back into that box. Whoever was doing this, whoever had come for her, her family, or the ranch, would have to deal with me now.

Theo tugged at my hand, and guilt buzzed through me like a jet taking off from a carrier deck. Strong and fierce and fast. How could I protect Fallon and go after the asshole pulling these stunts while keeping Theo out of harm's way too? Maybe I should have gone to Vegas first and dropped him off with Mom. But I'd become his stable ground, his safety net, and if I disappeared on him for days, that might cause even more damage.

"I'm hungry," he told me.

We'd been up for hours. The hard bed and loud noises from the parking lot of the motel in Santa Clarita where we'd stopped last night had kept us both up. Eventually, I'd given up on the idea of sleep in the wee hours, poured us into the truck, and headed for the ranch, knowing we'd have a first-class breakfast waiting for us.

All thoughts of food had been shoved from my brain when I'd seen the fire trucks and smelled the charred remains of the cabin. Seeing Fallon being held up by Kurt and a firefighter, I'd almost lost my mind. The fear—the absolute despair—that had coiled through my heart had been so powerful I'd barely been able to park the truck without wrecking it.

For the torturous seconds when I'd thought Fallon had been hurt, my insides had felt as if they'd been ripped out and left for the carrion birds to devour, peck by brutal peck.

When I'd called her name and she'd turned that blackened face toward me…

It made my hands shake all over again.

Theo's stuffed dog hit my stomach, jolting me back to him.

"Dog is hungry too."

Goddamnit, I needed to pull my shit together.

"Let's see what we've got in the kitchen," I told him, linking his tiny hand with mine.

The house Fallon and her mom had designed a decade ago was decorated in the farmhouse chic that had been the rage at the time. It had whitewashed wood, gray leather, and stone-tile floors. It would have been monotone if they hadn't spiced it up with bright colored rugs and decorative pillows.

In the kitchen, the glass-fronted cabinets were filled with vibrant earthenware that stood out against the dark-flecked granite counters. Everything was neat and tidy compared to the mess I'd left in my house. I'd barely remembered to start the dishwasher before loading us into the truck and hitting the road after Dad's call. When I eventually returned home, the refrigerator would carry the disgusting aroma of rotten food—more proof I was losing my edge.

Fallon's stainless-steel refrigerator was nearly empty, just as she'd warned. But there was bread, a few eggs, and a block of cheddar. I placed Theo on the counter and had him monitor the toaster while I scrambled eggs and shredded cheese.

I was just setting the breakfast sandwiches in front of the barstools at the oversized island as Fallon walked down the hall. My hand stalled, and I almost dropped the last plate as I took her in.

She looked like the Fallon I'd always known and yet, somehow, even more devastatingly beautiful. Black jeans clung to her lean hips, and a man's blue suit vest molded to her torso, leaving just a sliver of tanned skin showing above her waistband. Her arms were bare, and the neckline of the vest dove down dramatically, showing off cleavage that seemed rounder and fuller than I'd ever noticed, even when I'd seen her in a bikini more times than I could count. My mouth watered. My dick pulsed.

Hunger coursed through me that had nothing to do with the meal I'd just made.

It was a hunger I'd never been able to sate. Promises bound me, and my goals prevented me from taking what I wanted.

I watched, mesmerized, as she took those blond waves, a shade of dark honey or sweet cognac when they were wet like this, and skillfully worked them into a long braid that ended below her breasts. As she twisted a thick band around the bottom, my hands shook with the desire to tear it out, run my fingers through the lush satin strands, and yank them back, exposing the long slope of her neck so I could feast on it.

As I fought my body's reaction to her, she closed the distance, eyes darting to the food I'd placed on the counter.

"You cooked?" Her lips twitched. "I'm not going to end up fighting you for the bathroom, am I?"

It was a long-standing joke between me and my team that I'd mistakenly shared with her. Soon after joining Silver One Squadron, I'd thrown a party at my house to bond the old and new crewmates, and I'd used baked beans that had gone bad.

No one had let me live it down. Not even her.

"Shut up, pee-girl," I retorted and got another jolt of pleasure when her cheeks pinkened. I liked her flushed and warm and…

No. Just no. I wasn't going there.

"I was five. And I warned you I had to go. I can't help it if you kept tickling me, and my bladder lost control. That's really different than cooking a meal that almost took out an entire squadron of SEALs."

Theo patted Fallon's arm. "Did you have an accident? Parker says everyone, even adults, have them."

Her entire face softened as she looked down at Theo and swept her hand through his hair. "It does happen, buddy." She picked up his stuffed animal from the counter, looking down at the bandaged leg hiding my stitch job. "Who's this, and what happened to him?"

"Dog." Theo's face got all pinched as if he might cry, but he sucked it back up and said, "A meanie hurt him, but Parker fixed it. He says we can take the bandage off soon."

Fallon's gaze met mine over Theo's head, and my jaw worked overtime, trying to keep my emotions from leaking out. Anger still at the preschool staff. Guilt that I'd left Theo there to begin with.

"Parker is really good at healing broken things." Her eyes filled, and I felt a prick return at the back of mine.

I cleared my throat, scooped Theo off the counter, and sat him on the middle barstool. "Eat your breakfast before it gets cold," I told him.

I'd taken two bites of mine before I risked looking up at Fallon again. She'd turned deathly pale beneath her sunny tan. She pushed the plate away.

"If you end up with botulism, it's your fault this time," I attempted a tease with a wave at the refrigerator. "Your food."

"What's botch-a-tasm?" Theo asked, inhaling the breakfast sandwich as if he'd never seen food before.

"It's a…microscopic bug that can get in bad food. I'm just teasing Fallon though. This food is fine." I proved it by stuffing more of my sandwich into my mouth.

Fallon's eyes grew enormous, and she grabbed her plate and slid it along the island to me. "I'm not hungry."

She got up and headed for the door where she'd left her boots and a worn black hat. "I need to get back."

"Give us two seconds to finish up, Ducky, and we'll go with you."

"I need air. I'll see you down at the main house."

As she stepped outside, I swore under my breath and jogged after her. I swung the door open in time to see her sink onto the bottom step of the porch, shoulders shuddering.

I looked back inside and saw Theo eyeing the sandwich she'd slid toward me. "Go ahead, bud. You can eat that one. Then go use the restroom, wash up, and come on out."

He smiled and dug in. I left the door open so I'd hear him if he needed me and joined Fallon on the step.

I shoved my shoulder into hers. "Talk."

"Why are you here, Parker? Don't you have enough on your plate?" Her eyes were pained. I knew that look. It was the one she got whenever she talked about being an obligation to her family rather than being someone they wanted and loved.

"Do you even have to ask?" I growled.

"You don't owe me anything!" Her cheeks flushed, and her eyes flashed. She was always stunning but even more so riled up with passion raging through her.

When I didn't say anything, her tone softened. "You didn't fail me by walking away that day in Willow Creek. What happened with Uncle Adam and Theresa would have still happened if you were there. Worse, they would have shot you as soon as they walked into the bar. I wouldn't have been able to live with myself if that had happened. I won't let anything happen to you now either. I don't want you here. Go take care of Theo."

Having Theo with me was a problem, but I'd figure it out just as I'd figured out everything with him in the last month.

I was deadly serious when I said, "I'm not leaving."

"I don't need a bodyguard."

"Too bad. You got one."

She grunted out a frustrated, inarticulate objection before saying, "You're not my boss, Frogman. You can't issue a command and expect me to follow it. I don't have to let you stay. Go home."

Her words hit me low and fierce in the groin because I wanted to give her commands that had nothing to do with whatever the hell was going on at the ranch. I wanted to demand she climax just before I dove over the edge myself.

That singular thought was what would damn me to hell for the rest of my life.

I leaned into her space more. "You really think you don't need protection? Let's recap exactly why you do, shall we? First, the man you sent to prison for eighteen months is out and pissed and cozying up to your loser boyfriend, who attempted to set you up for a drug rap you escaped by the hair on your chin. You've had two cows mutilated, one with a clear message saying you'd pay. Your tractor tire was sabotaged, and now you've had a building burn down. If anyone needs to leave, it's you while you let the authorities do their job. So why the hell are you still here?"

Fury swept through those golden eyes. "No one is going to send me scurrying from my ranch with my tail between my legs."

And that was what scared me more than anything in my life ever had. The thought of her standing there, hands on her hips, defiant chin thrust in the air, while someone came at her with a knife. Or a damn gun.

"This is my land, Parker. *Mine*. No one is going to steal it from me or scare me into running. I don't care how many explosives they leave, how many tires they cut, or how many condoms they poke holes in—"

Her little rant cut off abruptly, and she clamped her lips shut.

"What the fuck are you talking about? Condoms? Explosives?" Confusion leaked into every syllable as I realized I was missing more than one thread of this conversation.

She moved, pacing in front of me. "Beckett, the firefighter who was with Kurt and me when you arrived, showed us some kind of detonator he found in the cabin's wreckage. Whoever placed it there didn't care that they might have hurt someone…" She inhaled sharply. "Killed someone." She rubbed two fingers of her right hand over the thumb on the left. A sure sign she was tempted to chew on the nail like she had as a little girl. "It could have been your dad in there this morning, or you and Theo…if you'd been a day earlier, or the bomb had been set a day later…"

She clutched her stomach and whipped away from me. Her shoulders shuddered again. I hated seeing her like this. The last time I'd seen her this upset had been that night at the beach when she'd saved Celia Turner's life.

I stood up and did the one thing I knew I shouldn't but couldn't stop myself from doing anyway. I put my arms around her, pulling her into my chest. I rested my chin on the top of her head and tightened my arms when she struggled. After a second, she went limp, leaning into me and letting me hold her up the way she rarely let anyone.

"No one has been hurt yet," I told her softly. "We have time to stop this from getting worse."

"The cabin was destroyed." Her voice broke, and she caught a sob before she let it out. "It was the one place on the ranch that Dad loved."

"This isn't your fault," I said, hoping to soothe her.

She fought her way out of my arms and turned to face me. "It's mine to protect, Parker. Spence left it to me, and I walked away from it for years so I could, what? Play surfer? College girl? Let a man into my life who only wanted me for my money?" Every word was spoken with such self-loathing that it tore at me.

"Stop it," I growled. "I refuse to let you blame yourself for any of it. This place wouldn't even exist if it weren't for you! Rafe never would have rolled up his sleeves and worked side by side with you to save it if you hadn't convinced him it was the right thing to do. Your mom would have slipped away into addiction if you hadn't found a way to get her help. You are one of the strongest humans I've ever met. So do *not* berate yourself for acting your actual age for a few short years instead of being the mini adult you've always been."

Theo came out of the house, his eyes darting between Fallon and me, worry in them. I swallowed hard over the fury I felt. It wasn't directed at Fallon but at whoever had made her doubt herself. The asshole JJ. Whoever was attacking the ranch.

"You ready to go see some horses?" I asked him.

His eyes lit up. "Dogs too?"

I glanced over at Fallon, and she shrugged. "Teddy usually brings his dogs with him to work. The female, June, just had puppies, so she'll probably still be at his place, but it's likely he'll have Johnny with him."

"Puppies!" Theo exclaimed just as I said, "Johnny and June?"

My lips twitched, and I was relieved when I saw hers do the same.

"Teddy is a romantic. He says Johnny Cash and June Carter are his ultimate life goals."

I snorted. "Isn't he, like, fifty or something and still single?"

Fallon's expression turned wary. "Yeah. But before Mom's accident, I thought maybe..." She shook her head. "He's been a regular at the rehabilitation center since she's been there."

"Your mom and Teddy are hooking up?" It was hard to imagine the wild beauty, Lauren, dating the narrow-faced, red-haired, skinny cowboy.

"I'm not sure she'll let anyone close after what happened to her leg," Fallon said sadly.

"She's going through a lot right now, but people live long, happy lives without a limb. The prosthetics they make nowadays allow people to do nearly everything they did before."

She shrugged and started down the drive, veering off to take the steps and the worn path to the main house on foot.

"Fallon," I called out, irritation growing inside me as I realized she was just walking away from the house. "You aren't going to lock up?"

She rolled her eyes. "Shut the door, Parker. It locks automatically. I'll give you a code once I have it programmed in by the security team."

I mounted the porch, slammed the door a bit harder than I should have, scooped up Theo, and jogged down the path till I caught up with her. "The security team has some explaining to do."

She glanced over at me. "You're right. They do."

"Does the detective in San Diego still insist JJ is there?" I asked.

"When I talked to him after the tractor incident, yes."

"There are ways to trick an ankle monitor, Fallon. I could do it with my eyes closed."

Her eyes turned thoughtful. "A month ago, I would have said JJ didn't have that much tech savvy in him, but I'm not sure I ever really knew him." That bitter tone eked into her words again. The self-reproach.

"Who really ever knows anyone?" I said. "Who was it that said that quote you love? The one about people only seeing the version of us that we choose to show them?"

"You know who it is," she shot back. And I held back my smile.

"Eleanor Roosevelt?"

"Try again, Kermit."

"Oprah Winfrey?" She rolled her eyes at me, and I considered it one of my achievements for the day.

"I know, that chick from The Painted Daisies? The singer who died?"

She gave me an exasperated huff. "That would be Landry Kim, and no, it wasn't her or her sister, who *actually* writes their music. But you're getting closer. It was a singer."

"Country artist or pop?" I put as much loathing as I could into the words, and she finally slammed a fist into my shoulder like she had in the old days.

"You're a moron."

"Moron!" Theo chanted, shoving his dog in the air like he did whenever he was excited.

"Don't use that word," I told him. "It's another one only adults can use."

"Fallon's an adult?" he asked, eyes wide and innocent.

And that took all the lightness I'd been able to tease back into her and sent it sailing. Under her breath, she muttered, "Not according to every *man* in my life, and hell, maybe they're all right."

"Hell!" Theo said.

Fallon glanced over at him, and then she burst out laughing. "Kid, you're going to get me in trouble."

Theo shot her his bashful smile. "I don't like getting in trouble."

"Me either," she said, shaking her head.

We were almost at the back door of the castle when she shot me a look. "Please tell me you really do know who said it. Otherwise, all my years of trying to salvage your taste in music has been a complete waste."

"Zendaya?"

"I give up!"

I reached out and tweaked her braid. "I know, Ducky. It was your superhero, Taylor Swift."

Her eyes crinkled at the corner when she smiled. "You might just be savable after all."

Then, she swept into the back hall as it hit me that I wasn't savable at all. Because that look, the satisfaction that had flickered over her face, had me craving to put it there again in all the wrong ways, and I wasn't sure I'd ever rid myself of the desire to do so.

Chapter Fifteen
Fallon

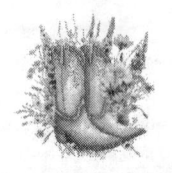

LANDSLIDE
Performed by Fleetwood Mac

FOUR YEARS AGO

> *HER: *** Link to Taylor Swift song****
>
> *HER: When you get back from wherever you're at, doing whatever the hell you're doing with your team, I want that to be the first thing you hear.*
>
> *HIM: SEAL comes home safely, only to be mortally wounded by a pop song.*

PRESENT DAY

The resort had five live-in staff at the hotel. The manager, the head chef, two maids, and a maintenance person. The remaining employees were locals who came on a rotating schedule, including many of our department heads. We'd converted the old servants' wing into a manager's office, a conference room, and studio apartments for the live-in staff.

As I entered the back of the castle with Parker and Theo on my tail, I headed straight for the manager's office. The teasing smile Parker had brought to my face slipped away as I considered what he'd said about needing a bodyguard. He might have been right, but as much as my body rejoiced at Parker here protecting me, I couldn't let him be the one to take on the responsibility.

I needed him to leave, and it wasn't just to keep them safe.

I wasn't sure my heart could take him being here.

How many sweet exchanges and delightful teases could I handle before I was begging him to take me again? Especially with the way my emotions were zigzagging all over the place these days.

I knocked on Andie's open office door and entered to find her pacing behind her desk. Her dark-auburn hair was in a tight bun, and her tailored pants and silk button-down were neat and unrumpled, but her gray eyes were tired and worn in a creamy face dotted with freckles across the nose. She had her phone to her ear, listening intently to the conversation on the other end. She shot me a worried look before glancing behind me to Parker.

"I understand. We hope to see you next year," she said before saying goodbye.

My stomach turned. "Was that a guest canceling their reservation?"

"No. It was the band we had planned for the Fourth of July celebration."

Frustration returned in full force, squeezing my chest. "Hell of a way for you to return from vacation, Andie. I'm sorry things are such a mess, but if worse comes to worst, we can set up the outdoor speakers and manage a playlist ourselves. It won't be the same, but it'll be music."

"We can, but I'll go down our list of usual bands and see if anyone can take their place on such short notice." Her eyes drifted to Parker again.

"You remember Parker Steele?" I asked.

"Of course. Nice to see you again." Her eyes lingered on him as many eyes did. After all, he was something to behold. But it was Theo who brought the wide smile to her face. "Who's this cutie?"

"I'm Feo," he said with an innocent bravado that tugged at my heart.

"Nice to meet you, Theo." She looked from him to Parker

and then back to me, grin disappearing. "Where do you want to start?"

"We need to put out a press release, but I want to meet with the sheriff first and see what he does and doesn't want us to say. Can you call a meeting with all the department heads? I'm pretty sure Olivia can keep our social media and ads focused on our summer activities instead of the bad news, but we need to brainstorm a canned response for the staff to have at the ready if they get questions."

"I already scheduled a meeting for eleven o'clock." She nodded.

"How are the guests holding up?"

"Most have been very kind. They were sad something like this happened and sorry for our loss rather than concerned for themselves. They're just grateful it was put out before it could spread. Do we know what happened?" Andie asked.

Some of the tightness in my chest eased knowing the guests weren't running for the hills…or rather back to their city life. But would they feel the same way if they knew the truth? That it hadn't been an accident? The resort was under attack on my watch, and I wasn't even sure what to do about it.

I told Andie about the device Beckett had found, and her expression turned grim. Parker shifted beside me, a barely perceptible move, but I would always be a thousand times more aware of him than any other human.

"Parker was supposed to stay in the cabin for the next few days." I barely held back the panic that tried to take hold at the thought of what might have happened if they'd already been there. I swallowed hard and then asked, "Do we have any other rooms open?"

"I'm staying with you," Parker said. His voice brooked no argument, and his eyes dared me to try to fight with him about it.

The idea of Parker staying with me in my house was even worse than him staying at the ranch.

Before I could respond, Andie said, "We're completely booked heading into the Fourth of July next week, but someone might cancel if the news that this wasn't an accident leaks out."

With a resigned sigh, I looked at Andie and asked, "Can you have one of the cots brought up to my house for Theo, and have Tami do a quick cleaning of Mom's room?"

"We don't need the cot," Parker said. "Theo ends up in my bed more times than not anyway."

Andie typed into her phone before looking up. "Done."

My phone buzzed, and when I pulled it from my pocket, I saw a message from Kurt saying Sheriff Wylee had finished talking to Beckett and was ready to meet with me.

"Can you pull all the files of any employee who left within the last year?" I asked Andie. "Especially any who left on bad terms? I want to go through them personally, but I suspect Sheriff Wylee will want to see them also."

She rubbed a hand to her forehead. "I can't think of anyone off the top of my head who was upset when they left, Fallon. And I especially can't think of anyone who would come after us like this." She paused, looking out the window and then back. "The staff will be as worried about their safety as the guests if this gets out."

"I'm meeting with the security team now," Parker said. "And Dad has authorized me to increase the team in order to catch this bastard before they strike again. I'll have more bodies here by tonight or tomorrow at the latest. Just intensifying our presence might be enough of a deterrent, but I also intend on closing whatever gaps they've been squeezing through."

As I headed for the door, I looked back and said, "Thanks for all you do, Andie. I'm sorry to throw more at you today, but I appreciate it."

"It's my job, Fallon, and you pay me generously to do it. This place runs so smoothly, I usually feel guilty taking your money." She gave me a wide smile that was supposed to be reassuring, but it only tied me in knots more.

I gave her a curt nod. "I'll see you at the meeting."

Parker and Theo followed me as we headed back outside.

The scent of smoke, charred wood, and burnt plastic hung in the air. My throat closed up once more when I saw the ugly remains of the cabin. *Damnit. Just damnit.*

Kurt and Sheriff Wylee were standing where the porch had once been. We'd just joined them when a soft bark had Theo pulling away from Parker and barreling straight for Johnny as he and Teddy rounded the barn.

"Theo, stop!" Parker yelled, fear in his tone.

But it was too late. Theo had already reached the dog, who wagged his tail furiously in greeting. Thankfully, Johnny was one of the friendliest animals I knew. In general, chinooks were good with people, but Johnny tended to think he was more human than canine. His short-haired, tawny coat shone, and dark, almond-shaped eyes glimmered with happiness at Theo's excitement.

Johnny had a dusting of darker brown along both the ridge of his muzzle and the tips of his short, floppy ears, while his chest was almost white. His mate, June, was even lighter than him, and the puppies they'd had were a fuzzy, furball mix of both parents.

Johnny was already licking Theo's face by the time Parker and I reached them. Theo giggled, a delighted, happy sound that rang through the seriousness of the air like magic.

"Theo, you can't just run up to strange dogs. Not all of them are friendly."

Theo certainly wasn't learning his lesson from Johnny as he draped an arm around the dog's neck and shoved his stuffed animal at him. "Dog meet dog!"

Teddy dropped to one knee by the boy. His beard had gotten thicker in the last few weeks, and it was smattered with gray streaks, just like his bright-red hair. Tall and lanky, I'd always thought of him as a sunflower that had grown too tall for its stem and was likely to droop over at any second. "You don't have to worry about Johnny, Parker. He makes lifelong friends with a mere brush of a hand." Teddy looked over at Theo. "Johnny, sit and say hello."

The dog planted his butt on the ground and held up a paw. Theo giggled again and shook the paw. "I'm Feo, and this is Dog," Theo told Johnny, and I swore the chinook grinned.

Teddy stuck his large hand in Theo's direction. "Not that you care, son, but I'm Teddy."

Theo smiled and shook his hand.

Teddy stood up, looked from Parker to me, and then behind us to the sheriff. "Why don't I take Theo into the barn and show him June and the puppies while y'all take care of business?"

"You brought the puppies?" I asked, surprised, just as Theo shouted, "Puppies!"

"I didn't know how long you'd need me here today after I heard what happened this morning, and I didn't want to leave them unattended for too long at the house."

Those damn tears kept finding their way back to my eyes. Everyone on my staff cared about this place. It made me despise all over again the way we'd let them go when the ranch had been failing before Spence had died. Kurt and Teddy and some of the other ranch hands had spent as much of their lives on the ranch as I had. It might not be a legacy they felt responsible for, but it was much more than a job to many of them. Dad had done his best to make up for our abandoning them when he'd hired our long-term employees back, giving each of them a nice resigning bonus. But a few of them had refused to return, and I couldn't blame them.

Maybe I needed to add those names to the file Andie was compiling. But all of that had happened ten years ago. Why would any of those people come after us now?

It didn't make any sense.

Parker seemed to weigh Teddy's offer hesitantly, even though he'd known the man for more than a decade. Even though being responsible for Theo was new to him, it would be hard for Parker to leave the boy in someone else's care.

I bumped his shoulder. "Go with them. I can catch you up on everything later."

His jaw worked overtime as he slid his teeth back and forth. I could see the pained indecision. Should he stick with me as my bodyguard or go with Theo? This was just one of the many reasons why I wished Jim hadn't called him. It wasn't fair to force Parker to decide between us.

"We'll just be right there." Teddy pointed to the horse barn. "Got a stall at the back all laid out with fresh hay for June and her babies."

"You show him a bunch of puppies, and I'll end up taking one home," Parker said with a tired resignation I'd never heard in his voice before.

Renewed worry spiraled through me. His life had imploded—in some ways worse than mine. Whoever was coming for me would be caught and put away, but Parker would now always be Theo's guardian. A father. The one thing he'd sworn he never wanted to be. I'd witnessed firsthand that kind of obligation as a child. I'd been Theo to Spencer. I didn't want that for either of them. The doubts. The responsibility.

Teddy chuckled at Parker's resigned tone. "Well, these puppies still have a week or so before they're ready to leave their mama." He looked down at Theo and offered him his hand. "Come on, kid, I'll show you the babies, but you'll have to be very gentle with them."

Theo literally squealed, his face bursting into a smile so large it was hard to look away from, but when I did, the affection on Parker's face stole my breath. The love there reminded me, in many ways, of the look Spencer had directed my way before he'd died. It made me instantly ashamed for thinking I'd only been a duty to my stepdad.

Parker watched as Teddy and Theo strode away, Johnny trotting along beside them.

I touched Parker's arm. "You know he'll be just fine with Teddy. He and Kurt raised me almost as much as Mom and Spence did."

His jaw worked overtime again before he turned on a heel and made his way back to where Kurt and Sheriff Wylee were waiting for us. I followed with my heart full of conflicting emotions.

Sheriff Wylee shifted to take us in as we approached. He was nearing seventy, if he wasn't already there, and he was large and round, with white hair almost the same color as his skin. It made him the perfect person to play the clichéd Santa at

Christmas.

He'd been the sheriff when my dad had been a kid, holding the position for nearly four decades now. He knew everyone and everything about Rivers and its people. He didn't fit into most small-town, law-enforcement stereotypes in that he wasn't an asshole who had too big of an ego and territorial issues. His only objective was keeping our community safe, and he used whatever help and resources came along to make it happen.

His face was concerned as he greeted me with a tip of his hat. "Fallon." He extended his hand toward Parker. "I didn't realize you had a son, Parker."

If you hadn't spent a lifetime scrutinizing Parker the way I had, you wouldn't have caught the flinch that crossed his face. It was a barely imperceptible flash before it was gone.

"I just recently became Theo's guardian. He was my teammate's son. We lost Will last month," he responded.

Understanding crossed the sheriff's face. "I'm damn sorry to hear that."

For a beat, an awkward silence hung in the air that no one knew how to bridge before I purposefully stepped into the void, turning the topic back to this morning's horrible event. "Beckett said he found a timing device of some kind?"

"We sent it off to the lab for testing," Wylee answered, looking almost as grateful as Parker that I'd turned the conversation away from the loss of his friend. "Fire marshal found a couple more pieces of shrapnel he thinks were part of the bomb's casing. We'll see if we can get any prints or DNA, but I wouldn't count on it with the heat of the blast. Still, we might get lucky and find a matching bomb signature in the fed's database."

"I requested the security team scour our video footage," Kurt added, throwing a thumb in the direction of the security hut. "I figured the sheriff and Parker would want to see whatever the cameras caught."

We all turned and headed down the worn path that led to the hut. Computer monitors and servers took up most of the room, but there was a locked gun case in the corner and a tiny kitchenette at the back. Our security team ensured we had twenty-four-hour coverage on the estate, but the hut itself was sometimes left empty while the team made their rounds in the wee hours.

We hadn't had any significant issues at the ranch since Uncle Adam and Theresa Puzo had rained their terror on us. Sometimes, when we had a very high-profile wedding, we needed extra security to keep the fans and paparazzi at bay, and we'd had a few minor guest issues here and there, but nothing that was atypical for a resort of our size.

Our head of security, Lance, was bent over the shoulder of another team member, eyes glued to the multiple screens as we came in. He straightened and turned to greet us with the same grim look that had been on all the staff's faces this morning. I hated it.

Dark-haired and olive-skinned, Lance had years of experience at much larger venues. Five years ago, he'd left Dad's Vegas resort and come here so he could raise his kids in a small town like the one he'd grown up in outside Denver.

Looking at Parker, Lance crossed his arms over his chest and bit out, "Before you even ask, Parker, I'll tell you the same thing I told your dad. We didn't miss anything."

"And yet we have a burned-down cabin, a slashed tractor tire, and two mutilated cows," Parker snapped back.

Lance didn't respond, but his eyes flashed with anger—whether it was at the situation or Parker, I couldn't tell.

"We'll need all the video sent to us," Wylee told Lance. "Everything from the time the first cow showed up mutilated."

"That's hundreds of hours," I said to Wylee. "You're not staffed to crawl through that much footage."

"We're all-hands-on-deck, Fallon. No one in my department is sitting on their asses while you've got trouble here. When we're not on shift, each of us will take turns looking through it."

"Let me see if I can wrangle some off-the-book support to analyze the video as well," Parker said. Then, he put his hand on the shoulder of the guy running the camera and said, "Stop! Go back."

I eased up next to him and saw, with a shiver up my spine, the same thing he did—me going into Levi's cabin.

I frowned. When had I last been in the cabin? Maybe when Dad had stayed there after we'd returned from San Diego? Definitely before Sadie and my siblings had shown up for my birthday and then all flown off to Australia.

"When was this?" I asked.

"Last night. 9:05," the guy at the camera said.

Everything seemed to slow down as something pulled low in my belly. Fear mixed with confusion. "I wasn't in the cabin last night." I turned to Parker, repeating, "I wasn't anywhere near it."

"I hardly think you'd plant a device to burn down your own property," Sheriff Wylee said, joining us. "Don't need the money, right?" The way his voice crept up, making the statement into a question, sent another shiver over my skin and reminded me of Detective Lake in San Diego throwing the bored-little-rich-girl routine at me.

It spiked my annoyance into full fury mode. "No. I don't need the damn money. And I wouldn't burn down part of my legacy."

The sheriff patted me on the shoulder. "Calm down. No one is accusing you of anything."

But the doubt was already there. I could see it.

"I wasn't in the damn cabin last night," I said. "I was…" My voice trailed off. Where was I? I'd fallen asleep on the couch, hadn't I? I'd helped bale the alfalfa yesterday, and I'd barely made it home and showered before collapsing on the couch with the television remote in hand. I'd woken up in the middle of the night with static on the screen and crawled into bed before passing out again.

"Fallon?" Parker prompted.

"Home. I was home. I fell asleep on the couch."

No one said anything, but there was a rustle of clothes as the men shifted awkwardly.

"We have the security system on the house. It'll show when I entered my code and that I didn't leave until this morning," I explained, irritated at even the idea of having to prove myself.

But as I looked around the cabin, my suspicions grew. Someone *had* put me on that screen, which meant it had to be someone with access to our systems. Someone with the skill to do it. But why would they? What could anyone possibly gain from trying to pin this on me?

I couldn't see JJ and Ace doing anything this crafty. They'd just come straight for me.

I swallowed hard, that bitter taste growing and coating my tongue until I didn't think I'd ever be able to eat or drink again without tasting it.

"The video has obviously been messed with, right? I wasn't here." I turned to Parker, sending him a look that pleaded with him to believe me.

He nodded. "I'll send it to Cranky. He'll tell us when and how the video was modified." He turned to Wylee. "You should send the footage to an official video forensic team. Going through the proper channels will take longer, but you'll have legal evidence to back up whatever Cranky finds out for me."

"Who the hell is Cranky?" Wylee asked.

"Member of my SEAL team. He's in charge of all our tech and surveillance. He knows how to do things with code you wouldn't even think was possible."

"Sadie's sister-in-law knows people at the NSA," I said quietly. "If I had her ask, they'd take a look too."

Wylee nodded. "I'd reach out to whoever you can. Getting as many eyes as we can on the evidence will help build our court case when we nail the son of a bitch."

My stomach flopped. Getting the NSA involved meant talking to Dad and coming clean about what had been happening since he'd left while also, somehow, convincing him not to come running back from Australia. If he did, Sadie would come too because there was no way she'd let him or me face any of this without her at our sides. And that meant my siblings would be here. In danger. No way would I allow that. Would the idea of keeping Sadie, Spencey, and Caro out of danger be enough to keep Dad away?

I had to put off telling them about any of it for as long as possible, and I had to convince Jim, Parker, and Kurt to do the same.

Suddenly, I felt trapped, buried under a heavy weight, just as I had over breakfast with Parker. I couldn't breathe. I needed air…respite…something.

I hurried out of the security hut, anxious to get away. To smell the pine trees and the wildflowers instead of burnt wood. To feel the wind on my face instead of confused looks. To feel anything but desperation, fear, and a horrible sense of failure.

Chapter Sixteen

Parker

WHAT COWBOYS ARE FOR
Performed by Brandon Davis

EIGHT YEARS AGO

> *HER: I caught her with a new prescription.*

> *HIM: Did she take any?*

> *HER: She says no, but she flushed them before I could count them. She finally agreed to rehab.*

> *HIM: Who's staying with you?*

> *HER: I don't need anyone. We have an entire staff of people.*

> *HIM: Fallon. Who the hell is staying with you?*

> *HER: You sound like Dad. He and Sadie are coming, but I wish they'd just stay in Willow Creek. The performing arts center is so close to being complete. That should be their focus.*

PRESENT DAY

I watched as Fallon shoved her way out of the cabin with the same desperation that she'd left her house at breakfast. She was unraveling, and I knew her well enough to realize she was escaping so no one would see it.

I wanted to stay and go through the footage myself.

What I did was follow the blond lightning bolt my body ached to console.

She was nearly at the barn when I grabbed her arm and pulled her around to face me. "Stop."

"Don't tell me what to do!" she huffed, yanking herself free. "Every person in there is now wondering if I'm involved with this."

"No one thinks that!"

"Please. I saw it all over Wylee's face. You even—"

"Looked confused. I don't fucking believe you'd set fire to this place," I insisted. "Wylee felt the same way. Confusion isn't doubt. So, tell me, Ducky, why the hell are you doubting *yourself*."

The flicker crossed her face again, the same one I'd seen while she'd been staring at the screen as if she'd lost something she couldn't find, as if she was trying to capture a fleeting memory.

She swallowed. "I… I…" She shook her head, spun on her heel, and headed for the barn. "I have a staff meeting to prepare for and damage control to perform."

"Fallon," I growled out.

She ignored me.

Instead, she headed into the barn and stopped just inside the door to check a clipboard hung on a peg near the door. Two men in cowboy hats, T-shirts, and worn boots stepped forward to say how sorry they were about the fire. One of them told Fallon that none of the guests had backed out of any activities for the day. Every trail ride, boating adventure, and hiking experience was booked to the max.

Her face was impassive while she got the rundown, but I saw her shoulders lift ever so slightly in relief. Whatever was happening to her and the ranch hadn't scared away the existing clients—at least not yet.

While she talked, I messaged Cranky, making sure he was aware the footage was coming and that I needed him to identify time gaps, black holes, or areas where the footage had been altered. I also wanted him to identify if there'd been any shifts in any of the security cameras' directions that couldn't be explained by Mother Nature.

The sound of Theo's giggle drew me from my phone, and I crossed over to the stall it had come from. When I peered over the door, my heart lurched at the sweet picture that greeted me. Theo sat in the hay beside another chinook, nursing four puppies. Johnny sat on Theo's opposite side, tail thumping while two more puppies pounced on it. The expression on Theo's face was pure joy. Pure magic.

I snapped a photo as a lump formed in my throat. Will would have loved to see Theo like this. *I'm doing my best, Will. He's as happy as I can make him after losing you. I don't know how you refused to get him a dog for so damn long, but what the hell am I going to do with a kid and a puppy?*

Teddy stepped in next to me, leaning his arm on the stall door, and said quietly, "He has a natural knack with animals. Even the horses seemed drawn to him as we walked around. Why don't you leave him with me for a few hours? He can help me with the feeding schedule and mucking the stalls. Basic stuff."

"You don't have time to be a babysitter," I replied.

"He's no problem at all, Parker. Besides, we both know there are very few people on this earth Fallon will let close enough to help her."

My chin jerked up, eyes meeting his. We stared each other down. My pulse raced, thinking of all the ways I wanted to get close to Fallon, ways I shouldn't want and yet hadn't been able to stop myself from craving.

When I didn't respond, he said, "You know, I'm not talking about that security bullshit or the day-to-day duties of the ranch, right?"

He never took his eyes off mine. I got what he was saying. Fallon rarely let anyone inside her walls to help maneuver the minefield of her emotions. If Maisey or Sadie were here, she *might* let them in, and even that was a big might. But for some reason, she'd always opened up to me. She'd always shared her darkest secrets as well as her hopes and fears.

At least, she had until that one fucking night had erected a new wall, this one between us.

Once she'd started texting me again, our texts had gone back to the usual banter we'd always dished out to each other, but it had all been surface level. She hadn't even told me what had happened with JJ in San Diego. I'd only heard my dad's third-hand version of it.

Climbing over the wall she'd raised since then wasn't going to be easy. But what choice did I have? None. I couldn't walk away from her any more than I could walk away from Theo—not if I wanted to still respect myself come morning.

I moved into the stall, crouched beside Theo, and ruffled his hair. He looked up with that wide grin that would forever get him exactly what he wanted with me. "I'm going to help Fallon for a while. Teddy said you could stay with him and help with the dogs and the horses if you'd like."

His grin grew impossibly wider. "I can help?"

"Yes. But you have to do exactly what Teddy says. The horses are big and can hurt you if you don't stand in the right place or you do something to spook them. And you can't run off just because you see something you like. You do only what Teddy says and stay right with him."

"Okay, Parker. I'll be good!" He made a cross over his chest with his little fingers.

My throat clogged. "You're always good, bud. You just get too excited sometimes and forget to listen. So let's put on those superpower listening ears we've talked about." I pretended to take the fake ears out of my pocket and made a big production of removing his old ones and placing on super bionic ones I'd been teasing him about for days now, screwing them on before tickling his neck.

He giggled, touching his ears. "Superpower actu-vated!"

"You got it."

I rose and turned to see Fallon watching me. Her expression looked as if she'd just witnessed something rare and magical. But it disappeared when Teddy bumped her arm and said, "Parker is with you today. Theo and I are going to do cowboy stuff."

Theo laughed again. I ruffled his hair one more time and then stepped out of the stall.

"Let me give you my number in case Theo needs me," I told Teddy. "He's not allergic to anything that I know of, and he's a healthy kid overall."

Teddy took out his phone, logged my number in, and then texted me so I had his as well.

"We'll be fine," Teddy reassured me. "You two go figure out what the hell is happening at the ranch before Lauren decides to leave the rehab center to try fixing it herself."

Fallon's face turned dark. "For heaven's sake, don't tell Mom."

He looked surprised and angry at her comment. "Excuse me?"

"The resort isn't hers to worry about, Teddy."

He stepped forward, his voice turning into a dark growl I never expected to hear from the easygoing man. "What the hell is that supposed to mean? Your mom has worked her ass off for this ranch. She's dedicated her life to it. And what does she have to show for it? A missing leg and a barely habitable house her grandfather owned that no one maintained."

Fallon looked chagrinned, and my nerves, already strung tight, jumped up another notch. I shifted, ready to step between them if I needed to.

Fallon's voice was full of regret when she said, "I didn't mean she didn't belong here, and you know it, Teddy."

He stared at her for a long moment before dragging a large hand over his face. He shook his head. "I know. I know. She's just been through so damn much."

I wanted to add that the majority of Lauren's pain and anguish had been because of her own bad choices. But before I could say anything, Fallon had laid a gentle hand on the man's arm and said, "I don't want her to leave the center before she has her prosthetic and has learned how to maneuver with it. She can't do anything here but worry, and we both know what worrying does to her. She's already in such a shaky place, Teddy. I'd never forgive myself if she started using—"

Her voice broke off, and she bit her lip as if fighting tears again.

Without finishing her thought, she headed toward the house with that powerful stride of hers. Strong and determined, she was a force to be reckoned with. A power that would be fierce and beautiful if our bodies were twined.

I shoved those thoughts aside and glanced from Teddy to Theo in the stall with the dogs. Doubts, obligations, and desires pulled me in multiple directions.

"I'm sorry, Parker." Teddy's voice was truly contrite. "I shouldn't have implied that girl was pushing her mama off the ranch. It's just, now that Fallon's turned twenty-four and the estate has become hers, the little say Lauren had about the place is gone. She lost her leg *and* her purpose. I just…" He choked on his own emotions.

"She's not a girl," I told him. "I'm not sure Fallon was ever allowed to be one. You and I both know it."

Teddy didn't respond at first. He looked out the barn door in the direction Fallon had gone. "I've never seen two women so strong and so determined and yet so unable to ask for help. The old Hurly place is falling down, but Lauren won't ask Fallon for the money to fix it. She won't let Fallon spend an ounce of her inheritance on anything but her own dreams. How can they love each other so much without realizing they'd both hang the moon for the other?"

I shook my head. I didn't have an answer for him. Fallon and her mother's relationship had always been this way—fraught with land mines.

Teddy looked back in at Theo, who was talking quietly to the dogs. "I may not know what to do with Fallon, but I can take care of this little guy and the animals I've had under my responsibility for longer than I remember. Go. Take care of her, Parker. You're the only one here who can."

And just like that, the full weight of my dual responsibilities slammed back into me.

How would I ever take care of them both without feeling like I was sacrificing one of them?

But Theo was happier than I'd seen him since learning to ride his bike, and Teddy had my number and could call if Theo needed me. Whereas the firebrand who'd stormed off toward the house would never admit to needing anyone, even when it was clear she did.

It was so infuriating I wanted to kiss her until she caved, until she admitted she absolutely did need someone—needed me—just as she had before everything had gotten screwed up between us.

I whirled around and jogged toward the house with a lifetime's worth of anguish eating me up inside, with a month's worth of new responsibilities clogging my view. The only way to fix this newest war inside me, the one battling it out between Fallon and Theo, was if I found who was behind the things happening at the ranch. Then, I could leave Fallon to her own stubborn determination and get the hell out of Rivers before my willpower crumbled completely.

♪ ♪ ♪

At the staff meeting, Andie and Fallon reassured the employees as best they could, came up with a canned response for them to use with guests, and promised to keep everyone abreast of the investigation. When everyone had headed back to their jobs with tasks in hand, Fallon and I set up in the conference room to dig into the former staff and existing employees.

I used Fallon's laptop and plugged each name into Dad's background-checking software, searching for criminal records and gathering information from various sources, including social media platforms. While Dad's app didn't contain the same level of information the top-secret databases we used in the teams did, it was enough to weed people out.

I'd planned on sending any names with red flags to Cranky, but not a single one of the former employees had any. No one had unusually large debts that would insinuate a drug or gambling problem. No one had ties to known gangs or drug cartels. And only one of the employees had left on anything close to bad terms after repeated complaints from guests that he was too "handsy."

The truth was, most people liked working at the Harrington Ranch—not only because they paid their staff far more than most employers in the area but also because they treated their employees like family.

With the former staff a dead end, we moved on to the list of current employees with almost as little luck. A teen named Chuck had been arrested for stealing a hat from the local convenience store and been suspended from school for three days after pulling the fire alarm. Normal, troubled-teen sort of incidents, but nothing that would put him on my radar for killing cows and burning down buildings. A couple of the ranch hands, including Teddy, had been charged with driving under the influence, but nothing recent. Teddy's last charge had been fifteen years ago, long before the ranch had even been in trouble when Fallon's stepdad had been alive.

Pushing aside the computer, I stretched my arms over my head and twisted from side to side. My body was screaming for activity, for a workout.

Across the table, Fallon's brows were furrowed, her shoulders hunched.

"What's put that look on your face?"

She straightened, face turning into a blank mask. "What look?"

"The one you give me when I say country is the lamest form of music."

She huffed. "I've proven you wrong too many times to count. Your ears are dead from listening to that acid metal you call music."

Instead of defending my genre of choice, I prompted, "What's going through your oversized brain, Ducky?"

"The only time we've ever had these kinds of problems on the ranch was when Uncle Adam hooked up with Theresa Puzo."

"Adam is in jail. Theresa is dead," I reminded her, but I felt that tug at the back of my neck that told me not to discount what she was saying. It was the same tug that had saved my life a few times. An instinct that couldn't and shouldn't be ignored.

"I know Dad and Lorenzo tolerate each other now for Sadie's sake, but Ike and Theresa's side of the Puzo family still loathes my father." She twirled a finger around her thumb.

"It's been ten years since that all went down," I said, but it wasn't with the same confidence I wanted it to be, and she read it.

"Lorenzo was in San Diego the day I was arrested."

"Dad mentioned it." I told her what we'd learned about Puzo's cousin who'd gotten out of jail in March and was working for a construction company out there.

Fallon frowned. "Dad went all Dad-like on Lorenzo and demanded to know if someone in his family had come after me, which only made me wonder, have there been other attempts by Theresa and Ike's side of the family in the last ten years that your dad or mine hasn't told us about?"

I could easily see Rafe keeping things from Fallon that he didn't want her to know, but they wouldn't have kept any of it from me. Not when I was in San Diego and could protect her. They'd have wanted me to keep my eyes wide open if there was even the slightest chance the Puzos were still coming for Rafe and his family.

"It's worth looking into, right?" she asked. "Because I seriously don't have any other ideas. And if my only options are JJ and that drug addict Ace or the Puzos, the Puzos would have way more resources at their disposal than two beach bums. That security video was modified, and the cow... Can you seriously see JJ killing a cow?"

Fallon was right. If I had to weigh JJ on one side and the Puzo family on the other, the Puzos were just the type to burn people's worlds down.

"It's a good lead," I told her. "I'll see what else Dad can dig up. Maybe have Sheriff Wylee investigate it too. Ten years seems an awfully long time to wait to come after any of you for revenge though."

"Theresa waited almost as long to come after Dad," she said before turning back to her laptop.

I didn't mention it, but she hadn't brought up her mother's brother sitting in jail in Tennessee. Adam Hurly had just as much reason, if not more, to come after Rafe, Lauren, and the ranch. But he'd been arrested, tried, and sentenced for first-degree murder, kidnapping, and embezzlement. He was stuck in prison for life with all the money he'd stolen from the ranch accounted for. And as far as I knew, Lauren hadn't once interacted with her brother since he'd taken Fallon and Sadie hostage at gunpoint, killed his partner, and then been thwarted by Sadie's and Fallon's bravery.

My gaze settled on Fallon, taking in every nuance and change since I'd seen her last. Dark shadows hung beneath her eyes, and the vibrant light that normally shifted around her like some goddamn halo was dimmer today. She needed a break. She needed to get her mind off all her responsibilities and the violence that had once again shown up at her door.

I pushed away from the table. "Let's go."

"What?" she glanced up, startled.

"We're done dealing with this for today. We need food." I waved at the barely touched sandwiches her staff had brought in earlier. "And we need some physical activity before our bodies congeal." Her eyes flared, and as much as I hated myself for it, I was happy to know her thoughts had gone to where mine always did when it came to her—the one type of activity we couldn't engage in. "I know I'm damn irresistible, but get your mind out of the gutter, Ducky. I simply meant, let's pick up some food and Theo and drag some inner tubes down to the falls."

"You want to go tubing?" Surprise filled her voice. "We haven't done that in…" She trailed off. I couldn't remember how long either. Years.

She shook her head. "I can't. Not only do we still have files to get through"—she waved at the paper and computers—"but it wouldn't look right to the staff. I can't just go gallivanting off to play in the water while everything is falling apart."

"Nothing is falling apart, Fallon. And your staff needs you

to role model resilience. They need to see it's okay to continue living even in the face of tragedy. Plus, if you're seen out there enjoying yourself, any worries your guests have will disappear."

She hesitated. But I'd be damned if I let her sit here, dwelling on everything that happened and internalizing it as somehow being her fault. Whoever was doing this, Fallon wasn't responsible. She'd done the right thing every fucking time something terrible had made its way into her life.

Determined to get her out of the chair and this office with no windows, I pressed further. "Let's go, Marquess. You can spare a few hours to entertain me and the kid."

She finally stood up, defiance straightening her back and raising her chin. "Harrington. If you're going to shorten my name, use the Harrington portion. It's my goddamn legacy, after all."

And I wondered if that was part of what was weighing on her. If she'd inherited a legacy she no longer wanted and would never admit to after forcing Rafe to spend millions of dollars to save it.

She'd never even breathed such a thought to me. If anything, she'd insisted the opposite, that she loved the land and the home she'd been given. She was determined to make both her Hurly and Harrington sides proud, as well as her dad and the Marquess name he'd taken on from his mother. Years of convoluted, twisted dramas had coalesced into Fallon being the sole remaining heir on all sides, and she'd always told me she wanted it that way. She wanted to take the bad of their past and turn it into something so good everyone forgot the turbulence of the ranch's history.

But maybe her years in San Diego, going after different dreams, had shown her a different life than the one she'd once wanted. I'd never thought it would be possible for either of us to consider our lives having alternate endings than the ones we'd envisioned. We'd both been focused on one dream, one goal, one purpose, for as long as we'd known each other. It was yet another of the many ways we were alike and one of the many reasons our friendship had been so strong.

For the first time in my twenty-nine years, my goals and dreams were being threatened. I'd been handed Theo to raise—a child I had insisted I would never have because I would never want to leave one behind for months at a time. Will had said he was leaving the teams to ensure his son didn't lose both parents. What would happen to the kid if he lost them *and* his new guardian?

My gut turned sour.

Somehow, I had to figure out a way to right the ship without giving up everything I'd always thought I wanted. Maybe that was all Fallon needed too—time to figure out what her new normal looked like. Maybe we both just needed time to once more bend our lives toward the goals that had first shaped us.

Chapter Seventeen

Fallon

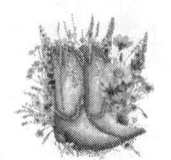

WANT TO
Performed by Sugarland

SIX YEARS AGO

> *HER: Dad said you're coming with Jim and Whitney to the ranch.*

> *HIM: I have five days. It was perfect timing.*

> *HER: I've got three new bookshelves that need assembling for my room.*

> *HIM: What do I get as payment for my manual labor?*

> *HIM: Never mind. Don't answer that.*

> *HER: *** Chicken emoji *** I'll have the inner tubes filled and ready to take us down the river. When we get to the snack bar at the bottom, all the food and drink is on me.*

PRESENT DAY

After slathering Theo with sunscreen, Parker strapped a tiny life vest on him as I watched from my spot on a tube in the river. The sun filtering through the trees cast them in a mix of light and shadow, making them seem more painting than real. A watercolor image of a loving dad and his kid.

It squeezed my heart and had me jerking my eyes up to the sky, trying to control the rush of affection and longing that swept through me.

Twisting the inner tube slightly away from them, I kept one foot tethered to the river's rocky shore so I wouldn't float away without them. The sound of the waterfall hitting the rocks muted Theo's chatter. Mist rose from a deep eddy at the base of the fall, filling the air with rainbows. It coated my skin with a cool spray that barely eased the sweltering heat. After weeks of unseasonably cool weather, summer had slammed down over Rivers in full force.

The heat meant there were a million things to do at the ranch—livestock and crops to ensure were watered and cared for, painting of fences and buildings, repairs to a few roofs. I shouldn't be here, lollygagging along on a river ride.

As I started to get out of the tube, Parker's voice halted me. "No."

I raised a brow in his direction, and he met my irritated gaze with a cool one over the top of his sunglasses. "Sit your ass back down and cool off, Ducky."

"Ass!" Theo screamed.

I couldn't help the chuckle that escaped me.

I could and should fight with him on his attitude and demands, but suddenly, I was overwhelmingly tired again. So I did the easiest thing I could. I sat back down. Maybe Parker was right. Maybe my guests and employees needed to see me doing this simply for the reassurance it would provide. The staff meeting had been tense with worry, but no one had threatened to leave. If anything, everyone had buckled down and recommitted themselves simply because it seemed we were under attack.

It had choked me up then, and it did all over again.

Why the hell couldn't I keep the tears at bay these days?

I looked down and tugged at the life vest that was pulling too tightly across my chest. In my teen days, I wouldn't have even bothered with one as Maisey and I made this same loop from the falls down to the lake on the tubes. But now I had to be a good role model for our guests.

I clicked open the strap, loosened it, and then locked it back into place, wondering why everything felt just a hair too small these days—even my bathing suit. My breasts had spilled out almost embarrassingly from the top when I'd put it on, prompting me to cover it with a tank top. While I hadn't put this particular suit on since Rae had shipped all my items from the apartment, I had worn it to the beach with her in May, and it had fit fine. The weight gain had to have been bloating from my upcoming period—or stress eating.

Except, you've hardly been eating at all.

I pushed that thought away, eyes settling on Parker again as he pulled off his T-shirt. Seeing him like this, all skin and carved muscles, literally made my mouth water and my core clench. He was the most beautiful man I'd ever seen. He'd always been that way, even as a teenager, but his years as a Navy SEAL had sculpted him into perfection.

It wasn't just the cuts and grooves that made him so stunning. It was his pure masculinity. The smattering of chest hair that led down to the waistband of his swim trunks and the delicious V that disappeared below the band. The sinful bulge below that had forever tempted me to explore, to see what he looked like completely bare.

He absolutely did not need the life vest he donned. Parker had been through much worse in his training, and very likely on his missions, than our lazy river could ever offer up. He wore it for the same reason I did—for my guests and our insurance policy—but I suspected it was also for Theo. So the little boy would wear his without argument after seeing Parker in one too.

Parker shoved his and Theo's shoes, shirts, and sunscreen into the water-safe bag I'd brought, then handed it over to me to snap onto the hook of my tube while he sat in his. He held out his hand for Theo, who glanced at Parker with a flash of uncertainty before crawling into his lap.

I reached over and touched the little boy's hand. "Do you like to swim?"

Theo cocked his head. "Mommy says pools are dirty."

"But you went to the beach with your dad, and he was

teaching you how to swim," Parker reminded him. "Remember riding the foamie while he pushed you?"

I wasn't sure if it was the reminder of his dad that made Theo's frown grow or the mention of the beach.

"This is way easier than swimming or surfing," I told Theo. "It's more like a slow ride at an amusement park. All you have to do is sit back and let the water take you. You'll see beautiful scenery and maybe some animals, and right before the river dumps us into the lake, there's a little slope that makes you feel like you're floating in the air. That's my favorite part."

I hadn't done this in so long that I'd forgotten the simple joy of meandering along the current with nothing to do but enjoy the view. I'd been too busy—and not just with college. Even when I'd been here, my focus had been on making sure the ranch succeeded after Dad had poured so much money into it, especially knowing he'd only done it for me.

"You ready?" Parker asked Theo.

The little boy nodded, and Parker pushed off from the shore with a bare foot. The current immediately grabbed their tube, but it wasn't a fast or scary rush. I shoved off and nearly collided with them. Parker grabbed hold of my tube, and just like I had when I was a kid, I hooked my foot into the handle of his, joining us.

The smile that took over Parker's face stole my breath. The sun beat down on him, turning his dark hair into shades of silver and deep sapphire. I wished I could see his eyes, but they were tucked behind tinted sunglasses. I'd just have to imagine the corners crinkling in that way they did when Parker was truly happy.

Theo's little face still looked hesitant as we moved along the surface. He was a lanky kid, with long legs peeking out of swim trunks smattered with cartoon dogs, but his arms and thighs had a surprising amount of muscle for a kid his age. Those muscles flexed as he clung to a handle of the tube with one hand and Parker's elbow with the other. I was fairly certain it wasn't fear but uncertainty that had him gripping so tightly. This was a new experience, something he was doing without his dad as a safety net.

I turned away, unable to look at them without my heart hurting for all they'd lost.

A shadow of a large bird crossed over us, and I looked up in time to see a hawk coast by, wings at full span. Catching an updraft, he barely seemed to move his wings but was still propelled upward at a surprising speed.

It wasn't quiet—the river gurgled, trees rustled, birds chirped and chittered—and yet it felt quieter than anywhere I'd been in weeks. Solemn and peaceful. The heat of the day made everything seem more languid. A dream in slow motion.

I scooted down until I could rest my neck on the tube, closed my eyes, and just let the rocking of the river soothe me.

It didn't take long for Theo to relax as well. He went from tense silence to a million questions at warp speed. What kind of tree was that? Did the wolves come down to the river? Who did all this land belong to?

"Fallon owns it all," Parker said.

I leaned my head to the side and watched as Theo's little mouth dropped open. Then he asked solemnly, "Are you a princess?"

I laughed. "Only if princesses sling poop for a living."

"Poop is hel-fy." The little boy sounded just like Teddy. Or maybe just like Spence had sounded when he'd been alive.

My smile grew. "Yep, it is healthy. It's when animals don't poop that you've got to worry."

"I want to own a ranch. I want all the animals."

"Fallon is going to be a veterinarian. Those are doctors for animals," Parker told him.

My stomach twisted, a mix of joy and pain. I wouldn't finish the program or get my license, but I'd still open the refuge.

"I know what a veg-utarian is," Theo said proudly, and I bit back a laugh.

"Veterinarian. Not a vegetable eater," Parker said, lips twitching.

"I know. That's what I said," the little boy replied. Then, he squealed with joy, pointing to the shore.

A mama deer lifted her head, warily eyeing us as we came around the bend. Her ears twitched while the rest of her remained frozen. Beside her, twin fawns continued to drink. Their spots were mostly gone, but they were still tiny.

"Deer!" Theo shouted.

The mama bounded toward the tree line, and her babies followed.

"Come back, deer!" Theo squirmed in Parker's lap, rocking both our tubes and threatening to tip us over.

"Easy does it, buddy," Parker said, attempting to stabilize us. "You keep shouting, and you're going to scare all the wildlife away. They like it best when it's quiet."

Theo sat for several seconds, and then he dropped his voice to a whisper and asked, "How many animals do you have, Fallon?"

"I'm not sure of the exact number anymore." I frowned, not liking that answer. "About a hundred cattle, thirty horses, twenty sheep, a handful of goats, and two dozen chickens."

"But how many deer? And birds? Do you have bears?"

"I don't own any of the wildlife. They own themselves. But it's my duty to take care of the land they inhabit so they can continue to live here without being hunted or forced to move."

"Fallon is opening a refuge here too," Parker told him, and my heart twisted remembering all the times we'd talked about it. "That means she's going to save animals who don't have a place to go at the end of their life or when they're sick."

The image of the cow with the words carved into her side slid through me again. It wouldn't be right to bring more animals here if they'd be hurt. I had to figure out what was going on, not just for myself and my guests, but for the future of the ranch and the dreams I still wanted to make a reality.

Caught in my thoughts, I wasn't prepared for the water that doused my face. I sputtered, ripping off my sunglasses and glaring at Parker as he laughed.

"You did *not* just do that," I demanded.

"You were getting all hot and bothered over there."

"As if!" I unhooked my foot from his tube, dipped my feet

in the river, and kicked hard enough to send water over both him and Theo.

They laughed, free and deep and joyous, and it took the darkness I'd fallen back into and ripped it away.

"Kick, buddy, kick," Parker said. The little boy's feet barely touched the river, but Parker's enormous ones sent a tidal wave in my direction. I was drenched from head to toe, but I was smiling in return. In the old days, I would have done my best to tip Parker's tube, but I didn't want to scare Theo. Instead, I simply splashed with my hands and feet as we approached the downslope to the lake.

"Hold on tight," I said to Theo as we went over the tiny crest.

It really did feel a bit like flying as we careened over. The tube turned dizzily, and I closed my eyes, riding it out. Theo's laughter rang out once more, joining Parker's deep boom, and my insides filled with happiness. When was the last time I'd felt like this? Loose and content and truly present in the moment?

I wanted to hang on to it, wanted to keep it and wrap it around me so I didn't have to think about the nastiness waiting for me once we landed ashore.

As we plunged into the lake from the river, the sound of a boat drew my eyes. A teen was up behind it on water skis, flying by just outside the swim zone roped off by buoys. The languid peace of the lazy river was left behind as more noise crashed into me. Laughter. Music. The rev of Jet Skis and other boats.

People crowded the pebbled beach by the dock, sunning on lounge chairs or relaxing under umbrellas. The snack bar had barbecue smoke pouring from its chimney, filling the air with an aroma that made my stomach growl for the first time in days.

Nearing the dock, I flipped out of the tube, grabbed the handle, and swam for the ladder. Parker eased out of his tube, leaving Theo inside it while pulling the boy in. We'd replaced the old splintered dock from my childhood with a composite one years ago, and my tube slid along it as I tossed it up. I turned back to Parker, steadying his tube while he helped Theo onto the ladder.

As I followed the little boy up, my skin tingled with

Parker's gaze lingering on me. A lifetime of awareness was magnified by a very new and very strange discomfort with my body. I unsnapped my vest and reached into the towel box we rolled onto the dock each day for our guests. I wrapped one around my chest and took two more out for Parker and Theo.

The little boy was eyeing the snack bar with something like longing as Parker took the towels from me. Instead of helping dry Theo off, he turned those sunglass-covered eyes on me, taking me in from the top of my wet braid, down to my chipped, bubblegum-pink nail polish, and then back up. His gaze lingered on the towel I'd wrapped around my torso.

Parker's smile turned into a frown, and he stepped closer to me, voice dropping as he asked, "Since when are you embarrassed of your body, Ducky?"

"What?"

"Covering yourself up in a tank top and now wrapping yourself in a towel. Where's the Fallon who strutted along a packed beach, not giving a shit who saw her in a tiny bikini?" He was worried. I heard it beating in every syllable.

I wasn't embarrassed. Was I? I had nothing to be ashamed of. So what if I'd put on a couple of pounds? Who the hell knew how I'd gained it with the pace I'd been working at since I'd come home, but I had.

"Look, Kermit, don't start with me."

Parker reached out, grabbed the edge of the towel, and yanked it so I spun like a top toward the edge of the dock. I barely registered I was going over the side before I latched on to his wrist and took him with me.

We landed in the water with enough force that it dragged us under the surface. My glasses went flying, and I barely caught them before they sank to the bottom. I kicked out, foot colliding with Parker's leg before rushing for the surface. I came up sputtering.

"Jerk. You almost made me lose my favorite sunglasses!" I splashed water at him as if I was annoyed, but my lips twisted upward, contradicting my words.

"You're way too uptight these days, Ducky. Let's see what

we can do to loosen you up."

Before I could object, he'd picked me up and launched me into the sky, sending me and my glasses sailing. It reminded me of my dad doing this exact same thing. The first time Dad had come back to the ranch, he'd joined Maisey, Sadie, and me at the lake, playing with us in the water as if he didn't have a care in the world. That day, I'd realized just how much he'd lost by leaving me here with Mom and Spencer. How much we'd both lost. I'd never thought those lost memories had mattered to him before then, but he'd been making it up to me ever since.

As I surfaced once again, Theo's little voice squealed, "Me, me, me!" as he jumped up and down at the end of the dock. "I want to fly too!"

Just as Parker turned toward the ladder, I leaped onto his back and pushed him under. It was only because I'd surprised him that I succeeded. Theo's little face registered shock before he started laughing as Parker burst through the surface.

He'd lost his glasses too, and now I could see every inch of the sly smile that creased his eyes and promised payback. That smile, that joy, pierced me like an arrow. It was another image of him that I'd keep locked in a secret place reserved exclusively for him.

"You lucked out with that sneak attack, Ducky."

"I thought you Frogmen were always ready," I taunted. "Besides, that's payment for *actually* making me lose my favorite glasses."

I looked through the stirred-up water, trying to catch a glimpse of them. The lake was normally clear, especially this close to shore, but there was too much activity today.

He tugged my arm, yanking me to his chest, and our eyes met. Heat. Yearning. Happiness.

"You know what happens to sneaks, don't you?" His voice was all sultry. A sensual dare.

"They win?" I taunted back.

His mouth came dangerously close to mine—so close I could feel the buzz that snapped between us. Then, his lips changed direction, breath coasting over my ear as he said,

"They go in the torture chamber."

His hand slid under my tank top, and he tickled me, fingers gliding over all the sensitive spots he'd found when we were little. I tried to jerk back, laughing and pushing at his hands, even as they drifted upward until his knuckles brushed the undersides of my breasts. The electricity that spun through me was almost as strong as the tickle.

I gasped and gurgled, still attempting to stop him, but he was relentless. Ruthless.

My lungs burned for air.

I knew of only one way to stop him. One thing that always got him to pull back when our play brushed over a dangerous edge. I attempted another gasp of air before sinking under the water and slipping through his fingers as he tried to recapture me. I kicked downward until my face was just at the waistband of his trunks.

I ran my palms along his inner thighs, letting my fingertips dance along a sensitive spot I'd found once by accident. I was delighted to see him respond. The bulge that appeared inviting me to do more than tickle.

Parker let out a muttered groan muffled by the water, and two strong hands gripped me under my armpits, hauling me to the surface. We were chest to chest, hip to hip again, and our mouths were right back to being dangerously close. Temptation hung in the air, turning those steel eyes dark and murky. When would he ever give in to this feeling? Why did he resist the pull when it would be so much easier to cave?

"Don't start something you can't finish, Ducky." The growl that escaped those firm, full lips only lit me up inside.

"Parker, me! I want to play too!" Theo protested.

But Parker remained completely focused on me, searching for something that had my pulse beating frantically.

I moved slowly, sucking my finger into my mouth, and those gray eyes turned even stormier as he watched. I had all of two seconds before he caught on to my intent. When I popped my finger out and stuck it into his ear, his expression went from broody lust to stunned surprise. I laughed, knowing I'd likely regret reinstituting our long-forgotten wet-willy contest, but reveling in having caught him off guard yet again.

I used his shock to escape, kicking away from him. As I reached the dock, I looked back with a raised brow and said, "If I remember, Kermit, it was always you who backed away from the finish line. I had no problem finding my way across it."

I had the intense pleasure of hearing him growl, but I pulled a card from his book and ignored the sizzling air between us. Instead, I held my arms up for Theo. "Jump, I'll catch you, and we'll show Parker what it's like when two superheroes gang up on him."

Theo giggled and took the plunge. The hook on his life vest snagged my skin, dragging along my chest, and I barely bit back a yelp. But the pain completely disappeared when the little boy wrapped his arms around my neck and whispered, "I like you."

And just like that, I fell completely in love with yet another boy who would never be mine.

Chapter Eighteen
Parker

SO MANY SUMMERS
Performed by Brad Paisley

NINE YEARS AGO

HER: Is kissing supposed to feel like someone put wet worms on your lips?

HIM: Who the hell are you kissing, Ducky?

HER: Just answer the question.

HIM: Don't make me call your dad.

HER: Fine. I'll ask someone else.

HIM: If some dumbass teenager kissed you, and it felt like worms, you need to run away now. Run as fast as you can, and do not look back.

PRESENT DAY

Get a grip, dipshit.

The taunt sounded like my old lieutenant at the Academy. Or maybe it was my dad's voice and Rafe's and mine all combined as I had to adjust myself discreetly under the water. If Theo hadn't called out, who knew what I would have done to those pretty pink lips taunting me. Wet and warm and ready for the taking.

How many times had she made it clear they could be mine?

That all of her could be mine?

I cooled my jets by counting to thirty and reminding myself of all the reasons it wasn't a good idea to tangle our bodies together.

I'd spent years protecting her and often failed.

Rafe would be furious if I messed with his daughter.

My dad would be disappointed.

And the *coup de grâce*, I had a SEAL team waiting for me to figure my shit out so I could return to base and start training again.

When I looked back at the dock, Fallon was holding Theo after catching him with ease as he dove into her arms. She said something to him that made him giggle, and for a moment, the joy radiating around them made an idea flit around the periphery of my mind. A way of keeping them both. A way to make us whole. But the idea was so shocking and fleeting that it disappeared before I could fully hang on to it. But it left a new and unexpected craving in its wake.

Family. Home.

Fucking things a SEAL knew better than to make a reality because the mission was your life. The team was your family. The job was your focus. Not people. Not someone waiting at home, worried you wouldn't come back.

I'd sworn to my dying grandfather I'd continue his legacy.

I didn't have a chance to dwell on the fading vision or how it opposed everything I'd believed I wanted as two bodies launched themselves at me. Fallon and Theo pushed and splashed and tried to sink me. I fought back, careful with Theo so as not to hurt him, even more cautious with Fallon as I attempted to keep my hands off those tantalizing places on her body that had made me lose my head while tickling her.

For the next thirty minutes, we splashed and played. Fallon and I took turns throwing Theo softly into the air, his life vest keeping him from sinking fully as he landed with a joyous chortle in the lake.

When goosebumps broke out along his arms, I called a halt. As the two of them climbed back onto the dock, I dove down below, scouring the lake for our lost glasses. It took me several long minutes, breath growing tight, before I finally found them and came up victorious.

I pulled myself up on the dock and made a dramatic bow as I presented Fallon with hers. "Your prize, princess."

She rolled her eyes and snatched them away, but any retort was cut off by Theo exclaiming, "I'm hungry!"

His eyes were fixed, hopefully, on the snack bar.

"You're always hungry," I teased, rubbing him down with a towel. "It's like you have an empty hole inside you instead of a stomach. Let me check." I blew raspberries above his belly button, and he went off into chortles again.

When I pulled back, Fallon was watching us, sunglasses over her eyes so I couldn't read her thoughts, but her face had turned serious once more.

I raised a brow, looking purposefully at the towel she'd dried off with. Instead of wrapping it around her body, she tossed me a defiant look and threw it into the used towel bin. Then, she shoved her feet into the shoes she'd pulled from the waterproof bag and sauntered across the pebbled beach toward the snack bar.

I barely got Theo to put his shoes on before he raced after her. I grabbed the rest of our belongings and the three life vests, following behind them.

"Snag a table. I'll be right back," Fallon said with a wave at some of the open spots.

She didn't stop at the register to order. Instead, she opened a side door of the hut and disappeared. Through the window, I saw her talking to the cook and the girl behind the counter. They both laughed at whatever she'd said. That was the Fallon I'd grown up with. She could talk to anyone and put them at ease, but if you crossed her or someone she cared about, heaven have mercy on your soul.

Theo and I sat at one of the tables shaded by a blue-and-yellow striped umbrella. He looked exhausted, and I hoped it meant that, for once, he wouldn't wake up in the middle of the night.

When Fallon came out of the snack bar, she had a tray loaded with nachos, warm pretzel bites, and three frozen lemonades. It was a smorgasbord of junk food I'd done my best not to serve Theo after that first desperate week when he'd come to live with me.

"You keep feeding Theo stuff like this, and he's going to want to live with you forever. Aren't you, bud?"

His eyes twinkled as he nodded, grabbing the cup of pretzel bites and clutching it to his chest as if he were afraid I'd rip it away. My lips twitched, and I dug into the plate of nachos covered in smoked carne asada, real cheese, and a homemade salsa that made my mouth water. I had access to plenty of top-notch Mexican food in San Diego, but this carne asada was one of the best I'd ever had.

"You guys even do junk food the five-star way," I commented between bites.

Fallon scooped some up, pleasure coating her face as she chewed. It made my insides tighten all over again, and I was thankful the table hid my body's reaction to her.

"At first, Francois was appalled at the idea of serving any so-called junk food," she told me. "He said he was a Michelin-starred chef and had his standards. But then, Dad threatened to hire a second chef who'd have equal space in his kitchen, and he caved like a sandcastle under a wave. Now, Francois sets the menu, but he makes one of the sous chefs, Ren, do any cooking he doesn't deem worthy of his time."

"My hats off to Chef Ren for doing it right." I watched as Theo stuffed another pretzel bite into his mouth. "But I fear this snack is coming so late in the day that I'll never get this guy to eat anything healthy for dinner."

"Hel-fy stinks. Vega-tubles stink," Theo said with a sad shake of his head.

"I bet I can make you like them," Fallon told him, and I groaned, knowing Theo was going to eat her alive. The kid really abhorred vegetables—red, green, orange, or otherwise.

"A bet?" Looking at him, I could see Theo's little mind whirling with all the bets I'd already made with him and lost on this same topic. "If I win, I get a prize?"

"You don't know what you're doing," I warned Fallon, and she just shot me a grin.

"What do you want if you win?"

"A puppy!" He shoved his hand in the air and then looked at the empty space where his stuffed animal normally was tucked. He'd nearly disintegrated into tears at the thought of leaving Dog at the house, and it had taken all of Fallon's and my cajoling to get him to come on the adventure without it.

Fallon's face turned all soft and gooey, and my gut clenched in a moment of panic. "No dogs, Fallon."

They both shot me a glare that said I was a party pooper. I'd eventually lose this battle. Theo was going to get his damn puppy, but I had to figure out how I'd take care of him and a dog when I was deployed before I agreed.

"How about, if you win, I let you name the foal that's going to be born any day now?" she offered.

"Foal?" Theo's brows furrowed.

"A baby horse," I said.

His face lit up. "Would it be mine?"

Her smile widened. "You'd have to eat a lot of vegetables to win an entire horse. But you could visit it anytime you're here. And once it's grown up and we've trained it, you can ride it."

Theo's face was one big grin as he said, "I'm going to win. I hate veg-utables."

"What does Fallon get if she wins?" I asked Theo.

He turned thoughtful. "I can draw her a picture. Daddy always said I was a real good drawer."

Before I could say I didn't think that was an even bet, Fallon stuck her hand out, and they were shaking on it.

And four hours later, after we'd eaten dinner in the hotel's dining room, and Theo had tasted a little pastry he'd fallen in love with and had been appalled to find out was full of vegetables, he did his part and drew her a picture. He sat at the coffee table in her house with his little eyes drooping as he did it, and when he finished, he crawled onto the couch between Fallon and me, shoving the paper at her.

She took it gently, scrutinizing it carefully. Her face made all kinds of weird expressions as she fought off a wave of emotions. Her voice was rough as she said, "This is the best picture anyone has ever given me."

Theo beamed and then looked at me with a yawn. "I want to go to bed."

Shock reverberated through me. Not once in the month he'd been with me had the kid offered to go to bed on his own.

"Okay, then, say goodnight to Fallon, and I'll tuck you in."

He hugged Fallon, clutched his stuffed animal to his chest, and headed down the hall to Lauren's room. By the time we'd returned from the lake, someone had changed the sheets and put up a cot, even though I'd told them not to bother.

"Cot or bed?" I asked Theo.

He eyed the cot as if it was a strange toy and then just climbed into the king-sized bed.

I pulled the covers up to his chin, took a book out of a backpack of toys we'd brought with us, and started to read it to him. He was asleep before I even got halfway through it. I left the bathroom door partially open in lieu of the nightlight I'd forgotten before shutting off the bedroom lights and heading back into the great room.

Fallon had pulled a blanket off the back of the couch, curled up in the corner, and turned on the television. And just like Theo, she'd already passed out. She'd taken her braid out when we'd come home, and her blond hair was a mess of curls cascading about a face that had turned soft and relaxed in sleep. It made her look younger than she normally did—or maybe she actually looked her age when asleep.

She'd changed into a pair of sleep shorts and an oversized T-shirt, and the whole time Theo had been drawing, the damn top had been slipping off her shoulder, taunting me with glimpses of bare skin, reminding me of just how smooth it had been under my fingers while we'd played at the lake.

I looked away from her, eyes catching on the picture she'd left on the coffee table.

Three stick figures in a blue blob that must have been

water. The people had strangely large smiles on their round faces, and Theo had drawn weirdly contorted hearts all around Fallon's head. Seeing it, seeing the love Theo had tried to capture, tugged at the fleeting images that had flashed by me this afternoon.

Family. We looked like a goddamn family. An impossible one.

Like a magnet drawn to north, my gaze landed on Fallon once more. Her exhaustion had taken her under with the same force Theo's had. Before I could stop myself, I was twining a silky strand through my fingers. Her hair had always been deceptive. The thick waves looked like they'd be coarse, but they were actually soft and smooth.

The longer I watched her, the larger the ache in my chest grew, until it was threatening to tumble over the edge with the force of an avalanche.

I'd always thought the person who ended up with Fallon would be the luckiest man on this planet, and I'd been pissed she'd let the loser JJ be that man for too many years. He hadn't deserved her. Not once. But maybe the truth was no man would be worthy of her. This fierce beauty deserved someone who'd climb buildings and soar through the sky for her—a true superhero.

I hated that she'd lost some of that teenage fierceness while living in San Diego. I'd seen it slowly and steadily decline over the last six years, but now, maybe because I hadn't been around her as much in the last few years, the loss stood out even more.

Coming home to the ranch hadn't returned it to her like it should have. Not yet. But I'd seen shimmering signs of it today. In her smile. In the dare she'd issued. In the way she'd touched me under the water.

My body grew taut all over again just thinking about it.

Fuck. It was time she went to bed. Time she locked herself in her room and let me shut myself in the one across the hall and forget the words she'd tossed at me.

If I remember, Kermit, it was always you who backed away from the finish line. I had no problem finding my way across it.

My frustration at both of us had me scooping her into my arms with more force than I'd intended. She murmured in her sleep, something soft and incomprehensible, but she didn't wake. She rolled her head onto my shoulder, lips parting, as I stalked down the hall and kicked open her bedroom door.

A light was on in the bathroom, a single beam streaming across the emerald-green linens. I shifted her so I could pull back the covers and then set her down. When I went to step back, her fingers curled into my shirt, locking me in place, and when I looked at her, sleepy eyes greeted me.

"What are you doing?" she asked, voice low and sexy without even trying.

"Putting you to bed."

"I'm not four, Parker. I'm not a child." Her lids fluttered closed as if they were too heavy to keep open. "I'm not sure I ever was." The words were raw and pained, but they were also the truth. Hadn't I thought it myself earlier when arguing with Teddy?

I tried to move away again, but her grip on my shirt tightened. "Let go, Ducky."

Long lashes opened, and the longing I saw inside those amber eyes almost knocked me off my feet. A craving as strong and alive and as intense as the one that beat in me.

"Chicken," she said, voice thick with emotions and tangled with lust. "No… Chickens are actually pretty obsessive when they see something they want. They don't back down. You're more a cow…meandering away at the first sign of danger."

"And you're supposed to be the danger?" The words slipped out before I could call them back, gruff and angry because we both knew the truth. She was dangerous. She'd always been.

She taunted me with a raised brow and eyes that fell to my mouth. Frustration burned. Didn't she know how much control it took to hold back? To not claim her? To refuse every offer she'd sent my way? I wasn't a fucking coward. It had taken more effort than it had ever taken me to hold up a boat in BUD/S to push her away each and every time we'd gotten this close.

"I must be pretty dangerous if I can make a SEAL run," she said breathily.

I wasn't sure if I'd moved or she'd moved, or if gravity had somehow pulled us together, but our lips ended up so close that if I even replied, our mouths would brush. Dread filled me. A sinking feeling I'd lost this battle. That I couldn't fight it anymore. But I didn't move. I didn't take the last breath that would cause our lips to touch. I just watched, drowning in the hunger of her eyes, as every fiber in my being told me to sink into them. Into her. To finally take what was mine.

Except, she wasn't mine to take.

She wasn't mine.

She wasn't mine.

She wasn't mine.

She closed her eyes again, letting go of my shirt, releasing me, and putting space between us once more. I found myself hating the inches that now existed between our lips when, moments ago, I'd been dreading our closeness.

"Don't worry, Frogman. I promised myself I'd never give you the chance to reject me again. So don't consider this an offer. You're off the hook for good when it comes to me."

I hated that almost as much as the space between us. I didn't want to be off the hook. I wanted to be on it, dangling from a line that only Fallon controlled. I wanted her reeling me in, inch by inch.

I still didn't move as my body and mind and heart all warred with each other.

Take her. Leave her. Love her.

It was the last thought that had me jerking away.

Love her? Where the fuck had that come from?

I did love her. Like one loved family. Friends. People who were important to you.

And maybe, sometimes, in the dark corners of my mind, I'd thought there could be something more…before promises and honor had stopped me from taking what she'd offered.

The love my parents had, or her dad and Sadie had, wasn't something I could have with Fallon. Not only because it was very rare for anyone to have that timeless, all-consuming love, but because I wouldn't leave a family to fend for themselves while I went off to fight wars no one on this planet knew we were fighting.

I stepped away as I always had, telling myself I was doing the right thing, the brave thing. But as I strode from her room and shut the door, I feared she might have been right. I really was a chicken. A fucking coward.

Chapter Nineteen
Fallon

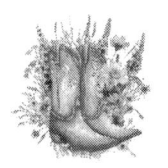

I DARE YOU TO LOVE
Performed by Trisha Yearwood

THREE AND A HALF YEARS AGO

HIM: Please tell me you aren't really dating the Patrick-Swayze-in-Point-Break wannabe.

    HER: Don't be jealous. It doesn't fit your SEAL vibe.

HIM: Not jealous, Ducky. You do remember Patrick was the bad guy in that movie, right?

    HER: JJ is harmless. A golden retriever.

HIM: Even golden retrievers can bite.

    HER: God, I hope so.

    HER: Did I scare you away?

    HER: You're such a prude.

HIM: Only with you.

PRESENT DAY

The next morning, while the sky was still a deep gray, I scurried out of the house like a rabbit chased by a cougar. Embarrassment trailed behind me once again. After Parker had walked out of my room, I'd tossed and turned and berated myself until I'd fallen into a fitful sleep. A nightmare followed me into the morning. Sadie and I at the bar, but instead of her answering the back door that early morning, it was Parker, and it was his body that hit the ground after a shot rang out. His eyes that had the light snuffed out of them.

I'd woken up to a racing pulse and an empty, nauseated feeling in my stomach.

As I got ready for the day, the terror from the nightmare burned away, leaving fury at myself and at Parker for how we'd ended the night. How did this one man have the power to humiliate me so many times? And why hadn't I learned my lesson by now?

I could say I hadn't offered myself up to him again, that I'd even told him I was absolutely *not* offering myself up, but the truth was, I had issued another dare he'd declined. I wasn't naïve enough to think I hadn't tempted him. I'd seen the heat and lust in his eyes. I'd heard the groan when I'd touched him in the lake, but for some reason, he could never seem to climb the wall that he'd placed between us.

It was his damn honor. Some misplaced loyalty for my dad or me or his team.

I hated it. Or rather, I wanted to hate it when, really, his honor was part of the reason why I'd always loved Parker.

Which was the exact reason I should never have let myself slip into a relationship with JJ that had lasted on and off for years. JJ had always been jealous of Parker, and I'd tried to prove to us both that what I felt for him was just childhood affection.

And yet, it had never been that simple.

Maybe before Parker had shown up when I was fourteen, right as everything had gone down with Dad, Sadie, and the Puzos, it had just been friendship and childish adoration. But having a Naval Academy cadet, muscled and gorgeous, tasked by our fathers to guard me like a hero from a fiction novel, had pushed all my teenage hormones into overdrive. After that, all I could feel when I was around him was a burning fire that needed to be quenched.

I'd never felt that same intensity with JJ. I'd been attracted to him. I'd let him be my first, and we'd had good sex. But it hadn't been life-altering. It hadn't swept me into a tidal wave where I couldn't tell which way was up. And just a simple touch from Parker could do that to me. A simple look could flip me around until I was doing the opposite of everything I'd promised myself.

When I walked into the barn, Kevin was frowning over a clipboard, which held the daily list of guest excursions. He looked up at me, scratching his dark-brown scruff and looking very much the stereotypical cowboy in a plaid shirt, Wranglers, and beat-up boots. As head of guest adventures, he made sure every activity we offered was safe, run by experienced guides, and left people with smiles on their faces, even when they'd spent the day shoveling shit. I wasn't sure how he did it, but he could convince anyone the worst ranch task was a delight.

"Morning," I said, heading straight for his office in a converted stall and the coffee I knew he'd have brewing there. We'd tried to make an office for him next to Kurt's in the ranch-hand house, but Kevin had insisted he wanted to stay close to the action.

"Going to be a scorcher today," he said, following me.

The compostable cup was only half full when I stopped pouring. The smell, normally a sweet addiction, turned my gut. I tried to take a sip, and my body rejected it furiously. I fought back the nausea before I looked up to find him scrutinizing me.

"You okay?"

"It's been a long couple of weeks," I told him. "What had you all squinty-eyed when I came in?" I changed the subject, glancing down at the clipboard he'd brought with him.

"Carrie called in sick. I had her slated to take a set of new riders up the river path to the picnic area near the caves. I'd fill in, but I'm already taking over Randy's fishing trip. He's been out since last week."

My stomach tightened for a completely different reason. "Is she afraid to come to work rather than truly being sick?"

He didn't respond with an immediate no, which only made my chest ache as much as my stomach. Eventually, he shook his head. "I don't think so. Bess told me there's been a bunch of staff at the mercantile calling in sick too. Something is going around."

Kevin's wife ran the largest gift shop on Main Street, stuffed to the gills with rustic mountain knickknacks and old forty-niner merchandise the tourists ate up. But it was her voluntary role as president of the Parent-Teacher Association that kept her finger on the pulse of what was going on in Rivers.

I set the coffee down and stepped away, hoping to put distance between me and the smell.

"I can take the beginner trip," I told him. I had a list of things to do today, not the least of which was to finish going through the employee files to try to figure out if it was one of them, rather than JJ or Ace, who'd slaughtered my cow and burned down my cabin. But taking the group up to the caves and back would put distance between me and my humiliation.

Kevin scratched his chin. "You sure? You've already got a lot on your plate."

"Don't we all? That's the way it's always been here, but I wouldn't trade it for the world," I told him. And it was the truth. I loved the pace and the level of activity and how it challenged me every single day. I'd just allowed myself to forget it for a few years.

Kevin grinned. "Me either."

"I can help out." The soft voice had me jumping nearly out of my skin. I whirled to find Chuck at the stall door.

"Jesus, you scared the daylights out of me."

He looked as he always did, like a gawky kid who needed to grow into his body, but there was something sad about his eyes today. "I know I haven't been here as long as the other guides, but I know all the stories. And I've learned a lot about the plants and wildlife. I can do this."

Kevin and I shared a look, and he took the lead in responding. "Thanks, Chuck, but we don't put anyone out on their own with guests until we're sure they can handle it."

Chuck looked so devastated that it even made me feel sad.

"Why don't you come with me on this ride? You can record some of my conversations and take notes. After, you can write down what you'd say if you took a group out on your own and present it to Kevin. If he likes it, we'll see about getting you trained."

The teen's face lit up. "Really?"

I nodded. "Of course. We want our employees to love being here, to want to share that love with our guests. Seems like you've proven that to us several times this summer."

"I'll get Daisy saddled up for you." He looked at Kevin and asked, "Can I take Henry the Fifth out?"

That horse had a temper if not managed right, but I didn't know Chuck's riding skills the way Kevin did, so when he agreed, I didn't say anything. I just let the kid go and get the horses ready, while I went over the list of guests and their riding experience with Kevin.

An hour later, I was just putting the final guest up on one of our gentlest horses when Parker found me. He was scowling as he let go of Theo's hand, and the boy ran straight toward the barn, shouting about the puppies Teddy had left there last night.

I could feel Parker glowering at me as I finished with the guest and sent her to join the others waiting for me at the end of the drive. Chuck was already with the group, and he said something that made them all laugh. Maybe the kid had more to him than anyone knew.

I had my hand on Daisy's pommel, ready to mount, before I risked looking directly at Parker. "I'm about to head out. What can I do for you?"

His hand landed on top of mine, and the tension that drifted between us had Daisy shifting and stomping a back hoof. She was the calmest horse I'd ever known, but she could read my moods better than most of the humans in my life.

"What part of being your bodyguard did I leave unclear?" he growled. Not a hair of the laughter and teasing we'd shared yesterday afternoon was left in his tone. That was just fine with me. It was easier for me to put my guard up, to not offer myself up on a silver platter, when he was grouchy and snarling.

My jaw tightened. "I don't need a bodyguard."

"Don't treat me like I'm a damn guest. I'm here to protect

you." I wasn't sure what he was more pissed about—that I'd snuck out without telling him or that I'd ordered room service to be delivered so he and Theo would have breakfast this morning.

"Letting you and Theo sleep in was just common courtesy."

"Bullshit." He leaned in, and I had nowhere to go with my back up against my horse. He lowered his voice in a way that caused it to rumble through my chest and stoke those fires I was attempting to bury. "You left because of what happened last night."

My eyes darted to his mouth and back up. "*Nothing* happened last night."

"When will you realize, me turning you down isn't because I don't want you?" As soon as the words were out, he looked like he'd swallowed a bug. He stepped back, face shuttering completely.

"You're forgetting, I didn't offer you a damn thing." I glared at him, hating that we both knew it was a lie.

He crossed his arms over his chest and shoved his chin in the direction of the group waiting for me. "Who from security is going with you on this little adventure?"

"I have Chuck with me."

"The teenager?" Parker snapped in disbelief.

"I don't need anyone else. If I drag security along with us, it will worry the guests more than they already are," I hissed. "Whoever this is hasn't come at me in the daylight hours. They've taken the cowardly way out and gone after my cattle and me in the middle of the night. You want to do something for me today? Figure out how they keep getting around the cameras."

"You're not going by yourself." He stated it like it was a cold, hard fact.

"You keep forgetting you're not my dad or my boss."

A throat clearing had us both jerking around and hissing, "What?" in unison.

Teddy stood there, trying to fight off a grin. "Just wanted

to ask if it would be okay for Theo to hang with me again today."

The little boy danced from foot to foot behind him. "Teddy is going to teach me to ride a pony. A real live pony."

Parker looked like he wanted to decline. And my foolish heart softened at the torn look on his face. He didn't want anyone to shoulder his responsibilities—not for Theo or anyone else. I hated he felt he had to carry the full burden on his own, as if trusting others to help him care for the little boy was somehow a failure.

With a five-thousand-acre ranch and hundreds of employees I'd considered mine from the time Spence had died, I understood the heavy weight of responsibility better than anyone. Except, I'd always *wanted* it to be mine. I'd even resented how Mom had worked herself to the bone for it between relapses. But the truth was, I'd never been able to fully count on her to put the ranch and me first when the drugs had called. I'd thought I would always put the ranch first, but I'd failed too. I'd stepped away from it for the years I'd been at college, barely giving it a thought, and now that it was fully mine, it was crumbling around the edges, as if I wasn't juggling all the balls at just the right pace.

I didn't want Parker to feel that way, as if he'd drop the ball at any minute if he chose me over Theo or vice versa. It was with a resigned recognition I realized I didn't want to feel that way either, afraid to let someone catch a ball for me. I wasn't sure I could fix my own issues today, but I could help Parker with his.

I put a hand on his arm. "Go talk to the security team. Figure out if Wylee and Cranky have found out anything. That's how you can help me best today."

He shook his head. "I can do that after we get back." He turned to Teddy. "I need a horse."

I snorted. "When was the last time you even rode, Kermit?"

He ignored me, heading for the barn.

Teddy waited, looking from me to the barn and then back. I let out a frustrated sigh before saying, "Fine. Give him Dandy.

He's easygoing and won't spook if Parker is too hard on the reins." Teddy nodded, still fighting his smile. I swung myself into the saddle and then looked down at him. "I'm starting out. Tell Parker if he wants to come so damn bad, he'll have to catch up."

Maybe he'd fall off and realize he couldn't actually do everything, that even SEALs had their limits.

I clicked my tongue at Daisy, and she followed the command like she had for years. Here in the saddle, I always felt strong and confident. Daisy and I moved like one, reading each other, knowing from every quiver of muscle exactly what the other needed. The quarter horse and I had grown up together, learning Western riding and trick riding with thousands of hours of practice.

The competitions I'd entered in college had been sedate, nothing like the wild tricks I'd done to entertain our first resort guests back as a teen. Those twice-weekly shows had been placed on hold while I'd been at college, only revived on special occasions, like the Fourth of July. Maybe, now that I was back for good, I'd reinstate them on a more permanent basis. Daisy and I would both need an outlet for our energy. Maybe I could even rope Maisey into picking her routine back up when she wasn't working at the hospital.

I pressed my knees into Daisy's sides, and she picked up her pace, cantering across the yard to join the group of eight, plus Chuck, who were waiting for me.

"Sorry about that, folks. It seems like we have a late joiner." I looked back to the barn, but there was still no sign of Parker. "Anyone have any questions before we start?"

Everyone shook their heads, and I took the lead, directing Daisy off the paved road onto a worn path that led to the river. We'd wind our way along it up into the mountains until we ended at the picnic area near the caves. We wouldn't go inside them. They were deep and narrow, and you could easily get lost if you didn't know your way around, but the guests ate up the rumors about bandits using them in the eighteen hundreds. I'd played around with creating an excursion that took them through it, but the insurance waivers had been too much at the time. Maybe someday.

The fast-paced pounding of hooves warned me of Parker's approach, but I didn't turn to acknowledge him. I was still annoyed—at myself and at him.

The trail was wide enough here to travel two by two, and a man with glasses sidled up next to me on one of our most easygoing mares. "Hey. Is it really true your family won the ranch in a poker match? And that pirates left the diamonds you found?"

I smiled. "Yes, my great-great-grandpa Harrington won the ranch with a royal flush. But I'm a descendant of both men who played that game, so I guess you can say the land found its way home again. And no, pirates didn't leave the diamonds. That was all volcanic activity. We were just lucky enough to have kimberlite pipes bring the diamonds to the surface."

His eyes turned greedy. "Any diamonds still around?"

Since turning the ranch into a resort, we'd had dozens of guests sneak out and try to dig up diamonds. For the most part, it was harmless, but sometimes they took it too far, destroying the land and getting hurt in the process.

"No. Believe me, my ancestors wouldn't have stopped mining if they'd thought there was even one shiny gem left."

He was going to ask more, but I cut him off, pulling Daisy to a stop to talk to the entire group about the plants and trees native to this part of California. I shared some of the medicinal qualities found in yarrow and the leaves of sequoia trees before moving us forward again and telling them they'd get to see one of the oldest sequoias in the area on this trip.

I stopped frequently so guests could take pictures of the various views, and by the time we arrived at the picnic area by the caves, they were all pink-cheeked and smiling. As they pulled the lunches packed for them by the hotel staff from their saddle bags, Chuck directed them to the picnic tables and told them a story about the bandits who'd used the caves for hideouts and how he'd spent time inside, searching for buried loot.

Pleased to realize he really did know all the old stories, even if I didn't want him encouraging the guests to go searching for treasure on their own, I left him to it and made my way to check the horses. Running my hands down them, I made sure none of the novice riders had accidentally injured them. Each horse nosed into the bag I had slung across me, searching for the treats they'd find there.

Parker fell into step with me, nodded toward the guests, and said, "You're really good with them."

I raised a brow. "Are you being nice because you got your way?"

His eyes twinkled, crinkling at the corners as he fought off a smile.

"I'm usually nice. Believe it or not, my team thinks I'm the calmest, most easygoing of the entire group. You're the only one who makes me growly."

The way his voice deepened at the end of his admission had that longing inside me flaring to life again. And because I didn't want him to see it, I looked away first.

"Okay, Baywatch," I taunted.

He huffed out a half laugh. "I should never have told you they called me that."

"You do remember the time you acted exactly like Parker Stevenson and his pals at the beach, right? You rescued that woman flailing around in the water as if she was being chased by a shark when it was only a fish." I tried to say it with a straight face but ended up hiding my mouth behind my hand.

"She clung to me like a koala cub."

"I overheard her friends saying she'd found out you were a SEAL and decided the whole damsel-in-distress routine was the way to your heart."

He flushed, a delightful blush I rarely saw, and it sent curls of pleasure through me.

I shoved his shoulder with mine and said, "You took her home."

His eyes grew serious. "Not the way you're implying. I caught on soon enough to what she really wanted. She wanted the movie ending, the prestige of having a Navy SEAL's ring on her finger, but she didn't really want me, and I certainly didn't want forever after with her. The women I take to bed know exactly what I'm offering. One night. That's it."

"Big bad SEAL showing his lack of courage again," I said.

"Excuse me?" His eyes widened in surprised confusion.

"Love takes courage, Parker. Risking yourself in a relationship takes bravery. You have to give part of yourself to the other person and hope they'll keep it safe. You say you don't want anyone waiting for you, that you don't want anyone to be hurt if something happens to you on a mission, but really, your one-night-only rule ensures *you'll* never get hurt either."

He didn't like I'd called him out on the truth, and so when he snapped back at me, I didn't take it personally, even though the words stung. "And how'd the risk work out for you with JJ?"

I just gave him a small shrug. Then, I moved away to retrieve the bagged lunch from my saddlebag. "You didn't get a meal from the kitchen. You can share mine."

"Fallon." I heard the apology in his voice, but he didn't say more.

I was glad he didn't. I needed the Parker who pissed me off or the friend I could tease with me today. Not the one I wanted in my bed. It was the only way I'd get through him being on the ranch without continuing to humiliate myself more.

Chapter Twenty
Parker

OUT OF NOWHERE
Performed by Canaan Cox

FOUR YEARS AGO

HIM: Will is officially in love with his new baby boy and in hate with Althea. She's a money-grabbing cheater. This is the exact reason I'll never be in a serious relationship.

HER: Not everyone's relationships turn sour. Not every woman is after something. Your parents and my dad and Sadie are perfect examples of forever after working out.

HIM: Rare species, soon to be extinct.

HER: Only if humanity lets it.

HIM: I'll never understand how you can be so positive about relationships when your family is the perfect example of how fucked up they can be.

Minutes passed.

HIM: I'm sorry. That was uncalled for. I'm frustrated for Will. Ignore me.

PRESENT DAY

I watched as Fallon rallied the guests and got them back on their horses with an ease that came not only from years of experience but also from that inner confidence she'd always exuded. Her words about love and relationships had hit me harder than I'd expected, especially coming from a woman who'd spent her childhood feeling loved but not wanted. That strange dichotomy had left permanent marks on her soul.

She wasn't wrong about relationships taking courage or the fact I wasn't willing to risk my heart. But it wasn't just mine I was protecting. I wouldn't risk her heart—any woman's, I corrected—when I could see no positive end to dragging someone into this lifestyle with me.

And yet, plenty of my fellow teammates were married. Had kids. Had lives they came home to that helped them forget what they'd seen and done while on assignment, unlike the stale silence that always greeted me when I walked in the door after a mission. But a good chunk of SEAL marriages ended in divorce. Then again, didn't all marriages? Divorce rates were sky-high across the board, no matter your profession.

I wasn't sure how I felt about all those little flashes of *what if* that had been taunting me since I'd arrived at the ranch—or the fact it was Fallon I saw at my side in those momentary lapses of judgment.

As the group turned back toward the castle, I brought up the rear again. Fallon stopped less often on the return, letting the guests carry the weight of the conversation among themselves or shouting out questions to her that she answered with knowledge and patience.

The view was beautiful, but Fallon seemed to shine above it all.

She was stunning—casual and at ease, with her aged cowboy hat tipped back to show sparkling, amber eyes. Her muscular arms were on display in a short-sleeve button-down shirt the color of mint ice cream. It was tucked into saddle-worn jeans that showed off delightful curves. Her gloved hands were so light on the reins it was like they didn't even need to be there.

She belonged on that horse, here in this place, with

mountains and streams shimmering around her. The way she and Daisy moved, as if they were one, made it easy to imagine Fallon as a centaur, carrying all the wisdom those mythical creatures were often portrayed as having.

But thoughts of her as a centaur only brought images of her bare from the waist up. Hell, bare completely. Riding a horse naked would hardly be comfortable for anyone, but the image of her just like that, with her hair flowing behind her as she and Daisy raced across flowered fields…damn if it wasn't the shit of fantasies.

A loud crack broke the air. A few guests let out yelps. The horses snorted and stomped nervously with their reins jingling. I had to pull my head out of dreamlike images of a naked Fallon before it registered the sound as a fucking gunshot.

Hunters. Did they have hunting excursions on the ranch these days?

When a second blast sent dirt flying at the horses' feet, some of the guests screamed, and a sudden and overwhelming fear flooded my veins.

Fallon!

Someone was taking shots at her—at all of us—and we were out in the open. Completely exposed.

At the front of the pack, Fallon and Daisy turned slightly as another blast sprayed dirt up her horse's fetlock.

My chest filled with panic before I locked it down and let my training take over.

"Head for the trees!" I commanded.

Chuck shook himself out of the shell shock first, hollering to the guests to follow him as he kicked his horse into a gallop toward the tree line. Some guests followed, dropping low in their saddles.

Another shot kicked up grass between Daisy and another horse. The woman on its back jerked her reins furiously. Fueled by its own fear, and its rider's, the horse took off. The unprepared woman slipped sideways in the saddle, dangling half on and half off. The off-kilter weight only panicked the horse more.

Fallon didn't even hesitate. She simply spurred Daisy after them.

Every instinct in my body screamed to follow her, to get Fallon to fucking safety.

But the ugly truth was that she'd never be safe if I didn't stop the asshole who was doing this.

Fury had me urging Dandy in the direction of the shots. The far ridgeline was lined with plenty of trees and boulders, providing cover for the shooter. It was at least three hundred yards away, which meant it had to be someone who knew their way around rifles.

Another blast brought more screams and shouts from behind me, and my focus lasered in on the objective—to stop the gunman. I pushed Dandy forward at a pace I wasn't necessarily comfortable with when I rarely rode these days, but I had to get to the shooter before he killed someone.

Fallon.

Fuck.

What would I do if I lost her?

I shouldn't have left her.

But I didn't turn around. I focused on the job. On finding the shooter. And when I did, I'd beat him to a pulp for scaring her. For bringing the blue shadows to her eyes and dimming her light.

As I reached the base of the hill, where the trees took over and the ground grew craggy, another shot reverberated through the air—this one directed at me. It sent birds flying from the nearby branches, wings beating furiously.

I slipped off Dandy and sprinted up the slope toward the last blast.

A rustling had me jerking to a stop. I attempted to control my breathing while listening for movement I couldn't see. The hillside had gone eerily quiet. Nothing. Not even a bee buzzed.

Then, pebbles bounced down the hillside above me.

I ran without once slowing, keeping out of sight whenever possible.

I caught a glimpse of dark hair before it disappeared over

the crest of the hill and increased my pace.

A motor kickstarted. Multi-cylinder.

Damnit. He was getting away.

My thighs protested as I thrust myself up the slope at an even more brutal pace. I dragged myself over a final boulder just in time to see an endurance bike kicking up gravel and dirt as it disappeared down the fire road.

"Fuck!" I shouted into the silence left behind.

I ripped my phone from my back pocket, calling the security office. I cut Lance off as he answered. "Get a team to the fire road on the northwest side of the estate. A shooter is escaping on a red off-road motorcycle. No helmet. Brown hair. Brown jacket. No license plate. Heading toward the lake rather than Rivers."

"Shooter?" Lance hissed.

"Go, Lance. Fucking go."

The line went dead. I laced my fingers behind my head, steadied my breathing, and then did a slow spin, taking in the area. I picked my way down the hill in the direction the shooter had come from, watching for footprints so I wouldn't smudge them, all while looking for any other clues that would identify who this had been. I stopped at a large clump of rocks jutting out at the point of the hillside. If I were aiming into the valley, this was where I'd set up. It had the perfect view of the trail as it emerged from the trees.

Except, he couldn't have known Fallon would be leading the excursion ahead of time. Kevin had told me she'd filled in at the last minute. So, what had been his game plan?

I scanned the ground. The shooter had left scuff marks where he'd lain between the boulders. Indents from the butt and the pistol grip setting in the dirt. Some boot prints. A handful of expended shell casings.

Not a professional, then. A professional would have taken the casings with them and swept the ground of any trace.

I raised my gaze to the field, noting how the guests had gathered in a circle with their horses, and my stomach dropped.

Someone was on the ground in the middle of the huddle.

Between their feet, I caught a flash of mint green sprawled amongst the flowers.

For a second, the entire world froze—and my heart along with it.

Pain spiraled through every vein.

It wasn't her.

Goddamnit.

It could *not* be her!

I leaped over the side of the boulder, my military boots sliding along the pine needles and loose rocks. Branches slapped me in my face as I hurtled down the hillside, gaining speed until I almost couldn't control the pace. The distance seemed impossible.

Memories of Fallon flashed through my mind on repeat. Smiles. Tears. Sass. Sultry looks.

Pain tore through me at everything I'd fucking denied us.

For what?

"Fallon!" I screamed just as I burst through the trees, and some of the guests jerked around, fear spreading across their faces until they saw it was me.

I hauled ass over the field and shoved my way through the group, heart torn between racing and stopping, a stuttering that made it hard to breathe.

Chuck was on the ground next to Fallon, holding her hand. Her eyes were shut, and her face was deathly pale.

Fuck. Fuck. Fuck.

I gritted my teeth, trying to pull myself together in order to do the one thing Fallon would count on me to do—get her guests to safety.

"Everyone on your horses. Get back to the hotel," I ordered.

The woman Fallon had chased down was crying uncontrollably as one of the other guests patted her shoulder.

"I called 9-1-1," Chuck said, his voice shaky.

His face was almost as pale as Fallon's as tears streamed down it. He nervously wiped the back of his cheek as I knelt beside her. I fought every urge screaming at me to pull her into my arms and yell at her to fucking wake up.

Instead, I assessed her carefully from head to toe. No blood. Thank God! There was no blood and no hole torn through her clothes. She hadn't been hit with a bullet, but she had a massive knot at her temple that was already turning an ugly shade of black and blue. She was breathing, chest rising and falling, but she looked so still and lifeless it was terrifying.

"What happened?" I demanded.

Chuck's voice was full of fear and awe as he explained, "She was like a superhero. She launched onto Sue's horse and pulled Sue back into the saddle before reining in the horse. They'd both just gotten off when another gunshot..." The teen's voice disappeared.

The woman Fallon had saved took over. "The horse freaked out. It reared up, knocking her in the head with its hoof. She went down like... I've never seen..." She broke into sobs again.

A head wound. A nasty damn head wound.

Her neck needed to be secured. She needed an MRI.

But, hell, the relief swam through me because it was better than a hole in her chest.

I looked around at the group, who still hadn't moved. They were standing there in shock. Tense and scared. "Go. Damn it. Get on the horses, and head back to the hotel."

Chuck stood, looking down at Fallon again with tears still streaming. "I'll t-take them."

"Make sure the EMTs know where to come, and tell them to send a backboard." I gave the kid a firm look, one that said *do not fucking fail me*.

He pulled his shoulders back and got the guests mounted and moving.

The woman Fallon had chased down just stood there.

"I can't... I can't get back on..." she cried.

Chuck took her by the elbow. "Come on, Sue. We'll walk the horses back."

"What if we're shot at again?" she wept.

"The shooter left," I growled. "But the safest place you can be right now is at the hotel."

As soon as Chuck had the two of them heading toward the resort, I planted my ass on the ground and grabbed Fallon's hand. "Wake up, Ducky. Wake the fuck up before I'm forced to call Rafe. You and I both know you'd hate that."

Nothing. Just the continued slow rise and fall of her chest.

Guilt, anger, and fear all washed through me in a heady mix that made me want to pound my boxing bag until my fingers bled. I slammed my fist onto the ground.

"Wake the fuck up!"

Her pupils danced behind closed lids.

I'd wasted so much time with her. I'd spent the last few years running as hard as I could the opposite way. I'd put as much distance between us as possible. For what? For honor? For a promise I'd made when we were fricking teenagers?

Because I'd lacked the courage to make us something unforgettable. Something timeless.

I'd denied us the pleasure and relief of sating the hunger that crawled through us whenever we were together. I'd denied myself the comfort of coming home to someone who cared about me more than they cared about another living soul. I'd pushed and shoved and refused her dares when all I'd really wanted was to give in to the fire that burned between us.

And I'd nearly lost her.

My throat closed.

I could still lose her if she didn't wake up.

If I lost her without ever really having touched her, without ever truly making her mine, I'd hate myself more than I ever would for breaking a stupid promise I'd given as a green-ass cadet. She needed to know she was much more than a duty. She needed to know I cared about her. Cared was a stupid word. What I felt was a need so deep it was greater than the necessity for air.

I brought her palm to my mouth and placed the softest of kisses there. "Don't you fucking leave me before I can accept your dare, Fallon. Don't even think about it."

A flutter of eyelashes sent my chest into a dizzying spiral.

I leaned in, brushing my lips gently along her cheek. "Open those goddamn eyes, Ducky."

A wild and unrestrained relief soared through me when she did just that. Confusion danced through them.

"What happened?" she croaked.

She tried to move, and a pained groan escaped her.

I put my hand on her chest, stopping her. "Stay still."

Her free hand went to her temple. "My head."

"Took a nasty kick," I said. "Don't move until the EMTs get here."

Fire returned to her eyes. "You did not call an ambulance!"

Her furious response eased the pain and torture inside me. My chest lightened. Thank God.

She tried to move again, and I let go of her hand to hold her down. "It was Chuck who called them, but I'm glad he did. You shouldn't move until an EMT can check you for a neck or spinal injury."

"I got smashed in the head with a hoof, Frogman, not kicked in the back." She fought me, and instead of hurting her more, I let her sit up. Her eyes swam, and she closed them, swallowing hard as nausea overtook her. "It's embarrassing. I know better than to get kicked by one of my own goddamn horses."

"You were being shot at. That makes people do all sorts of things that are out of character."

Her eyes flew open. "You went after them—"

"Got away on an off-road motorcycle. I sent Lance to the old fire road to see if he could catch up with them."

She swore under her breath. Then, she gripped my arm. "Help me up."

"Fallon."

"Help me up, Parker. I need to walk back on my own feet if I'm going to withstand this humiliation. And the guests..." She shook her head and went even paler than before. I wasn't even sure how that was possible. She touched the enormous knot, wincing.

Debate warred inside me. She needed to be checked out. While the hit had been to her head, it didn't rule out spinal damage. The fall to the ground could have injured her as much as the kick, but I knew that expression on her face. The fierce determination. She'd get up on her own if I didn't help.

I gripped her elbows and eased her to her feet.

She swayed, unsteady, and my arms surrounded her.

I drew her into my chest and said gently, "Give it a minute for everything to stop spinning."

Fallon wasn't the only one who needed the reminder. My entire world was spinning. Relief mixed with fury for whoever had done this, and behind it, fear lingered like an ugly aftertaste. Not just for her and her safety, but for me. For the wash of feelings and thoughts that had flooded me when I'd seen her on the ground. When, for a few seconds, I'd been forced to imagine my world without her and found that idea more terrifying than even the idea of not returning to my platoon.

I'd thought nothing would make me give up my spot on the teams and the promise I'd sworn to my dying grandfather. Not a damn thing. And yet, I'd been a breath away from making a bargain with the devil to do just that if it meant she was okay.

I didn't know what to do with this new information. And I always fucking knew what to do.

At least, I had until Will had died and flipped my world upside down.

Since then, my life had taken steps further and further away from what I'd planned. Seeing Fallon sprawled on the ground, feeling the intense loss of something I'd never had the courage to make mine, had sent my world spiraling another dozen steps away from what I'd envisioned for myself.

I would have stood there, wrapped around her, until the EMTs arrived, if Fallon hadn't moved. She pushed against my chest and took a tentative step back. I instantly wanted to drag her into my arms again. I wanted to hold on until I was convinced she was strong enough to aim fire and brimstone at me once more.

Confusion danced in her eyes as they met mine. "When I was knocked out…did you…" She swiped her cheek and then shook her head and winced again. "Never mind."

She turned slowly, inhaling sharply before she took another step away from me. She whistled, and Daisy immediately trotted over to her. Fallon would have leaped into the saddle if I hadn't caught her by the wrist. "Don't even think about it."

Her eyes met mine, flashing with heat again. "Excuse me?"

"You need to get checked out before you go bouncing around on the back of a horse. No more jiggling that beautiful brain of yours until a doctor approves it."

"I've taken plenty of falls off my horse. I always get back on."

"Except, this wasn't a fall off your damn horse. You were unconscious, Fallon—for at least five minutes, if not longer. You need a full workup. MRI, CAT scan, the entire shebang."

She started to argue, and I did the only thing I could think of to stop her—I put my mouth on hers. I forced myself to be gentle, to savor the softness as I barely brushed our lips together. But it sent a cataclysmic wave of heat and longing spinning through my chest and straight to my groin. Warning signs danced in my mind, and I started to pull back, but her hand fisted in my hair, pushing our mouths together more.

She kissed just like she did everything in her life. With a rush of energy. With an intensity that screamed power and control and confidence.

I lost my hold on reality, on the fact she was injured. I slanted my mouth to take better possession, slipping my tongue between her soft heat, where I encountered heaven. Salty seas and sweet yarrow and coyote mint blooms. A burst of ocean and land. Being lost in her was like being lost in sunlight dancing over the water, sparkles of light shimmering and blinding you for a brief moment.

A moment you'd never forget. A moment you savored.

And I did just that—treasured the minutes spent kissing the one woman I'd promised myself I never would. Our brief mouth-to-mouth in a bar years ago was nothing compared to this, and that had been a fire I'd never quenched.

The longer I spent with my body and heart and soul tangled with her, the deeper I fell. I was lost in a well I'd never be able to climb out of, that I'd never *want* to climb out of, because now that I was here, now that I'd tasted perfect bliss, I never wanted to leave. I needed to keep this feeling. I needed to keep her and make her mine forever.

Chapter Twenty-one
Fallon

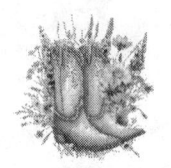

I WON'T LAST A DAY WITHOUT YOU
Performed by Katie Peslis & Jay Rouse

FOUR YEARS AGO

> *HER: Why'd you leave so early?*
>
> *HIM: Did you need an audience for the JJ and Fallon show?*
>
> *HER: What's that supposed to mean?*
>
> *HIM: Nothing. I'm still wound tight from the mission. It was better that I left before I said something I'd regret.*

PRESENT DAY

Parker was kissing me.

I was kissing Parker.

And holy hell, was it better than I'd remembered. Better than the brief one full of surprise and longing that I'd given him in a dive bar.

This was lightning and thunder. Stormy skies and the best of sunlit days.

Every single particle of my being was vibrating with life. Joy and pleasure swept through me.

Everything I'd ever wanted, every dream I'd had, and every favorite memory was nothing compared to these stunning seconds when our mouths were joined.

It was so beautiful it hurt and, conversely, wiped away every anguish.

I couldn't think. All I could do was lose myself to the wild rush of yearning that whipped through me as he deepened the kiss. He took complete control of my body and soul and heart.

Every nerve screamed the truth—we were finally right where we belonged.

Parker had finally kissed me.

I hadn't dared him, hadn't made the first move.

He'd. Kissed. Me.

All I'd had to do was get knocked unconscious to make it happen.

That simple thought allowed embarrassment to roll back in. With it came my anger at whoever had shot at me and my guests and frustration at Parker for choosing this ugly moment to give in.

I let go of Parker and took a step back.

Our eyes locked, deep storms blending with my warm fires. Desire, so large it was almost visible, whipped through the air between us.

"Damn you," I whispered.

He dragged a hand over his face. "Ducky, I'm sorry."

I punched him in the chest, and knowing it wouldn't hurt his solid wall of muscles only angered me more. I wanted to leave a mark. "Don't you dare apologize for kissing me. That isn't why I was cussing you out."

He watched me, a nervousness to him I couldn't remember having ever seen in Parker before.

"I'm just saying you could have chosen a better moment."

For two heartbeats we stayed that way, with yearning and frustration and hope still spinning between us, and then, his lips quirked. He rolled his face up to the sky and let out a chuckle that landed in my belly with almost the same force as the kiss. His laugh had always done that—pummeled me with joy and affection.

A shout across the field drew our eyes to where two EMTs jogged our way. One had a backboard strapped to him, and the other carried a large medical kit.

Everything that the kiss had kept at bay came slamming back into me.

We'd been shot at. My guests had been in danger.

And even though it wasn't still happening, in my head, I heard the sound of the rifle echoing across the land, and it woke dangerous memories. Hearing the same sound a decade ago. The terrifying helplessness and fear that had consumed me, knowing Dad and Sadie were being shot at and running for cover. The loud report of a pistol shot at close range with my uncle pulling the trigger. A sickening thud as Theresa Puzo collapsed to the floor with blood pooling out of her.

My vision swam. A tremor ran up my spine, and my hands began to shake.

I tried to fight it off, not only the physical reaction but the memories and the emotions they dragged with them. I did my best to toss them behind the same door where I kept all my traumatic moments. But the door felt flimsy and fragile, as if it would burst open again at the smallest provocation.

When I glanced at Parker, he'd already shuttered away every emotion. He was back to being the Navy SEAL—feet wide, arms crossed over his mammoth chest, jaw tight. But I knew from experience, from watching my dad hide his emotions all my life, from doing the same myself, that just because Parker had tucked them away, it didn't mean they weren't beating inside him, trying to escape their cage.

But there was one emotion I wouldn't let either of us keep locked up anymore. I silently swore we'd get back to the desire the kiss had raised.

I wouldn't let him start this and then try to forget it happened—not when it was the single most beautiful kiss I'd ever had. The entire world had slid into perfect focus when his mouth had been on mine. We would have that again.

"I'll make you a promise, Kermit," I said quietly as the two men drew closer. His gaze met mine before flicking away. "I'll go to the damn hospital, have them run their stupid tests, but when I get back, we pick up where that kiss left off."

"You're going to the hospital if I have to strap you to that backboard and carry you there myself." I started to protest, and he stepped closer, tweaking my braid. It was the same gentle tug he'd done my whole life, but it shot pain straight to my temple, causing me to gasp. "And that, right there, is why you're going to the emergency room."

"Fine," I snapped. "But I expect to be rewarded for it."

His gaze fell to my mouth, and heat shot through my chest.

I dragged my eyes away before stepping toward the EMTs. The quicker we got this over with, the quicker I could get back to what Parker had started.

♪ ♪ ♪

Hours later, I was still in the hospital, waiting impatiently in the emergency room for a doctor to return with some of my test results. They'd done a full battery of tests, bloodwork, urine samples, and ordered a CT scan, which had felt like overkill. After all, I'd been knocked in the head before.

The longer I sat there, the harder it was to keep at bay the memories of another emergency room in Tennessee, where I'd been more worried about Sadie's injuries than mine. She'd taken the brunt of the violence in trying to defend me.

The tremors I'd forced away in the field returned, and my stomach twisted nastily again.

I hated thinking about that day. Uncle Adam had done nothing but watch as Theresa Puzo had clocked me with the grip of her pistol. Then, he'd hurt Sadie, hitting and kicking her, while I'd been stuck in a chair with Theresa's gun aimed at me.

My chest grew tight as emotions and tears tried to escape.

The gunshot that day had been…evil. I had no other words to describe it. It had been different than any shot I'd ever heard, even when I'd pulled the trigger many times myself. Guns were just another tool a rancher had to be familiar with. Uncle Spencer had shown me the mercy that came from putting a dying cow out of its misery, but that day in the bar with Sadie, everything had been different.

Today, it had sounded the same way.

Another chill ran up my spine.

The blasts echoing over the field had held that same darkness. Maybe it was because the shots had been directed at humans. Maybe it was because they were as far from mercy as possible.

All I knew was, the longer I sat in a stupid hospital room waiting, the more the memories tried to swallow me, tried to sink their greedy, ugly grasp into me.

I didn't want ugly.

I wanted the heaven I'd found in Parker's embrace.

When Parker poked his head in to check on me, the worry in his eyes meant the ugliness hung around us like a heavy cloak. I loathed it. I wanted the heat back. The desire. The lust. Instead, Parker had returned to his SEAL persona. He was cold and factual as he dealt with Sheriff Wylee and the ranch's security.

The buzz of my phone had me jerking in surprise, even though I'd been gripping the device like it was a lifeline the entire time I'd been in the emergency room.

DAD: What the hell is going on, Ducky?

Tears pricked. I closed my eyes. Embarrassment and failure spiraled through me.

I couldn't respond. I should have been pissed at whoever had told Dad, but I couldn't find it in me.

DAD: Just tell me you're okay.

Thankfully, an attendant came to take me for the CT scan before I could respond. I handed Parker my phone before I was wheeled away.

"Can you text Dad back for me?"

He gave me that hooded look, the one draped with concern, and I closed my eyes against it.

When I came back from the scan, I didn't ask for my phone back. I didn't ask what Dad had said or whether he was racing back from Australia to rescue me. It was cowardly, but I didn't think I could handle his concern on top of Parker's without completely falling apart.

I didn't want to hear Dad say this wasn't my fault. Because the truth was, I'd brought this back with me from San Diego, and I'd been in charge of the boat when it had begun to sink. I hadn't bailed it out quickly enough, and now our guests were checking out and running away. Who could blame them? Who would stay after being shot at? No one. Not even the guests who hadn't been on the ride today would put themselves in harm's way by sticking around.

Parker's phone buzzed again. "Wylee," he said with a frown and stepped out of the room yet again.

The doctor returned while he was gone. She wheeled a stool over to the side of the bed and sat beside me. "How are you feeling?"

"Other than my head pounding like a stampede's going through it, I'm okay."

"Nausea?"

I bit my cheek. Yes, but I didn't want to tell her I'd been battling it for days.

"I'd like to keep you overnight," she said.

I started to shake my head and caught myself, knowing it would hurt like hell. "I'd much rather go home."

"The man with you, Parker, is it? He'll stay with you and follow our instructions for checking on you throughout the night?" she asked.

I wanted Parker to stay up all night for other reasons—much better ones that had to do with the intensity of our kiss. But I could hardly tell the doctor I was going home, hoping to have a wild round of sex. She'd never let me out the door.

"He will," I said. The truth was, I doubted I could send him away, even if I tried. And that thought took the passion of our kiss and sent it sailing. Because it meant I was an obligation again. A responsibility. Duty rather than love.

"How long have the two of you been dating?"

Surprise brought my eyes to hers.

She chuckled. "I'd have to be blind not to see that you care about each other. And the heat in his eyes when he looks at you…" She waved a hand in front of her face. "Hot potatoes."

For all of two seconds, everything felt lighter. Brighter. More hopeful. But then, she took it away with her next words.

"It'll make it easier for you to tell him about the baby."

My mouth popped open. "Wh-what?"

Every single thought I'd pushed away in denial came flooding back. The nausea. The soreness in my breasts. My pure exhaustion. The couple of pounds I'd gained. The way my stomach was a solid knot, hard and unyielding in an unfamiliar way.

No. Goddamnit. No.

This could not be happening.

JJ could not be tearing apart my life even more. Not now. Not when I was this close to making Parker mine like I'd always wanted.

A baby.

I was having a baby.

Holy shit. My head spun, the world went fuzzy, and then the doctor was there, easing me back onto the bed.

"Just take a slow, steady breath, Fallon." Her words were gentle. Concerned. And it caused those damn tears I'd barely been holding back to rush forward. "I thought maybe you knew."

I wasn't ready to be a mom. Not now. Not yet.

Not when I was failing so utterly and completely at everything.

I swallowed hard. "I… There have been a few moments in the last week or so I wondered, but I've been under a lot of stress, so I just thought it was that."

She patted my arm. "Is this news going to ease that stress or add to it?"

I chuckled, but it wasn't full of humor. It was dark and pained, and it allowed her to draw her own conclusions.

"Okay, then. I'll get you some pamphlets that list your options and provide you with the names of my recommended

OB-GYNs. I'll be right back."

I closed my eyes again, tears rushing down my cheeks as my own words that I'd tossed at JJ taunted me. *I'm not pregnant. But even if I was, I'd never keep it. Not if it was yours.*

I'd said it simply because I knew he'd try to get his hooks into me if there was a baby. He'd try to dip his hand into my inheritance as the father of my child, demanding child support and more. Look at what had happened with Will and Althea… My lungs squeezed tight as an even worse thought hit me. He'd have a say in how the baby was raised. He'd share his twisted ethics and make our child someone without honor.

Shit. Shit. Shit.

My hand landed on my stomach.

A baby.

His baby. The thought made bile rise in my throat.

But it was also mine. A piece of me. It had my DNA. Dad's DNA.

It would have fierce determination and strong will.

But it would also have Hurly DNA from my mom's side. And if I was being honest with myself, that DNA was tainted. Gamblers. Thieves. Murderers. Even Mom hadn't escaped the long list of bad traits, adding prescription drug addiction to the list.

My family was a screwed-up mess of bad decisions, obsessions, and felonies.

It wasn't like I'd escaped the darkness either. Mistake after mistake after mistake.

The curtain whipped along on the track, and I opened my eyes. The doctor came in, and I slowly sat up. She handed me a brown bag.

"This has all the information you'll need. It also has a few days' worth of prenatal vitamins, a brochure on natural remedies for morning sickness, and suggestions on a healthy diet for you and the baby." Her eyes were kind. "Give yourself time to adjust and think things through before you decide what to do. I recommend knowing what you want before you broach it with your boyfriend."

"He's…" I trailed off. It didn't matter what she thought. "Okay."

Parker stepped in behind the doctor, his eyes finding me immediately, settling on my wet cheeks. "Fallon?" Concern bled into my name, but he whirled to face the doctor before I could respond. "What's wrong with her?"

The doctor's face went blank. "I'm sorry. I can't discuss a patient's health without their permission."

Parker stepped toward her, a glower on his face, but my words stopped him. "Just the shock finally settling in, Parker. She's told me I can go home. Concussion is the worst of it."

"Yes. You'll have to watch her. Let me print out the instructions for you. I'll be right back." She scurried around Parker.

He stalked over to me and picked up my hand. "Ducky, I know you. This isn't the shock."

I couldn't meet his gaze. I felt it burning into me, but all it did was make me want to cry more. Because I'd finally gotten what I wanted. I'd finally gotten Parker, and now there was no way I could keep him. No way I could even finish what he'd started with one life-altering kiss in a field. Not when I was having a baby he'd never wanted. A baby that belonged to someone else.

To JJ.

Those thoughts caused the sinking feeling in my chest to grow as I realized the truth. I'd already made my decision. I couldn't get rid of the baby. Not even knowing JJ might be able to get his hooks into me and the child if and when he found out about it.

I'd just have to find a way to keep JJ from discovering the truth. I wouldn't put his name on the birth certificate. I wouldn't contact him. I wouldn't post about the baby online. I'd only keep the ranch's social media accounts and close all my personal ones.

But another wave of panic rode through me, knowing I wouldn't be able to keep the baby a secret forever. It wasn't like I could run away and hide. I had a resort to run. An estate to manage. A refuge to build.

And if JJ ever showed up and demanded a DNA test, he'd find out the truth.

And what the hell would I do then?

Chapter Twenty-two
Parker

FALL
Performed by Clay Walker

FOUR YEARS AGO

HIM: Will left me with Theo for two minutes today, and the kid puked and shit through a diaper. My clothes are ruined, and my house reeks. Tell me again why you see babies in your future?

> *HER: Did he hold your pinky? Or smile up at you? Did you snuggle with him while he slept? Those times with Spencey were the best.*

> *HER: Plus, I want the ranch to go to the next generation of Harringtons. I'd never require my kid to stay here, but I hope they'll want it as much as I do.*

HIM: I guess I can understand that. I'd like to pass my family's SEAL legacy on, but it would be unfair to have a kid when they'd only see me a handful of days each year.

> *HER: You could be like all those old actors who have kids in their sixties. You'd be retired with your Bull Frog trophy already on a shelf by then.*

HIM: I'll still be in peak shape when they force me out the door, so it's possible.

HER: It isn't your career but your ego that's going to kill you someday.

PRESENT DAY

They hadn't let me go with Fallon in the ambulance. It was a protocol I hated but respected, and it had allowed me to check in on Theo. Teddy had him holed up in the barn, out of sight, safe and sound. My responsibility to him, to keeping Will's son safe, tore through me, at odds with my desperate need to go after Fallon.

When Theo seemed to sense my torment, I tickled him and did my best to downplay what had happened before heading to my truck parked at Fallon's with Lance jogging at my side. We made plans for the added security arriving later, the investigation, and the additional cameras I wanted set up.

I was calm and collected on the outside, but inside, I was a fucking mess. Thinking of Fallon. In my mind, seeing her on the ground. Seeing the ugly knot on her head. Seeing the fear and fury in her eyes.

I'd almost lost her. Fucking hell. I'd almost lost her.

I slammed my hand on the steering wheel.

The only damn good thing that had come from today was our earth-shattering kiss. I'd finally done what I should have years ago—I'd kissed her. Claimed her.

I didn't regret it, but she'd been right. It had been a shitty-ass time for me to do so.

When my phone rang, my dad's face on the screen, I almost rejected the call, the bitter taste of failure in my mouth.

"How is she?" he demanded.

"I'm just pulling into the hospital parking lot. She was awake, talking, and pissed when they took her in the ambulance."

"So, normal Fallon," Dad said, trying to lighten the mood, but it couldn't hide his worry.

"This was a scare tactic, Dad. They could easily have hit someone. We were wide open."

"Or they aren't skilled with guns."

Which brought us back to JJ and Ace. I was waiting to hear back from Wylee and the detective in San Diego to ensure the two men were right where they should be.

"Backup is arriving later today and more tomorrow," he said. "For now, focus on Fallon."

I couldn't respond as his words brought back all the ways I really wanted to focus on her. The ways I should have been focusing on her for years now, ways Dad wouldn't approve.

"Park?" Dad prompted.

"I almost lost her…" It was choked. Angry. Full of guilt.

Dad inhaled sharply. "We didn't. She's here. Now, we just need to do our damn job and catch this son of a bitch."

Frustration bloomed that I did my best to keep a lid on. At myself. Our dads. The asshole coming for her. I shoved the truck door shut and strode toward the emergency room doors.

"I'll call you later."

"Park—"

"I gotta go."

I hung up on him for the first time in my entire life.

When I found Fallon already stuffed into an ER cubicle, she wasn't falling apart, but there was a haunted look in her eyes. And it hit me how much this entire damn day must have brought back her worst moments. I'd had guns aimed my way, been in the heat of battle, and the shots today had only panicked me because of Fallon. Because of the innocent people being targeted.

But Fallon wasn't a SEAL, and the last time she'd had a gun pointed at her, she'd witnessed someone die. As the hours went by, while the doctors kept her for observation and waited for test results, she started to wilt. It was more than exhaustion I read in the slope of her shoulders. This was that damned weight of responsibility she was good at taking on. This time for some asshole who'd come for her and the ranch.

What I wanted—no, needed—was to take her home, order

an entire team to surround her house, and lock her away until we caught the bastard doing this. But she'd never let me. She'd hate it if I caged her, and I didn't know what that meant for either of us once I finally got her home.

Every time my phone buzzed in my pocket, I cursed, having to leave her to take the damn call, having to return to the cold, hard facts while dealing with the sheriff, the security team, and my dad when all I wanted to do was pull her into my arms and insist that I'd make everything okay.

But could I? I hadn't protected her again today. She'd been out in the open…

I shook my head as I returned to her room, for what felt like the hundredth time, in time to see Fallon being wheeled away for yet another scan. When she gave me her phone and asked me to handle her dad, it puzzled me for longer than it should have.

For as long as I'd known Fallon, she'd craved her father's attention. She hadn't ever wanted him telling her what to do, but she'd wanted his love and affection—at least, the Fallon I'd known as a child had. But then again, she hadn't been that lost, abandoned teen in a long time. Three years ago, I'd clung to the idea of her still being young in order to save myself from a fall I'd subconsciously known was coming. But she was a grown woman, the owner of a ranch where she oversaw hundreds of employees, and she wouldn't want her daddy rushing in to save her. Not now. Now, it would only make her feel like she'd failed.

It was another thing Fallon and I had in common. The weight of our regrets hung on us, regardless of whether we were truly responsible for them or not.

Just as I started to return Rafe's text, the phone vibrated with a call, his image filling the screen. I answered, cut him off when he demanded to talk to her, and gave him as much information as I could. She was stable. They were running tests.

"Damnit," he'd demanded. "Why the hell did I have to hear about all of this from your dad today? The tractor accident, the cabin, and now this? Why didn't she tell me herself?"

"The last thing Fallon wants is for you to come running

back from Australia to take care of this."

Rafe was quiet. "She's always been too damn independent for her own good. But I promised her she wouldn't ever face anything alone again, and I mean to keep that promise."

"She's not fucking alone." The surety and fury in my tone must have told him more than I'd intended, because his response turned sharp.

"Neither of you are kids, Parker, but—"

"Stop before you say something both of us will regret. I won't let Fallon be hurt again on my watch, Rafe. I'm not saying that out of some damn obligation to you or my dad. I'm saying that because she means more to me than any person on this planet."

That moment when I'd thought she'd been shot swam in front of me yet again. The absolute desolation I'd felt. I never wanted to feel that way again. If it meant breaking old promises I'd made as a clueless teenager, so be it. I didn't know what it meant for Fallon or me or our futures, but I wouldn't let another day slip by without facing the truth, without facing the risks loving someone presented with courage and bravery—and Fallon.

"I see." Rafe's voice was deep, full of emotions. "That asshole JJ did a number on her, Parker."

"I know." What I didn't say was that I'd done a number on her too. I'd added to her scars, and I hated myself for it. Rafe may have promised her he'd never let her face anything bad alone again, but right now, with the stench of antiseptic surrounding me, I vowed I'd never hurt her again.

"With Theo thrust upon you, your life has been tossed up in the air," Rafe said.

I ran a hand over my head. I hadn't even thought about Theo when I'd been thinking about Fallon. My emotions and plans were all over the goddamn place. Dad had said sometimes a grenade landed in your life, and it was only in the wreckage that you saw what it had brought you. I understood that a bit better today than I had a month ago. That Parker, the one who hadn't had his life torn apart, would never have felt the love I had now for Theo, the pride I'd had in teaching him to ride his bike, or the pure joy of snuggling with him at night while we read books. The old me would never have kissed Fallon and burned from the inside out with a passion and intensity that topped the exhilaration of a skydive in midnight skies.

When I finally responded, my voice was thick. "What I'm telling you about Fallon has nothing to do with Theo or the way my career is up in the air. What I feel for Fallon…"

Rafe's sudden laughter cut me off, surprising the shit out of me.

"Damnit, I've lost another bet with my wife because of you," he said over more chuckles.

"Excuse me?"

"She told me a decade ago I had to pull my head out of my ass and see what was happening right in front of my eyes with you and my daughter."

"Nothing has happened," I quickly interjected. I didn't want him to think I'd gone back on the promise I'd made when Fallon was fourteen. "We've been friends. That's it."

It was the truth. Nothing had happened that day she'd kissed me in the bar. Nothing had happened until one world-altering moment and a cataclysmic kiss of a lifetime had changed everything.

"I appreciate the sacrifice," he said with dry sarcasm. "If someone had come along and told me Sadie couldn't be mine, I would have pounded them into the ground. But you, letting Fallon experience life and have a normal college experience, giving her a chance to grow into a strong, vibrant woman without the intensity of a soulmate kind of love blindfolding her and limiting her options…that tells me more than anything just how much you care about her."

Love. Soulmates. The words hung in the air and sent a chill up my back. Not because they felt wrong but because they felt so damn right.

It was everything I'd told myself for twenty-nine years I didn't want.

But it had never been true. I just hadn't wanted it without her.

Now, I wanted a chance at forever. I wanted to be one of the few couples whose relationship stood the test of time. The ones others looked to with envy, wishing they had the same.

But for Fallon, being with me meant dealing with my career and being apart for months while I was deployed and knee-deep in dangerous missions. It now came with a beautiful little boy who'd lost everything and who I'd also given promises to.

"You'll tell me if I should come back." It was a command, not a question, but it didn't bother me that Rafe had issued it. I understood exactly why he had.

"I will. But right now, you showing up will only make Fallon feel worse."

"I hate that you're right." We let it sit between us for a moment. "Tell her to call me when she gets home."

We hung up, and I turned back to the series of texts that had arrived while I'd been on the phone with Rafe.

The motorcycle and its rider had been long gone by the time Lance and the team had hit the fire road. But Sheriff Wylee was collecting evidence, and the team was scanning the video footage we did have for any clues. I wanted the new cameras the team was bringing today to be installed as covertly as possible so this asshole couldn't avoid them.

Cranky had sent me a list of footage he thought had been messed with, as well as a list of cameras that had been shifted in ways Mother Nature couldn't have caused. He'd promised to dive further into the altered video to see if we could recover a digital footprint that might lead us to the attacker.

I shoved my phone in my pocket and returned to Fallon's room. My heart sank when I saw her cheeks were wet with tears. Fallon didn't cry. Not often. I wasn't sure who'd taught her it was a weakness, but she held her tears back with a ferocity that would have made her a formidable contender for a SEAL team if she'd chosen that route.

The doctor wouldn't tell me the truth when I demanded it, but I'd get it out of Fallon. She was upset about something besides the shooting and her injuries. I'd take her home, tuck her up in bed, and use any means to get the truth out of her.

My body tensed once more, thinking of the new and glorious ways I might be able to torture her with pleasure until she told me the truth—ways I'd always stopped myself from even considering but now laid before me like a prize.

I'd let her heal, I'd make sure she was okay, and then I wouldn't hold back.

After the doctor returned with a printed list of instructions and the signed release orders, I was tempted to sweep Fallon into my arms and storm out of the hospital. Instead, I took her hand and walked her to my truck.

I opened the passenger door and assessed her as she eased into the seat. She was hurting from more than just the kick in the head. Maybe it was from the fall, but I thought it went beyond even that. She was moving differently. Awkward. As if she didn't know what to think about her own body anymore.

She was silent on the ride back to the ranch, and as much as I wanted to push her, I let her be. We had time for me to get to the bottom of things.

When we pulled onto the road leading to her house rather than the resort, she frowned at me. "Where are you going?"

"Home. To put you to bed like the good doctor ordered."

"I have staff to meet with and plans to make."

"You pay all those people a shit ton of money to handle things. They'll live without you for a day," I told her.

"Goddamnit, Parker, this isn't some band deciding not to show up. We had a major attack take place on my ranch. My guests experienced the worst thing many of them have ever experienced. They deserve my time and attention. Their families deserve it. My employees deserve it."

"And what do you deserve? Exhaustion? Burnout? Irreversible brain damage because you don't allow yourself to heal?" I growled. "Fuck that. I'll take you back to the hospital and have them handcuff you to the bed before I'll let you destroy yourself. Nothing is worth that happening. Not even this goddamn ranch."

Fury burned in her eyes as I parked the pickup in front of her house. "Everything I've done my entire life has been for this legacy, so don't you dare tell me what it's worth."

She jumped out of the vehicle and most likely would have headed to the path leading to the resort if her legs hadn't buckled. Surprise crossed her face when she landed on her hands and knees. I swore, slammed the truck door, and sprinted around the front. She struggled to get to her feet, and I simply scooped her into my arms and carried her up the steps.

When she didn't scream at me to put her down, worry coasted through me all over again.

I punched in the code she'd given me, opened the door, and then scanned the open space for signs of a threat. I put her down gently on the couch.

"Stay here while I clear the house," I ordered.

I silently checked both suites and returned to find her with her eyes closed, head resting on the back of the couch. She was deathly pale once more.

I moved to her, drawn as I'd always been but denied. I let myself touch her, gently brushing my fingers through her messy hair. Her eyes popped open. What I saw there—the desolation and fear—speared me in the heart. A brutal stab I was sure would bleed out.

"You need sleep," I told her softly.

Her throat bobbed, and for a moment, I thought she was going to cry again. "I do. But I also need to see my team. I'll have them come here for a quick meeting, then I'll rest."

My teeth slid together, and the force of the grinding shot pain through my jaw.

"I need my phone, Parker."

I debated, but having her agree to stay here was better than her running down the hill. I withdrew it from my pocket and handed it over.

She spent a few moments texting and then put the phone down.

"I have an hour. I'm going to wash the dirt and hospital scent off me," she said.

This time, when she stood, she did it slowly, giving herself time to adjust. While I didn't argue with her, I did follow her down the hall. Inside her room, she looked over her shoulder.

"What are you doing?"

"Making sure you don't crash and burn."

She stepped slowly into the walk-in closet and returned with a stack of clothes before heading for the bathroom. When I followed her to that door too, she turned around, and the first sign of a smile crept over her face.

"You coming inside? Going to watch me strip? Maybe get in the shower with me? Wash my hair?"

Those were all the wrong words for her to say, because I wanted to do just that. See her naked. Watch the water pour over her slopes and valleys. Push her up against the tiled wall and take what was mine. Even knowing that couldn't happen today, it didn't stop my body from reacting.

I stepped closer instead of away as she'd expected, and her nostrils flared. I put one hand on her waist and pulled her so our hips touched, and that same damn electricity that always found us lit me up.

For the first time in my life, I didn't curse it. I rejoiced in it. All of it. The heat. The absolute need. My hand went to her chin, capturing it and letting my thumb glide over her lower lip.

"Showering together will have to wait for another day." Desire leaked into every word.

She stared at me for a moment before nipping at my thumb, and my body went up in flames. "Don't make promises you won't keep, Frogman."

I lowered my mouth until our lips were almost brushing. "We will be showering together, Fallon. That isn't a promise. It's a fact. Get used to it. But it won't be when you can barely stand and have employees showing up. It's going to be when I can take my damn time, when I can have you up against the tile, and on the damn floor, and on all fours in the bed."

A tremor went through her, and her eyes slammed shut. She inhaled and exhaled deeply. Then she pushed me away and pulled the door partially shut. When she looked at me again, the desolation had returned to those honeyed eyes. "Unfortunately, Park, I think that ship has sailed. You were right all along. It's better if we're just friends."

I was so stunned, so fucking knocked sideways, I simply stood there while she shut the door in my face. I stared at the wood for far too long, processing her words. After the kiss on the field, she'd insisted it wouldn't be the last one.

What had changed?

What had happened at the hospital? What had the doctor said? Did she tell Fallon she had some goddamn disease? Something permanent? Something that would put that despair in her eyes?

I turned the handle to find she hadn't locked it. When I walked in, she yelped, covering her bra and panty-clad body with one hand and reaching for the sink to steady herself with the other. It shouldn't have been any different than seeing her in a bikini, which I'd done more times than I could count, and yet it was different, because I'd dropped the barrier I'd always held up between us. Now, I wanted to do more than look. I wanted to touch every single inch of her. I wanted to know, not just where she was ticklish, but every spot that turned her on.

I stalked over to her, careless with her in a way I shouldn't have been as I cupped her neck, tipped her chin, and devoured her mouth. This kiss wasn't like the one on the field. This was angry and frustrated and full of promise. I would have her. She would be mine. She was already fucking mine. She'd been mine for more years than I could count. Just as I'd always been hers. I'd always known it deep inside me, even when I'd denied it. Denied her.

No more.

I plundered her mouth with an intensity that had her gasping and clinging to my arms. I held her steady and let the tidal wave consume us. Drowning in the emotions. Sweeping us into unsteady seas.

It took more willpower than I'd ever used before to stop myself. To step back.

For a brief moment, I regretted it, until I saw the desolation on her face had disappeared, and in its place desire and lust burned.

"Our ship hasn't sailed, Ducky. And when it does, we'll be on it. Together."

Her mouth popped open.

"Now get in the damn shower before I call your team and tell them not to bother showing up."

That did exactly what I wanted it to do. It brought the defiance back, straightening her back.

"Take your high-handed commands and get the hell out of my bathroom."

I grinned at her. "I'll be right outside the door. If you get dizzy in the shower, just holler, and I'll come get you."

Fallon's huff was a twist of exasperation and laughter. "Whatever happened to flip your switch is sort of scary."

That wiped away my humor, but I kept the smile plastered on my face because I didn't want her to think of what had happened in the field or send her into a spiral of sadness after I'd achieved a laugh. But she was right. It had been terrifying.

"Go slow so you don't get dizzy and fall—unless you want me to see you naked before I have a chance to shower you with romance." She let out another frustrated huff. "And, Fallon, you better get used to it. To me. I'm not going anywhere."

I shut the door before she could respond. But she was likely thinking the same damn thing I was—exactly how long would I be there before command called me back to base? It was the same question I'd been asking myself about Theo, but with Fallon, it had another layer to it because there was no way I could leave until we'd figured out who was coming after her.

I'd go AWOL before I left her unprotected.

The thoughts of my career going down the drain if I did just that reminded me of something I'd somehow forgotten. I wasn't alone. I had a team of men who had my back. Screw the cop in San Diego. My teammates would gladly pay a visit to JJ and Ace for me. They'd make sure the losers were still sitting in San Diego, waiting for JJ's trial. But they'd also find out if one or both of them were behind these stunts.

I yanked my phone from my pocket, opening a group chat. I could count on my team. They'd have my back.

And if this wasn't JJ or Ace, we'd go down the list of suspects, one by one, until we figured out exactly who'd pulled the trigger today.

Then I'd end them.

Chapter Twenty-three
Fallon

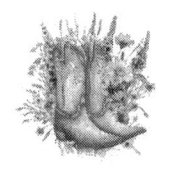

GOOD NEWS
Performed by Shaboozey

TEN YEARS AGO

>*HER: I can't sleep.*

HIM: It's been a traumatic day. That's not a surprise.

>*HER: Can we take a walk? Down to the waterfall?*

HIM: It's not a good idea to leave the house. Our dads would have our heads.

>*HER: I need out of these four walls. I need to smell the fresh air and see the stars. I need to believe there'll be an end to this that doesn't leave me broken.*

HIM: Nothing can break you, Ducky. You're the strongest human I know.

PRESENT DAY

I stared down at my body as the water poured over my shoulders. I pushed on the tightness in my stomach. I'd wanted a baby—at least two. After watching the awe and amazement on Dad's and Sadie's faces while they stared at my siblings after they'd been born, I'd ached for that to be mine someday. To feel that same adoration and love for something I created.

And I'd only be lying to myself if I said it wasn't Parker I'd imagined sitting on the bed next to me after delivering my own.

It had been a childish dream from a lovesick teenager.

One I'd known couldn't come true. And now, even more so because I was having a baby, but it wasn't Parker's. There was no way I could put this on him. Not when he'd never wanted kids and was struggling to balance his life with the one he'd already been entrusted with. No way I'd add to those burdens.

Which meant, when I had this baby, I'd be alone.

I guessed that wasn't any different than how I'd spent most of my life.

Get a grip! my conscience screamed. Those ridiculous thoughts were the leftovers of the troubled teenager I'd once been. And they'd never been completely true. Yes, my family had been a mangled mess of knots, but I'd always been loved. I'd had Spence for the first fourteen years of my life, and he'd been more of a dad to me than my own father until he'd died. Spencer had loved me, showered me with praise, and taught me everything he knew about farming and the ranch and the land—or as much as he could when I'd still been a kid.

And Mom had never held back her affection when she'd been clear-headed. Every time she came out of another battle with addiction, she'd tried to make it up to me. She loved me, but fighting her demons had taken most of her strength and focus.

Even Dad had proven himself and his love at the time I'd needed it most. When I'd felt the most alone, he'd returned to the ranch solely for me. He'd ensured I kept the one thing I'd always wanted.

So it was time I jerked myself out of my pity party and moved on, got past the childhood baggage. I had to do it if I intended to raise a child without my scars bleeding into them.

I glanced at the antique clock on the bathroom vanity and realized I'd spent far too long under the steady stream. If I didn't hurry up, Parker would return thinking I'd keeled over in the shower. I washed my hair as quickly and as gently as possible, wincing every time I came near the large knot on my temple. I washed off the rest of the dirt and grime from lying on the ground and then stepped out of the shower.

The large mirrors reflected a pale face, making the bruise on my forehead stand out even more.

I tried to comb my hair and then gave up because pulling on the tangles hurt too much.

I wobbled, exhaustion and dizziness tugging at me. I planted my hands on the counter and stared into the mirror, gaze settling on my lips and feeling again the two amazing kisses Parker had given me. They'd scoured themselves into me and would remain there forever.

He'd promised me more. He'd promised romance and naked bodies.

Teenaged Fallon was screaming with excitement, doing three-hundred-and-sixty-degree turns on Daisy's virtual back. Adult Fallon, who'd just found out she was carrying someone else's baby, was desperately sad. To come so close to all my dreams, to have them a kiss away, only to have them ripped away by an asshole who had supposedly loved me and then tried to sabotage my life, was just too much.

Brutally harsh.

Almost as harsh as the shots fired at me and my guests.

A tremor ran up my spine.

What the hell was I going to do? Not only about the danger to me and my guests but Parker's admission? Once he got something in his sight, he didn't let go. Even if I tried to push him away, he'd pursue me with that single-minded focus of his I'd always craved to have centered on me. The only way to get him to stop was to tell him the truth.

And I wasn't sure I was ready to tell anyone yet.

A sharp rap on the door brought me back to my current problem—the staff showing up and the public relations nightmare of a shooting on the resort grounds.

"Fallon?" Concern dripped through Parker's voice. That

wasn't anything new. He'd always been worried about me. He'd always cared. I'd just hoped one day that caring would turn into something more. And now he was trying to offer it, and I felt obliged to reject it so he wouldn't take on another responsibility that wasn't his.

How had I imagined it working out in those childish dreams? Had I really imagined him changing his mind about relationships and kids just to sweep me off my feet and give me the family I craved?

Is this how my mom had felt when she'd found herself pregnant with Dad's baby when she was really in love with Spencer? So much of what had happened to my mother had been because of her own choices and those of her family that it had made it hard to feel a lot of compassion. But now, I felt an empathy I'd never wanted. And yet, it hadn't stopped me from wishing for something good to happen in her life. Something not tied to the ranch or me or Dad or the cursed Hurly and Harrington legacies she insisted on honoring. I'd hoped she'd start wanting more for herself than the land that would never be hers.

What I hadn't wanted was to understand her choices. And I certainly had no desire to be her, repeating a cycle her mother and grandmother had started—marrying because you were pregnant.

Another rap on the door was followed by the rattling of the handle. I opened it before Parker could storm in. He scanned me from head to toe and back, lingering on the bruise.

I'd dressed in a pair of loose leggings and an oversized T-shirt. It wasn't professional. It didn't scream *boss*, but it was all I could manage.

"Sheriff Wylee is here," Parker said.

I didn't answer. I just stepped around him, keeping my pace slow and steady so I didn't nearly pass out again like I had when I'd stepped out of his truck.

In the great room, Wylee was pacing in front of the windows overlooking the resort. The bright light made me wince as he turned toward me, twisting his hat in his hands. The look he gave me sent a curl of dread up my spine. It was cold instead of concerned. Hard instead of soft.

"Have you found the shooter?" I asked.

"Not yet," he said curtly, watching as I eased over to the couch.

"You own a Remington bolt-action rifle?" he asked.

Parker made an inarticulate noise from where he stood behind me—a grunt of disapproval.

"You know I do, Sheriff. You examined all the ranch's guns after the incident with Dad and Sadie a decade ago. Do you think I scared the hell out of my guests by shooting at myself today?" I kept my tone factual. Stiff. I wouldn't react to his insinuation, even if I wanted to punch him in the face for even thinking it.

For a second, he looked chagrinned. Then, he sat on the chair next to me, confusion between his brows. "What we've found doesn't make any damn sense, Fallon."

"And what exactly is it that you've found?" Parker demanded.

"Fallon's prints on the shell casings along with her prints on the inside of the detonation device from the cabin."

Maybe it was because I'd experienced one too many shocks in the same day, or one too many in the last few weeks, but I couldn't stop the bubble of incredulous laughter that escaped me.

Parker planted himself next to me. "This is bullshit."

Wylee looked from him to me. "I'm not saying it makes sense, Parker. I'm saying these are the facts."

A fresh wave of sadness flashed through me as the truth hit. The same truth that had hit me in the security hut the day before. "This is someone I know. Someone with access to me and the estate. Someone who would have the keycode to the gun cabinet in the security hut."

"We haven't uncovered a single red flag that would implicate any of the employees," Parker said. "We have a few more to go through, but nothing stood out."

Wylee didn't respond, and that chill that had settled in, that dread, grew to a whole new level.

"There's more," Wylee said.

"More than me trying to burn down my goddamn ranch? And what, go in cahoots with someone trying to kill me and my guests?"

"You didn't get hurt though, did you?" Wylee said softly.

"Fuck you, Wylee. Fallon isn't behind this." Parker stood, and I grabbed his hand, holding him back before he could do something stupid.

"We found the car that drove your mom off the cliff. It was buried in the back brush off the highway. An anonymous caller called it in."

It should have been a relief. It should have been a step in the right direction after the hit and run had gone unsolved for over three months, but instead, the heavy lump in my chest enlarged.

"It was a stolen Toyota Land Cruiser taken from the San Diego airport a week before the accident," Wylee said. "No prints, but it did have a receipt inside from a coffee shop near the stables where you kept Daisy, along with a USD sweatshirt that had a long blond hair on it."

It wasn't just dread now but fear that crawled through me. It felt like I was sitting in the interrogation room of the San Diego police station all over again, faced with people thinking I was the worst kind of human. A thief. A drug dealer. And now an attempted murderer.

My brain whirled, trying to pull the pieces together, trying to figure out who would do this. Who would try to frame me while taking the ranch down at the same time? It couldn't be JJ. It didn't make sense. Wylee had said the car had been stolen a whole week before Mom's accident, and that was just after JJ had proposed. He'd wanted to marry me. So what would he have gained in running Mom off a cliff?

A memory tugged at the back of my brain—something I wasn't sure I would have ever recalled if I wasn't faced with all these quiet accusations. "The alarm at the stable in San Diego went off one night. The owner called everyone out to check on our horses and the equipment we had stored there. The only thing I was missing was a sweatshirt."

Wylee frowned. "That's pretty damn convenient."

"Convenient!" Parker exploded. "What the hell would her motive be to do any of this?"

Wylee ran a hand over his jaw. "That's the piece I can't quite put together, and it bothers me. You were already set to inherit the ranch, not your mom, so you'd have no reason to get rid of her."

Anger broke through the panic and fear. "Go to hell."

I stood, and the world spun. I had to grab on to Parker's arm so I wouldn't fall into the glass coffee table.

Wylee stood as well. Again, he looked momentarily ashamed, but then his face went blank again. "I'm glad to see that reaction out of you, Fallon. I want to believe the fierce kid I knew is still the woman before me, but the facts are piling up in ways that don't match. And the truth is, we haven't seen much of you in the last six years. I don't know who you are anymore."

It tore at my insides that I wasn't sure I knew myself either. But I'd be damned if I let him see that.

"If you think, for even one second, I could do any of this to my family, my staff, and my guests, then you never knew me at all," I spat. "Get the hell out, and don't come back until you can apologize and give me the name of the person who did this to me and mine."

Wylee headed for the door, snapped his hat on his head, and said, "I'll validate the break-in with the stable owner in San Diego, and I'll give you a list of the components of the timing device with your prints on them. Maybe you can figure out how you came in contact with them. But we have the video showing you at the cabin the night before it blew, so if you have a lawyer, you might want to think about contacting them."

He closed the door quietly behind him, and I just stared at it with a vision gone blurry with tears. More damn tears.

Parker tugged me to him, and I went with ease. I wrapped my arms around his waist and rested my cheek against his chest. His warmth bled into me. His strength held me up.

A sob escaped before I could catch it.

He sat, pulling me into his lap, and I let him. He grabbed my chin, forcing me to meet his gaze. His was steel glazed with fire. "We're going to figure this out. We need to widen the list of suspects, anyone in San Diego who you might have had a beef with, not just JJ and Ace. Whoever this is doesn't just want to hurt you. They want you arrested. They want you to lose everything."

"Celia." Her name was out before I'd really even thought about it. But once it was, I realized it was a very real possibility. "No one has seen her in months, but she stalked me, Parker, everywhere, including the stables where I kept Daisy. She was nearly feral when I testified against Ace. They had to remove her from the courtroom."

Parker was quiet for a moment. "I'll ask Cranky and the guys to find out what Ace knows about her whereabouts when they have their *conversation* with him and JJ."

"Excuse me?" I frowned, pushing up so I could see his face. "You can't have them beat up. If you do, everyone will definitely think I was involved and that you're my accomplice."

He guffawed. "My guys won't leave a mark, but we'll get what we need out of those two douchebags."

Parker wiped the tears from my face with gentle thumbs, and it made my stomach bottom out. Not only from the tenderness of the move but from the look in his eye. The one I'd always wanted to see that was full of promise. Full of much more than just affection.

I dragged myself away from him, and he watched me with narrowed eyes.

"Fallon—"

A knock on the door had us turning in that direction. The room spun with it, and I had to grab onto the arm of the couch to stop myself from falling. I hated it. Hated the weakness almost as much as I'd hated the nausea swamping me for days now. I needed it to stop. I needed full use of my faculties to figure out what the hell was going on.

Through the wavy glass on the front door, I caught a glimpse of Teddy. I made my way over and opened it with Parker grunting his disapproval behind me.

Theo ran in first, straight for Parker, his face all smiles.

"I rode a pony!" he screamed, dancing around. The tiny voice smashed into my skull, but I still smiled. How could you not when faced with so much excitement?

Parker picked him up, and his lips broke into a smile as large as Theo's. "Did you? I can't wait to hear all about it." Then, he stuck his nose in Theo's neck, snuffling, and the little boy laughed. "Man, do you smell like a horse or what? I think you need a bath."

"Teddy says if you don't smell at the end of the day, you didn't do your job right."

Parker looked over at Teddy, who barely hid his smile. "Maybe Teddy needs to be the one to dunk you underwater and do your laundry."

Teddy had left the door open, and I watched as the ranch van pulled up behind him—the one we used to transport guests back and forth to the airport. Kurt was behind the wheel, and Lance was in the front passenger seat. As the vehicle came to a stop, the side door slid open, and more of my management team, including Andie, Francois, and Olivia, piled out.

I hadn't figured out what to say to them yet. I'd been sideswiped by Wylee and his accusations. I needed to get my arms around all of this before it blew up in ways that were more permanent and lasting than the loss of a cabin. Before it ended the legacy my parents had worked so hard to save for me.

My head hurt. But the pain in my chest, the throbbing in my heart, was worse.

For the first time in as long as I could remember, I didn't want to face any of it. I wanted to tuck my head under the covers and forget everything that had happened since graduation.

♪ ♪ ♪

Somewhere in the last fifteen minutes, my body had started to give out. The angry spike of adrenaline Wylee's visit had given me had disappeared, leaving me even more exhausted. I felt like I was drowning, an undertow pulling me under.

Except, I didn't have the energy to fight it. I just wanted it to take me under.

"With the resort shut down, what will happen to the Fourth of July festivities?" Andie asked. I hadn't taken a bullet today, but I still felt as if I had a hole in my heart that grew with every decision we'd made since my staff had arrived at the house.

We'd agreed to officially close the resort for the next two weeks. It was in the middle of our busiest time, but it was the only thing to do. I wouldn't keep guests on the ranch if I couldn't guarantee their safety.

With a gut clenched tight, I'd also told Andie to refund all the current guests their money and offer them a future complimentary stay. For those on the excursion with me today, we'd provide additional compensation for pain and suffering. Some of the guests had already left, and I'd call each of them tomorrow. For the guests who were still here while rearranging their travel plans, I'd meet with them before they departed.

The hole inside me grew, knowing we'd also have to break the tradition we'd started eight years ago. Since the resort opened, we'd hosted the town's Fourth of July events. Rivers's residents and guests had mingled on the ranch, participating in various sporting competitions, shopping at craft and food booths, and dancing in the twilight by the lake. The night always ended with a fireworks display watched from temporary bleachers assembled on either side of the lake.

Calling the celebration off was just one more failure weighing me down.

"I'll call the mayor tomorrow," I said. "We might be able to move everything downtown and hold some of the events at the county park." I watched while Andie took meticulous notes and then met each of the staff's concerned gazes. "We'll need a skeleton crew to maintain the resort and care for the animals. Any suggestions?"

If none of the staff agreed to stay, I could handle most of the priority tasks myself. I'd done it before. After Spencer had died, Mom and I had handled all the animals and the crops for months before Dad had shown up and rehired our ranch hands. Worst case, I could call Dad, and he and Sadie would show up to help. But the idea of bringing them and my siblings into this mess, into possible danger, made the sour taste in my mouth return.

"You've already agreed to continue paying the entire staff while we're closed, all the way through the end of July if needed," Kurt said dryly, as if the fact they were still getting paid should be enough for folks to show up when they might be used for target practice.

"We can offer a bonus to anyone who agrees to stay," Kevin suggested.

"That's a good idea," I responded. It would be yet another hit to our bottom line, but I'd cover it from my personal accounts. I could take the loss, but not indefinitely and not if I ever wanted to get the large animal rescue up and going without turning to Dad for help, and he'd already provided me enough. My job was to manage what I'd been given, not keep running back to the well for more.

"We've got additional guards arriving tonight and tomorrow. They'll be setting up more cameras and instituting some other undisclosed security measures. Hopefully, that will reassure any staff who agrees to stay," Parker said, speaking up for the first time. He'd mostly just sat, watching me with those intense eyes, waiting for me to stumble. I was almost there.

"Speaking of staff," Lance said, clearing his throat. "There was a man at the lake earlier who rescued a swimmer with a cramp. He was wearing an outfit that looked a hell of a lot like one of our security uniforms but wasn't." Lance showed Parker a photograph from his phone. "He isn't your shooter, is he?"

Parker shook his head. "No. Too short. And his hair is too light. What was his excuse?"

"Said he was hired to watch over things and then shut down tighter than a clamshell," Lance said.

"Where is he?" Parker demanded.

"Had to let him go. Really didn't have anything to hold him on, especially seeing as he'd just rescued a guest," Lance said. "I did send his name and details to Wylee, and he said he'd pull him in for questioning."

"Send me what you got, and I'll dig into it on my end,"

Parker said.

Silence settled down, and I cleared my throat, pushing through the haze of weariness one more time. "Andie, set up an all-hands-on-deck meeting for tomorrow morning. Let them know we expect everyone here, even if they weren't scheduled to work. They can ask questions, and we can reassure them they'll still have a paycheck while we find this guy."

Everyone started collecting their things and heading for the door.

"One more thing," Parker said, and everyone turned to look at him. "Wylee—" And for the first time in the last hour, panic shot through me. I didn't want him to tell the staff what the sheriff had said. I didn't want them to know I was being targeted in more ways than just a gun. Not yet. His eyes narrowed, but he cleared his throat and changed tactics. "We've had a few cameras messed with—"

"By the old Hurly house and some near the fire road," Lance cut him off, his tone defensive. "We'd already noted it before you showed up. We just haven't had a chance to check them out yet."

Lance's tone sent a shiver up my spine. Not necessarily at him, but at the simple reminder it might be one of these people in this very room who were involved with what was happening. Someone had hated me enough, or had been paid enough, to sabotage me and set me up for an attempted murder charge. Someone with access to our cameras and our gun cabinet. And Lance had access to all of it.

Parker narrowed his eyes on my head of security. Lance was a husband and a father. He and his family had merged into the Rivers community with ease. His wife was on the PTA with Kevin's wife. Their kids were involved in sports. Why would he come after me? Why would he destroy the ranch that was his livelihood?

God. I hated doubting my people.

I hated everything about this.

Every. Single. Piece. Of. It.

Teddy cleared his throat. "I'm heading over to the Hurly

house tomorrow for Lauren. She's looking for an old family album. I don't know much about all your tech equipment, but I can move a damn camera so it's facing the direction you need."

Lance nodded at him. "I'll give you the angles."

Parker opened the front door and gave them all a pointed look. In another lifetime—one that had ended mere hours ago—I would have harassed him for sending my staff on their way. Now, I was just too exhausted and overwhelmed to object.

The team left, telling me to get some rest with eyes full of concern.

Except, there was a good chance one of them was faking that concern. One of them, or one of the hundred or so who would show up at the meeting tomorrow, had turned against me—for some reason I couldn't even fathom. Money? A perceived slight?

Ever since I'd reminded Parker about Celia, my brain hadn't gotten her out of my head.

Whenever I'd run into her while she'd been tailing me in those months after Ace's arrest, there'd been venom in her eyes. A rattlesnake, coiled and waiting. One I'd been stupid enough to think had slithered away into the forest, never to be seen again.

I'd even felt half worried, half guilty that something horrible might have happened to her.

Now, it felt like another thing I'd missed. Another failure in the ongoing list of them.

Chapter Twenty-four
Fallon

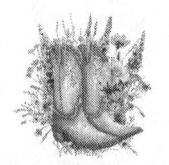

WICKED GAME
Performed by Chris Isaak

SEVEN YEARS AGO

HIM: *** Link to "Wicked Game" by HIM ***

HIM: If you listen to that song and can still tell me metal can't portray love, I'll know you're lying.

> *HER: Kermit, that song was written and first released by Chris Isaak nearly a decade before your band made it. Country for the win yet again.*

PRESENT DAY

When everyone had left, I crossed my arms on the table and rested my aching head on them. My body was screaming for rest. My soul was screaming for a respite.

Strong hands landed on my shoulders, fingers probing into my tense muscles.

I wanted to fall into it, but guilt and my new little secret held me stiff.

A moment later, a tiny palm landed on my arm. I opened my eyes to find Theo looking at me with sad eyes. "You have a bad owie."

I sat up, but Parker didn't remove his hands. He continued

the massage, moving over my neck and down my shoulders. It was tantalizing in all the ways it shouldn't be, especially not with a little kid staring up at me.

I was a hot mess.

"I'll be okay," I told Theo.

"Parker's making us grilled cheese. It's my favvv-or-ite thing in the whole world."

"He is, is he?" I shifted so I could see Parker's face, and it caused his hands to finally leave my body. "How are you doing that with no food in the house?"

"While you're resting, Theo and I are running to the grocery store."

Before I could protest, he swept me into his arms. Theo giggled.

"Put me down," I said, but it had no real heat to it, not with the fatigue wearing me down.

As he strode toward my bedroom, I asked, "How many times are you going to do this?" He raised a brow in question. "Carry me like some fragile bride over the threshold?"

His lips twitched as Theo ran around us in circles, giggling.

"You're a princess, Fallon! And Parker's the prince. A fairy godmother is coming to protect you wif magic." His voice was so high and excited that it screeched through me, shooting pain to my temple. I couldn't stop my grimace.

"Remember how I said we needed to be quiet because of Fallon's owie? Why don't we start protecting her by you using your whisper voice," Parker told him.

Theo's eyes widened, and he shoved Dog against his mouth, mumbling from behind it, "Okay, Park. Sorry, Fallon."

Parker dragged back the bedding, set me down, and then pulled the covers up to my chin. Theo ducked under Parker's arm to sit next to me. He looked at his stuffed animal and then set it on my chest. "Dog isn't magic, but he helps me when I'm sad. He can nap with you."

A lump grew in my throat that made it hard to swallow. I ran a finger over the animal's matted fur. "That's really sweet of you to offer, Theo, but—"

"She'll take good care of him while we're at the store," Parker said, sending me a warning look before putting a hand on the little boy's head. "Go get your shoes on."

Theo looked at the stuffed animal hesitantly, then at me, before his face turned determined. He ran out of the room.

"He should take Dog with him," I said.

Parker tenderly tucked a strand of my hair behind my ear. "Leaving Dog is a huge step for him. You need to let him do it."

"I don't want either of you to be nice to me. I can't handle it right now."

He huffed out a dark laugh. "So, what? You want someone who will kick you when you're already down? Is that what JJ did?"

He said JJ's name like it was poison on his tongue.

I didn't respond. Couldn't. JJ had never literally kicked me, but he'd also rarely offered a helping hand either. I'd thought I was the center of his world, that for once I'd had someone's complete focus, but looking back, I could see all the times he'd been more concerned about himself than me. I could see all the times he'd let me down. Like after Mom's accident, when I'd asked him to get my assignments from my professors, and he hadn't. Or forgetting something I'd asked him to pick up at the store, so I had to run out and get it myself. Or accidentally leaving my surfboard behind, so I was left on the sand instead of on the waves with him. And every time, he'd had an excuse. A charming way of soothing my ruffled feathers.

I'd been so busy berating myself for letting things linger between us, for not loving him enough, for not seeing who he really was, that I'd missed the reality. What had happened between us wasn't *only* my fault. JJ had done his best to make sure I saw the suave golden retriever instead of the conniving German shepherd. He'd hidden his true self just as much as I had.

Why had I let myself shoulder so much guilt for what had happened between us?

I was done with that guilt. We'd both screwed up, but I

hadn't tried to ruin his life the way he'd tried to ruin mine. That was all on him.

Parker's face turned dark the longer I went without responding.

"It's about damn time someone put you first, Fallon. I'll gladly and happily step up to the plate."

It hurt so incredibly bad to hear him say it. To want it. But to know I couldn't have it. So instead of accepting it, instead of leaning in to what I heard him offering, I tossed it back with a cruel taunt.

"But as soon as you deploy, you'll be gone. It's an easy offer to make when you know it has an expiration date."

His face shuttered. "You're right. I haven't figured it all out yet. Not with you. Not with Theo. But I will."

He took a step back, and I immediately felt contrite. Exhaustion and heartache were making me bitchy and had me taking things out on the one person who'd never deserved it. Parker had always had my back. Even when he'd rejected me, it was because he thought he was doing what was best for me.

"Parker…" His name was full of apology and sorrow.

How many times had I opened my heart and body to him and felt the sting of his rejection? I didn't want to do the same to him, but I also couldn't handle accepting it. Not only because of the baby I was growing inside me that wasn't his but because what I'd said held the truth. He'd only be here temporarily, and having him in all the ways I'd always wanted only to let him go again might just end me.

He looked back at me from the doorway. "Get some rest, Ducky. Let that brain of yours have a break. We'll talk more later."

I listened as he and Theo chatted in hushed voices until the front door clicked shut behind them. I closed my eyes but didn't think I'd sleep. My brain whirled, replaying the entire enormity of the day's events on repeat. The shots. The kisses. Wylee's accusations. My staff's frustration. The knowledge that one of them had definitely had a hand in the attacks. But eventually, my weary body took control, and I fell into a deep sleep—dark and dreamless.

♪ ♪ ♪

"Wake up!" An impatient female voice dragged me from the darkness.

My lids were heavy, and it was hard to force them open. When I did, I saw pale-green eyes the color of sage glaring at me from beneath a soft-brown fringe.

"Maisey?" I croaked.

My best friend shoved a water glass at me and ordered, "Drink."

I sat up, and the room didn't spin quite as severely as it had earlier in the day. "What time is it?"

"A little after seven," she huffed. "I would have been here sooner if you'd thought to give me a call. Do you know how stupid I felt showing up for my shift at the hospital, only to find out my best friend had been used for target practice?" She didn't let me respond before demanding, "How are you feeling?"

"Like I've been hit in the head with a hoof. And your yelling isn't helping."

She pulled a bottle out of the pocket of her scrubs and shook out two pills. "Take these."

When we'd been little kids, Maisey hadn't set her mind on a single career like I had. It wasn't until her mom ended up with cancer, and Maisey spent months as a teenager helping care for her that everything changed. After her mom died, Maisey had been single-minded in her determination to become a nurse.

"I thought I wasn't allowed pain pills," I said.

"Acetaminophen is fine in the first twenty-four hours, but don't expect it to do miracles. It'll only take the edge off."

Silence settled in between us as she continued to frown at me.

"Where are Parker and Theo?" I asked.

"Eating dinner. Parker was going to bring you some, but I wanted to see how you were doing before you ate." She waved her hand. "Scoot over."

"When did you get so bossy?" I asked, but I did as she commanded, and she climbed in beside me.

Sweet memories flooded me of us doing just this many times in high school. I'd missed my best friend more than I'd let myself acknowledge. We'd spent our entire childhood twined together and then had college pull us in different directions. We still texted, called, and visited each other as much as we could, and we still shared all our deepest, darkest secrets, but it wasn't quite the same as seeing each other nearly every day.

After she settled her back to the headboard, I leaned the unhurt side of my head onto her shoulder.

"What the hell is going on, Fallon?" she asked, but it was gentle and soft this time instead of harsh and upset. "First the tractor, and then the cabin, and now this?"

I'd barely texted her about the fire before the rumors had spread through Rivers. I was lucky she'd been pulling a double shift and hadn't shown up. Now, I told her everything about the incidents and Wylee's accusations. The only things I held back were Parker's change of heart and the baby I was carrying. They still felt too unreal to share yet.

"Wylee has lost his mind if he thinks you're involved. He needs to pull his head out and start doing his actual job of protecting you," she snarled, but it dissolved into an unexpected smirk. "Although, with a Navy SEAL staying in your house, I'm not sure you need more protection."

I shoved her shoulder.

"Too bad we couldn't figure out a way for your mom's room to be off-limits. Then, we'd have the perfect, one-bed, forced-proximity situation I love in romance novels."

I laughed. "What would we do with Theo? Lock him in a closet?"

She smiled. "Kids sleep. How do you think married couples make more than one baby?"

We were laughing when a soft rap on the door was followed by Parker entering the room. He had a plate in his hands. "Did Nurse Maisey approve dinner?"

She grimaced. "I hate my name sometimes. Nurse Maisey sounds like a bad cartoon. Or like I'm going to go all Nurse Ratched and lobotomize someone for standing up to me."

Parker chuckled.

He handed me the plate, and in response, my stomach growled at the scent of a perfectly toasted grilled cheese. He'd included a scoop of freshly cut fruit salad with it, but the sandwich was what I dove into. Every molecule in my body seemed to rejoice.

"Theo's right. You do make a mean grilled cheese," I said after inhaling several bites.

Parker's eyes bounced between Maisey and me. "Would you like one, Maisey?"

She shook her head. "No, I ate before I left the house. Working in the ER, you never know if you'll get a chance to breathe, let alone eat."

"Do you have to get back?" He crossed his arms over his chest, darting a look at me that said he wanted to finish our conversation from earlier.

"I called off. I'm spending the night," Maisey said, and I almost laughed at Parker's barely masked disappointment. "No way I'm leaving Fallon here without a trained medical professional looking over her. She'd try to convince everyone she was fine and start baling hay."

Parker chuckled, and it landed low in my belly as always.

"Okay, then. I'll just leave you two to catch up while Theo and I do all the guy things." He looked around the bed. "Do you still have Dog? He'll never get to sleep without it."

I pulled up the covers and found the stuffed animal tucked by my side. I handed it over. "Make sure he knows how much it helped."

Parker stared at me again for a long moment, as if he wanted to say something else, but then headed back toward the door. "Let me know if either of you need anything. I sleep light these days."

As soon as he was gone, Maisey whispered, "Holy hell. The heat vibrating between the two of you has grown in epic proportions. If I trusted you more, I'd leave you two to your own devices. But seeing as you're both the strong and muscly type, your sex life would be way too active for your concussion. I'm doing you a favor by staying so you don't end up prolonging your recovery and have long-lasting side effects."

She was right. It was for the best—but for an entirely different reason than she'd given. I had to figure out a way to make him retract all his enticing offers without telling him the truth. And that wasn't anything I'd ever been good at—keeping things from him. Or Maisey. They were the only two people on this planet who'd always seen through my pretenses.

I stabbed a piece of watermelon, and I'd barely put it in my mouth before my body objected. The grilled cheese had gone down fine, but even the smell of the watermelon had me barreling for the bathroom. I tried to go slow, but everything spun.

I landed on my knees by the toilet with Maisey right behind me.

I heaved, but nothing came up.

"Shit!" Maisey said. "I expected some nausea, Fallon, but I'd rather not see actual vomiting."

I sat back, leaning against the cool wall. Everything hurt. My body and my soul.

"It isn't the concussion causing the nausea," I told her, and my hand involuntarily went to my stomach.

"What do you—" She cut herself off and sank to the floor beside me with a flabbergasted look. "Holy shit. That asshole. That asshole!" She pounded the floor.

Maisey was the only person besides those in the interrogation room who knew what JJ had done, partly because I'd been too humiliated and angry to tell anyone, and partly because I'd thought it hadn't mattered since I'd had a period.

But now, here I was with a life I couldn't yet feel growing inside me. A life I was incredibly protective of already.

I wanted to shelter it from the knowing looks it would get from people around town, just like the ones I'd gotten growing up. I didn't want them to know their life had started with an act of betrayal, like mine had. I also didn't want them to have a dad who'd use them as a bargaining chip if he found out about them. And yet, how would I ever keep the baby from knowing the truth? When they asked about their dad, what would I tell them? A lie?

"You know what's worse?" I whispered to my best friend.

"What could be worse than being impregnated by an asshole poking holes in your condoms, being shot at, and being accused of the attempted murder of your own mother?"

"Thanks for summing up the shittiness of my life so thoroughly," I said dryly. Then, I looked at her, and the tears leaked out. "Parker... Parker finally let his guard down and kissed me. He admitted he wanted me."

"Oh my God, *he* kissed *you*?"

I nodded. "Twice."

"And?" she asked breathlessly, knowing—as only a best friend for life could—just how much I'd always wanted him to initiate a kiss, to not back away from the electricity burning between us.

"Universe-spinning, life-altering good." Just thinking of our kisses made my entire body light up, pushing away the nausea until the truth crashed back down.

"I'm jealous. I've never had that kind of a kiss," she said mournfully.

"Don't be jealous. I have to walk away from it." It hurt more than I could ever have imagined anything could.

"What?" She looked at me, flabbergasted. "Why?"

"I'm pregnant with another man's baby, Maise," I told her sadly. "What am I going to do? Date Parker while I grow to the size of a basketball? Expect him to massage my feet while I grow another man's kid inside me?"

Realization hit, and her face turned red with anger. "That fucker. I want to kill him with my bare hands."

"Me too. At least if JJ were dead, he'd never find out about the baby. I can't let him know he succeeded, Maisey. He can never, ever know," I said fiercely.

Maisey and I just sat shoulder to shoulder, contemplating

life as we had many times growing up. Finally, when the cold of the tile started to eat its way through us, she helped me up and back into the bed.

We turned on the television, and knowing me as she did, she pulled up a streaming service and found my old comfort show. The one I'd returned to over and over through the years. Buffy's face on the screen eased the tension in my body. If she could save the entire Earth from devastation as a teenager, I could certainly figure a way out of my current troubles as an adult.

"You could marry him," Maisey said.

I jerked my gaze from the TV. "No fucking way am I marrying the asshole who got me pregnant and is going to prison for drug dealing and identity theft."

Maisey's mouth dropped open. "As if I'd ever suggest you marry that loser. No. I'm talking about Parker."

I snorted. "Just because he's decided he wants to have sex with me doesn't mean he's changed his mind about love and marriage and kids. Parker has always been clear he didn't want any of it."

She frowned and then shrugged. "But he already has a kid now. What's he going to do with Theo when he's deployed? Is he resigning his commission? If you married Parker, like ASAP, and JJ ever came sniffing around, you could tell him it was Parker's baby. You know he'd believe it. He always thought you were sleeping with Parker anyway. And you could keep Theo while Parker was off on assignment."

"You're suggesting I offer Parker some kind of fake marriage, like in a romance book?"

She raised a single eyebrow. "I'm not sure how much 'fake' there would be in the 'fake marriage.' The steam between the two of you is real."

I barely stopped myself from shaking my head, knowing it would hurt too much.

"Thanks for suggesting it, Maise, but I promised myself I wouldn't continue the cycle the women in my family are known for. I won't marry someone just because I'm pregnant." When she started to say something, I talked over her. "I don't want my kid growing up wondering, if they hadn't been born, if our lives would have been different. Look at my dad. All he wanted was to breed and train horses, and I ruined that for him. I know too painfully well what it's like being the reason your parent didn't get what he wanted."

Maisey squeezed my hand. "That's one way to look at it, Fallon. But *you* weren't the reason your dad left. He left because your mom married Spencer. And when I see your dad, I don't see a man wallowing in lost dreams. Sure, his dreams changed, but I think that's normal. It's the rare person who actually follows the path they decide on when they're a little kid. If you asked him, I think your dad would tell you he's happier now than he could have been staying here on the ranch. He built an entire empire, married his soulmate, and created two more beautiful babies. Even more, following that path has allowed him to give *you* your dreams, and I think he'd say that was worth it. What parent doesn't want to help their kid get everything they want?"

Her words settled hard in my chest just as the ones Parker had said about JJ did. Had I allowed myself to hold on to responsibility, to take blame, to feel regret, for things that I never should have shouldered? Worse, had I misjudged both my parents? Maybe Mom hadn't worked her ass off on the ranch as some attempt to reclaim her Hurly family legacy, but simply because she knew how important it was to me. But twenty-four years of baggage wouldn't let me toss all my previous convictions aside that easily.

Still, long after my friend had fallen asleep, my mind continued to whirl with all the implications of Maisey's talk. The concussion care instructions the ER doctor had given said to keep both thinking and activity light for the first few days, but it was impossible to stop my brain.

And the worst of Maisey's comments refusing to be banished was the one about Parker.

Because the longer I thought about it, the more marrying Parker seemed like a real solution to both our troubles. I'd already fallen hard for Theo. I could adopt him and give him a good home on the ranch. He'd have all the dogs and animals he wanted. And Parker could remain on the teams. Sure, he'd have a family waiting for him like he'd never wanted, but he already had Theo anyway. Life had already taken some of his choices from him.

No. It was a ridiculous idea, wasn't it?

When I finally fell asleep, it wasn't the deep and dreamless one I'd had that afternoon. Instead, it was full of taunted wishes and happily ever afters that couldn't come true.

Chapter Twenty-five
Parker

LET IT BE ME
Performed by Ray LaMontagne

FIVE YEARS AGO

>HER: *Cranky is a good-looking guy.*

HIM: *No.*

>HER: *No? No what? You don't even know what I was thinking.*

HIM: *We both know what you were thinking. So I'll repeat it with extra meaning— NO!*

PRESENT DAY

"*You're supposed to be resting,*" I groused as I scowled at Fallon sitting on a hay bale just outside the barn.

If you gave her a cursory glance, she looked the same as she always did, dressed in dark jeans, a tank, and her cowboy hat. But when you scrutinized her, as I'd been doing all morning, you saw she was unusually pale and shaky. Her sunglasses shaded her eyes and hid the dark shadows, and her hat hid the ugly knot with its purple-and-black coloring, but I knew they were there. I'd barely been able to take my eyes off them as she'd pushed the eggs I'd made around on her plate.

Stay out of bright lights, and get lots of rest. That was what the doctor had prescribed for the first forty-eight hours, but Fallon had done very little of either.

"I'll go back to the house after the staff meeting," she said.

She'd met with the last remaining guests this morning in the lobby, hugging them, apologizing, letting them know how sorry she was that the worst had happened while they'd been staying with her. Some of them had been polite, shaking it off as not her responsibility, and others had looked like they might sue her for everything she owned.

Now, she was waiting to meet with the resort's employees. While they'd slowly been gathering around the barn, the hum of conversation had grown. It felt uneasy. A hint of fear lingered in the air.

Eventually, Andie told Fallon everyone had checked in, and Fallon stood up on the bale. Raised above the crowd, she was an easy target, and I had to fist my hands in order to resist the temptation to jerk her back down. I focused instead on scanning our surroundings for danger before turning to assess the people assembled.

Somewhere in this midst, a traitor lurked.

Either they'd pulled the trigger themselves, or they'd helped whoever had.

As Fallon shared the plan for the resort's shutdown, paid leaves, and bonuses for those who volunteered for the skeleton crew, I examined each face for any sign of responsibility.

"Forgive me for saying this, Fallon, but are a few weeks really going to make a difference?" a tall man asked, and my vision narrowed in on him.

"We hope to have the person in custody by then," she told him with a surety I knew she felt far from.

I heard the murmur just as she did, a whispered voice that said, "Yeah, but what if it's you?"

How the fuck had anyone already heard about Wylee's accusation? And why the hell would anyone who knew Fallon believe it?

I stepped closer, reaching for Fallon's hand, but she batted it away. "I see some of you have been listening to ugly rumors.

This land is mine. It's been mine since I was a teenager. Mom and Dad may have helped me shape it, but it's my legacy. Anyone who believes I'd do anything to hurt this place or the people who work here can resign today. No hard feelings. I'll give you a nice severance package and a reference, but I won't have you working here if you don't believe in me and mine."

Movement at the back of the crowd had my eyes jumping to Chuck. He was fidgeting, face as white as snow. Sweat glistened on his brow. Every instinct in my body leaped to attention. *The kid knew something.*

He tugged at his baseball cap, kicked the dirt, and then headed into the barn.

Fallon answered a few more questions before handing over the logistics to Andie. As she stepped down, I grabbed Fallon's hand and hauled her toward the barn.

She protested, but I ignored her, determined to find Chuck before he disappeared.

Theo's giggle and Teddy's deep laugh from the stall with the puppies greeted us, and guilt hit me square in the chest again—for giving Theo so little of my time in the last few days, for dragging him to a place where people were getting shot. I couldn't solve it at the moment, but somehow, I'd have to do better. For all of us.

Movement near Daisy's stall drew my gaze. Chuck was petting the horse over her stall door. I made a beeline for him, and Fallon followed with a whispered, "What's going on, Parker?"

I didn't touch the kid, but I shifted into his space enough that unease had him taking a step back. His eyes darted behind me to Fallon.

"H-how are you feeling, Ms. Har—Fallon?" he asked.

"She's got a concussion, and the sheriff thinks she's responsible for all this bullshit. How do you think she's feeling?" I demanded.

"Parker!"

I ignored her indignant exclamation.

"How about you tell me why you look like a kid caught

with his hand in the till?" I growled.

Chuck started crying, shoulders shaking.

"Damnit, Parker, you scared the bejesus out of him," she said. She pushed me to the side and grabbed Chuck's arm, leading him toward Kevin's office stall. She made him sit on a stool and grabbed a cup of water from the dispenser.

The kid took a few sips and then looked up at us with scared eyes. "No one was supposed to get hurt."

My stomach clenched. Goddamnit.

"I-I... He told me he was working for you the first time we met. He said you thought someone was s-stealing. N-no one could know he was investigating, or you wouldn't catch them in the act. I swear I w-wouldn't have h-helped him otherwise. I wouldn't have! This place is the first place I've ever felt at h-home. As if I b-belonged." He shook his head fiercely, but his eyes were frightened.

Fallon squatted and grabbed his hand, squeezing. "I know, Chuck. It's clear as day to me and everyone else that you were meant to work here. You're a natural with the horses and the guests. Just tell us what you know."

"He asked me for the security codes..."

Fallon frowned. "How did you have them?"

Chuck flushed and looked away. "I'm... I've always been sort of invisible. I can get in and out of places. People hardly see me. I caught Kevin punching in a code here and there. And one of the security guards never even tries to hide it."

The security guard was fired. I'd let Kevin go too, but I thought Fallon might fight me on that one.

"And this man...he knew you had the codes?" I demanded.

"He said he'd been watching me and that I was a s-suspect because of my shoplifting and how I was able to get into places I shouldn't have been. He said the time I'd been spending up in the caves made it seem like I was hiding stuff there, and if I didn't h-help him, it would prove I was the one s-stealing." I snorted, and the kid's chin went up. "I thought I was helping!"

"Don't worry about Parker, Chuck. Just keep talking," Fallon said gently. "When was this?"

"The first day you came back from San Diego. But I'd seen him before. When I was here training over spring break, I saw him talking to some of the guests and just thought he was one of them."

"Okay. So you gave him the alarm codes. Then what?" Fallon prompted.

"A-after...he said I had a record and that I'd h-helped him commit a crime, so if I didn't continue to help him, he'd make sure I went to jail." His voice hitched. "My mom's sick, you know. She works part time at the emporium downtown, but I help with just about everything around the house. If I went to j-jail...wh-who would take care of her?"

Fuck. Whoever this was had played on this kid's fears about his mom and jail. But even knowing that, I couldn't quite forgive him when he'd put Fallon and the ranch at risk to save his own ass. My empathy was almost nonexistent, whereas Fallon looked like she might cry right along with the teen.

"Do you know his name?" Fallon asked softly. "Did he tell you why he was doing this?"

"Wh-when he first approached me, he said he was undercover. He went by the name Terry. L-later h-he said the H-harringtons had stolen from his family. Th-that you were all evil and r-ruined his and other people's lives. I spat at him wh-when he said that, told him he was a liar, and he clocked me." Chuck rubbed his cheek.

"I'm so sorry, Chuck," Fallon said, her voice all kindness while my anger grew inch by inch. "You must have felt so scared and alone."

"I didn't know he took the r-rifle, Fallon. I swear...I would have t-told you. N-no one was supposed to g-get hurt."

"Fallon almost died multiple times," I snarled.

The kid sobbed. "He said it was just payback for some stolen money."

My mind went straight to her Uncle Adam. Shit, was this him? Fallon's uncle was still in jail. He'd never see the outside of a prison again, but he could have hired someone to do this. The feds thought they'd seized all his offshore accounts with the money he'd embezzled from the ranch, but maybe they'd missed one. Maybe he still had enough money to hire a hitman.

But why wait ten years? What had changed that would push him into acting now that Fallon had control of the ranch?

"When was the last time you saw him?" I demanded.

"Day before the cabin explosion."

"You'll look through the video feeds from that day and see if you can identify him. If not, you'll work with a sketch artist so we can get an image of him," I ordered.

"I'll do wh-whatever I can, but he always wore a hat and glasses," Chuck said. "He had long sleeves on, even when it was hot. And he had a big, bushy beard, so I'm not sure if I'll recognize him without any of that."

"You're still going to try," I said coldly.

Chuck nodded and wiped his nose with the back of his hand. "Am I g-going to jail?"

"That depends on the sheriff," I said just as Fallon said, "No."

I glared at her.

"Parker?" Kurt's voice had me spinning to face him with a snarl. Taking in Chuck's puffy face and my grimness, his lips flattened into a straight line. "Two guys are here to see you, but what's going on in here?"

Most of the Marquess Enterprises security team had shown up last night. I'd debriefed them over the phone from Fallon's place. They had a list of things to do today, including installing over fifty new cameras and patrolling the property in new, random shifts only I was privy to. Once Wylee had dropped his accusations, Dad and I had agreed the new arrivals would report only to me. Part of their job would be to question the existing security team and any staff who remained as part of the skeleton crew. Whoever this was wouldn't walk away from the ranch now, and in order to remain below suspicion, they'd have to sign up to help or stand out like a sore thumb.

I glanced again at Chuck's teary-eyed face and then headed for the barn doors.

"I'll let Fallon catch you up. But, Kurt, we need to keep a

lid on what Chuck has told us until we catch this fucker."

When I stepped outside, the sun blinded me, and I raised my hand just as a fist pummeled me in the shoulder. In two seconds, I'd gripped the wrist and twisted the man's arm behind his back, only to release it when I heard Cranky's rough voice chuckling.

"Damn, you don't mess around, Baywatch."

Next to him, Sweeney's lips twitched, eyes hiding behind the same tinted sunglasses Cranky wore. Both men were over six feet tall with shoulders the size of a linebacker's, but that was where their physical similarities ended. Sweeney was dark-skinned to Cranky's pure white. Sweeney had hair that curled into knots when not shaved down to the scalp, and Cranky's was straight and ice-blond.

"What the hell are you two doing here?" I asked, but inside, relief swelled.

"Leave no man behind," Sweeney said. "That doesn't just mean while we're on assignment, shithead."

"You talk to JJ and Ace Turner?" I demanded.

"We had a nice long conversation with those assholes." Cranky grinned. "Six men in black clothes and ski masks had them pissing their pants."

"And?"

"JJ insisted he's been in San Diego since his arrest. I had a look at his ankle monitor anyway. No one messed with it," Cranky said.

I looked to Sweeney. "So, you believe JJ? He isn't behind any of this?"

"He told us the truth." Sweeney's mouth tightened. "He doesn't know shit about what's happening here."

"But not Ace?" I demanded.

"He clearly hates Fallon. I won't repeat the things he called her." Fury spiked again, dark and ugly, but I just bit my cheek and let Sweeney continue. "He insisted he hadn't left town, but he was smug about it, as if he knew we couldn't prove it. I left Pigpen sitting on the place, and right after we left, two men showed up in a black Escalade. Ace joined them, and they headed to a construction company. Ever heard of Lopez Construction?"

I shook my head. "Are they Ace's drug connection?"

Cranky chimed in. "Definitely. I may have tapped into some facial recognition software I wasn't exactly supposed to use for personal reasons and found out one of the guys was Jesus Lopez. He's muscle for the owner of the construction company, who also happens to have ties to a seriously nasty cartel in Mexico. Never got a clean capture of the second guy, but I'm working on tapping cameras around their job sites and offices."

My conversation with Dad came back about Lorenzo's cousin going to work for a construction company in the LA area. "This construction company do work in LA?"

"Major hub there, why?" Cranky raised an eyebrow at my questioning him.

"Fuck."

"You know him?"

"One of Puzo's cousins got out of jail and went to work for a construction company in LA."

Did this really have nothing to do with Fallon? Was it about the Puzos and the hatred they had for her dad? Rafe's house in Tennessee had been broken into, and like I'd told my dad, I didn't believe in coincidences.

"You have pictures of them?" I asked.

"Do bears poo in the woods?" Cranky asked, yanking out his phone.

I grimaced. "You and your shit analogies. Let's see if our inside man knows any of them." I grabbed the phone and swiveled around to head back into the barn.

"You've identified your insider?" Sweeney's voice was gruff.

I didn't respond, but as we walked into Kevin's office and they saw the puffy-eyed teen, Cranky snorted. "You've got to be kidding me."

Chuck looked up, and fear swarmed across his face as his gaze swung from me to my equally muscled friends. Kurt stood up, stepping between my teammates and Fallon in a protective move that reassured me that at least this one man on the estate was on her side.

Fallon put her hand on Kurt's arm. "These are some of Parker's teammates."

The tension in Kurt's shoulders eased slightly.

"Sweeney, Cranky, this is Kurt and Chuck." I waved to the two men.

"Fallon, Fallon, Fallon," Cranky said, shifting so he could take her in again. "My girl, how dare you drag our Baywatch into all the action without asking us to tag along."

Fallon gave out an exasperated laugh. "You Frogmen are a bunch of adrenaline junkies."

"Damn straight," Cranky said as Sweeney said, "Fuck no."

It only made her laugh, and for that, I was thankful. It was the first laugh I'd heard from her since last night when she and Maisey had been tucked up in her bed. Who knew I could be jealous of a one-hundred-and-ten-pound nurse? But I had been. Because I'd had plans of staying with Fallon last night. Of keeping her not only safe but personally making sure she relaxed and got the rest she needed to heal. I'd known exactly what I'd do to make her relax, and instead, I'd been in a bed across the way with Theo jamming his knees in my spine.

Behind us, a little kid's excited voice had us all turning.

"Parker, Teddy says I can have the masked puppy as long as you say yes!"

Theo ran straight for me, and Teddy followed behind, his lips twitching once again.

Theo slid to a stop when he caught sight of Cranky and Sweeney.

Sweeney lowered to his haunches and held out his hand. "Hey, little man. I've missed your lucky high fives."

Barreling into Sweeney with a smile, Theo slammed his tiny hand into my friend's palm with all his might. "No high fives. Mine are five fousands. I give five fousands!"

Sweeney shook his hand as if it hurt. "You sure as heck do." He surreptitiously slid Theo a roll of Starbursts he'd pulled from who knew where.

Cranky reached down and held out his palm. "Don't leave me hanging, bud. I can't be left behind in the lucky dollar race with Sweeney."

Theo smacked Cranky's hand too. "The pain. Oh, the pain." Cranky fell on his ass, dragging Theo with him. "It hurts so good, man. Hurts so good."

Theo burst into laughter, tucking a second roll of candy into his pockets. Before Will had died, I would have added my own candy to Theo's stack. I'd have filled the kid with sugar and then sent him back to his dad to deal with. Now, I'd be the one who had to calm him down when my teammates left and he was riding a sugar high.

When I looked up from the shenanigans of my teammates and Theo, I caught Fallon's gaze. She was smiling, but she looked washed out again. Exhausted. And all the humor and lightness of the moment deflated for me. She needed rest.

"Okay, fun and games are over," I said. "Fallon needs to get back to bed."

"I'll happily take her to bed," Cranky said, setting Theo aside and snapping to attention with his innuendo hanging in the air.

Fallon laughed. "You know, Cranky, the way I feel right now, it wouldn't be fair to you. You'd only get half of me today."

"Half of you, sweetheart, is ten times better than most women."

"No one is taking Fallon to bed but me," I growled and then wanted to slam my fist into my own face as every single pair of eyes in the barn jerked to me, including hers. Kurt and Sweeney barely held back their smiles, Teddy and Chuck frowned, and Cranky let out a huge laugh.

Ten minutes ago, I'd been relieved to see my teammates show up, and now I was ready for them to get the hell out of Rivers so I could figure out the rest of my life. And that singular thought brought to the forefront exactly what my subconscious had already figured out about my future.

The Moments You Were Mine

Those fleeting flashes of family I'd always denied wanting were suddenly exactly what I craved.

Chapter Twenty-six
Parker

SELFISH
Performed by Jordan Davis

FOUR WEEKS AGO

> HER: *You and Theo are on my mind. I just wanted you to know I'm here for whatever you need.*
>
> HER: *And before you respond with some fifth-grade-boy innuendo. That wasn't an offer of sex.*
>
> HIM: *I'm not sure I'll ever have sex again. I don't know how Will did it.*
>
> HER: *Had sex after Theo?*
>
> HIM: *Trusted anyone else not to pull one over on him.*

PRESENT DAY

Before I could maneuver Fallon out of the barn, Andie and Kevin joined us. Her hotel manager had a tablet out, ready to give Fallon an update on which of the staff had agreed to stay while the ranch was closed. While I also needed the names to pass along to the new security team for investigation, I could do that later. Right now, it was more important to wrap things up so Fallon could get back to resting.

I stepped close to her and dropped my head to whisper, "Five minutes, Fallon. If you're not done in five, I won't give a shit about saving face for you in front of your employees. I'll pick you up and carry you out of this barn without a single qualm."

Her head turned, our lips coming dangerously close to touching, and my entire body tightened in anticipation. But the flick of annoyance in her eyes told me, even if the situation hadn't, that there wasn't a kiss coming.

"How many times do I have to remind you that you're not the boss of me?" she growled softly.

Sparks zapped between us.

Keeping my voice as low as possible, I told her, "I can guarantee you'll like me bossing you around." And I was rewarded with a flush that covered her cheeks, aggravation twined with lust.

I stepped away to let Fallon get her update from Andie, pulled Chuck from his chair, and hauled him over to my teammates. "I need you to take a look at some pictures."

Cranky brought up his phone and showed him the pictures of Ace and Jesus Lopez.

The teen shook his head. "These guys are way skinnier than the guy I met with."

As he reduced the picture, the one next to it popped up. It was a mug shot of Ike Puzo I'd sent to my team when we'd been compiling a list of people with a grudge against Fallon and her family.

Chuck's fingers stalled, and a buzz went up along my spine—intuition that I'd trusted more times than I could count in the field.

"He look like your guy?" I asked.

"I don't know. Like I said, he always wore sunglasses and had that bushy beard."

The Puzos had an entire clan of siblings and cousins who all resembled each other with dark hair, tanned skin, and dark eyes inherited from their Italian ancestors. I hadn't grabbed a mug shot of Tony Cantori, the cousin who'd gotten out of jail earlier this year, but I was sure Dad had one.

I sent my father a text just as Fallon stepped out of the makeshift office with Andie and Kevin. Andie glanced down at the photo of Ike still open on Cranky's phone.

"Is this the person doing all this?" she asked with a frown, pulling the phone to her before showing it to Kevin. "Isn't this the guy from One-Eyed Frank's who I turned down? Remember, he got kind of pissy and grabbed my arm? I was grateful you and Bess stepped in."

Kevin scratched his chin. "That was back in, what? March? He left with that couple who were fighting. The scruffy guy and the tiny brunette."

"It can't be Ike. He's in prison. But his cousin Tony got out in March," I told them.

Fallon grabbed my arm, squeezing. "March? Parker... Mom..." She swallowed hard, eyes turning glossy.

Fuck.

My phone vibrated. Dad had sent an image of Tony Cantori like I'd asked, but it was his written reply that had that buzz spiking along my spine again. "Dad says Tony died in a house fire. Burnt to a crisp in May." Jesus. May. Right when Puzo showed up in California. I looked up at Cranky and Sweeney. "If Tony went to work for a Mexican cartel, Puzo wouldn't have taken that lying down."

I turned my phone to Andie and showed her the picture Dad had sent me of Tony. "Is this the guy you saw in March?"

She looked from Cranky's phone with Ike's mug shot to mine. "They look a lot alike."

But what, if anything, did this have to do with what was happening to Fallon now? The attacks on her seemed intensely personal. They'd set Fallon up to take the fall, not Rafe. And if it had been Tony who'd been here in March, why would he run Lauren off the road? Was this Ike Puzo pulling strings from prison to get revenge against Rafe and striking out against anyone related to him? Why not simply send someone here to kill Rafe ten years ago when he'd still been living at the ranch?

Did it really matter why? What I needed was for it to stop.

So, I'd call Dad and have him pay a visit to Ike in prison as soon as it could be arranged.

When I glanced over at Fallon again, she looked impossibly paler than before. She needed to be in bed if she was going to heal.

"Can you take Theo to the truck?" I asked her. "Give me two minutes to finish here, and I'll take you both home."

Her gaze held mine for a few seconds, and it was a testament to how shaken up and tired she was that she didn't even argue. She just looked down at Theo, gave him a small smile, and grabbed his hand. "Come on. You can tell me about the puppy Teddy gave you. What are you going to name him?"

My chest ached, and I almost growled my objection to the entire puppy idea, but instead, I bit my cheek and watched them walk out into the light. I followed them as far as the barn door, ensuring they made it safely to my truck.

They looked right together, like they belonged, but keeping Theo near Fallon was putting him in danger. When Dad had first called and I'd driven with Theo to the ranch, I hadn't expected things to be this bad, to swing this out of control. The double-edged sword of responsibility and guilt dueled it out inside me again.

I needed to find and stop whoever this was, for both their sakes.

I turned back to my teammates and Fallon's staff, saying, "She needs rest. If she doesn't, she may have long-term impacts from the concussion. You all have my number. I'd rather you contact me instead of her for the next twenty-four hours. If I can't figure out whatever you need, I'll ask her, but she needs a chance to heal."

"Is Rafe coming?" Kurt asked.

"I talked him out of it yesterday, and I'll keep putting him off. The last thing we need is more of the family here and in danger, and I hope he'll see it that way too."

"Maybe Fallon should take off for a while also," Teddy said. His face was grim. "If this guy was responsible for Lauren..." His hands clenched into fists, eyes dark with fury.

"I don't think she'll leave," I said, imagining the fight I'd have if I tried to convince her it was the right thing, but I'd still give it a go. "Having fewer people on the ranch will make it easier to identify whoever it is that's behind this and if anyone else besides Chuck has been helping them."

I made a point of saying it and meeting the eyes of each of her staff who were in the barn. I hoped to hell and back one of these people hadn't betrayed Fallon in addition to Chuck. It would devastate her. She'd been through enough loss and betrayal, but I wasn't convinced a pimply teen was the only one who'd given this guy access to the ranch. Someone had known the schedule of the security team in order for the shooter to get into the gun locker, take the rifle, and get out undiscovered. And someone had known the schedule had changed at the last minute and that it was Fallon and Chuck leading that ride yesterday morning.

"We'll handle things here," Kurt insisted. "You just take care of our girl."

I cringed inside at the term girl, knowing what he meant but equally frustrated that all of us, me included, had seen Fallon as just that for way too long.

As I walked out of the barn with Cranky and Sweeney, discussing plans to meet up later for a follow-up strategy session, Andie joined us. She offered to show them to rooms in the hotel. With most of the guests having departed already, they'd have their choice.

By the time I finally got into the truck, Fallon's eyes were closed, her head resting on the seat back while Theo chatted away behind her. My concerns grew when she still didn't scold me for my high-handed command in sending her out of the barn, and they continued to expand when we got back to her place, and she went straight to her bedroom without a word.

I set Theo up at the coffee table with some toys and coloring books. Then, I turned a dog show on the TV so that it would mask some of my conversation with Dad.

He answered on the first ring, and I caught him up on what we'd found out this morning.

"I'll contact the prison this morning and see how soon I

can get in to see Ike."

"I want to be there."

"I'd feel better if you stuck with Fallon," he said.

I didn't want to leave her either, but maybe I could kill two birds with one stone. If I took her with me to Las Vegas, she'd be away from the ranch and out of the bull's-eye for at least a day or two. "Make the arrangements for Fallon and I both to see him."

"No. Absolutely not," Dad snapped. "He'd get off on that."

"Just listen. Someone needs to visit Adam Hurly in Tennessee and make sure he isn't the one pulling the strings. Chuck said the guy was talking about money stolen from him. That's fucking Adam. If you head back east, Fallon and I could meet with Ike. If it's Ike who's targeting her, seeing Fallon show up in his space will provoke him. We'll get a reaction, one I'm good at reading, Dad."

The line was silent for a minute as my father considered all the options. Instead of answering me directly, he asked the same question I still couldn't answer. "Why wait ten years?"

"I know. It doesn't make any sense for either Adam or Ike to come at them now. And why come after Fallon and not Rafe? We're still missing something. But if Tony Cantori was working for the same men Ace Turner is, it was absolutely not a coincidence and most likely led to his death. I'm not sure we can rule any of them out. Not even JJ."

"Honestly, I can't see it being JJ. Not only does he not have the skills or *cahones*, but what would he get out of it? She really had nothing to do with his arrest. Ace, on the other hand, didn't hide how pissed he was."

"And his wife, Celia. Have you found her yet?"

"Not a trace."

"So we're nowhere," I said, frustration blooming.

Dad's voice held the same exasperation I felt. "We know what happened to Lauren wasn't an accident, and we didn't know it was related before this. We can spiral back, pull in all the data, and we'll find an answer, Park. In the meantime, I'm sending someone to protect Lauren at the rehab facility, and I'll get Rafe up to speed."

"Keep him away, Dad. We don't need him showing up with Sadie and the kids and putting them at risk too," I said. "And you and I both know Sadie won't let him come on his own."

She might not put her kids at risk by bringing them to the ranch, but Fallon's stepmom wouldn't leave Rafe's or Fallon's sides if she thought they were in danger. She'd proven just what lengths she'd go to in order to protect them when she'd taken a beating for Fallon and shot Adam in the shoulder before he could hurt either of them further. Sadie was a fighter. She fought for the people she loved with every fiber of her being. I respected the hell out of her for it.

The guilt of that day still hung on me. It should have been me who'd taken the beating, not them. Rafe had sent me with Fallon and Sadie specifically to protect them, and I'd left hours before my replacement had arrived. When I'd found out Fallon had been hurt, almost killed, I'd questioned my ability to be a SEAL. I'd left someone unprotected, and they'd almost died.

It was the one and only time I'd considered leaving the Naval Academy and giving up my dreams. It had been Will who'd talked me into staying. When Fallon ended up at the University of San Diego with me stationed there, it had felt like a second chance to redeem myself, to protect her when I'd failed before. But I hadn't. I'd let JJ close to her for three years when I could have done something about it. I could have done exactly what she'd wanted the night I'd found her at the bar and taken her home.

If I had, she would have been mine and not his.

None of this would have happened.

That ate me up from the inside out.

I'd wasted so much time with her and caused her untold amounts of anguish.

Dad's voice drew me away from the path of self-reproach I'd started down. "Let me call the warden at Ike's prison and see if we can speed up the approval process for the two of you. I'm already on the list for Adam's jail. I made damn sure I could see him whenever I wanted."

That surprised me. "You've met with him before now?"

"Twice," Dad said. "He was sending letters to Lauren, and I ensured he stopped. Then, he had his cellmate send letters to Fallon, and I returned and talked to him *and* his friend."

That foreboding I'd felt earlier returned. "Fallon never mentioned it." And I was sure she would have told me if her uncle had contacted her.

"Neither Lauren nor Fallon ever saw the letters. Rafe and I intercepted them."

So Fallon had been right. Our dads had kept things from us. It pissed me off as much as I understood why they'd done it.

"What did the letters say?"

"Nothing, really. Long rambles about the Hurlys and Harringtons being in some symbiotic relationship. What happened to one happened to the other."

A chill went up my spine. "Adam is in jail. He wants a Harrington in jail too? Wants Fallon in jail? That would hurt Rafe far more than Rafe going to prison himself."

Dad inhaled sharply. "Damnit. Maybe."

We discussed the possibilities for a few more minutes before saying our goodbyes. He promised to let me know what he heard back from Ike's warden.

I shoved my phone in my pocket, mind spinning with all the puzzle pieces that we had and the ones we were missing. Something still felt off. Something I couldn't quite see yet.

Lost in my thoughts, it took several minutes before the panorama from the windows of the ranch spread out below me finally registered. With the rivers, mountains, and castle twining together, it was a stunning glimpse of Eden. But just like in the Bible story, betrayal had rocked the land.

When she looked at it, Fallon saw much more than the physical rocks and trees and water. She saw a legacy worthy of continuing for future generations. She felt a responsibility to the forest and wildlife as much as the man-made structures.

My earliest years had been spent on naval bases, but I barely remembered those locations. The home I remembered most was the one we'd had in Las Vegas. Dad had settled us there before he'd even met Rafe. It was a tract home in a nice neighborhood.

We could have afforded to move to an even better neighborhood after Rafe's business took off and Dad became a shareholder in a multi-billion-dollar enterprise, but we hadn't. We'd stayed right where we were and lived a very typical American existence. Mom worked at a local women's shelter, Dad worked for Rafe, and I went to public school, played football, and took a leadership role in the campus ROTC.

Fallon had never known normal. She'd never been an average kid or an average teenager.

Not because of the screwed-up love triangle she'd been born out of, but because she'd been an heiress even when the ranch was nearly bankrupt. She'd been Rafe's only child until she was fifteen, the sole heir to Rafe's fortunes. Even now, with two siblings, the money she'd eventually inherit from him would mean neither she nor her future children would ever have to worry about money, as long as they played it smart.

But she'd never acted like an heiress. Growing up on the ranch had grounded her. The hard work she'd put in each day had ensured she hadn't thought she was better than others. She'd shoveled shit and hay and ran the tractor like any good farmer's daughter. She'd put in the time earning what she'd inherited.

I refused to let anyone take it from her. Refused to let someone send her running permanently or lock her in prison for crimes she hadn't committed. For simply being the last remaining ancestor of a feud that had gone on too long between the Hurlys and the Harringtons—or the goddamn Puzos.

I also refused to leave her. Never again would I make the mistake I'd made in Tennessee ten years ago or three years ago in San Diego. She'd be safe, and she'd be mine.

♫ ♫ ♫

I spent the rest of Saturday and all of Sunday running the investigation from Fallon's home. Her staff had respected my wishes and sent their questions and updates to me rather than her. I knew Fallon would be pissed when she finally realized it, but she'd spent much of the last twenty-four hours doing exactly what the doctor had recommended, sleeping and resting in a darkened room.

Her parents had called several times. The conversations with her mother had been tense and frustrating, but that was nothing new. I wasn't sure how much of the truth Fallon had given her about what was happening. Since Spencer had died, everyone had treated Lauren with kid gloves, and it had only gotten worse after the accident.

The conversations with Sadie had been full of laughter as much as tears, but it was Rafe who'd called the most, and she'd been exhausted after every one of them, the burdens of the ranch hanging over her even more.

When Rafe called again on Sunday evening, I took the phone away and told him that he needed to let Fallon rest. He'd been as pissed at my gall as she'd been. But once I'd calmed him down, he'd said he was grateful I was looking out for her and making sure she actually gave herself a chance to heal.

As I tucked Theo into bed, I had to fight back my frustration at another day spent getting nowhere. I forced myself to smile, to show him only the love he deserved. And after he fell asleep, I went in to check on Fallon for the hundredth time.

She was doing the same thing she'd done for two days now—watching her favorite TV show. I wasn't sure how she could look so exhausted after all the sleep she'd gotten, but she did. Her eyes still looked bruised, and her face was still pale. The ugly knot on her head seemed even more pronounced. It made my chest ache.

I joined her on the bed for the first time, sliding over until we were shoulder to shoulder and our heads shared a single pillow. She glanced at me warily.

"I'm going down to the ranch tomorrow," she said, lifting her chin, eyes flashing with defiance.

"Give it one more day, Ducky," I said softly. "You still look like hell."

She shoved at me with her shoulder. "You sure know how to charm the pants off a girl."

Our eyes met, and she bit her lip as if realizing what she'd said. It drew my gaze to the soft, pink flesh. I wanted to taste it again. Wanted to devour it. Wanted to burn myself into her in ways that left us both scorched. Marked. Branded.

Even more, I wanted the flashes of family I saw when I was with her to be permanent. I never wanted to come home to a stale, silent apartment again. But could I really leave her and Theo for months at a time, knowing every moment I was gone they were worrying about me? Knowing the worst could happen with one tiny slipup? Knowing they could end up at yet another funeral after they'd already been to one too many? Worse, knowing I wouldn't be here if and when they needed me. Not just for protection from unseen killers but to soothe hurt feelings and help with the day-to-day chores of life.

I cleared the emotions clogging my throat and looked toward the television while I passed along the latest update I'd gotten from Cranky. "Video footage puts JJ at the coffee shop the same day as the receipt left in the car that ran your mom off the road."

She muted the show. "You really think this is JJ?"

"Honestly, not nearly as much as I think this could be Ace. Even if JJ is pissed at you for breaking up with him and turning on him, what does he get out of ruining the ranch?"

"He didn't want me to keep it," she said.

"What?" My eyes jerked back to her.

Fallon swallowed, suddenly seeming nervous. She twisted her fingers around her thumb before running it along the edge of the comforter. "He wanted me to sell the ranch and build a life with him in San Diego."

I scoffed. Anyone who knew Fallon realized she'd never leave the ranch for good. San Diego had simply been a means to an end.

"So you think he's trying to, what? Ruin the ranch, run it into the ground so you'll go running back to San Diego? Even now? With him going to jail?" It seemed ridiculous.

"What if he put it all into motion before the police arrested us?" she said.

"He had to know there was no way you'd stay in San Diego forever."

"That's exactly what he thought. He assumed if I was pregnant, I'd choose him and marriage and San Diego over raising a child on my own. He knew I'd hate everyone in Rivers looking down on my kid like they'd always looked down on me."

My stomach turned cold, and my lungs squeezed so tight it was hard to grunt out, "You were trying to have a baby together?"

Fallon laughed, but it wasn't light and humorous. It was dark and pained and raw. "No. I didn't want a baby, but he did."

I frowned. I couldn't follow the dots she was trying to connect for me any more than I could connect the dots about who was doing all this. It pissed me off because I was usually the guy my team relied on to do just that. "What are you saying?"

She looked at me quickly and then darted her gaze away. "He was sabotaging our condoms."

Instant, hot rage washed through my veins. I had an uncontrollable urge to destroy him. An urge that would be difficult to contain if I ever ran into the asshole again.

"What the actual fuck?" I growled.

"He rented an apartment in the Kleindyke building and filled it with brand-new furniture, including an entire nursery."

I stared at her, disbelief and hate and fury mixing in.

"You see," she said, swallowing hard before continuing, "if I was pregnant, if I had *his* kid, and we got married, he'd be able to sink his hooks into my money. He'd always be entitled to some of it via alimony and child support. He'd finally have the wealth he'd always wanted just so he could rub it in the face of everyone who'd put him down growing up. He didn't want an actual kid—I really don't think he did—but he wanted what would come with it." She was accelerating as she talked as if she was speeding up a ramp before getting onto a freeway. But then she stopped, took a huge breath, and said, "That's why he can never, ever, ever find out that he succeeded."

She placed a hand protectively over her stomach.

And every thought went out of my head except one.

She was pregnant.

Fallon was having a baby.

Chapter Twenty-seven
Fallon

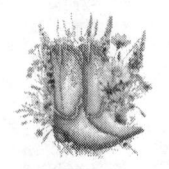

THERE YOU ARE
Performed by Martina McBride

ONE YEAR AGO

>*HER: I need the sea and air and a moment of freedom. Pick me up at five a.m. tomorrow so we can hit the waves?*

>*HIM: What's wrong?*

>*HER: I just need to get out of my own head for a while.*

>*HIM: It'll be just the two of us?*

>*HER: Just the two of us.*

PRESENT DAY

When I risked looking into Parker's face, his lips were tight, and his eyes raged. He started to roll away, as if he was going to leave.

"I'll fucking kill him."

I grabbed his arm, and he stilled, turning back to me with a face I barely recognized as his.

This was not the emotionless Navy SEAL I saw so often but an enraged one. The man who did what had to be done to defend a country he believed could still be righted, no matter how bad our government got. This was the man who did the worst out of duty. He would end JJ's life if I whispered I wanted it done.

He'd protect me. He'd protect the baby.

My chest squeezed tight at those words. How long had I wanted that? For Parker to be mine? For us to have a future together that ended with marriage and children?

He'd said he wanted me. He'd finally admitted it.

But would it change now that he knew I was having another man's baby? Would he look at me differently? Would he close down once he realized being with me meant yet another child he hadn't asked to have or raise?

What would happen if I offered up the wild idea Maisey had placed in my head that I hadn't stopped thinking about since? Not even everything that had happened on the ranch, not even the thought of Ace or the Puzos sending someone here to hurt me, had stopped the idea from spinning around inside my brain all weekend.

"You're pregnant?" he said, glancing down to where my hand rested on my stomach.

Those stupid, useless tears that had been with me for a month now rushed in. I barely caught them, holding them back by closing my eyes as I simply nodded.

A warm hand cupped my cheek, fingers stroking. My body ignited as it always had when we touched, and when I opened my lids, it was to find dark, stormy grays burning into me.

"Who have you told?" Parker asked.

"Only Maisey."

He didn't say anything else. He just stared at me as if he could pull every thought from my brain with just his gaze, all while he caressed my cheek with a gentleness that would be my undoing.

I pulled his hand into mine, setting them on my chest.

"Maisey suggested something pretty outlandish," I told him. "A way I might be able to keep JJ from finding out about the baby—or at least, putting him off it if he ever finds out I have one."

Parker shifted our hands so our fingers twined together,

linking us, merging us. It made those damn tears prick again.

"A bullet in his head will make sure of it." He said it calmly. Matter-of-factly. No debate.

My lips twitched upward. "Thanks for offering, but I think we already have enough going on without a murder rap adding to it."

"No one will know, Fallon. It's my job to get in and out without anyone being the wiser."

"You can't kill a U.S. citizen on U.S. soil without consequences." When he started to respond, I interrupted. "I don't want you to become a murderer for me, Parker. I couldn't live with that. And as much as I hate JJ and everything he stands for, I wouldn't want to be a part of killing someone. I saw…" I inhaled, memories of that day with Sadie washing over me. Hearing the gun go off as Uncle Adam shot Theresa in cold blood. Watching her body jerk. Hearing the sound of her gurgling. The way she hit the ground. No. I wouldn't ever want Parker to do that for me. Not in cold blood. If he did that when he was on a mission, in defense of our country, it was bad enough. I wouldn't let him take JJ's life on my behalf. "I don't want that weighing on my soul."

His face was grim when he asked, "What did Maisey suggest?"

I hated this. I hated asking him to do this. While it was true it would solve some of our problems, it would also start a slew of different ones. But I'd spent the last two days thinking about it, weighing our options. I could ease his burden of caring for Theo alone, but I'd be adding two more lives to his shoulders. I could promise we wouldn't be a bother and tell him that he didn't even have to come home to the ranch when he wasn't deployed, but I knew Parker well enough to know he wouldn't do that. The honorable man he was deep inside would never agree to marry me and then just walk away.

"She suggested…" My body started trembling, and I bit my lip, trying to control it. Parker's brows scrunched.

"Ducky?" He brought our twined fingers to his lips and placed a soft kiss on the back of my hand. It only made me want to cry more. To come so close to having everything I'd wanted only to ruin it by throwing this at him? It was so unfair. In the list of unfair things that had happened to me in my life, this was at the top.

I inhaled a shaky breath. "She suggested you and I might be able to solve both of our problems by getting married."

His entire being stilled, stormy eyes turning almost black. But he never removed his gaze from mine.

When it felt like a lifetime had gone by, and he hadn't responded, I jumped into the silence. "It would just be on paper. So if JJ ever came looking, I could show the marriage certificate and the date and say the baby was yours. If he asked for a DNA test, I don't know what I'd do, but for the most part, I'm sure I could persuade him the baby wasn't his. I mean, he was always jealous of you. He always thought—"

"Yes."

Surprise hit me square in the chest. "What?"

"Let's do it. Let's get married."

"Just like that?"

"Just like that," he said firmly.

"Wh-what about never wanting to get married or have kids? Don't just toss an immediate yes back at me, Parker. You need to think about this. You'd have two kids tied to you who weren't yours. I'd need the baby to have your name, have you listed as the father on the birth certificate, so it would make it more difficult for JJ to come after me."

"Okay."

Every response he'd spoken was sure. Solid. Unwavering. Instead of relieving me, it pissed me off. Not because I'd wanted him to say no, but because I was throwing a bomb into the middle of his well-thought-out life, and he wasn't even blinking at it.

"Listen, Kermit—"

This time, he cut me off with a kiss. His mouth landed on mine with nearly the same fierceness as it had held in my bathroom after the shooting. It was strong. Unyielding. Demanding I shut up but also demanding something else, something I wasn't sure I could truly let myself believe in yet.

He wanted me. He wanted me regardless of the fucked-up nature of my life, regardless of the fact a baby was growing inside me who didn't belong to him.

When I started to pull away, one hand went to the back of my head, holding me in place, and he deepened the kiss. His tongue slid inside, taking control, soothing and enflaming all at the same time. Goosebumps coated my skin, tingling from the top of my head down to the soles of my feet. I wrapped my arms around his neck, dragged our bodies closer, and dove in, demanding and taking as much as I was giving.

His fingers dug into the skin at my waist, and the warmth from his touch traveled up my body, a thundering wave of desire crashing over me. I hooked my leg over his hip, drawing us closer. One of us moaned. Maybe both of us did.

The entire world froze while we got lost in hands and lips and teeth as they learned each other's curves and slopes and inner recesses. While the heart I'd given Parker a lifetime ago finally found its way home. While our souls rejoiced and danced to a beat faster and stronger and more intense than even the one our bodies moved to.

When he finally broke the kiss with a sharp inhale, it was me who refused to let him stop this time.

I needed this.

I needed him.

I needed to get lost in the wave before the surf broke and reality came crashing in as our boards met the sandy shore.

I shoved my mouth back at his, and he made an inarticulate noise, a grunt of pleasure and pain before rough palms slid below the hem of my shirt, skimming along soft skin. His fingers settled on my breasts, twisting and plucking. My core clenched, and a stunning flame rippled through me, burning me from the inside out.

I twisted, trying to get closer, and my head banged the headboard, causing a hiss to escape.

He jerked back, putting some space between us, even while his hands remained on my body.

"Not like this," he growled. "Not when you're still

recovering. I want all your passion, Fallon, but I also want you firing on all eight cylinders when I finally make you mine."

His lips were a vibrant red from our kiss, and his eyes were the color of skies that had been singed by lightning.

I swallowed hard. I'd wanted to hear those words from him for so long, and having them now was both painfully beautiful and painfully cruel.

I looked away and repeated what I'd said earlier. "It could be just a paper marriage, Parker. I know this isn't what you wanted. You didn't want me any more than you wanted marriage or kids."

He pushed his fingers under my chin, forcing me to meet his gaze as his hand pulled mine to the bulge in his jeans—hard and large and straining to escape.

"Does that feel like I don't want you?"

I couldn't respond. A knot had formed in my throat as large as the one on my head.

"Let's get a few things straight. First, I've fucking wanted you for years." I tried to shake my head, but both his hand and the pain from the concussion stopped me. "I wanted you. But I thought I couldn't have you because of a stupid promise and my career." When I started to reply, he cut me off with another quick kiss and a nip to my bottom lip. "Second, there's no damn way this will be a paper-only marriage. It would be impossible to keep it that way after I've gotten a taste of you, after hearing the little inhale you make when I kiss you. So if you don't want to share my bed, if you don't want to spend your nights twined with me, then you need to back away now, and we'll find another solution to your problem."

"*Our* problems," I said, annoyance welling. "I wouldn't even suggest getting married if I didn't think I could help you and Theo too. He deserves stability after everything he's been through. He deserves to know someone chose him rather than feeling like he was just an obligation someone took on. I'm choosing him, and I'll make sure he always knows it."

Parker's lips curved upward. "There's my girl."

I narrowed my eyes at him. "You wanted to set a few

things straight? Fine. Let's start with the fact that I am not, nor have I been for a long time, a *girl*."

He hooked a leg over mine and, in a swift move, drew me closer so I was tight against his body, until I could feel the hardness beneath his jeans pushing into my thighs. "Believe me. I'm very aware of that fact. I shouldn't have said girl. I've been pissed at Teddy and Kurt and the others for using the term. You're absolutely not a girl, Fallon. You're a stunning force of nature."

A flutter whooshed through my stomach. Intense desire. Longing.

Those feelings had always gone unrequited with Parker.

And for a brief moment, I felt a heady sense of satisfaction. I'd gotten what I wanted. I'd gotten him. But as quickly as the thought came, it vanished, replaced by guilt.

I touched his face. "I feel like I'm trapping you. That someday, some year down the road, you'll look at me and realize it and end up hating me." Annoyingly, my voice cracked at the end.

He cupped my cheek. "If your crappy taste in music hasn't made me hate you yet, nothing else can."

He was trying to lighten the mood, trying to make me laugh, and I gave him a weak one. But inside, worry still festered.

When I didn't respond, he said, "We'll leave for Vegas tomorrow."

"Tomorrow?" I breathed out.

"How far along are you, Ducky? If we wait even a few more days, will JJ be able to tell it's a lie? That there was no way I could be the one who got you pregnant when he failed?"

"Five weeks. That was the doctor's guess. I'm at least five weeks along."

His eyes narrowed. "We really can't wait any longer, then, can we? And this actually works perfectly with something else I wanted to talk to you about."

He told me about his dad visiting Adam and wanting us to visit Ike in prison. "Plus, if you leave for a few days and the incidents stop, we'll know whoever this is was coming after you and not the ranch."

I didn't really want to leave now. It would feel like I was abandoning everyone I cared about, leaving them to face the music while I ran. As if reading my mind and sensing my hesitancy, Parker pressed. "You aren't running. You're actually trying to solve this by going to see Ike. And if whoever is doing this is really gunning for you, they'll follow you and leave everyone here alone."

The notion of someone following me and trying to hurt me again returned that dark intensity to his face—the SEAL ready to do what was necessary. It shouldn't thrill me as much as it did.

"Plus, if we go to Vegas, I can leave Theo with Mom for a few days to keep him away from all this," he said. "My parents offered to take him before, but I didn't want to leave him when he was just starting to come out of his shell. I didn't want him to think he was losing me just like he'd lost his parents."

"Parker…" My voice was full of apology.

He slid a hand through my hair. "This isn't your fault. Don't take that on. I just didn't expect things here to be this bad. It's better if he's nowhere near us at the moment."

I couldn't argue with his logic. If something happened to Theo because of me, I'd never forgive myself. But the same went for Parker. Or any of the people I was responsible for.

Maybe I really should leave. Run away. Go have my baby in some secluded location. But then, if JJ ever found out, he'd know the baby was his, even if I didn't put his name on the birth certificate.

To protect the unborn little one inside me, I had to do this. I had to take this risk with Parker.

That twisted a knife inside my heart all over again.

Was this what my dad had felt when he'd decided to leave me with Spencer and Mom? Impossible choices that always risked someone?

"Stop overthinking this." His voice was quiet and sure again, just like when he'd told me he would marry me.

"Are we going to tell your mom when we get there? About us getting married?"

His hand was still in my hair, stroking, soothing.

"We can't keep it hidden. If you want this to fool JJ, then we have to tell everyone and anyone we can."

My lungs squeezed tighter. "How are we going to explain it without telling everyone I'm pregnant?"

"The truth. That after denying our feelings for years, we don't want to wait another moment to start our life together."

They were beautiful words, ones that should have made me feel elated. Instead, they hurt because no matter how long I stared into his eyes, I couldn't tell if they were words he'd come up with to convince others or if they were really the truth.

He leaned in and kissed me. This one was different. It was strong and firm and held a promise. A vow. As if we'd already said *I do*.

"From here on, Ducky, you're not alone. You and me—we're in this together. And I swear you'll be safe. The baby will be safe, and Theo will be too. None of you will ever be hurt again on my watch."

And as much as he wanted that to ease my worries, it did the opposite.

Because once again, I'd become a duty. An obligation. A responsibility.

I closed my eyes and evened out my breathing, pretending to sleep.

But my heart wouldn't stop berating my brain for getting me into this mess. It was too late to back out. I'd do anything to protect my baby, even risk everything I'd ever wanted for myself, which is exactly what my dad had done for me.

A cycle on repeat. Unwed pregnancy. People sacrificing themselves and their dreams.

Heartache and betrayal.

I swore the cycle wouldn't continue with my child.

This would be the last time anyone in this family had to give up their dreams. The last time anyone felt like they were nothing more than an obligation that had to be fulfilled.

Chapter Twenty-eight
Parker

BE YOUR EVERYTHING
Performed by Boys Like Girls

FIVE YEARS AGO

HIM: You know what girlie pop song I hate most?

HER: 'Thinking Out Loud'?

HIM: That's a good guess for many of the same reasons. But no, it's '(I've Had) The Time of My Life.' Every frickin' time it comes on, some girl thinks I should sing it to her.

HER: Stop wearing your Navy Whites to the bar, and you'll eliminate half the problem.

PRESENT DAY

I woke from a nightmare where Will's face contorted just as the bomb went off at his feet. The agony of knowing he was dead before I could even make it across the charred street to his side still filled me as my eyes flew open. It took a few seconds for the warmth at my side to bring me back from the dark of that moment. To bring me back to the Harrington ranch, with me in Fallon's bed, having agreed to marry her.

We'd fallen asleep with the television on, the sound muted, and now the screen flickered, sending a wash of light and dark across the room as Buffy and her friends tried once again to save the day. Fallon's head rested on my shoulder, her side tucked into mine. Sometime during the night, my hand had spread wide over her stomach, as if I was already trying to protect the life growing inside her.

A baby. A little piece of Fallon who would be impossible not to love, just as it was impossible not to love Fallon herself. Because that was the simple truth. I loved her. I wasn't sure there'd been a moment since she'd been brought into my life that I hadn't. It may not have been the kind of love it was today, the unyielding, all-consuming love that fueled desire and passion and hope, but it had always been love.

She thought I was doing this to protect her and the baby and maybe as a way of shrugging out from under the burden of caring for Theo alone. And while all of that was true, none of those were the real reason I'd said yes.

When she'd suggested getting married, everything in my world had righted itself after weeks of feeling scattered. The puzzle had slid together into a perfect whole right next to the flashes of family I found myself craving. I absolutely wanted a life with Fallon. I wanted to wake up at her side and face the challenges of the world next to her. I wanted her bravery and determination to fuel me every day, making me a better man. I wanted to be worthy of her.

This wasn't me accepting a new obligation.

This was me being lucky enough to catch a falling star and keep it.

She needed to know it. She needed to hear it from me.

But she wasn't ready.

If I pushed and told her now that I loved her, she'd think it was my way of making her feel better about forcing this marriage on me.

I didn't feel forced. If anything, I felt relieved.

This was what I wanted. Her.

I'd tell her, and soon, but not yet. I'd wait until I was sure she'd really hear it.

Besides, I still had some decisions to make.

I wasn't sure why it had taken me so long to realize making

Fallon smile, making her laugh, making her climax, and giving her the partner she deserved was more important than any mission I'd ever done for my country. Serving hundreds of millions of people would never be as important as serving one. It would never be as important as making a woman who'd always felt like an obligation feel like she was my very reason for breathing.

I'd been so focused, so closed-minded in my pursuit of my career goal, I'd missed what was really important. It wasn't the mission. It was what you came home to. That was why my house had always felt so empty when I'd gotten home. Your loved ones were the reason you were fighting when you were out in the field, because you were fighting for their freedom to love and laugh and thrive. Being home with them was the reward.

The question was, would I risk Fallon's happiness, Theo's, and the baby's by continuing to put myself in danger? Could I step back onto the tarmac, get on a plane, and carry a gun into a battle, knowing I might not come home to them? Did I even want that for myself? Or was I just holding on to an oath to a dying man?

I loved being part of the teams. I loved every minute we spent challenging each other to be better than the best and to accomplish the impossible as a unit. I loved the actual work and the camaraderie that came with it.

What would I do if I wasn't a SEAL?

Ride on the coattails of my heiress wife?

It would be no better than JJ wanting Fallon for her money.

A sour taste ran through my mouth at that thought. Metallic. Ugly.

Dad was stepping down, retiring from Marquess Enterprises, and Noah was taking over for him. I could easily go to work for them and fill in any holes, but that thought didn't bring me joy.

Fallon shifted next to me, and a little breathy exhale drew my gaze to her face.

She was so goddamn beautiful. Dazzling asleep, but even

more so when she was awake and that vibrant energy filled her, drove her, sparkled from her. It had mostly been missing since I'd arrived at the ranch. I'd seen mere hints of it, and I was determined to bring it back full time, to ensure those rays shifted out of her like confetti—like fucking fireworks—every single day.

I'd do anything to make it happen.

Her eyelids fluttered as she dragged herself from the sleeping world to the real one. When she was fully awake, her gaze locked on mine. Surprise lit those warm depths and then a small smile. "I thought it was all a dream."

I brushed my lips lightly over hers. Hunger raged through me. How long would I be able to wait before I couldn't hold back any longer? A day? Two?

Before I knew it, I was softly singing the lines from "House of Sleep" about never sleeping alone and about my real dreams.

She swallowed hard, a soft and wistful look in her eyes, even though her tone was all saucy tease when she spoke. "You really singing Amorphis to me this early in the morning, Kermit? It's no '(I've Had) The Time of My Life,' so you must really want my morning sickness to turn into actual vomit."

I chuckled. "There's hope for you yet if you at least recognize the song and artist. I won't give up hope of making a metalhead out of you before the end of the next decade."

"Fat chance. Country will always be where it's at, but I'll take some eighties and nineties pop songs as an alternative."

I nipped at her bottom lip in response, and when I went to pull away, she locked me to her with a hand to the back of my head just like I'd done with her last night. She deepened the kiss, tongue sliding inside, demanding I respond. It was no sacrifice to do just that. I rolled her on her back and lost myself in the taste and feel and smell of her, hands and mouth and teeth discovering all the spots on her that made her pulse race beneath my fingertips.

I spent an eternity savoring the simplicity of our kiss before I realized it wasn't going to be enough. Not this morning. Not with the realizations I'd made while she'd slept.

I needed to give her something. I needed to start showing her exactly what I felt. What I wanted. The life I needed to have at her side.

When I yanked the thin straps of her tank down and moved my mouth to a taut tip, she gasped. And that sound filled me with as much determination as it did lust. I might not take her fully, I might not plant myself inside her as hard and deep as I wanted to, but I would give her a memory to hold on to. Relief. Respite. Joy.

As I continued my devotion to her breasts, my palm slid under her sleep shorts, diving below the waistband of her underwear to find the sweet heat at her core. She arched into me, a moan escaping.

I pulled back to take in the sight of her, eyes flashing with fire.

And the look of her this way, flush and warm and sleepy, just about sent me over the edge like some pubescent boy at his first make-out session.

I took her mouth once more. Devouring. Claiming. Cherishing. All the while, my fingers soothed and circled and plunged.

"Parker," she keened as if trying to hold back, as if trying to collect herself.

"Let go, Fallon. Let go of it all for a few seconds and just feel. The slide of my hand. The quiver building inside." I kissed her with long, slow strokes of my tongue that echoed the movement of my fingers. "The exquisite moment when the light explodes, and there's nothing else but this. Me. You. Bliss."

I'd barely finished the words before her body convulsed, and she let out a gorgeous little cry that made me want to start all over again just to hear it on repeat for the rest of my life.

When every single quiver had been eked from her, my hands stilled, and I watched as her lids fluttered open. Flames burned within those depths, as if the climax she'd just experienced had done nothing but fan the fire rather than sate it.

Damn, did I want to spend the rest of the day getting lost

in that blaze. I wanted to go up in smoke right along with her.

Instead, I pulled away. I rolled off the bed, adjusted my painfully hard dick, and then looked down at her with a grin.

"Get your ass up, Ducky. We have a long drive ahead of us. If we make good time, I figure you can be my wife by twenty hundred hours."

She sat up, brushed at her hair, and then crawled over on all fours to the edge of the bed. My mouth went dry as she kneeled in front of me, placing one hand on my chest. "Are you trying to make an honest woman of me before you take me, Kermit?" She squeezed me through my jeans. "It's a little too late for that."

She'd meant it as a joke, but I knew her well enough to realize she was also criticizing herself for getting pregnant while not married. Just like her mom. Just like her grandmother. I'd forgotten the time she'd told me how her family had a history of putting the cart before the horse. Maybe these days, no one would give it much thought, but Fallon had wanted to break the cycle.

I grabbed her wrists, bringing her hand to my mouth and kissing the palm. I met her gaze with a steady one. "You'll be married before the end of the day, Ducky. Married before this kid comes. And you and me, maybe we'll make another baby to keep this one and Theo company."

Her chin dropped, mouth popping open.

I tapped it closed and smiled. Then, I smacked her on the ass.

"Get ready. Pack a bag. We'll be gone a couple of days."

Then, I strolled out of the room, whistling.

My life had flipped on its head a month ago. I'd been locked under the overturned boat, struggling for air, but I'd finally righted the ship. I'd finally realized that marrying Fallon Marquess-Harrington was what I'd been put on this earth to do.

♫ ♫ ♫

Instead of driving to Vegas, Fallon suggested taking the

Cessna parked in the ranch's hangar at the small, private airfield nearby. It would save us nearly six hours in a car with a four-year-old, and I couldn't argue with it.

Theo was upset about leaving the ranch and the puppies, but I promised him we'd be back before he knew it. He looked doubtful, and I wondered what his parents had promised him the last time they'd seen him. Had Will promised Theo would see him in a few days? Weeks? How many promises had been broken already in his little life?

I was determined to keep mine.

We drove my truck inside the hangar, right up next to the plane, and I loaded our bags and Theo's car seat into the Cessna while Fallon started her pre-flight checklist. She walked the outside of the plane, talked to the control tower, and ran every diagnostic with a single-minded focus I respected.

Her stepdad had taught her how to drive, fly, and maintain just about every piece of equipment they used on the ranch. Now, watching her concentrate as she went through the checklist, I found myself turned on all over again. The baby growing inside her didn't know how lucky it was to have her on its side, but someday, I'd remind him or her of it when they were rebelling and thinking their parents were the worst.

Parents. Plural. Because I was going to be right there at Fallon's side raising the child with her.

I kept waiting to feel panicked by these random thoughts, but I wasn't. Maybe I never would be, simply because I was making the right choice.

I strapped Theo's car seat into the spot behind Fallon and took the front seat next to her. I looked back at Theo when the engines kicked, and his face burst into a smile.

We taxied out of the hangar and down the runway.

Fallon spoke to the tower via her headset and then shot me a grin, which she extended to Theo. "You all set, boys?"

Theo hugged Dog, giggled, and nodded. I winked at her.

And then we sped down the runway and lifted off. The little whoosh I always felt in the pit of my stomach when we left the ground greeted me. It felt like new possibilities. New challenges.

Theo squealed in delight, waving his stuffed animal at the window and the view of the mountains as we rose, rose, rose. The sky was clear, not a cloud in sight.

One of the things I loved most as a SEAL was plunging out of a plane, feeling nothing but air and gravity tugging at you. Even in the dead of the night, when I needed night vision goggles to see the landing zone, it was a heady experience. You had to trust the equipment, trust yourself to have examined and packed it correctly. Those few moments of free fall were almost religious. Life. Death. The incongruous fragility and strength of humanity.

More people should experience that thrill. They should come face-to-face with our fallible limitations, as well as the strangely beautiful knowledge that humans had figured out how to best even the very forces of gravity for a few short minutes.

Maybe I could give that to people by offering skydiving excursions for guests at the ranch. Or maybe a prep course for military hopefuls?

Sweeney had mentioned resigning his commission when his current contract was up. Would he be interested in starting a business with me? Could we open a skydiving center here? In Rivers?

My stomach twisted, nauseated at the idea of leaving the teams but also excited at the idea of creating new dreams for the first time in my life.

Theo's laughter brought me back to him and Fallon. I'd missed something they'd said, and I hated it. I wanted to know everything they said and did and felt. How much more would I miss if I was gone for months at a time? How much would Theo and the baby have grown and changed before I came back to them?

I gave them my full attention as Theo asked Fallon a thousand questions about flying. She answered every one with patience and ease.

"Someday, I'll teach you how to fly," she promised.

Pure delight coated the little boy's face. "Really?"

"Sure."

I turned to Theo. "You like the ranch, right, bud?" He nodded. "How would you feel about living there forever?"

His smile disappeared. "But I live with you."

Shit. I'd absolutely screwed that up. "And you still would. What if you and I lived with Fallon all the time?"

Fallon frowned. We hadn't talked about where we'd live, and once Lauren got out of rehab, she'd move back into the house. Plus, the baby was going to need a room. Fallon and I still had more things to figure out than we'd settled, and I was jumping ahead twenty paces by telling Theo we'd all live together.

"Can I have the masked puppy? And a pony?"

"You'd have to learn to take care of them," Fallon answered. "Animals are a responsibility. You have to feed and water and clean up after them every single day, even when you're sick or tired or grumpy."

"I will! I will!" Theo nodded his head.

"We'll talk about it. Maybe start with one and see how you do," I said.

When I looked back at Fallon, her brows were pulled tight.

Damn. Had I pushed too hard and too fast? I'd acted more like her than me, jumping in feet first rather than planning a strategy of attack. But as the miles zoomed by below us, and we drew closer and closer to Vegas, the certainty I was doing the right thing, that we were doing the right thing, only grew stronger.

Fallon would be mine. Theo and the baby would be mine.

We'd be a family. I'd be part of a new team—one I'd never considered being a part of before. And just like free-falling while waiting to deploy my chute, I was excited at the new challenges and possibilities spread out below me. I was determined to hit the ground on my feet. I wouldn't mess this up for any of us.

Chapter Twenty-nine
Fallon

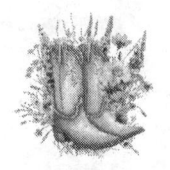

WHEN YOU SAY NOTHING AT ALL
Performed by Alison Krauss & Union Station

ELEVEN YEARS AGO

> *HER: Do you believe in curses?*

> *HIM: No. Not any more than I believe in fate. Why?*

> *HER: Uncle Adam says my family is cursed. That the poker game where the Hurlys lost the land to the Harringtons twisted our futures. He says it's why so many Hurlys and Harringtons have died in tragic ways and far too early in their lives. And now the ranch is nearly bankrupt. I'm struggling to find one good thing that's happened since the land switched hands. I can't find it. I think he might be right.*

> *HIM: You. You're the good thing, Fallon. Maybe everything had to happen just as it did so you'd be born. All I know is the world is better because you're in it.*

PRESENT DAY

My head and heart were spinning a bit, and it had nothing to do with the altitude or the nausea that had flitted through me this morning. It was the speed at which Parker was moving. He'd gone from saying yes to my ridiculous proposal, to getting married today, and now living together at the ranch at warp speed, faster than the Cessna was traveling toward Las Vegas.

I'd gotten what I wanted. But it felt empty in many ways.

A consolation prize.

Then, I remembered the way he'd touched me this morning. The look in his eyes as he'd told me to let go hadn't seemed like a participation trophy. He'd looked at me as I'd always wanted him to—as if there was love there.

Did he love me? In that way my dad loved Sadie? The way Spence had loved my mom? The way Parker's parents loved each other? My lungs almost forgot to breathe at even the possibility. A tiny piece of me tried to celebrate the idea before I squashed it. Talk about speeding ahead.

But he said he'd wanted me for years. I'd felt that longing time and again, hadn't I? I'd even told him he was a coward for not taking what he wanted. The sexual tension had flitted between us long before it should have. He'd just always had the strength to say no.

Holy crap, were we really doing this? Getting married and telling our families we wanted to spend our lives together? I'd barely broken up with the man I'd been living with. Would our parents believe us? Would they really think I'd gotten pregnant with Parker's child almost immediately after getting hitched?

Unease traveled through me.

I could convince Mom. I had years of practice showing her only what I wanted her to see, but Dad and Sadie…I wasn't so sure. And Parker was extremely close to his parents. They had a relationship I'd always envied, built on love and respect and trust. Now, I was asking him to lie to them—forever.

My stomach flipped again.

Maybe we could tell the Steeles. But if we did, Jim would tell Dad and my father didn't keep secrets from Sadie. Someone would slip somewhere along the way. That old saying about the only way to keep a secret was to tell no one was true.

The entire flight, I couldn't shed the back-and-forth doubts.

After we'd landed and loaded our bags in the SUV we kept parked in our Vegas hangar, my emotions still hadn't settled. Parker insisted on driving, and I was more worn out than I wanted to admit, so I didn't fight him on it. I just handed him the key fob and climbed into the passenger seat.

The Steele residence was a simple two-story in a middle-class subdivision that had been new at the time his parents had bought it but bordered on antiquated now. As we pulled into the drive of the stone-and-stucco house, the same thought hit me that always had whenever I'd been here over the years—it was a home in a way the castle I'd spent my childhood in had never been.

It wasn't like there hadn't been love in my home. My parents and Spencer had absolutely loved me, and none of them had clipped my wings as I'd tried to spread them. If anything, I'd been given more room and space than most kids. So, I wasn't sure what had always made Parker's home seem different. All I knew was walking into it felt like being doused with a blanket of love and acceptance.

Maybe the simple fact that betrayal hadn't started his family the way it had mine was the reason.

When we got to the door, Parker's mom was waiting for us in the opening.

Whitney was taller than me, almost six feet, and she looked younger than her actual age of fifty-five. She had dark hair and pale-blue eyes that were scrunched now in concern. She assessed us in a way that both her husband and son were good at doing, as if living with Navy SEALs for most of her life had worn off on her.

After hearing Parker's dad had gotten us in to see Ike Puzo the following day, she'd expected our arrival, but she didn't know we were also there to get married. Would she be happy or confused?

When Whitney saw Theo, her entire face lit up.

"There's my sweet grandson," she said, holding out her arms.

Theo ran into them, and my heart lurched. She'd already accepted him as part of her family. When she looked at my baby, I knew she'd do the same, regardless of whether or not the baby was Parker's.

Whitney put Theo down and then unleashed her hugs on Parker.

When she turned to me and squeezed me, she whispered, "I'm so sorry for everything that's happened."

And those stupid tears I couldn't seem to shake threatened once more. At least I could blame them on my hormones working overtime now.

We followed her into the great room. It hadn't changed in the twenty years I'd been coming here for dinners with Dad. The inside screamed the same middle-class charm as the outside. Well-made and well-used furniture filled the space, bookcases at least a decade past fashionable housed knickknacks, and framed pictures of Parker and his family in different settings were scattered along the walls. Some of those photos included Dad and me from when we'd vacationed with the Steeles.

"I've got a lasagna prepped for tonight and sandwich fixings for lunch if you're hungry," Whitney said, bypassing the living area to head straight for the adjoining kitchen.

The warm wood of the cabinets and the gold granite island and counters hadn't changed any more than the rest of the house. But instead of looking outdated, as it could have, it simply screamed comfort to me.

"Mom, I need to—"

"Go get the bags from the car," I interrupted Parker. His brows furrowed, and his gaze burned into me. I shook my head ever so slightly.

Whitney turned from pulling items out of the refrigerator. "Okay, I have you in the guest room at the top of the stairs, Fallon. I figured Theo can stay with Parker for a couple of nights." She turned to the little boy. "Want to help me cut out sugar cookie doggies while Parker and Fallon get your things?"

"Yes!" Theo shouted, stuffing his dog in the air as he

always did when excited. His enthusiasm had my lips twitching again, just as his million questions on the plane ride had. The kid had carved himself into my heart just as he had Whitney's.

"Wash your hands," she told him.

He hurried over to a stool she'd already placed by the sink. With a flash, I remembered times when I'd done the same thing. I wasn't even sure how old I'd been. I just remembered it had felt different than when I'd helped Mom cook. That had always felt like a chore. Whitney had made it feel like a reward.

Parker and I made our way outside to the SUV as my nerves continued to rattle.

"What's going on? Why'd you stop me from telling my mom about us?" he demanded as we hauled our bags from the back. When he tried to take mine from me, adding it to the stack of his and Theo's, I just glared at him. His jaw clenched, but he let me shoulder my own.

As we returned to the house, I stopped him on the steps with a hand to his elbow.

"I just wanted to give you a chance to change your mind before you tell your mom anything." I swallowed. "Everything is so ugly right now in my life… Sometimes, I'm not sure I'll ever escape it. My family has a history of bad things finding us. It's like fate has decided we don't deserve anything good. Maybe Uncle Adam was right. Maybe the day my great-great-grandfather Harrington won the Hurly land in a poker match did curse us."

He dropped his duffels, pulled mine from my shoulder, and drew me close. With our bodies touching, it was hard to remember all the reasons I should let him out of the promise he'd made.

"I'll never believe that murdering son of a bitch was right about anything," he growled. "Plus, I don't believe in curses, and fate isn't a one-way path. It might give us a shove in a certain direction, but I believe our free will drives the outcomes of our lives more than anything supernatural. We decide what happens."

He was so sure. How had he gotten to the acceptance of our marriage so quickly? After living his whole life telling me he would never get hitched. It was like he was the Parker I'd always known and loved from afar and yet someone else entirely.

I met his gaze and said, "I hate the idea of you lying to your parents."

He didn't respond. Instead, he kissed me like he had this morning and last night, fierce and determined and tender. It was as if he was issuing a new promise every time our lips touched.

His eyes were dark and stormy when he pulled back just enough to look down into my face. "I'm not lying to my parents." I started to protest, and he nipped my bottom lip before continuing, "I understand why it's hard for you to accept that I'm not doing this simply as some answer to our problems. For as long as we've known each other, I've insisted I didn't want a serious relationship, let alone a wife and kids, and now it seems like I've done a one-eighty."

My chest tightened, and seeing the panic that was raging, seeing the doubts, his eyes softened. He tipped his forehead into mine, and my body melted at the tenderness of the move.

"So, let's be clear," he said quietly. "The real reason I'm doing this is because seeing you on the ground the other day, thinking you'd been shot..." He swallowed hard before continuing. "It terrified me, Ducky. It was like I'd been going through life with a hood over my eyes, and someone finally yanked it off. The simple truth is, I can't live without you in my life...not as just my friend or even a lover, but as *my* person. The one I belong to and who belongs to me. The person I wake up next to every day and plan a future with. Our future. Yours, mine, Theo's, and our baby's."

The sweetness of the words tore through me, but it was the 'our' he'd placed before the word baby that broke me. Tears poured down my cheeks. Parker's words were everything I needed to hear—everything anyone would want to hear from the person they'd loved for as long as they could remember. He made it clear he wasn't just accepting me but accepting the child inside me as easily as Whitney had accepted Theo, as easy as Spencer had accepted me when he'd married my mom.

So why did I continue to feel like nothing more than an

obligation?

Was it simply the baggage of my childhood? Something broken in me that wouldn't allow myself to be more? Not just to him but to anyone. Was that really why I'd never let my guard down with JJ? Maybe it wasn't just my infatuation with Parker that had held me back, but the feeling that I wasn't worthy of being someone's everything.

"Don't cry." His voice was deep and gritty and pained. He kissed the tears, and it only made them flow faster. "I hate it when you cry, because it means I haven't done my job. I haven't taken the pain away."

I wrapped my arms around his neck and moved so our mouths collided. I devoured him the way he'd consumed me this morning and tried to infuse the kiss with all the feelings I'd always had for him, but also the same promises he was making to me. I would do my best to make sure he never regretted this decision.

"It's not your job to take away the pain, Parker. Not as my friend or my lover or my husb-band," I stuttered over the word. "We just have to help each other through the challenges this life throws at us until we get to the other side of them."

We stared into each other's eyes for so long that I thought the world had stopped.

Then, he was kissing me again, as if there would never be another time for us to do just this.

We were still locked in the embrace when the door of the house opened behind us, and Whitney said, "Hey, Parker, did you—"

We twisted around to see the astonishment on her face. She recovered quickly and, to my surprise, grinned.

"Are you going to stand outside kissing all day, or are you going to come inside and have lunch?"

There was laughter in her voice and maybe even a hint of joy. I'd expected Jim and Whitney to be concerned about this sudden change in Parker's and my relationship, especially considering everything happening with me and the ranch. But when I was brave enough to meet her eyes, I saw nothing but happiness.

Would it change when she learned we were rushing to get married? Or when she found out about the baby? Or the fact Parker was talking about living with me at the ranch as if he'd already left his SEAL team behind? Because that was what he was talking about, wasn't it? That was what waking up at my side every day would entail. But I wasn't going to let him do that. I wouldn't let him be my dad, turning away from everything he'd grown up wanting, no matter what Maisey had said. I'd make sure Parker still lived his dreams and accomplished his goals, even if it took him from us and the ranch for months at a time.

Chapter Thirty
Parker

IF YOU LOVE HER
Performed by Forest Blakk

NINE YEARS AGO

> HER: *I wish you were here for the wedding.*

> HIM: *Dad said he'd never seen Rafe so happy.*

> HER: *Sadie unlocked something in him. Maybe I should be hurt that I wasn't enough to make him really happy, but I'm not. I'm grateful Sadie's love allowed him to open himself up. She's made us a family again.*

> HIM: *You were always a family, Ducky. Your dad would have always gone to the ends of the earth for you.*

> HER: *Maybe because he felt he had to, but family should be more than an obligation. Sadie has given us that. She's given us the freedom to really love one another.*

PRESENT DAY

When we stepped inside, Mom was still grinning. As if seeing me kiss Fallon on our doorstep wasn't the least bit disturbing. As if she was *happy* to have found us locked in an embrace.

Would she feel the same way when I told her we were getting married? And not at some distant point, months in the future, but today.

She hadn't seemed disgusted by my inability to keep my mouth and hands to myself. Had Mom always known, just as Rafe had hinted Sadie had, that Fallon and I were an inevitability? Was I the only one who'd been blind to it? Not the feelings or the desire—I'd known those were there for years—but the rightness of a future with her. How had I not known that the love I felt for her was exactly the forever kind of love my parents had?

"Where's Theo?" I asked.

"Bathroom," Mom said, heading back toward the kitchen. "Your dad called. He needs to talk to you about seeing Ike but said you weren't picking up." She shot us a look. "I'll let you be the one to tell him *why* you were ignoring his call."

Fallon cleared her throat. "I'm going to put my bags away."

Mom sent another smirk in our direction. "I guess you'll be staying with Parker, and Theo will be in the guest room."

"I'll call him after we get settled," I told Mom before scurrying down the hall after Fallon, feeling a bit like the time Mom had caught me with my dick in my hand as a preteen.

I caught up with Fallon just as she started into the guest room. I grabbed her elbow and propelled her into my old bedroom, a door down.

My room didn't look the same as it had when I'd been a teenager. Mom had replaced the SEAL and military posters with black-and-white photographs of some of Rafe's stunning buildings around the world, including the casino here in Vegas. But it had the same queen-sized bed and a navy comforter similar to the one I'd once used.

"You really think it's a good idea for us to share a room at your parents' house before we…you know…?" Her voice drifted away.

"We're getting married, Fallon. I already told you my conditions. We do this, real and all in, or we don't do it at all.

Outside on the steps, you gave me an out, but I don't want it. I haven't changed my mind. Have you?"

Her gaze was pained when she met mine. Dark and shadowed and tortured. My hand surrounded her neck, thumb settling on her pulse as I leaned in to brush her lips with mine. I couldn't stop myself from doing it after years of denying myself.

"Tell me that doesn't set you ablaze," I said as I pulled back, "that you don't want to spend the rest of your life sharing a bed with me, and I'll call it off."

The pulse in her throat thudded against my thumb as I searched her face for the truth. She closed her eyes, hiding from me.

But her voice was painfully quiet when she finally spoke. "I'm afraid."

"The Fallon I know and love has never been a chicken. It's impossible for you to start now." As her eyes flashed open, I realized what I'd said—the love I'd carelessly tossed out instead of planning and saying it purposefully. I tried to gloss over it for now, promising myself I'd give her those words in the way she deserved when she was ready. "Don't make me dare you."

She snorted out a half laugh. "I always win our dares."

"Or I always let you think you win our dares." It wasn't true, but I liked the irritation it fueled in those warm eyes. It brought back the confident Fallon I'd loved in a completely non-platonic way for far longer than I'd ever realized. "Tonight, Ducky. We're going to say 'I do,' and that'll put us on a new path. One where you and I decide our futures together. No fate. No curse. You and me."

She squeezed my wrist before breathing out, "Okay." She let go and stepped away from me. "I need a minute before I can face your mom again."

She grabbed her bag and headed into the Jack-and-Jill bathroom that joined my old room and the guest room. For two seconds, I was tempted to follow her, to push a bit harder and make sure she realized I meant what I said and that there was no reason to be scared.

The curse she talked about was non-existent. As soon as we figured out who was responsible for this recent string of attacks and put them behind bars, she'd see it had nothing to do with supernatural forces.

And then, I'd spend the rest of my life making sure she never felt cursed again.

I grabbed Theo's backpack of toys and strode out of the room. I wanted to talk to Mom before Fallon came out so my mother's reaction didn't increase Fallon's nerves. I dropped Theo's bag on the couch in the great room and marched into the kitchen on a new mission.

Mom was beside Theo, watching him push a dog-shaped cookie cutter into the dough she'd rolled out. She glanced up at me, that knowing smile returning to her face.

"So, it's finally happened," she said matter-of-factly. "Do Rafe and your dad know?"

"Rafe, sort of. Dad, no."

Theo finished, and Mom helped him transfer the cookies to a baking sheet.

"When can I eat 'em?" he asked, squatting to look into the oven.

Mom chortled. "They need about ten minutes to cook and a few minutes to cool."

"Wash your hands one more time, and then get your toys out of the bag I left on the couch," I told him. "You and Dog can play while you wait."

After he left the sink, I watched him from the island as he went into the other room and searched his toy bag. I glanced toward the hallway to ensure Fallon wasn't coming out yet and then turned back to Mom.

"We're getting married."

Mom's brows jerked up, nearly reaching her hairline, and I chuckled.

I ran a hand over the scruff on my jaw that I hadn't shaved this morning in my hurry to get us out of Rivers and to Las Vegas.

"Tonight," I added.

Her mouth popped open. "Now, hold on—"

I shook my head. "No. We've wasted years already because I was too much of a coward to stand up to Rafe and Dad. She could have died the other day, Mom, and I would never have known what it was like to be hers and for her to be mine. I refuse to wait any longer. I refuse to waste more time just so you and Sadie and Lauren can plan some damned wedding."

"Don't cuss at me."

Mom put up with a lot as a military wife and mother, but cussing was where she'd always drawn the line.

"I know your father and Rafe talked to you when you were teenagers," she said quietly. "I wasn't thrilled about how they made you promise not to do something that everyone knew was inevitable. But that was different, Parker. She was too young, and there was too much of an age gap between you then. Not in years, but in experiences."

"I know," I said, because I did. I understood fully why our fathers had warned me off. But I'd stuck to the promise for too long. I'd made the mistake of turning her down repeatedly, and it had sent her running back into JJ's arms. I wasn't sure I could forgive myself for that. If I hadn't been an idiot, the baby inside her might have my DNA instead of his.

When I didn't say anything else, Mom's eyes softened. She placed a hand on my arm and squeezed gently. "Is this what Fallon wants? A quick Vegas elopement without her family standing up with her?"

I gave her a curt nod. "Yes."

She stared at me for a long moment. She tilted her head and considered me. "I can see this as a typical Fallon move. She's always tried to prove she didn't need anyone, but this isn't you. You live your life as a unit. Your teammates and your family would like to be there for you as you take this huge step."

She was right. I'd never thought about getting married, but if I had, I would have wanted my people—the people I trusted with both my life and well-being—to be there with me. But the situation wouldn't allow it, and that was the one piece I couldn't tell her. No one could know the baby wasn't mine. No one. Not even the people we trusted most.

"I'm sorry, but I'm not budging on tonight. This is the way we've chosen to handle it."

"Handle it." She frowned again. "Like it's an assignment."

Fuck. It was. But it also wasn't. I inhaled deeply, moved closer, and dropped my arm around her shoulders. "I love her, Mom."

Her eyes filled instantly. She nodded. "I know. Mothers know these things." She patted my cheek softly. "Your dad is trying to make it home by tomorrow night, but he can't see Adam at the prison until one o'clock. Wait one or two days more. Let him be here for both of you."

"I'm not waiting for Dad. I'm not waiting for anyone. I promised her we wouldn't waste another day. If we tell everyone, they'll all demand to be here, and I'm done listening to anyone else's demands when it comes to Fallon."

She sighed almost wistfully. "That's the most romantic thing you've ever said. It fills my mom heart with pride." Then she grimaced and continued, "If I'm going to take the heat for knowing about this and not telling anyone, I better get it as right as I can. We'll get the license and the rings after lunch, and then I'll go with Fallon to pick out a wedding dress of some kind. If you don't have your Navy Whites with you, you *will* wear a tuxedo. I'll at least have photos to give everyone when they scream at me. The chapel at The Fortress might not be available on such short notice, but I'll make some calls."

The Fortress was Marquess Enterprise's hotel and casino here in Las Vegas. Designed to resemble the tidal island of Mont Saint Michel in France from the spirals and towers of the abbey at the top of the island all the way down to the sea walls, it dripped with wealth and sophistication.

Rafe had opened the casino about a year before everything had blown up on the ranch with Spencer's murder. He still maintained a private penthouse at the top of the hotel's tower that the family used whenever they were in Las Vegas, even though he and Sadie lived primarily in Tennessee.

Fallon's relationship with her dad had improved in recent years, but for a long time, she'd thought she was nothing more than a duty to him.

Realization hit me in the chest like a bomb going off. This was why she'd given me yet another "out" on the front porch. She knew I loved her, just like her dad and stepdad had loved her, but she still wasn't convinced that I wasn't doing this out of duty. She was worried it was just another time she was someone's obligation. For as long as I'd known she battled feeling this way, I should have picked up on it sooner.

The shit thing was, I *was* doing it out of honor and duty, but it wasn't the primary reason I was marrying her. The real reason was the truth that I'd told both my mother and Fallon. I couldn't stand the idea of not waking up with her at my side. The only reason that mattered was that I loved her. Fallon needed to not only hear it in a way that made her believe it, but I needed to show her in a way that left it completely irrefutable. Somehow, before the end of the day, I had to convince her this was more about us than any damn obligation.

♫ ♫ ♫

By the time Fallon came out of the bedroom, Mom and I had placed several calls to get the ball rolling on our marriage. My mother gushed over Fallon so much that she turned bright red, sending me desperate looks to save her. But I had no intention of stopping my mother from making Fallon feel as special as she deserved on her wedding day.

"I'll follow you to the Marriage License Bureau," Mom said. "And then Fallon and I will go find the perfect dress."

She hustled out of the room to grab her purse and keys, and Fallon crossed the kitchen to slam me on the shoulder with a fist. She didn't hold back, and it actually stung, but my only response was a grin.

"Shopping? Really? How did you rope me into this while I was out of the room?"

"Mom was right about one thing, Fallon." I pulled her into my arms. "Even though we're doing this fast, it doesn't mean we can't take a few minutes to do it right. Just make sure you don't overdo it physically today." I brushed my lips gently over the bruise at her temple. "I don't want you relapsing."

Plus, I had ideas for tonight. Our wedding night. Ideas that might just bring that flush back to Fallon's cheeks for completely different reasons. Ideas that would have her crying out in bliss. The climax she'd had this morning was nothing. I could top that. I *would* top that.

"What are you and Theo doing while I'm shopping?" she asked.

"I don't have my Whites with me, so I'm getting a tux," I answered, but that wasn't all I had on my list of things to accomplish. I hoped she wouldn't be upset when she found out about some of it, but it would be too late at that point. And if worse came to worse, I'd dare her not to back down. The Fallon I knew wouldn't. She'd raise that stubborn chin of hers and walk down the aisle just to prove she could.

Theo left his toys behind on the couch and joined us, glancing warily at Fallon and me wrapped up together. "Dog is bored."

"Well, good thing we're about to head out. We have a list of errands, and I'll need your help keeping me on task," I said. It was the same way I'd gotten through all the errands with him back in San Diego, by giving him his own job. I picked him up before wrapping my free arm back around Fallon's waist and pulling the three of us together. "I have a very important question for you, bud."

He tilted his head sideways. "Yeah?"

"I need someone to be my best man. That's a friend who stands by your side when you get married. Would you like to be my best man?"

His eyes grew wide. "You're getting married? To Fallon?"

"Yes."

"And we're going to live with her at the ranch? With the doggies and the ponies?"

"Don't forget the chickens and the cows," I told him with a smile.

"Okay! Let's do it!" Theo yelled, shoving Dog in the air.

I hugged them both tight. This new life wasn't something

I'd planned, but it would be better than anything I'd ever imagined for myself.

I put him down and told him to get his shoes on.

When I looked up, Fallon's face was a sea of conflicted emotions.

"What's wrong, Ducky?"

"What does this mean for you, Parker? For your team—"

I cut her off with a kiss like I'd done several times in the last few days, because sometimes it was the only way to stop her from spiraling into a thousand arguments and what-ifs. "I know we haven't discussed everything, but I promise we will. After. For now, let's concentrate on getting the marriage license and our wedding gear before heading to The Fortress."

"The Fortress?" Her brows furrowed.

"Mom placed a call. As luck would have it, their chapel wasn't in use today. I guess no one wanted to get married the Monday before the Fourth of July. They've slotted us in with the officiant at eight o'clock. That means we have seven hours to pull this off. Dress, hair, and makeup for you. I've got the rest."

"The rest?" Her frown grew.

I kissed the spot between her brows. "Stop overthinking this, Ducky. For once in your life, let someone else handle the bulk of the plans. Relax. Have fun."

Chapter Thirty-one
Fallon

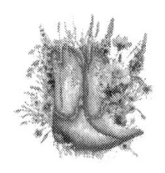

AMAZED
Performed by Lonestar

SEVEN YEARS AGO

> HER: Why is it that women have to wear uncomfortable things like strapless bras and four-inch heels to be qualified as dressed up, but a guy gets to wear pants and flats?

HIM: Is this for prom? What teen wannabe is taking you? And has your mom or your dad had 'the talk' with you?

> HER: I'm seventeen, not ten, Frogman. I've had the sex talk.

HIM: So you know how all teen guys hope to close out their prom night with one thing?

> HER: Maybe all teen WOMEN want to close the night out with the same thing.

HIM: Do not give in to the lure of one night, Ducky. The walk of shame isn't worth it.

> HER: Only a misogynist hypocrite would say I'd be doing a walk of shame when he's had more one-night stands than I could count.

HIM: Just trust me on this. Prom night is not the night for you.

> HER: You offering me an alternative?

PRESENT DAY

How did I get here?

I stared into the mirror and wondered for the thousandth time if I was doing the right thing.

Then, I took a breath and reminded myself of everything Parker had said earlier, especially when he'd said he loved me. Sure, it had been in passing, as if it was already a foregone conclusion, but he'd said it. And he'd said he wanted to be with me, wanted me in his bed, waking up next to him every morning. Hearing him talk that way, hearing those sweet words, was a beautiful dream come true.

Until I thought of the baby and why he'd jumped off the ledge.

But Parker had sounded so sure when he said that wasn't the only reason he was doing this. Seeing me on the ground after the bullets had flown had supposedly pulled back his blinders. But would I ever know for sure?

Why couldn't I just let go of the doubts and enjoy this moment?

Looking into Whitney's tri-fold mirror in her bedroom suite proved I'd gotten what I'd always dreamed. I was getting married. To Parker.

The door behind me opened, and my future mother-in-law came in with a glowing smile that hadn't once faded since Parker had told her about our marriage.

She'd been happy every second of our afternoon together, gushingly so. When we were looking for dresses in an exclusive mall off The Strip, she'd told me, more than once, how she'd always thought this would happen. She was thrilled we were making a family for ourselves—one that included Theo.

Now, she took me in from head to toe, in that way that reminded me of her son, before she said, "You look absolutely gorgeous, Fallon. Parker is going to lose his mind."

I looked back at my reflection.

The Cheongsam-styled dress I'd bought was the palest of

aquas, just a shade above white. It was sleeveless with a Mandarin collar and sheer keyhole side and back inserts. The sheer inserts were topped with intricate flower appliques in shades of silver and a darker aqua with tiny seed pearls at their centers. The dress had an organza top layer that floated from my waist to my calves and an inner satin lining that ended above my knee.

As soon as the sales clerk had brought it from the back, I'd known it was the one. Not just the right one for this spontaneous Vegas wedding, but the one I would have chosen no matter how long we'd planned the ceremony.

Even more perfect, I'd brought my favorite dark-teal cowboy boots with me, and they would match perfectly. The flowers on the boots even looked like they belonged in a matched set with the ones sewn on the bodice.

Fate.

That word shifted something inside me.

I tugged at a long curl that had been artfully left out of the updo. Whitney had finagled a hair and makeup team from the spa at Dad's hotel to work me into their schedule, paying extra for a house call. The stylist had taken my normal braid and upleveled it. She'd twisted my hair into several small braids and then piled them together in an elegant knot at my crown, leaving plenty of long, loose tendrils curling down my back and over my shoulders. She'd worked the angle of my hair upfront to hide the knot at my temple as best she could, and the makeup folks had carefully applied cover-up over it. The bruising and swelling were still noticeable, but only if you really looked.

"You don't need jewelry with the neckline of that dress," Whitney said. "But I thought you might like this cuff to be your 'something borrowed.'"

She took my hand and slid the bracelet on before I could object. The gracefully twined vines and flowers of silver wound from my wrist up to almost my elbow. It was as feminine and lovely as the floral appliques on my dress.

My throat momentarily closed.

Reading my wild emotions, Whitney risked messing up my hair and makeup to hug me. "You're sure, Fallon. This is how you want to do it?"

I didn't hesitate. "Yes."

I hoped it sounded as firm and confident as I wanted.

Her phone alarm jangled. "That's us, then."

I grabbed the small clutch I'd bought with the dress that now contained my phone and a few essentials. I wouldn't need anything else for this short jaunt downtown to The Fortress. We'd be back in a few hours, and I'd no longer just be Fallon Marquess-Harrington, but Fallon Marquess-Harrington-Steele. I'd have to choose what name to use going forward. Should I keep something from my heritage, or was it time to start a new era? Was it time for a family called the Steeles to take over? Maybe that was all it would take to break the curse Uncle Adam insisted lingered over us.

But I didn't have to decide tonight. It could wait.

We made our way out of Whitney's room and down to the first floor. My head swiveled, searching the great room for Parker, but there was no sign of him or Theo. They'd been absent when we'd returned from shopping as well.

"He's meeting us at the chapel," Whitney responded to my unanswered question.

My nerves jangled. The independent piece of me that had sworn I could do anything on my own hated needing him here to calm my nerves, but I did.

I needed my doubts to be soothed by more charming words and a kiss that held the promises we were making to each other.

I followed Whitney out of the house to a limousine parked at the curb. The logo etched into the back window showed it was one of Dad's used to pick up the high rollers who stayed at his casino. The way we'd been using Dad's staff today, he was certain to hear about the wedding before the night was over.

Would he be angry I'd done this without him? That he hadn't had the chance to walk me down the aisle? It couldn't be helped, but I did feel a twinge inside. If things had been different, I would have wanted him here, even if I'd never wanted a full-blown wedding.

After climbing into the limo, I asked, "Did you tell Jim?

Or my parents?"

She shook her head. "No. I respected Parker's wishes, and he told me he'd handle it."

"I'm sorry we put you in the middle of this, but thank you," I said, my voice clogging again. Would these hormones ever stop raging? How much worse would it get before I delivered the baby? "And not just for keeping it to yourself, but for helping me find this lovely dress and trying to make this day special for me. For both of us."

She squeezed my hand. "I love you, Fallon. You've always been family to me, and I am so grateful, so very, very grateful, that you've helped Parker see the light. I've been waiting for him to realize he didn't have to sacrifice love and family in order to serve his country. I was terrified that when Jim and I were gone someday, he'd be alone."

"I would never have let him be alone," I insisted.

She smiled and dabbed at the corners of her eyes. "I know. But having *him* realize it too…that's the real win, isn't it? It's the silver lining that's come from the ugliness happening at the ranch."

I'd tried fervently to put the ranch and the troubles there behind me today. I'd had enough to worry about with us taking this huge step. The doubts and insecurities around this decision were enough for one day. Tomorrow, we'd visit Ike in jail and deal with more of my problems.

Inside The Fortress, the sounds and smells and energy of Dad's resort greeted us. While the outside looked like a French abbey town, the inside was a blend of eighteenth-century luxury and 1920s Art-Deco charm. Gold gilded nearly every surface, hand-painted murals filled the walls, plush carpets graced the floors, and marble columns glimmered like diamonds.

Getting married here, in the opulence of my dad's casino would not have been my first choice. I would have preferred the waterfall at the ranch, with an arch of wildflowers over us and sunlight shimmering through the trees, but maybe this was better. Maybe this quick little jaunt saved me from arguing with Mom about the simplicity of the wedding.

That twinge of something that was a mix of guilt and

wistfulness wound through me once more because my family wasn't here.

No matter what kind of wedding we were having, the most important part of the dream had come true. At the end of the aisle tonight, the groom waiting for me would be Parker. And that was the real reason I'd turned JJ down when he'd proposed and why I should have broken up with him long before things had gotten so far out of control. In all my dreams of a far-off wedding day, it had always been Parker who was waiting for me.

The stained-glass doors of the chapel opened to reveal Parker and Theo just inside.

One look at Parker and my heart stumbled to a stop. He'd slicked his dark hair back, making his square jaw even more prominent. The scruff he'd boasted all day was gone, leaving his skin smooth and silky. A black tuxedo was molded to his broad chest and shoulders, and he'd, somehow, found a vest that almost perfectly matched my pale-aqua dress.

His eyes widened as he took me in, using that slow, head-to-toe scan that always set my insides ablaze. Lust. Yearning. Love. And I did love him. More than I could ever express. He was the only person who I'd ever let see the real mess inside me. Not even Maisey had seen my cruelest, darkest thoughts. Parker knew them and still liked me, still wanted me.

"Wow," he breathed out before closing the distance, lifting my hand to his mouth and kissing the knuckles. The old-time, gentlemanly move set my pulse racing and kicked my stuttering heart into overdrive. "You're stunning, Fallon. A goddamn star bursting into existence. A phenomenon I'm somehow lucky enough to have at my side."

Whitney sighed behind me, but I couldn't break my gaze from Parker's. I was locked in an embrace with him that had nothing to do with our bodies and everything to do with our souls.

"Even cussing, it's clear you got some charm from your father, after all," his mom said.

"Fallon *is* a princess!" Theo exclaimed, and finally, my eyes tore themselves away from Parker to look down at Theo.

His tux was an adorable matching mini of Parker's. He held out a tiny gift bag for me. "We couldn't find a fairy godmother, but Parker says it still has magic to protect you."

My chest swelled with emotion as I took in the two beautiful humans who, after today, I'd forever be able to claim as mine. When I couldn't respond over the lump in my throat, Theo shoved the bag at me again. I slowly took it, pulling the tissue paper out and unwrapping the tiny object within.

The bracelet was nothing like the one Whitney had let me borrow. This one was two leather bands woven together with beads. On the beads were letters—an F, P, T, and B and ones that spelled out *The Steele Family*. It took one too many heartbeats for me to realize the B was for the baby.

I knelt and pulled Theo to me, kissing his cheek. "It's the best gift anyone has ever given me, Theo. I'm so honored to be a part of your family."

The kid flushed and patted my cheek before tucking himself back up against Parker's leg.

When I stood up, Parker's smile was so wide, so happy, so calm, most of my nerves disappeared. I was here with him. We were getting married. He truly wanted me. That was all that mattered. Everything else was just unnecessary static.

Parker held his arm out for me and said, "You ready, Ducky?"

I nodded, smiling at him as I slid my palm onto his jacket sleeve.

Whitney held a hand out to Theo and said, "Walk me down the aisle, best man."

He giggled and did just that, almost running to get to the altar at the end.

I'd been so caught up in Theo and Parker, in the magnificence that was us becoming a family, I hadn't even looked past the chapel's entrance. What I saw brought a fresh round of tears to my eyes. Wildflowers were scattered everywhere. Bouquets of bluebells, yarrow, and goldfields were mixed with cattails and ferns and tied together with bright-teal bows. Somehow, impossibly, Parker had brought the ranch to me.

He'd known what I'd needed without me saying a word.

But it wasn't the flowers that caused the tears to finally crest. It was the body at the end of the aisle, waiting next to the officiant.

Maisey.

My best friend was there.

I swallowed hard and wiped at the tears with the knuckle of my free hand as Parker said, "Don't cry, Ducky. Please don't cry."

I looked up at him, meeting gray eyes awash with love, and the last of my remaining doubts went sailing to the sky. I'd always belonged to Parker, and he'd always belonged to me. That wasn't going to change, no matter if we said "I do" now or later or never. I cleared the thickness from my throat and said, "They're happy tears, Parker. I don't know how to thank you."

"I didn't do it just for you. I did it for both of us. So we wouldn't remember today as some secretive, rushed event, but as something we chose. Something we both wanted and celebrated with people we love at our sides."

"Keep it up, and I'll never stop crying."

Before he could respond, we'd made it to the officiant and Maisey. She handed me a bouquet of wildflowers and gave me a saucy smile. "You didn't think you'd actually get married without me, did you?"

She wore a simple summer dress of creamy yellow, and her brown hair was up in a messy bun, but she looked happy and beautiful. I pulled away from Parker to hug her.

"Stop, you're going to crush yourself," she said, but her voice sounded as achy and raw as I felt.

I let her go and turned back to Parker to see he was messing with his phone.

"One more thing before we get started," he said.

Parker swiped some more, and suddenly, the two large screens hanging on the walls on either side of the altar came alive.

"What are you doing?" I asked Parker.

"Hold on," he said while his fingers moved. The large screens came to life, revealing a virtual conference software program, and my confusion grew. Parker logged in as the meeting's host, and the image showed the chapel with me standing next to him.

I started to ask again what he was doing until, one by one, other attendees joined the meeting.

My pulse jumped as Dad and Sadie appeared, squished together on a screen. My father's brows were furrowed together as tightly as Jim's were when he emerged in the next square. Mom looked puzzled in her room at the rehabilitation center, but at least her eyes were clear of any drugs. Then, more people joined the meeting—Parker's teammates, Kurt, Teddy, Andie, Kevin, and even Rae.

My heart had already felt like it was full to the top, but it swelled impossibly more as I realized what he'd done. Parker had gotten our family here. For us… For me… Just like he'd gotten the wildflowers and Maisey. He'd made sure we did this with the people we loved watching on.

I swallowed hard and grabbed his free hand. When his eyes met mine, I saw in them the one thing I needed most. I saw love. It hadn't been just an offhanded throw-out comment earlier, and it wasn't the platonic love of a long-time friendship. It was the forever kind of love he'd once said only a rare couple was lucky to have.

And we were one of them.

"What the hell is going on?" Dad demanded, his voice ringing down from the screens. "Parker sends us some cryptic message insisting we sign into this meeting immediately, and instead of seeing you at the ranch, dealing with the shit there, I see you in the goddamn chapel at The Fortress. With. Fallon."

Dad's voice cracked as if he'd already answered his own questions. He knew, just as everyone else did, what was happening.

Parker slid his phone into his pants pocket and then grabbed both my hands, turning me to face him. He didn't talk to the screens or the dozen or so people watching. Instead, he spoke directly to me.

"The other day, I almost lost the most precious thing in my life, the one person I was supposed to spend forever with, and I realized I'd already lost more minutes than I could count with her. Minutes I could never get back. But from this day forward, I pledge to never lose another."

"Parker…" My voice trailed away. I didn't know what to say.

He kept his gaze locked on me as he said, "While I wasn't willing to wait another minute to marry her and ensure we'd claimed each other as our own, it was important to both of us that we have the people we love at our sides as we took this step. This was the best compromise I could come up with. So thank you for joining us as we say our *I dos*."

A cacophony of voices tried to talk over each other, but Dad's voice won out with a loud, "Damnit."

Parker chuckled. "And with that, I'm putting you all on mute."

He pulled his phone out, tapped a button, and put it away again. He turned to the officiant and nodded. Parker tangled our fingers together and brought our joined hands to his chest. The heat of his body comforted me. The strong and masculine and earthy scent of him brought me home. This was where I belonged. With him.

"We are gathered here today…"

I didn't hear the rest. I was lost in Parker's gaze and his touch and the warmth of his smile. I was lost in the beating of my heart that echoed the thump of his below my palm.

Without personal vows planned, we simply repeated the ones offered to us, but the look in Parker's eyes was more special than any words could ever have been. The way he uttered each one told me he meant every single syllable. He was promising me I'd never be alone again.

The ring he slid on my finger was a band of white diamonds with a small, square-cut yellow diamond at its center. It looked like the ones my family had mined on the ranch decades ago, and I had no clue how he'd found it. I hadn't bought him a ring, but when it was my turn, he handed me a simple platinum band, and I slid it onto his finger with a sense of rightness I hadn't experienced in months…maybe years.

Parker and I had finally arrived at this moment as if it had been ordained. It had just taken us a while to find our footing on the path guiding us here.

"You may kiss the bride."

Parker smiled his widest smile. The one that crinkled his eyes and spoke of pure joy. The eighth wonder of the world.

He wrapped an arm around my waist, drew me closer, tipped my chin up, and kissed me. It should have been light and brief with the audience we had, but it wasn't. He devoured me just as he had been doing since he'd first kissed me in the field. And I pushed my lips back into his, claiming him with the same intensity.

What felt like a lifetime later, Whitney cleared her throat, and we broke apart, faces filled with goofy, happy smiles.

"Wife," Parker said, and my entire chest melted into nothingness at that single word.

"Frogman," I said back.

He rolled his eyes and then threw his head back and laughed.

It drew my gaze to the screen behind him. The faces of our friends and loved ones had moved from shock to pleasure. Mom and Sadie wiped their eyes. Jim beamed at us. Only Dad still seemed pissed but also, strangely pleased.

"Maybe you'd like to unmute them?" Whitney suggested.

Parker did and then pulled me close to him again. Theo ran in circles around us while we fielded an array of questions and congratulations.

"Whitney," Jim's voice interrupted, "you have some 'splaining to do, my love."

"You can't blame her, Jim," I jumped in. "She tried to slow us down, but we didn't want to be slowed."

"Only you, Fallon," Mom said. Her tone was exasperated, but I also heard love in it. Neither was a surprise. For most of my life, I'd done things my way—ways she didn't understand.

"We'll have a reception for them later," Whitney said. "After everything is resolved at the ranch."

That set off another round of voices trying to talk over each other in that weird, virtual meeting sort of way.

But Whitney's words had dimmed the moment some. It brought back the allegations hanging over me and the danger waiting for us. The same danger that would now put Parker and Theo at risk.

Knowing me as well as he did, Parker read the slip in my mood. He squeezed my hip and leaned in to kiss my temple. He whispered in my ear, a low, guttural, "No."

I looked up at him, lips twitching. "No, what?"

"Don't think about any of that right now. Not tonight. Not on our wedding day. Only good thoughts today, Wife."

I laughed and said quietly, "Still not the boss of me, Kermit. Even with your ring on my finger."

He grinned and chuckled. "I wouldn't have it any other way."

Chapter Thirty-two
Parker

I SWEAR

Performed by John Michael Montgomery

FIVE YEARS AGO

>*HER: Will and his bae don't seem to mesh all that well, do they?*

HIM: What the hell is a BAE?

>*HER: You're a disgrace to your generation, Parker. What are you, fifty instead of twenty-five? It means lover. Partner. Like, instead of calling someone baby, which we all know can be downright insulting.*

HIM: I can promise you that no one has complained when I've called them baby.

>*HER: But then again, you don't really stick around to find out, do you?*

PRESENT DAY

After we'd let our families and friends talk to us for much too long, I'd ended the virtual meeting with a promise that we'd let them hold a reception for us later in the year. Mom insisted on taking us to dinner with Theo and Maisey at the hotel's Michelin-starred restaurant. Customers had to make reservations a minimum of six months in advance, so I knew it was only because of who Fallon was that Mom had been able to swing a table.

I sat next to Fallon in a quiet booth at the back of the fancy restaurant and couldn't stop myself from touching her. I kept our fingers twined as much as possible, and when that didn't work, I had my thigh pressed into hers or my arm behind her on the back of the booth.

She looked beautiful—such a ridiculously underrated word for the truth of her. It wasn't just the hair and makeup and dress. It was something inside her that was glowing stronger than it ever had. That light I'd thought had been dimmed when I'd first arrived on the ranch had returned but with a new vehemence. A spectacular force.

She was mine.

She'd always been mine, but I'd let myself deny it for too long.

Stupid, when I'd never considered myself stupid.

After the entrees had been served, eaten, and removed, the chef brought out a fraisier cake that was Fallon's favorite, along with a wildly expensive bottle of champagne, adding his good wishes to the rest of the staff's. The strawberry sponge cake layered with pastry cream and topped with marzipan was almost too sweet for me, but watching Fallon lick the fork with her eyes closed became one of my new favorite moments. Before, I would have looked away. I would have forbidden myself from thinking about all the ways I could put that same look on her face with my hands and my mouth. Now, I reveled in it.

After Mom and Maisey gave teary-eyed toasts, and Theo started to fade as the minutes ticked further past his bedtime, we finally left the restaurant. I dropped Fallon's hand to hug Theo. "I'll see you tomorrow, bud. Just like we talked about, right?"

For a moment, uncertainty crossed his face.

"Wait, what?" Fallon shot confused looks between us.

Mom reached for Theo. "Maisey, Theo, and I are having a movie day tomorrow, aren't we? All the best dog movies we can find, but only the ones with happy endings. We'll eat lots of popcorn and plenty of the sugar cookies we made."

I cringed, thinking of Theo's fallout after a junk-food binge, but it was Fallon who objected. "But I don't have my things, and—"

"I packed them all up while you were with the stylist and sent them along to Parker here at the hotel," my mother said. She leaned in and kissed Fallon on the cheek. "You deserve a wedding night, Fallon. Both of you."

Fallon's cheeks flushed. Maisey hugged her, whispering something that made Fallon blush even more as Mom pulled me into another quick embrace.

We watched as the trio made their way down the carpeted hall toward the front of the hotel, with Theo waving Dog at us in a way that tugged at my heart. It was our first night apart since he'd come to live with me. Would he be okay? Who would he sleep with if he woke in the middle of the night? I'd given Mom the rundown, but I wouldn't be there…

And that was always a SEAL's worst nightmare—not being there when your team needed you.

"Parker, this is silly," Fallon said softly, pulling my hand into hers.

I looked down at her, those amber eyes shimmering with that warm light that had finally returned, and my chest settled. Theo was with my mom, and there was literally no one other than my dad who I'd trust more with him. Theo would be just fine. And Mom was right—Fallon and I deserved a wedding night.

I didn't toss the *deserved* word around very often. It was overused, frequently hiding a sense of entitlement that actually hadn't been earned. But I wanted tonight to be special for my wife.

My wife.

Those words were so foreign to me and yet so completely right.

"Once we get to the suite, I'll show you just how *not* silly it is."

Then, I swept her off her feet and strode toward the

elevators.

She laughed. "Put me down."

"No."

Her gaze darted around us. "We're drawing attention."

"Good." When we came to stop at the elevator bank, I adjusted so I could push the button, and she tried to slide out of my arms. I tightened my grip and leaned down to kiss her on the forehead. "Stop wiggling. You're worse than Theo."

"I weigh about a hundred and twenty pounds *more* than Theo. You can't possibly carry me all the way to our room. Where is our room, by the way?"

"I carried a damn itty-bitty ship for hours in unrelenting waves. I think I can carry my wife a few feet."

She stopped moving, eyes falling to my lips before meeting mine again. "That word…it keeps hitting me in the chest."

"What word?" I knew, but I wanted her to say it.

"Wife."

And it hit me in the chest too. Pride and love and desire. I started to curse myself again for taking so long to get here and then halted those thoughts. I couldn't change the past, and dwelling on it would only make me bitter—not at her, but at me. From here on, I'd concentrate on making it up to her, on building a life worthy of her.

The doors opened, and I stepped inside, hitting the button for the suites at the top of the tower. We were still alone in the elevator when the doors closed, and I kissed her, slow and soft and mindful of the cameras in the corners.

Tearing my mouth from hers was harder than I expected. I brushed the good side of her temple with my lips again and then said, "I wouldn't know what it's like to hear that special word as you've yet to say the matching one."

She grinned at me and batted her lashes playfully. "What word? You mean, Kermit? Frogman?"

I growled.

Her smile grew. "Fine, fine. I know…" She inhaled, leaned up, and brought her mouth close to my ear, sending a wave of heat and lust down my spine. "Bae."

I pinched her side, none too gently, but she simply laughed.

"I will hear it, Fallon. Before tonight is over, you're going to be chanting it."

Her smile disappeared, flames bursting in her eyes. "Big promises, *Bae*."

The doors opened with a ding, and I strode toward the suite where Theo and I had gotten ready. I hadn't seen the items I'd ordered—we'd gone to the chapel before they'd been delivered—but I knew they'd be waiting for us, as top-notch customer service was one of the things Rafe's hotels were known for.

At the door, I had her dig in my pocket for the keycard, and as she pressed it against the reader, she said, "We could have stayed in Dad's penthouse."

"Not on our wedding night. I don't want to be thinking of your dad at all. Or mine. Or anyone but you."

The door shut behind us with a quiet click, and I marched straight past the suite's sitting area into the bedroom. A mahogany four-poster bed carved with vines and flowers took up the bulk of the space, but there was also a free-standing tub placed in front of windows that overlooked the lights of The Strip twenty floors below. A gold-gilded settee was at the foot of the bed, the deep rose velvet cushions matching the satin of the bed linens. It was floral and feminine and perfect for a wedding night.

The staff had scattered candles around the room as I'd requested. They were fake, but they still added ambiance to the dim lights. The sweet scent of the same wildflowers I'd filled the chapel with hung in the air, and a silver stand with champagne on ice sat in the corner.

I wanted Fallon to have romance tonight. This wasn't just us rushing to beat a clock clicking down on her pregnancy. This was a true wedding night with love leading us into a long future.

When I finally set her down, I didn't let her back away. Instead, I put one hand behind her head, wrapped the other around her waist, and took her mouth with a passion I hoped she'd feel all the way to her toes.

When I finally started to pull back, she protested, sinking her teeth into my bottom lip and taking control. I let her, enjoying the hungry way she explored and the heat of her touch, enjoying the thrust of her tongue and the savage, almost desperate lick into my mouth.

I pulled back enough to remove the clips and bands from her hair, running my fingers through her tresses until the blond waves danced around her breasts. I wanted to bury my face in those strands, to inhale that salty sea and floral aroma until it was burned into my senses. Instead, I slanted my mouth over hers once again. It was almost too much, having her, touching her, being engulfed in her scent and her love.

I was already painfully hard. Harder than I'd ever been and hungry for relief.

But my body would have to wait.

I needed to spend hours cherishing her first. Hours taunting and teasing her until she was desperate enough to say the word I craved.

She broke our kiss, looking around the room and taking in the flowers and candles and champagne before eyes burning with desire returned to mine. "I didn't expect all this."

I ran my thumb along her bottom lip. For two seconds, I let the asshole JJ enter my mind, pissed that he might not have given her any of this. Romance and flowers and sweet, sensual, slow sex in the flicker of candlelight.

"I demand you start expecting it," I said, voice rough and low.

"Yeah?" She cupped my cheek, and I leaned into the warmth of her stroke. "And what about you, Parker? What do you expect?"

"You'll always be able to tell me no, Fallon. I'll never expect you to say yes. But tonight, I want to taste you. Every single inch of you. To watch you climax around my tongue and my fingers before I take you up and over again while I'm buried deep inside you."

She pressed a hand to her chest as if the words had hurt. It rose and fell at almost a frantic pace. She tossed her purse aside and pressed herself against me. She wrapped her arms around my neck and set her mouth on mine. Strong. Hard. Fast.

I met her pace, her demands lick by lick, but I wasn't going to let her take this at her normal Fallon speed. I was determined to savor every single second of our first time together. I placed my lips on her neck, nipping and sucking as I found the dress's zipper and slowly tugged it down.

My hands slid into the opening at the back, gliding over silky skin before pushing the material over her shoulders. I eased back enough that the dress dropped to the floor, leaving her in nothing but a thong and her cowboy boots. Her bare nipples were hard and straining. A delightful feast just waiting for me. I dipped my head, lapping at one and then the other, and she moaned. That same enchanting sound I'd heard this morning.

I picked her up and set her on the bed before returning to my worship of her. I started with the hollow at the juncture of her ear and neck, making my way down to the sharp cut of her collarbone, the gentle valley between her breasts, the taut slope of her stomach, and the indent of her belly button, delighting in the birthmark I found right at her pelvic bone.

As I placed a kiss there, her hands tightened on my necktie, forcing me to meet her gaze. Something flashed in them. Humor mixed with longing and a surprising dash of hurt that had my hands freezing.

"Are you saying yes, Parker?"

My endorphin-overloaded brain couldn't follow her thoughts.

Her hips pressed into mine, and a hand cupped me through the tuxedo pants.

"You feel like you're saying *yes*, but I could have sworn you once told me you'd never say yes to me. That you would never break. Never ring a bell and give in."

I rested my chin on her stomach, despising I'd hurt her so deeply.

"I claim self-defense, Ducky. I'm sorry I hurt you to save

myself from breaking a promise I never should have made. But you have no idea how close I was to shattering that night." Her eyes turned stormy. "Or how much I hated it when I woke to find you gone. I thought I was protecting you, but instead, I sent you careening back into that loser's arms."

Goddamn tears flooded *my* eyes.

She brushed at my lashes, fingers rubbing the dampness.

"Show me what you would have done if you hadn't denied us both what we wanted." Her voice was low and sexy and sent a pulse to my dick that was almost my undoing.

And I did just what she demanded, gliding fingers and tongue over the slopes and valleys, and embedding the love I felt into every touch. I indulged myself in studying and learning her, pursuing her pleasure until she was panting and her hips were thrusting. I sucked on the scrap of silk at her core, and she mewed. The sexiest sound I'd ever heard.

"I need you inside me, Parker, and you're wearing too many clothes."

"Say it, Wife. Say the word I want, and I'll gladly remove the penguin suit."

Her eyes sparkled. "Kermit?"

I bit her thigh, and just like with the pinch, I wasn't exactly gentle.

She had the audacity to laugh once again, which made my determination grow.

I knew how to buckle down and get what I wanted. I could be unrelenting.

I dragged the tiny excuse for panties over her hips, trailing kisses over her skin as I revealed everything below them. I removed her boots and then stepped away from the bed to feast on the portrait she made with her hair spread along the pink satin of the bed linens, chest heaving.

As I stared, her hand settled low on her stomach, a protective motion.

I twined my fingers with hers, settling over the little bean growing inside her. That's what it would look like at this stage if I remembered right from the parenting books I'd read. I'd get to watch this child grow while inside her, and I was surprised at how much that excited me. How much I truly wanted to be a part of it all. I'd watch over this baby and be the best father it could ever have. I'd trained to accept nothing less than the best from myself.

The idea of not being a SEAL for much longer stabbed me in the gut, but it wasn't as severe as it should have been, because I had something even bigger and more important waiting for me, something filling that vague emptiness I'd been fighting.

Fatherhood. Marriage.

Love.

All kinds of love.

"Parker?" Fallon's brows furrowed together.

I leaned in and kissed her stomach softly. "I want this baby, Fallon. I want it almost as much as I want you. She isn't an obligation or a duty. Neither are you. You're both my purpose. My life. My loves."

Tears filled her eyes, and she sat up, grabbed my face, and kissed me. Then, she murmured against my lips, "Your words are almost enough to take me over the edge by themselves, Parker. I don't want that. I want to go over with you inside me. As one person. One unit. Our own little team."

I stripped out of the tuxedo as fast as possible. She watched while I did, taking in every inch of me, including the one part that was straining to make her mine.

"I'm clean, Fallon. I've been tested, but do you want me to wear a condom?"

She stared at me for a moment. "All my tests came back negative from the ER, and I don't think I can get pregnant twice."

For a moment, it took the magic from the air—the reason she was pregnant.

But I refused to let any of that ugliness bleed into our night. So I joined her on the bed, resuming the caressing and worshipping I'd started and forcing her to focus on only the beauty in this room with the two of us coming together.

As my fingers danced and glided along her skin, she

writhed, arching into me, gasping for air, and making a slight humming sound I wanted to hear on repeat for the rest of my life.

"Now, Parker," she demanded.

I stopped, whispering in her ear, "Say it, Wife."

"Bae, I'm going to be really unhappy if you don't finish what you started soon."

"Say it, and we'll both be far more than happy. We'll be ecstatic."

Her eyes flashed, that last, defiant piece of her refusing to give in. And I wanted her to keep that fierce independence, but I also wanted her to know she was safe to let go. That it was okay to let someone else drive. To have control. Here, she could give in, and it didn't make her less. It only made *us* more.

She turned her head, bit my shoulder, and dug her fingernails into my hips as she pressed our cores together. "Parker…"

It was the most erotic beg I'd ever heard. And I almost caved. I almost thrust into her and took what was mine so I could give her what was hers.

I bit her ear, nipped at her neck, and allowed my fingers to slide inside that wet heat.

Taunting. Tormenting. Taking her up yet again but never over the edge.

When I could almost feel the quiver of her around my fingers, I stopped once again and whispered, "Say it, Wife."

She slammed her palm down on the mattress. "Fine." Amber eyes met my steel ones. It wasn't the desire I focused on. It was the complete and utter love as she finally caved. "Husband."

I pushed into her in one hard thrust. She gasped in pleasure, her inner walls already clenching.

"Hold on, Wife. We have to catch the wave before we can ride it to shore," I said.

I'd never felt anything like this. My senses were on complete overload. The scent of her and me and the flowers. The mix of colors from her and the room. The warm flicker of the candles. The sound of skin sliding and the panting of breaths. It all twined into something unworldly, bigger than either of us. A power that filled the room as two became one. As souls touched. As hearts joined.

When she reached the peak, when she was already crying out and chanting *husband* as I'd promised she would, I lost all control. I was nothing but sensation, raw and wild and beautiful. And as I went over the peak, slamming into her one final time and letting go, I was blinded by love and light and hope.

Chapter Thirty-three
Fallon

HOW DO I LIVE
Performed by Trisha Yearwood

THREE YEARS AGO

HIM: *I don't get how everyone flies to some sweltering Caribbean island for their honeymoon. Even the surfing wouldn't be worth it.*

> HER: *Pigpen actually pulled the trigger?*

HIM: *Yep. Three Frogmen down.*

> HER: *I know you never want to do the deed and put a ring on someone's finger, but if you did, where would you go for your honeymoon?*

HIM: *A mountain lake. Somewhere temperate with stunning views and plenty of outdoor activities.*

> HER: *You literally just described the ranch.*

HIM: *I did, didn't I? But it's too hot in the summer. Maybe Lake Moraine in Canada. Kayaking and hiking during the day and making love all night.*

> HER: *I can tell you've never given this much thought, Kermit. I can almost guarantee a couple on their honeymoon isn't going to spend the day kayaking.*

PRESENT DAY

The sensuality of this moment, tangled with Parker, having reached the top and gone over together as one, was a little bit of heaven, full of visceral emotions I couldn't describe but lay savoring.

The sex with JJ had been good—at least, I'd thought it had been. But with Parker, it felt…holy. That might be blasphemous, even when I wasn't overly religious, but I couldn't help thinking it.

Fate.

I'd dangled that word to Parker just like I'd dangled the word cursed, but I'd never really understood it until now. Until he'd been inside me, and we'd become one. Not just physically but in every single molecule of our being.

When we parted, it was almost painful. I almost wept, and I wasn't sure I could blame it on baby hormones.

As he started moving away, I caught him by the hips and held him close.

His eyes met mine, and in the flicker of the candlelight, what I saw in those depths had my entire soul relaxing.

"I love you," I said. It wasn't a whisper. It wasn't hesitant. It was the simple truth.

"I know," he said. And I rolled my eyes and smacked his ass. He chuckled, but then his smile disappeared, and the same look returned to his eyes that I'd seen in the chapel. "I love you too. So much that I'm not even sure that's the right word for it. Love seems too benign. Too underrated."

My heart swooned even more than it had when I'd seen the romantic setting he'd assembled for me—for us.

His fingers lingered on the knot on my forehead, which was still an ugly mix of colors.

"I'm not sure this was the easy activity the doctor ordered," he said gently.

He pushed up and away from the bed, and the cool air of

the hotel air conditioner wasn't the only reason I felt cold. I wanted him with me always. How did people survive without their other half joined to them? It felt impossible.

"Where are you going?" I asked.

I watched as he strode toward the tub in front of the windows. His body was a work of art. Cut and defined. Hard and powerful. I could lie here forever watching him and be happy. That was as startling of a thought as the need to keep him close had been, because I usually didn't like to sit still for long any more than I liked to be smothered.

Parker turned on the tub's faucet, running his fingers in the water until it met with his approval before adding some liquid from one of the handful of bottles sitting in a tray hanging off the side. As the tub filled, he popped the cork on the champagne and poured it into two glasses. He set those on the tray as well.

Finally, he came back to me and stretched out his hand. "Wife."

I smiled and let him pull me up. The room spun a bit. It had been a really long day, and I hadn't had a chance to rest as I had this weekend. But there was no way I'd admit any of that to him, not when he'd gone over and above to make this night special.

Not when I finally had everything I'd ever wanted.

And that was when a new truth hit me. JJ had done me a favor, and whoever had shot at us had done me another, because those events had broken down the walls between Parker and me. We were finally where we belonged.

Parker swooped me into his arms again, and I chuckled. "My leg muscles are going to atrophy if you keep refusing to let me use them."

He nuzzled his nose into my neck. "Humor me while I get accustomed to being able to do this."

He set me in the tub and then stepped in behind me. The heat instantly soothed my tired muscles. The soft scent of citrus and clove filled the air, combining with the wildflowers that littered almost every surface. It could have been too much. It could have been overpowering. Instead, I knew it would be a scent I'd remember for the rest of my life as equaling love.

I rebraided my hair quickly to keep it out of the water a bit, and when I'd finished, Parker pulled me back into his chest. His fingers slowly caressed as his lips trailed kisses over my shoulders. My skin puckered into goosebumps, even though the water was steamy and warm.

He grabbed the two flutes, handing me one, which I would only take a sip of with the baby. I'd had none of the chef's at dinner. "Thank you for making tonight more than I ever imagined it could be." I swallowed hard. "Now, I need you to promise me something."

He didn't reply, but his brows furrowed.

"If…" I inhaled deeply, trying to get the courage to say what I needed. "If it becomes too much… me, the baby, the ranch, Theo… I need you to be honest about it. To tell me. I know this is an adjustment for you. You've gone from never wanting anything serious, let alone marriage, to having a ready-made family."

He tilted his head, thoughtful, and then said, "It's the strangest thing, Ducky, but nothing has ever felt more right in my life. Like, what I'd had before was all pretend, and this is what is real. I told you earlier, it's like someone yanked a hood from my head, and I can finally see."

"When do you expect the team to be called back?" I asked.

"I'm not going back."

He'd been talking this way all day—as if his career was over. I started to shake my head, but he cut me off.

"I was due to sign a new contract in September, but I'm not going to. I'll use up my vacation time until the paperwork goes through. I'm not leaving you."

With a shaky hand, I set the flute on the tray and awkwardly turned around in the water. "Please don't say that. Please don't do that. I'll never forgive myself for costing you your dream."

The lights of The Strip from outside the windows flickered across his face, casting colored shadows the candles in the room competed with, and in that mix of shadow and light, I caught a glimpse of the SEAL again. The honorable man so determined and strong and brave that it was impossible to doubt him.

"It's what I want, Ducky," he said, sincerity and sureness ringing in his tone. "Those old dreams...they feel like ones a child made. Self-centered. Inward-looking. I realize now, looking back over the last few years, my time on the teams has turned into nothing more than a job I was good at, and one I did with some people I liked. I kept feeling this ache when I was out in the field... this loneliness... I didn't even realize it, but I'd already started imagining new dreams—ones with you. It just took my life flipping sideways for the clouds to clear enough for me to see it."

I shook my head, fingers sliding along his jaw as my heart ached, but I wasn't sure who it was for. Him or me or us? The teams for losing him? "But what about the promise to your grandfather? To continue the Steele legacy."

"He forgave my dad for getting out, understood the reasons. I'd like to believe he'd forgive me too. That he loved me enough to want me to be happy more than he'd want me to get some useless trophy."

I didn't know how to respond, but my heart still ached.

"Those months when you stopped texting me..."

I started to apologize, and he put a wet finger to my lips to stop me before he continued, "I was more lost than I'd ever been. Hollow. Empty. I don't want to feel that way again. When I'm with you, that's when I feel complete. Whole. Learning to be a dad and a husband are the challenges that interest me now. And figuring out what comes next, what I'll do with the skills I've earned, is more exciting than I'd imagined it would be. I have some ideas. Actually, the flight here this morning presented me with some new possibilities."

I wrapped my legs around his waist, and the water sloshed closer to the top of the tub. The length of him pushed against me. Hard and ready. Distracting me.

"Are you going to tell me what those ideas were or make me guess?" I asked and then slowly trailed kisses down his jaw, along his neck, and over his shoulders. His entire body stiffened, large hands gripping my waist.

"I'm not sure I can form a coherent thought with you wrapped around me like this, Wife."

My hands surrounded him under the water, a slow, sudsy stroke that had him throwing his head back and groaning. Every part of me lit up at that picture, the simple fact it was *me* who'd made him react that way. I continued my trail of kisses, wet and open-mouthed, as my hands moved, finding a rhythm that had his hips thrusting in the water. A tiny wave crested and broke over the edge of the tub. We were going to make a mess. We were going to be those newlyweds who Dad's staff complained about, and I didn't care. This, me bringing him up and over the crest, was all that mattered.

When he was worked up, almost to the summit, I pulled back.

His head jerked up, dark eyes meeting mine, and I gave him my best saucy smile. "Tell me your plans, Kermit, and I'll finish what I started."

Before I could get in another stroke, he'd stood and snagged me in his arms once more. We were out of the tub and on the thick, plush carpet before I could protest. He was inside me, strong and hard and powerful, before I could do more than let out a titillated little laugh.

His eyes were dark as he moved above me. That feeling of coming home, of being one, of reaching nirvana, returned. This was what life was supposed to be like. Moving as one entity. One love. The universe took complete souls and broke them apart like a scientist splitting atoms, but when the halves found each other again, that was when the true power formed. When the atoms rejoined. When the souls glided back together.

When he was inside me, when we rode this wave, it felt like we were invincible, as if nothing in life could ever tear us apart.

I dug my nails into his hips and did my best to flip us. He didn't protest. He just moved with me and then watched with stormy eyes as I rode him. And when I finally crested the wave, he was right there with me. Pleasure and love and joy filled the room as I called out the new name, the new word, he'd been desperate to hear.

Husband.

He was my husband.

I was his wife.

Nothing on this earth, nothing in the universe, would break us apart.

♪ ♪ ♪

My eyes felt heavy when I woke with my back tucked up against Parker's chest and his hand spread wide across my abdomen. My body was beautifully sore. My heart happy. We'd made love again before the sky had started to lighten, and then he'd insisted on sleep. Or maybe my body had. I'd done too much the day before, but I didn't regret it.

This was completely worth it.

Nothing could be better than the sunlight filtering through the windows while the man I loved was wrapped around me.

I was happy.

It might have been the most inappropriate time for me to be so with the danger hovering around us, waiting to return, but I couldn't deny it. I was so happy my heart felt as if it had wings…as if, at any second, it would take flight.

Eventually, between rounds of lovemaking, Parker had told me his idea of starting a jump school. One used to train people before they joined the military but also for Special Forces units. The land around Rivers provided plenty of obstacles. He believed some of his teammates would join him as they wound up their SEAL careers. Sweeney had already planned on leaving and might join him sooner than the others.

I loved the idea. Loved that it meant he'd be with me, Theo, and the baby more than he'd be away, but I also couldn't help the twinge of worry at the pace at which he'd switched gears. It wasn't a one-eighty. It was more like stepping outside of his body and pulling on a new one.

A nip to my ear had me yelping.

"I can practically feel the vibration coming off that motor in your brain," Parker said. His voice was husky and low from sleep.

I was on my back with him above me before I could think of an adequate comeback.

I expected his mouth to land on mine. I expected his hands to slide over me. Instead, he stared for so long it felt like our souls collided before our bodies did.

"I'm where I want to be, Fallon." He'd read my mind again. How did he always do that? "More, I'm where I was always meant to be."

I kissed him in response. I didn't have any other words.

Just as he deepened the embrace, my stomach rumbled loudly, and we both chuckled.

Parker glanced over at the clock on the bedside table. "We have time for breakfast before leaving for the jail, but not for what else I had in mind."

He pulled us both from the bed and set me on my feet.

"Maybe I want the *what else* more than food," I said, raising a brow and taking in his naked form.

"No," he said and then smiled when I let out a grunt of annoyance. "My baby needs food to grow, Wife."

My heart did all sorts of cartwheels and tumbles. His baby. Wife. I might just die from the sweetness of it all.

He dragged me into the shower with him, which caused another slow embrace that quickly could have become more but he stopped once again. Before I was ready for it, we were back in reality, sitting at the café in Dad's hotel, ordering crepes on the terrace.

But it wasn't until we were in the SUV and heading north toward the prison that I thought to be nervous.

I'd never met Ike Puzo in person, but his twin sister had nearly ended my life and my dad's as payback for Dad's giving the Feds the evidence they needed to put Ike away. What would it be like to sit across from him, even knowing he was in jail and couldn't hurt me personally? Would the same evil I'd felt facing his sister be in the room with us?

I hadn't been nauseated this morning, but now the crepe I'd eaten twisted nastily.

Parker grabbed my fingers, bringing them to his mouth and kissing the knuckles before setting our joined hands on the center console. "Talk to me."

"If he's behind this, how will we get him to admit it?" I asked.

"I doubt he'll say anything that can directly incriminate him, but he'll hint at it," Parker said. "Like most bullies, he'll want you to know he's responsible for the pain he's caused. What's the point if he can't gloat about it?"

"I should act as if I'm terrified, don't you think?"

Parker considered it for a moment. "As much as it goes against my grain, or yours, to show him any of our emotions, you might be right. If he thinks you're there to beg him to stop or to bargain with him, he might tell us more than if we threaten more years on what's already a life sentence."

I nodded and turned to look at the high desert speeding by outside the windows. The rugged, harsh land made me miss the forest and meadows of the ranch with an ache that was almost painful. I wanted to be home. I wanted to be back with Parker and Theo and to have all of this behind us with only a beautiful future in front of us.

I would do anything I needed to get Ike to admit he was behind everything that had happened.

Except, we still had no clue why he would wait this long. Why wait ten years?

Parker's phone rang, and he hit the button on the steering wheel to accept the call.

"Hey, Park, you're almost at the prison?" Jim's voice rang through the speakers.

"About fifteen minutes out. You're on speaker. How did things go with Adam?" he asked.

"It didn't."

Parker and I shared a startled look.

"What do you mean it didn't?" Parker demanded.

"Adam is dead."

Chapter Thirty-four
Parker

HERO OF THE DAY
Performed by Metallica

TEN YEARS AGO

> HER: One good thing came out of this whole thing with Uncle Adam.

HIM: If you can see any good in being held at gunpoint and pistol-whipped, you're a better person than me.

> HER: The idea that Sadie could have died pushed Dad into going all in with her. You should see how happy he looks. Happier than I've ever seen him before.

HIM: Then you've never looked in a mirror when he's watching you. You bring him joy, Fallon. He loves you.

PRESENT DAY

I hadn't lied to Fallon the night before when I'd told her it felt like I was finally living my real life rather than a dream I'd made up as a kid. Being with her, looking forward to a future I didn't have all lined up with every I dotted and every T crossed, was exciting. Challenging. Interesting.

What I wasn't happy about was having this new vision I was creating stabbed at by some asshole we still hadn't named. Going to see Ike today was a step in the right direction, but I hated that Fallon would be in the same room with him, hated that we might have to let him see a fear neither she nor I would ever willingly give to an enemy.

I could feel her concern rippling like an undercurrent through the air on the drive.

When Dad called, it was almost a relief to have the silence broken. But that relief quickly changed to shock when he told us Adam was dead.

"What happened?" I asked.

"He was poisoned. Someone was putting a beta blocker in his food, and it caused his heart to give out," Dad said. "It's under investigation, and the prison's hospital and kitchen staff are being scrutinized and interviewed."

"Highly unlikely he's behind what's happening at the ranch, then."

"Unless it was a suicide. Maybe Adam orchestrated his revenge and then took himself out," Dad responded.

"No way Uncle Adam would kill himself," Fallon interjected, shaking her head. "He was too arrogant, too full of his own self-worth."

"Prison changes people," Dad told her. "But I don't disagree. This feels like another attack, making me believe it's directed at your family more than you personally. I'd say it moves us another step away from JJ, but it could still be Ace."

I hated JJ's name with a passion I'd never hated anything or anyone. Not even Adam, after kidnapping Fallon, had worked up this much loathing. Maybe it was because I knew JJ was the reason Ace had still been in Fallon's life. Or maybe it was because JJ had seen Fallon as I had last night—bare in heart and soul and skin. But then I corrected myself. JJ had never seen her heart and soul. She'd never given him either of those. Those had always been mine.

"It's even more important that we're on our way to see Ike, then," I said.

"Agreed."

It was quiet for a moment, and I was just about to end the call when Dad added on, "Changing the subject, I just want to make sure what happened yesterday with you two has nothing to do with this."

I heard the worry in his voice, and I was almost sure the question was directed more at me than her. But we both answered at the same time. My "Absolutely not" ringing with her "No."

Dad chuckled. "Okay, then. I'm only sorry part of your honeymoon will be spent dealing with this sorry excuse of a human in a jail cell."

"We'll take a real honeymoon after this is resolved," I told him and was surprised to mean it. That same surprise filled Fallon's eyes, but I just smiled at her. "Maybe we'll go to Lake Moraine and do some kayaking."

She did that little half-laugh that always made my lips twitch and warmed my heart.

"Give me a call when you're finished with the asshole," Dad said, and we hung up.

The quiet returned to the car, and I didn't break it until we parked in the prison's visitor lot. "I'd say I'm sorry Adam is dead, but I'm not. The only thing I'll be sorry about is if it's made you sad."

She turned to face me and shook her head. "Honestly, Uncle Adam has been dead to me for ten years. The moment he let Theresa hit me without stopping her and then followed that up by abusing and attempting to shoot Sadie, I no longer had an uncle."

I cupped her neck and tugged her closer so I could brush my mouth against hers. I mostly did it simply because I could, because it was a new addiction I'd never get tired of, but also so I could remind her that she was safe. I wouldn't let anyone hurt her again.

"It's still a shock," I said, "that someone killed him."

She nodded, brows furrowing in thought. "Why is it all happening now, Parker? What triggered it?"

I tipped my forehead into hers. "I don't know, but we'll figure it out, Ducky."

It irked me that I couldn't pull the pieces together yet, but finding out who'd put the beta blockers in Adam's food should lead us to this asshole's door.

I pulled back. "Ready?"

She glanced over at the tower hiding the men with guns and the bland cream-and-brown buildings inside the barbed-wire-topped fences. After a moment, she nodded.

"Leave everything but your ID in the SUV," I said and then jogged around the vehicle to open her door.

Once we were inside the prison walls, the dank desperation hit me. I'd been in much worse places on my missions—jails that had contained the smell of death and rot and piss—but the air here still held the anger, desolation, and fear I'd sensed in those faraway locations. Emotions that put everyone, from the guards down to the prisoners themselves, on edge. The worst could happen at any moment, and everyone expected it. If they didn't, if they got lax and dropped their defenses, that was when the real evil slid in.

After we were thoroughly scanned, the staff directed us to a waiting area where we sat in chairs screwed to the cement floors and waited for a guard to fetch us.

I put a hand on Fallon's bouncing knee and drew the fingers she was rubbing together into mine. "You don't have to do this. I can go in alone."

All her movement stopped. When she spoke, it was with a tremor of anger. "I want to face him. I want to look Ike in the eye as we ask him about the attacks. But what I want most is to see the man who tried to have my dad killed locked in a cage he'll stay in for the rest of his life."

A guard approached. "Visitors for Ike Puzo."

We both rose and followed him down a hallway lit by bright LED bulbs. Stark and bright, it allowed very few shadows to exist, but I could feel them anyway. They clung to the very air we breathed, trying to squirm their way inside your soul.

Dad had negotiated our use of an interview room generally reserved for lawyers meeting with their clients, and the guard opened a metal door to reveal a small space with cinderblock walls. A plain steel table was bolted to the floor with four plastic chairs, lightweight and unlikely to do any serious damage, on either side of it.

"The guard who brings Puzo will wait outside the opposite door," the officer waved to the door across from us. "I'll be right outside this one. When you're ready, knock or press the buzzer." He pointed to the black button on the wall next to the exit.

Then he was gone, leaving us locked in the small room.

My nerves tried to rattle to life, but I shut them down just as I did on our missions. Nerves didn't have a place here. I wasn't leaving this cell without having gotten something out of Puzo.

I assessed Fallon as she sat in one of the chairs. This morning, she'd been happy, her cheeks full of color that matched her vibrant pink tank top and her eyes shining with that magical inner glow. But that light was dimmed here. The shadows under her eyes seemed more prominent, just like the bruising at her temple. Ike would like what he saw, not only because she was beautiful but because she'd been hurt…because she was clearly troubled and suffering.

I hated it—hated she was here at all.

The door on the other side opened to reveal a guard, and behind him, a man shuffled in, legs and arms cuffed. The man was almost as tall as the guard, with broad shoulders and dark hair. His face was turned down rather than looking at us, and something spiked across my neck—a warning of something not quite right.

The guard shifted, and the prisoner stepped forward.

When he finally looked up, I expected to see anger and hate and maybe satisfaction in his eyes. Instead, I saw confusion.

One that matched mine.

"What the hell is this?" I growled.

The guard reacted, tension immediately straightening his shoulders, hand reaching for his baton. "You asked to see Ike Puzo, right?"

The prisoner's dark eyes took me in before jumping to Fallon. I pulled her from the chair and pushed her behind me. "We did. So go get him."

Surprise leaked over the guard's face. He glanced at the prisoner, brows drawn, and waved a hand. "This is him."

"This is not Ike fucking Puzo."

It hit me. The piece of the puzzle we'd all been missing. Andie had identified Ike Puzo when she'd seen his picture on Sweeney's phone the other day. He'd been in the bar, harassing her, and I'd thought it had been Tony Cantori before he'd been burned to a crisp.

Fucking hell. Ike had been out the entire time.

"Puzo-78. That's who this is." The guard was immediately defensive.

"Listen, asshole, this isn't Ike Puzo. This is Tony Cantori, his goddamn cousin. The one who was released earlier this year and supposedly died in a house fire. You morons let them switch places!" I was pissed, anger so deep and harsh filling me that I had trouble containing it. I had to fist my hands and lock my feet to the ground to keep myself from attacking one or both of the men.

The prisoner turned as if to run, as if to escape, but there was nowhere for him to go.

The guard spoke into his mic, voice urgent as he rambled away to his administrator. And while he concentrated on getting someone in charge, I finally moved. I shoved the inmate up against the wall, surrounded his neck with my hands, and squeezed tight enough to be a threat but not tight enough to prevent him from speaking.

"How much did he pay you to finish his sentence? And where the hell is he?"

Tony grinned, revealing rotting teeth. "I'm dying anyway." He showed me his hands. The fingers were bent awkwardly, and the tips were white. "Scleroderma slowly eating away at me. It seemed a fair exchange. He gets out and makes sure my wife and kid are set for life. I get to escape this hell my body has created. We figured we'd have at least a few months before anyone realized what had happened."

"Where is he?!" I shoved the guy against the wall so hard his head cracked against it.

He only cackled.

"If you think he'll take care of your wife, you're an idiot."

Something flashed in his eyes. Worry.

"Tell me where he is." I shoved my forearm into his throat, and he gasped.

"Ask. Ace."

The construction company. I'd thought Tony had met Ace through his job, post parole, but Ike already knew him. "How the hell does Ike know Ace?"

"Federal prison, man. Ace was here for that assault on national park grounds." Fuck. The piece we'd overlooked. How the hell had we all skipped right over the fact they'd served time together? "Once Ike and Ace both realized that a Marquess was responsible for putting each of them here—" His eyes drifted to Fallon, and I pushed my forearm tighter.

"Don't look at her. Don't even think about her."

"It focused Ike on getting out. He convinced Ace they'd get payback. With my family taken care of, everybody wins."

I pushed him away from me with a force that had him grimacing as he hit the wall again.

"I think Ike will have some fun with her tight little ass before he's done." Tony sent a grin in Fallon's direction. My fist connected with his jaw, and he spun sideways, a dark laugh filling the air.

"That's enough," the guard said, coming to stand next to me with his baton in hand.

One guard with a stupid-ass baton wouldn't prevent me from finishing off Tony, but it would ensure I had paperwork to do, ensure we were delayed in leaving. And I suddenly needed to get the hell out of there. I needed to get back to Rivers and find Ike Puzo before he did something more than mutilate a cow and burn down a building.

Fuck.

I spun around, strode over to Fallon, and hauled her to the door. I banged on it.

"Our administrator is on his way," the guard in the room said.

"Good for him. We're leaving."

The officer who'd walked us inside opened the door. His eyes jumped from the prisoner to his fellow officer and then to us.

I propelled Fallon past the guy into the hall.

The door banged shut behind us. The guard's heels clacked on the floor as he caught up. "You need to wait."

"Fuck that. This goddamn place released a convicted felon—one who has it out for my wife and her family. The last thing I'm doing is waiting around while you all pull your dicks out of your asses and try to figure out what happened."

As I charged down the hall, Fallon slid her hand into mine, squeezing. I finally looked down into her face. Fear resided there, but it was coated with the same burning anger lighting me up.

A man in a cheap suit and a regrettable goatee met us at the exit doors, blocking our path. It was unnecessary, as we couldn't leave until someone in the locked security room buzzed us through. "Mr. Steele, Ms. Harrington. If you could be so kind as to join me in my office."

I leaned toward him, and he took a step back. "No. You figure out what the hell went wrong on your own. My wife and I have more urgent business. We have people to protect because you failed at your job."

Inside, I was shaking with rage, but my voice was icy and calm.

The man hesitated.

"Our fathers"—my gaze darted to Fallon and back to the man—"both have the governor on speed dial. If you try to keep us here, I can guarantee it'll put the final nail in the shitty coffin that has become your career."

The man swallowed and then spun around to the windowed room where a guard sat. "Let them through."

I didn't say another word. I just strode through the doors as they buzzed open with Fallon's hand still clutched in mine.

"Goddamnit, Parker," Fallon hissed once we were out of the building. The full force of the midday sun in the Nevada desert hit us. Hot. Steamy. Burning like the anger I felt.

Burning like the guilt that knifed through me. How the fuck had we missed that Ace had spent time with Ike? They'd been in the same goddamn prison together, and not once had it come up on our radar. How many times would I fail her? How many times would I fail, and yet she'd still look at me like I was the hero of her story?

I nearly jogged to the SUV with Fallon's hand still wrapped in mine. Sliding into the vehicle, I ripped my phone out of the glove compartment and started the engine so the air-conditioning would kick in.

"He's been out. This whole time!" Fallon's voice was high-pitched, full of worry and genuine fear. "God. Mom. He went after Mom because Dad wasn't there…" She frowned. "But Dad was on the ranch for days after we came back from San Diego…" She shook her head, trying to pull it together.

"Ike was likely back East by then. Your dad's place was broken into, remember? And someone had to bribe whoever killed Adam. Bad luck for Ike that he showed up at your dad's house, ready to do him in, only to find him gone. That had to piss him the hell off."

"The first cow was mutilated while Dad was with me. He and Sadie and the kids left the next day."

"Maybe that was Ace. They're clearly working together. Or maybe they've been playing a cat-and-mouse game to torment all of you before pulling the trigger. Ike had to know it would hurt Rafe even more to ruin your name and the ranch's before he killed you. Rafe would come running back, and he'd have everyone in one place."

My heart fucking gave out even thinking about her being killed. That same terror I'd felt when I'd seen her on the ground after the shooting filled me.

Dad picked up on the first ring. "That was quick."

As I caught him up to speed, his swearing got worse and worse.

Fallon pulled out her phone and dialed her dad. It was hard to hear with both of us talking, so I stepped out into the hundred-degree heat.

"This explains the timing to some degree," Dad said. "Meeting Ace in prison encouraged him to act. They had eighteen months to hatch their plan together, and the timing was perfect with Tony coming up for parole."

"Someone inside let this happen," I snapped, looking back at the prison.

"It isn't necessarily someone dirty, Park," Dad replied. "Even with today's technology, there are still prisoners who escape using someone else as a cover. It's a real thing. It doesn't happen often, but once every few years, it occurs."

"Or he paid someone—maybe that weasel of an administrator who tried to stop us from leaving."

Dad's voice turned dark and protective. "They tried to stop you?"

"Not with violence. They didn't cuff us, but you could tell the shithead wanted to cover his ass before we screamed from the rooftops what happened."

"No way this gets covered up," Dad growled.

"Ace might be Ike's connection on the outside, but Ike would need to offer the cartel something in return for the cash and fake IDs he would have needed to pull this off. Especially once Tony was supposedly killed, and Ike could no longer use his IDs."

"Lorenzo was pissed that Tony was working for Lopez, dragging the family name back in with drug dealers. That's why we assumed he offed Cantori. But..."

Another round of fear hit my gut as Dad's voice faded away. Another possibility slithered out of the dark recess. "Do you think Lorenzo is really orchestrating this? Has he gone into business with the cartel?"

Dad didn't respond right away, carefully considering. "I

don't think so. Everything about Lorenzo Puzo is legit these days. But if Ike is on the loose, Lorenzo is in just as much danger as Rafe and Fallon. Ike hates everything his cousin has done. He blames him almost as much as he blames Rafe for what happened."

I opened the car door. "We're on our way to him. He can answer our questions face-to-face."

"I'll call Lance and the team at the ranch as well as Sheriff Wylee," Dad said. "You want me to tell Lorenzo you're coming to see him?"

"No. I want to see his reaction when I give him the news that Ike has escaped."

Fallon hung up with her dad as I slid in behind the wheel.

"Dad is making arrangements to come home." The fear that had taken back seat to her anger was at the forefront now, and it stoked my rage another notch. "God, Parker, Dad will make himself a target. He's trying to leave Sadie behind, but I heard her in the background, yelling at him. You know she won't let him come by himself."

She shook, tremors rattling her entire body.

I pulled her into my arms, the center console biting into us. I hated that I kept fucking failing her, hated she was experiencing any of this because we'd missed a crucial piece of information. I kissed her forehead, running a soothing hand over her hair. "We'll find and stop Ike before your dad even lands."

She pulled back and glared at me. "How? No one has even caught a whiff of him. No one even knew he was out. Only Chuck has seen him." Her eyes went wide, more terror filling in. "He'll kill Chuck. He's the only one who saw him at the ranch."

"Chuck couldn't ID him. The only thing he could say for certain was the guy had sunglasses, a hat, and a bushy beard." It was an attempt to reassure her, but I wasn't sure it worked.

Reluctantly, I let her go. I wanted to hold her until I could smooth away all her fears and trembling nerves, but we needed to move, needed to see Lorenzo and get back to Rivers.

"Dad is calling Lance, but call Kurt and Teddy. Make sure they keep an eye on Chuck too."

She did as I'd asked as we exited the prison lot. I put my pedal to the floor, speeding down the highway toward Vegas and Lorenzo Puzo with fury fueling me.

Chapter Thirty-five
Fallon

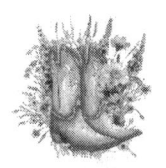

NOT READY TO BE NICE
Performed by Sasha Allen, The Voice

NINE YEARS AGO

> *HER: Spencer has been dead a year today. Sometimes, it feels like forever, and sometimes it feels like yesterday.*

> *HIM: I'm sorry, Ducky.*

> *HER: I can't decide if he'd love or hate what we're doing here. Dad has designed a flashy, Vegas-style fountain for the front yard. The centaurs move and everything. I think Spence would have literally pissed on it.*

> *HIM: Or he would have been grateful the land didn't end up in Puzo's hands.*

PRESENT DAY

Even though we'd stormed past his secretary, and Parker had immobilized his bodyguard in order to gain access to his office, Lorenzo still greeted us with a suave smile. He assessed us from those dark eyes as he stood behind the sleek desk in front of floor-to-ceiling windows with views of The Strip.

The bodyguard Parker had planted with his face in the carpet jumped up, hand going to his gun holstered below his jacket, but Lorenzo's dismissive words halted him. "That'll be all, Rick."

The man wasn't happy, but he left, shutting the door with a quiet click.

Lorenzo came around the desk, buttoning his suit jacket with one hand, and said, "Mr. Steele, Ms. Harrington—or should I say Mrs. Steele—what can I do for you?"

The fact he knew we'd gotten married sent a shiver along my neck. I didn't dare look at Parker, but I could feel the fury vibrating through him.

"Did you know?" Parker growled.

"Know about the wedding? Not until a little birdie sent me that interesting tidbit with today's report."

"About Ike, asshole."

Parker's curse wiped Lorenzo's smile away, but his voice was still smooth when he replied. "I play nice with Marquess these days. Let's not change that, shall we?" He waved a hand at the two chairs in front of his desk—black leather and chrome that matched the rest of his modern office. "Sit and tell me what's going on with Ike."

When neither Parker nor I moved, Lorenzo tucked his hands into his pockets and frowned.

"He traded places with Tony Cantori." Parker's voice was ice cold. "He's been out of jail since March."

Something flitted across Lorenzo's face, not quite fear but wariness. "I'd wondered, briefly, if it was actually Tony's body they found. It seemed too convenient that his wife and daughter were in Florida at the time of the fire. But then again, we all knew Tony was slowly dying. I assumed this was his way of ending his misery and ensuring Laticia got a tidy check from a life insurance policy."

The silence that lingered was heavy.

"He's working with Ace Turner and the Lopez cartel." Parker stated it as a fact, even though we had no proof. "Question is, are you in on it as well?"

Lorenzo turned his head, looking at the accent wall in his office filled with black-and-white photographs. The family pictures went back in time to when the Puzos had helped create Las Vegas with several other mob families. But the old images were mingled with newer ones of Lorenzo and the city's current elite.

"Since Theresa's death, I've made progress with Ike's side of the family. They know my goodwill and patronage lasts only as long as our feud remains buried. No one would help him." Lorenzo sounded confident, but another flicker of wariness crossed his face. "I couldn't understand why Tony would go to work for the cartel, but this explains it. With no one in the family willing to help him, Ike needed new connections."

Parker closed the distance in a flash of muscle and controlled fury. The move would have intimidated most people, but Lorenzo didn't even bat an eye as they stared each other down. They were complete opposites, but both radiated strength. Lorenzo's was hidden beneath a bespoke suit, while Parker's rippled from muscles pouring out of his black T-shirt and jeans.

When Parker spoke, his voice was dark and threatening. "If I find out you've even lifted a single pinky to help him in his vendetta, I will end you."

Lorenzo raised a brow. "You're becoming tiresome. Aren't SEALs renowned for their intelligence? This overly aggressive powerplay is the opposite of smart."

The two men stared each other down. My stomach, which had been doing ugly flips since Tony had walked into the prison interview room instead of Ike, did another round.

I grabbed Parker's elbow, tugging at it. "Let's go. He doesn't know anything."

For two seconds, I thought Parker might put his hands around Lorenzo's neck as he had Tony's back at the prison. I'd never seen Parker so aggressive. I'd seen him use his strength, but I'd never seen him raw and on edge like this.

He whirled around, grabbed my hand, and strode for the door. We'd barely opened it when Lorenzo's voice stopped us.

"Regardless of your impudence, I will do what I can to help you find Ike. I'm assuming he's the one causing trouble for you at the ranch? Spreading those lies about your involvement, Mrs. Steele?"

Parker's back stiffened, and he would have stormed back to Lorenzo if I hadn't used all my strength to hold him back.

"You know a lot about what's been happening for someone who hasn't been involved," I said.

"I always keep an eye on my family and my investments."

"Except, I'm not your family, and you have nothing to do with *my* ranch," I responded.

"Sadie and her children are my cousins. Your misfortunes fall on them and thus impacts me. Plus, Teddy Jones and I have a business arrangement he might be unable to repay if your ranch were to falter."

I couldn't hide the shock that hit me with the same force as the hoof I'd taken to the head. If I hadn't been standing next to Parker, I might have hit the ground. Instead, Parker's arm banded my waist and steadied me.

"What does Teddy have to do with you? With any of this?" I choked out.

Instead of answering me, Lorenzo waved as if dismissing us. "I'll be in touch if I find out anyone in my family has helped Ike."

The tremors running through me made it difficult to walk as Parker and I left the office. I started to comment, reeling from the news that somehow one of the men I'd trusted most had been working with Lorenzo, but Parker cut me off with a shake of his head. His eyes darted to the room's corners, where cameras recorded our movements.

We didn't talk again until we were in the SUV parked in the garage below Lorenzo's building.

In my head, I kept replaying every moment with Teddy since I'd returned to the ranch at the end of May. His smiles and his kindness to Theo. His obvious infatuation with Mom. He'd been around me my whole life, and I'd never once felt threatened or uncomfortable. I was weirded out a bit by the idea of him and Mom hooking up, but that was the extent of discomfort I'd ever felt around the man.

"Teddy..." I said, shaking my head. "I can't believe Teddy

has been working somehow with Lorenzo. For what reason? God...he's been cozying up to Mom. What did he hope to accomplish?"

"We'll find out. I'll call Sweeney and Cranky, and they'll interrogate him while we're on our way."

My immediate reaction was horror at the idea of Teddy being hurt. Regardless of what Lorenzo had said, Teddy was part of the Harrington Ranch family and deserved to explain his actions. Hadn't I wanted everyone to give me the benefit of the doubt when the evidence was stacking up against me? He deserved the same.

"You will not have him interrogated!" I exclaimed. "I'll talk to him. Me. He's my responsibility."

Parker didn't like my response. His face was grim, lips tight. "Fine. I'll let you have the first shot, but if he doesn't give us answers, or if we find he's had anything to do with you being shot at and terrorized, I will make him suffer."

It wasn't a threat. It was another promise—one that returned the churning bile in my stomach. Ace and Ike were working together. They'd bonded over a mutual hatred of me and my father. My family. They wanted to destroy everything and everyone I loved.

Fear spiraled inside me as my hand settled on my stomach. I could run, keep me and the baby safe, but this would never be over until Ike and Ace were back behind bars. It hit me. No one could find Ike, but we didn't need to find him. He would find me.

"I need to go home," I told him. "I need to be at the ranch."

Parker shook his head. "No. Not until we find out if Ike is still there."

"Either take me to the airport so I can fly us home, or I'll get out of the car and make my way there on my own."

His jaw worked overtime, and his hands clutched the steering wheel until his knuckles turned white. "I need to see Theo first. I promised him we'd be back today."

"He can't come with us, Parker." I shook my head. The fear I felt at the idea of Theo being close when Ace or Ike found me was beyond comprehension. It was torturous enough to imagine Parker being in my orbit when it happened, but at least he was trained to defend himself.

"I know," Parker finally said on a heavy exhale. "I'll leave him with Mom, but he needs to see me. He expected both his parents to return, and neither of them showed up ..." Parker's voice disappeared in a sea of emotions.

My heart constricted. I knew what it felt like to be abandoned. I'd felt it every time my dad had sent me back to Rivers without him and when Mom had disappeared behind her prescription drugs, leaving me to fend for myself. But Theo had experienced an even worse kind of abandonment. In dying, neither of his parents could repair the damage they'd left behind as my parents had tried to do over the years.

"You should stay with him," I said quietly. "He can't lose you too."

Parker's eyes narrowed at me, anger blazing. "If you think I'm letting you go back to the ranch and face Teddy and Ike—and whoever else is involved—on your own, you've lost your mind. Even if we hadn't said 'I do' and agreed to face this world together, I'd be at your side. You're not alone, goddamnit."

I bit my cheek until I tasted bitter metallic on my tongue. I just wanted this to be over before anyone else got hurt. But Parker was right. I couldn't face this alone. This wasn't something I could shovel my way out of. I didn't have the training or the knowledge to protect myself or the ranch from a man determined to destroy us.

A memory of Spencer hit me hard and fast. We'd been at the top of the mountain, looking down over the waterfall and the rivers as they twined toward the lake, and he'd said, *'It's a huge responsibility to care for this land, Fallon. Sometimes, you have to do the one thing you don't want—you have to rely on someone else. Don't make the same mistakes I have. Know when to bury your pride and ask for help.'*

For most of my life, I'd been determined to be the only one to decide what happened to the ranch. I'd resented Mom as she'd made decisions and controlled what I thought wasn't hers. I'd run to San Diego not only to honor my promise to my dad, but so I wouldn't have to watch my mom handle the reins until I could inherit them. I was sure I'd do it better once it was mine. I thought I'd be able to shoulder the entire legacy as Spencer had—on my own. But I'd forgotten his message somewhere along the way.

I needed to learn from the past—mine, Spencer's, and my ancestors. Maybe the curse Uncle Adam talked about wasn't from the poker game where one family had taken the land from another. Maybe it was simply pride. Arrogance.

I cupped Parker's cheek, running my thumb along his jaw. "Some of the worst mistakes my family and I have made were the moments we tried to face a battle alone. The legacy of the land doesn't just belong to me because of a deed and a bank account. It belongs to everyone who works the ranch, every person who loves it and invests their heart and soul into it. It's not mine to carry alone. Right now, I need you to help me keep it and the people there safe."

"I can't promise no one will get hurt, Ducky. Like you said, a battle is being waged against the ranch and your family, and there are always casualties in a war. But I promise to do everything in my power to ensure the ones who get hurt aren't you and yours. That it's Ace and Ike and anyone helping them who pays the price."

Renewed fear for Teddy wound through me and for Chuck. People who'd stepped across a line, maybe not even realizing they had.

Parker grabbed my wrist, kissed the palm of my hand, and then set it aside as he started the SUV and backed out of the parking spot.

We were going home. And for the first time in more years than I could count, that thought filled me with trepidation instead of peace.

Chapter Thirty-six
Fallon

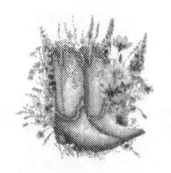

THE ARCHER
Performed by Taylor Swift

TEN YEARS AGO

HIM: Please tell me Dad heard wrong. Tell me you did not fly a fucking plane by yourself.

> *HER: Everyone is freaking out over nothing. It was harder to figure out how to get to and from the airports than it was for me to fly the Cessna. It practically flies itself.*

HIM: Ducky...that was fucking reckless. What the hell am I going to do with you?

> *HER: Go ahead, scold me like my parents. Be as hypocritical as them. Everyone expects me to be a goddamn adult when they need another pair of hands but calls me a reckless and impulsive kid when I actually make the tough calls and do what has to be done.*

Minutes passed.

> *HER: Sorry. I'm angry. And upset. Ignore me.*

Another few minutes went by.

> *HER: Taylor's right... 'who could leave me, but who could stay.' I make it unbearable.*

HIM: Don't do that. Do NOT belittle yourself.

L J Evans

You're just like her—your idol. You're ready for combat and showing everyone around you exactly what a hero should look like.

PRESENT DAY

The teary-eyed goodbye with Theo added another layer of somberness to the mood that had settled over Parker and me. The little boy retreated into himself, hugging Dog and nodding as if he already knew we weren't coming back, as if we'd already broken our promise. It was heartbreakingly sad.

The sorrow and fear all but swallowed me and made it almost impossible to focus on what I needed to do—fly home, question Teddy, and find Ike. I ended up having to review some of the items on my preflight checklist multiple times while the SEAL I'd married had already zeroed in on his next task.

While I talked with the tower, Parker downloaded everything he could find on Ike, his half of the Puzo family, Ace, and Lopez Construction. After we were in the air, he spent the entire flight digging through the research while I spent it anxiously coming up with a plan for my talk with Teddy.

It was dangerous to fly so distracted. Dangerous to be going home at all.

But I had to hold out hope that we'd be able to end this once and for all, now that we knew we were looking for Ike.

As we passed over the Sierras, I spoke with the tower and received the go-ahead to land. Much of what a pilot did was automated these days in the newer planes, more like watching a video game run versus actually flying. But the takeoffs and landings still required a steady hand and clear mind, especially as the airport in Rivers wasn't equipped for auto-landing. Those few moments were some of my favorite parts of being a pilot—the moment when I had complete control.

I started our descent, watching the horizon on our approach.

At about a thousand feet, two blasts rocked the plane in

quick succession. The cockpit shook, metal screeched on metal, and the wings dipped sideways.

A startled, frightened yelp escaped me.

The instrument panel lit up, alarms screamed, and my heart slammed against my rib cage.

Parker shouted, "What the fuck?"

I gripped the yoke, trying to steady it, as sweat instantly beaded along my forehead and dripped down my back. My gaze darted from one gauge to the next until it settled with dread on the landing gear warnings.

Panic surged, clutching at my lungs.

The landing gear. Something had happened to the landing gear.

A whisper of air coasted near my ear, and I swore I heard Spencer's soothing voice right next to me, swore I felt his hand on mine, guiding me through the counter roll to balance the wings. I focused on the horizon again, ignoring the smoke billowing outside the window and the dozens of ear-piercing alarms.

As I leveled us out, the runway approached chillingly fast. I had mere seconds to make a choice—land or take us back up?

Something was wrong with the wheels. If that were true, we'd crash no matter when we landed. And who knew what else had been damaged on the plane. Would we even make it into the air again if I pulled us up?

We were going to crash.

Goosebumps traveled over my skin.

"Get into the crash position," I said and was surprised my voice didn't shake.

Parker ignored me, demanding, "What can I do?"

Tears threatened as I remembered the sweet promise he'd made to Theo. *I swear, nothing on this earth will prevent me from coming back to get you, bud.*

And now, it would be my fault he broke it.

We were going to die.

My baby would die before she'd even had a chance to live.

Fear and despair tried to take hold.

Then determination kicked in. Pure obstinance.

No.

I could do this. I could fucking do this.

I could land without a wheel or two. It wouldn't be pretty. But I could do it.

I opened the channel to the tower. "Mayday. Mayday. Mayday. Rivers Tower, this is Cessna N18255. We've had an explosion on board. Landing gear damaged. We're at 909 feet and coming in on runway two. No time to dump the fuel. Emergency services required. Two adults on board."

Another set of chills wound up my sweaty spine. My hands shook, and I had to remind myself to breathe.

I'd barely stabilized the plane before the runway was there, the ground rushing up. I did what I'd always done, touching what should have been the first wheel to the tarmac. The moment we hit, the plane tilted. No second wheel caught, and we teetered like a chair with a broken leg. I struggled against the natural reaction to yank the yoke in the opposite direction. Instead, I countered it gently, but it was already too late. The imbalance was too much.

The plane landed on its right wing with another horrible screech of metal. My body went with it, my harness yanking me back and holding me in place so I didn't fall into Parker. His head slammed into the side window.

We careened down the runway on the plane's passenger side until we hit the edge of the tarmac and toppled off into the grass and dirt on the other side. The coarse terrain slowed us down enough that when we slammed into the concrete divider between the airport and the forest, it wasn't at full speed.

Stunned, I sat there for too long.

We were down. We were whole.

The airfield was too small for a full-time emergency crew. It would take them at least fifteen minutes to respond.

We had to get out of the plane, away from the fuel and the smoke.

"Parker!" I shook his shoulder. Blood dripped down from

a gash on his forehead, and panic bloomed inside me again. "Parker!"

I saw the rise and fall of his chest as my fingers landed on the pulse at his neck.

He was alive. God... Those damn tears flooded my eyes once more.

I had to get us out of here.

I braced my legs as I unlocked my harness so I wouldn't fall onto him. The plane rocked as I dropped so I was straddling him. When I bent to unlatch his belt, my brain objected. Already battered and smashed from the horse's hoof, it screamed at me for bouncing it around even more. With unsteady hands, I undid his seat belt and then straightened, reaching for the pilot's door that was now over my head.

The latch opened easily, but it took all my strength to counter gravity and fling it wide. The motion sent the plane into another dizzying sway that had me slamming into the instrument panel. I shoved myself away from it and turned back to Parker.

I pushed my shoulders under his armpit, using my legs to lift his dead weight. I'd tossed hay bales my whole life. I'd shoveled and dug and scraped my way through chores on the ranch. I had muscles, but they were out of shape from years in San Diego, and they groaned at trying to lift him.

"Parker, wake up," I hissed as his head rolled into me.

Somehow, I got him up out of the seat, but our weight sent the plane pitching again, and I almost dropped him into the back. I finally got him propped up against the pilot's seat while I eyed the door, trying to figure out a way to get him out first. Smoke and the scent of avgas drifted through the opening, burning my nose and making my eyes water more.

"Give me your hand," a deep voice said at the door. Relief filled me. Help had arrived. A mechanic or someone from the tower. The emergency crew couldn't possibly be here yet.

"Help me get him out first," I said, pushing Parker within reach of the man's hands.

"I'll come back for him. You first," he demanded. His face

was shadowed, the sun glaring behind him. I had a sense of dark hair and beard and nothing else.

"No. He's unconscious," I told him. "We get him out first."

The man swore, but he reached in farther and grabbed Parker's shoulders. I wrapped my arms around Parker's thighs and lifted. Between the two of us, we got him out the door. As he hauled Parker over the edge, I started to climb out and watched in alarm as the man carelessly dumped Parker on the tarmac near the back of the plane before turning to jog back to me.

He was wearing sunglasses and a baseball cap.

He wasn't anyone I'd seen at the airport, but then again, I hadn't been here often in the last few years.

He reached out a hand to help me as I jumped out. My feet had barely landed when the smoke and smell made me gag.

"We have to get away from the plane!"

I'd just pushed away from him, stepping toward Parker, when I heard the slide and release of a gun. The tip of a barrel landed on my temple, and I froze.

"We'll just leave him there." The voice was steady and dark. "If he dies, it's his fault for sticking his nose in where it doesn't belong."

My heart hammered against my rib cage. The adrenaline rush that had kicked in during the crash spun out of control, nearly taking my breath away. I turned slightly, trying to get a better look at the man I'd thought was our rescuer. He was exactly as Chuck had described him—a man hiding his features.

But I knew who he was now. Knew what he wanted. Dad. Me. All of us dead.

I swallowed hard, trying to move my feet, but they were lodged to the ground as if they were cement blocks. In the distance, I heard the faint sound of sirens. Fire engines. An ambulance. But they were still too far away to be of help.

"Give me your phone," he demanded.

"It's in the plane." I nodded to the wreck behind him. To my horror, I saw flames lick at the grass beneath it.

He thrust the gun into my temple once more, and the knot

there screamed in agony. His large, rough hands slid over my ass, checking my pockets to see if I was lying.

"I don't have it," I said, surprised when my voice sounded as calm as it had after the explosion. In truth, I was freaking the fuck out. Terror had me in its grip. For Parker, lying on the ground near the fire and fuel. For me, facing a man full of hate.

"Move," he said, shoving me toward the hangars. The action nearly sent me tumbling to the ground, but I caught myself and willed my feet to move.

My mind reeled. What was in the hangar? What could I use as a weapon?

How could I get away? Could I run? Would he just shoot me?

Would the fire truck make it in time to get Parker?

God. I wanted to scream Parker's name, wanted to wake him up.

But if I did, I didn't doubt Ike would simply shoot him before Parker even realized what was happening.

As we crossed the empty tarmac, there wasn't a soul in sight. Where was the tower crew? Had they gone for the fire suppressants kept on site? Would they get to Parker?

Once we reached the hangar, I started toward the side door, and he yanked my arm with enough force that I cried out. I hated myself for giving it to him, for letting him see my pain.

"Not inside." He pushed me toward a dark sedan parked next to the building. He popped the trunk and waved at me to climb in.

What could I do to delay? The sirens were getting closer. If I could just hold on a minute or two more, I'd have help.

Please just let them get to Parker before the plane explodes. Please, God, if anything, get him *to safety. For Theo. For my soul. For the Steeles.*

Parker would be wracked with guilt.

Dad would be distraught. Like Parker, he'd blame himself for not being with me when the worst had happened once again.

Mom would lose herself to drugs for sure.

My baby...my innocent child wouldn't even take a single breath.

I bit my cheek, holding back the tears. Ike might get my pain, he might be able to take my life, but he wouldn't see my sorrow.

Then, the realization hit. If Ike had wanted me dead, he would have already killed me. He would have shot Parker and me while we were inside the wrecked Cessna.

He needed me alive. For something.

The burn of bile grew up my throat as the truth landed. He needed me as bait. To lure Dad.

Which meant he was taking me somewhere until he could get Dad here. Somewhere help could follow. I just had to leave behind enough clues.

Parker would find them.

He'd fucking survive, and he'd come for me.

"Get in." Ike shoved me, and the back of my head hit the trunk lid. The world swirled until I thought I might actually vomit. As I put my hand to my head, the bracelet from Theo swung down my wrist. Lettered beads. The sweet gift. The sweetest message.

I swallowed over the lump in my throat and defied Ike as I tried to buy myself a few seconds. "No. You're going to kill me anyway. Just get it over with."

He laughed, dark and deadly, confirming my thoughts as he said, "Yes. But I need Daddy Dearest to show up first, and he needs to hear your voice to incentivize him to get his ass to Rivers."

"Fallon!" Parker's voice, groggy and unsure, traveled across the tarmac.

Ike shifted, keeping his gun trained on me as he pulled a second from his back and pointed it toward the runway, the burning plane, and Parker, who'd risen to his hands and knees. While Ike was distracted, I tugged on the bracelet with all my might, and it broke. The noise of the sirens as they approached hid the sound of some of the beads hitting the ground while I captured and shoved more of them into my pocket.

Ike glanced at me, and even with his eyes hidden behind his glasses, I felt the evil radiating from them. "I'll kill him if he reaches us before you get in."

I did what I was told and climbed into the trunk. He slammed it shut, and darkness swallowed me. The car rocked as he got in. The sirens had almost reached us as he started the engine and peeled out. My body rolled into the rear of the car, and I let out a pained groan.

I widened my feet against the side, bracing myself as the car sped up. I turned my attention to the trunk, letting my eyes adjust to the dark, scanning the space for the child-release latch. Hope flared when I found it, only to die when I pulled it and nothing happened. He must have disabled it, proving Ike wasn't stupid. Just vengeful.

I felt around, searching for the compartment, hoping to find a tire iron, anything I could use as a weapon, only to come up empty.

The windy back roads leaving the airport tossed me from side to side. I steadied myself as best I could as my chest grew tight with fear. Where was he taking me? What would he do to me when he got me there?

Dark thoughts, horrible thoughts from my past traumas blended with too much television.

I forced myself to focus on breathing. On the simple inhale and exhale. Forced myself to remember the most important thing. Parker was okay. I'd seen him rising to his knees.

He'd get away from the plane and the fire before the entire thing went up.

I had time.

Because Ike wouldn't kill me until I'd talked to Dad.

And that was his biggest mistake. It was the error that would sign his death warrant.

Because Parker would do anything to save me. My Navy SEAL. My bodyguard. My husband would rain hell down on this man for even touching me.

And I was going to leave him the clues to do it.

Chapter Thirty-seven
Parker

DON'T GIVE UP ON ME
Performed by Andy Grammer

TEN YEARS AGO

HIM: You're hurt. You're hurt because I left.

> *HER: I'm hurt because Theresa smacked me with her gun. That has nothing to do with you.*

HIM: I shouldn't have left you, damnit.

PRESENT DAY

I jerked awake with the scent of fuel filling my lungs and the haze of smoke burning my eyes. The crash! Fallon!

I rolled to my knees and screamed her name.

I stumbled to my feet. Blood trickled down my forehead that I ignored. I scanned the runway, flipping back to the plane's wreckage when I didn't see her.

I jogged toward the Cessna on unsteady feet. How had she gotten me out? And where the fuck was she?

Sirens shrieked. Too far away yet. Too damn far.

Flames licked at the tail of the plane. The dry grass of the runway ignited.

I pulled myself up into the open doorway. "Fallon!" I shouted.

It was empty. She wasn't inside.

Had she gone for help?

I spun around, eyes searching the runway and the buildings on the far side. A black sedan peeled away from the Harrington hangar.

Confusion settled like a fog over me for a second too long.

The blast on the plane. The crash.

It had all been planned. Carefully executed.

Goddamnit!

Why the fuck hadn't I checked the plane for bombs? Because I'd been too distracted by Theo's blank face, and Fallon's fear, and Puzo's goddamn games.

I forced my legs to move, racing across the tarmac just as the plane exploded behind me, sending me to my knees once again.

Fire engines lit up the runway, heading toward the flames.

I jerked myself to my feet and sprinted toward the hangar.

The side door was locked when I yanked on it. The roll-up door was down and bolted. I jogged in the direction the sedan had gone.

The tower. They'd have cameras. They'd have an ID on the license plate.

Something bright and shiny caught my eye. The realization of what it was hit me in the chest with the strength of a fist. Several of the beads from the bracelet Theo had insisted on buying Fallon were scattered on the ground.

He'd taken her.

She'd been taken on my watch.

I reached into my back pocket for my phone and came up empty.

Fuck, fuck, fuck.

I'd wasted too much time already. The sedan was long gone. He was at least five minutes ahead by now. My truck was locked in the goddamn hangar, which meant he'd be at least ten minutes away by the time I found a vehicle to go after him.

I turned back to where the fire truck had stopped by the

plane's wreckage. They'd already hauled their hoses out and were dousing the fire with foam retardant. An ambulance screeched to a halt next to the truck. Voices shouted out orders.

As I tore back across the tarmac, an EMT turned toward me. His eyes went wide. "Sir. Sir. Were you in the plane?"

"Phone. I need a goddamn phone!"

"Have a seat. We're trying to find the other person. Do you know where she is?" he asked.

I shoved his hands aside as he tried to propel me toward the back of the ambulance. "She's gone. He took her. I need a fucking phone!"

"Calm down. You're bleeding. Confused."

I swiped at my aching forehead and came away with blood. I'd have a knot that matched hers when I found her.

And I would. I would fucking find her.

I grabbed the man by his shoulders, flipped him around so his back was to my front and my arm was pressed into his neck, and demanded, "What I need is a phone. Hand yours over."

"Parker? It's Parker, right?"

My eyes jerked up to see a firefighter making his way toward us. His eyes were narrowed as he glanced from me to the EMT I had in a chokehold. The firefighter was the guy who'd been at Fallon's side the day of the cabin fire. He put a hand out as if to calm me down.

"I'm Beckett. This is Fallon's plane, right? Can you tell me where she is? She was onboard with you? Piloting?"

"She's been taken. I need a fucking phone."

Beckett's eyes narrowed. "Taken. Kidnapped?"

"For fuck's sake. Yes. I need a goddamn phone."

He whipped his out of his pocket. "Let Jon there go," he said with a nod toward the EMT. I shoved the man away from me, and he stepped back, anger pouring off him as he grabbed his throat.

Beckett placed a call. Wylee. He was calling the damn sheriff. I needed my team! I needed Cranky and Sweeney.

"I need to get to the ranch," I bellowed, but no one moved.

No one listened. I wasn't their commander. I wasn't their teammate. I needed mine.

Tortured thoughts of what Ike would do to her pounded through me.

I acted on instinct, heading for the driver's side of the ambulance.

"What the hell are you doing?" the EMT's buddy demanded as I pushed past him and into the driver's seat. I smacked my knees on the steering column. The keys were in the ignition. I started the ambulance as people yelled and shouted outside the door.

The last thing I saw as I put my foot to the gas was Beckett's scrunched face shouting into the phone he had clutched to his ear.

I was out on the road and heading toward the ranch when the ambulance's radio squawked.

"Parker Steele, this is Sheriff Wylee. Stealing an ambulance is not the way to go about this. We're assembling a team. We will find her."

I didn't respond, taking the corners as fast as I dared in an unfamiliar vehicle.

I'd failed her. *Again*.

I pounded my hand on the steering wheel. Once. Twice. A dozen times. I'd have bruises to add to the cut on my head and the pain radiating up my right shoulder. I didn't have a gun. But I had my hands, and I'd been trained to use them. I'd killed before using nothing more.

Where had he taken her? How long did I have before he ended her life? He needed her to lure Rafe here, and Rafe would expect to hear her voice, expect to know she was alive before he dragged his ass to California. Except, Rafe was already on his way.

Fuck.

I shook my head, focusing back on Fallon.

Ike would have to hide her somewhere.

Puzo had a place nearby, didn't he?

Goddamnit, I needed my teammates. I wasn't clearheaded

enough to see all the angles.

The longer it took me to reach the ranch, the farther away she'd be.

It seemed like an eternity before I flew through the gates and down the drive of the resort. I was screeching to a halt in the nearly empty parking lot before I remembered she'd shut the resort down. Thousands of acres of emptiness. Was he stupid enough to come back here? Would he think he was safe because he knew where some of the cameras were? But he didn't know about the new ones we'd installed. He couldn't. Not unless Lance was involved, and I hadn't seen any signs he'd turned on us.

Cranky jogged toward me as I climbed out of the ambulance.

"Fuck. You're hurt," he said.

I swiped at the blood again. "He took her. Ike took her."

He gave a curt nod. "Wylee called. We're pulling up the cameras now."

"Lorenzo Puzo has a place in the hills not far from here," I told him as we raced toward the security hut. "I need a gun. Comms."

"Slow down, Baywatch."

Anger and hate, primarily self-directed, spewed from me. "I'm not fucking Baywatch today. He took her. He has every intention of killing her. I have to find her before Rafe does exactly what Ike wants and shows up. If he does, Ike won't hesitate to put a bullet in both of them."

We'd just reached the security hut as a horse and rider flew up the crest beyond it. Every defensive instinct kicked in, and I shoved my teammate into the hut's exterior wall seconds before I realized it was only Chuck on the horse's back.

The kid was wild-eyed as he pulled the reins tight, jerking the horse to a stop as dirt kicked up around us.

"Fallon!" Chuck said, sliding off the horse. "He has Fallon!"

"Where?" I demanded, grabbing the kid's shoulders and shaking him. His eyes turned even wilder.

"I was watching the hawks through my binoculars," he said, pulling up the ones he had strapped around his neck. "I was across the river. It was closer to come here first. To get help."

"Where the fuck are they?"

"Off the fire road. Above where we were shot at. I was surprised to see her because I didn't know she was back yet. And then I saw the g-gun... He had it a-aimed at her. They d-disappeared into the trees."

I ripped open the hut's door. Lance and Sweeney were inside, bent over the screens, searching the cameras. I went directly to the gun cabinet, punched in the code I'd been given by my father, and yanked it open. The rifle was too big. It would only slow me down. I grabbed a leg and a chest holster, loading weapons into both. Cranky did the same next to me.

Behind me, Sweeney's deep voice said, "Stop. There."

I turned to the screen and saw the dark sedan I'd watched leave the airport stop in nearly the same spot where the offroad motorcycle had been parked the day of the shooting.

"Stupid to come here." Cranky swore under his breath.

I watched as the man got out of the passenger seat. Hat. Sunglasses. Gun tucked in his waistband like a loser. He popped the trunk and tossed zip ties inside as he pointed a second gun at her. I couldn't see her, couldn't see if she was hurt or bleeding from the crash. From his hands.

Rage consumed me.

Another few seconds went by as he spoke to Fallon while she was still inside the trunk before hauling her out. She stumbled, but he just grabbed her arm and dragged her along the dirt.

My fury turned into an all-consuming inferno.

Her hands were zip-tied, but he'd made the mistake of letting her tie them in front of her. It was easier to get out of them from that angle, although I doubted Fallon knew it. Still, it was another mistake in a sea of them Ike had made in the last hour.

Fallon's face was white as snow, and her hands shook as

she pushed her hair from her eyes.

Even hurt and afraid, her beauty shimmered around her. So fucking brave and strong.

And alone.

My chest nearly seized. I'd promised her, just as her dad had, that she wouldn't face anything horrible by herself again, and yet there she was. All fucking alone.

"Parker." Sweeney's voice drew my gaze from the screen to his eyes, full of the same rage and hate I was feeling. "Plan time."

"Rafe," I said. "We need to get him on the phone and warn him. Ike will make her call him. That's his endgame. Revenge against Rafe. Ace is the one who wanted Fallon." Fuck. Was Ace here? On the property too? I swallowed over the lump that formed in my throat. "This is all just fun and games to Ike until he gets his hands on the man who put him in prison, the man ultimately responsible for his sister's death. He won't kill Fallon until he's sure he has Rafe dangling from a hook and on his way. He'll need somewhere he can defend, somewhere he can keep her without anyone sneaking in from the rear."

"The caves." Chuck's shaky voice drew our gaze. He flinched under our scrutiny. He swallowed hard before continuing, "The caves the bandits used are in that direction."

He lifted his chin toward the cameras and the line of trees Ike and Fallon had disappeared into.

"How well do you know them?" I demanded.

"I know them well enough." The teen's voice had evened out, determination underlining it now.

The door of the hut bounced against the wall, and my gun was in my hand, aimed at the opening, before Kurt and Teddy drew to a stop.

Teddy—who had fucking something to do with Lorenzo.

All it took was two long strides for me to have him up against the wall with my forearm to his neck and my gun at his temple. Teddy's eyes grew wide with fear. Voices shouted at me. Cranky. Sweeney. Kurt.

"How much did you get?" My voice was a low, deadly

growl.

"What the hell?" Teddy choked out.

"Puzo. How much did you get for turning on her?"

Kurt stepped up and tried to yank my arm away. "Parker! What the hell? Stop!"

Cranky pulled Kurt back, and my arm pressed harder into Teddy's throat.

"Puzo threw you under the bus, Teddy," I snarled. "How much did you get, and what did you give him in return?"

"Fuck you," Teddy gasped. "You think I'd turn on her? On Fallon or Lauren? Fuck. You."

"What the hell is going on?" Kurt's voice was full of confusion and anger.

But it was nothing to the storm brewing in me.

"Parker, we can figure that out later. Right now, we need to make a plan," Sweeney said. His voice was calm. Serene. The team leader he'd always been in action. I was nowhere near my SEAL self. I was a bundle of emotions that ended up with deadly consequences.

Will had died for these same reasons—emotions clouding his judgment.

I shoved my forearm deeper into the man's throat before stepping back.

Teddy coughed, and his hands went to his throat as he sagged.

I turned my back on him and looked at Sweeney. "We'll follow their trail from the fire road just in case they don't go to the caves."

"Agreed. While you and I approach from there, Cranky and Lance can head directly to the caves from the river," Sweeney said, pulling up a map of the ranch on one of the monitors and dragging his finger along the path Fallon and I had gone with the excursion the day of the shooting.

"I'm coming," Kurt said, heading for the gun cabinet and pulling out the rifle. He was already loading it when Teddy joined him, pulling out a shotgun.

I tore it from his hands. "No. You don't get a weapon. And you will not be anywhere near her—ever again, if I have my say."

"Screw you," Teddy said, eyes full of a rage that matched my own. "She's like a daughter to me. If you think I'd do anything to hurt her or Lauren, you're an idiot."

Sirens filled the air.

I didn't have time for this. I needed to get out of here before the sheriff arrested me for taking the damn ambulance.

"Let's go," I said.

"Comms," Sweeney said, stopping me with a palm to my chest.

Behind us, the doorway filled with a huffing and puffing Wylee. "What the hell, Steele?" The sheriff's jovial Santa image dissolved into a furious demeanor that matched the mood in the room. "Why the hell would you waste my time, take me from a burning airplane and a double-murder scene to chase after you in a stolen ambulance?"

"Ike Puzo has Fallon," I said. I pointed to the screen Lance had frozen at a still image of the sedan.

Sweeney handed me a set of comms before handing others to Cranky, Kurt, and Lance.

"You can't head out after him without law enforcement," Wylee said. "He's suspected of killing two men in the tower at the airfield."

I just raised a brow. "You want to do something?" I waved a hand at Teddy. "Keep him the fuck away from me and this rescue mission."

Wylee glanced from me to Teddy with surprise. "Teddy?"

"It's not what he fucking thinks," the man snapped. "I'd never hurt her. Or Lauren. They're my family."

"Yeah, and Chuck here thought he was on the right side of the law too," I growled. I eyed the kid. He said he knew the caves, but how the hell could I trust him? He'd worked with Ike once before. What if he led us into a trap?

Goddamnit.

But he had come to get help after seeing Fallon at

gunpoint. It was easy to see the crush he had on her, and he'd been distraught when he'd thought she'd been hurt the day of the shooting.

I looked up at Kurt. "You know the layout of the caves?"

He wiped at his jaw. "It's been years since I spent any time in them. Mostly as a kid. I could get you around, but Chuck here probably knows them better than any of us."

The teen's shoulders straightened, and he raised his chin. "I can help you, Mr. Steele. I swear, I can."

"Fine." I looked out the door at the fading sun—another thing in my favor. Nighttime cover was a SEAL's friend. I turned back to Sweeney. "We got any night vision goggles here?"

He shook his head in the negative.

Damn.

Still. We were used to working at night. We'd make do.

I glanced at the screen one more time, focusing on Fallon's pale face.

Hold on, Ducky. I'm coming for you.

And if Ike had hurt even one more strand on her head, I'd make him suffer before I killed him.

Chapter Thirty-eight
Fallon

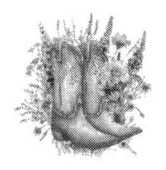

GUNPOWDER & LEAD
Performed by Miranda Lambert

TEN YEARS AGO

> *HER: Giles was Buffy's real dad. But he died and left her to fight alone.*
>
> *HIM: First, Buffy was never alone. She had the Scoobies. Second, we both know you're really talking about Spencer. So I'll just say that Spence was a good father, and I'm sorry you're feeling his loss, but don't give up on Rafe. He's no Hank Summers. Rafe will be there when you need him most. He loves you.*
>
> *HER: If I've learned one thing in this life, it's that you can love someone and still fail them.*

PRESENT DAY

The chill of the caves had already worked its way into my skin and bones, and the adrenaline that had fueled me earlier had slipped away. It meant I was shaking like a leaf. My mouth was dry, and I craved water as if it was a lost treasure. I was bleeding from a cut on my arm I must have gotten in the crash and hadn't noticed until I'd been sitting here for what had felt like an entire day already.

"Why the fuck isn't he answering?" Ike demanded, pacing

in front of me.

When we'd first arrived, he'd had me shackle my ankle to an iron rung pounded into the rock. It was old, probably used by the bandits who'd holed up here well before the Harringtons had owned the land, maybe even before the Hurlys had claimed it. If I wanted to escape, I had to get close enough to Ike to get the key from the front pocket of the sweatshirt he'd pulled on.

He didn't seem to care that I was freezing my ass off. But then, why would he when he only intended to kill me anyway?

After he'd made sure I was locked tight, he'd lit an LED lantern, and it had filled the cave with creepy shadows. Not far from me, a sleeping bag, a duffel, and a pile of food debris were scattered around. It angered me to see it, to know he'd been staying here for weeks, using my land as his base to taunt and terrorize me and mine.

Maybe I should have been afraid while I sat here shivering. Maybe I should have dreaded the moment Ike turned his hate and fury at me, but I wasn't. I was strangely calm because I knew what was coming for him.

The only thing that scared me was the idea of Parker or someone else I cared about getting hurt while trying to rescue me. Because they were all coming. Parker's teammates. Kurt. My security team.

I was not alone.

I'd never been alone, even though there'd been plenty of times as a kid I'd thought I was.

Instead, I was part of a team.

I'd do my part as one of the members. I'd free myself before Parker got here and distract Ike for long enough that Parker could disable him. I just had to get the key for the shackle tearing into my ankle to do it.

Ike stopped in front of me and hit redial on the satellite phone he was using to receive a signal this deep in the caves. When the call clearly went to voicemail, he shoved it toward me. "Tell Daddy to call back within twenty minutes, or I'll take a finger for every hour he makes me wait."

I shook my head, and he backhanded me. My head

whipped to the side. Thankfully, I didn't crash into the cave wall. I wasn't sure my concussed brain could handle much more.

He dug his fingers into the cut on my arm, and I couldn't hold back the cry of pain.

He stepped back and spoke into the phone, "You hear that, Marquess? That was the first finger. I'll take another if I don't hear back from you in an hour."

Blood dripped from a new cut on my lip, and I wiped it gently on my shoulder as I watched the key inch out farther from the pocket of his sweatshirt.

I had to get him closer again. I had to antagonize him enough to swipe at me once more. I was good at antagonizing people. It was a Fallon specialty.

"You should have taken your freedom and run," I said.

He twisted around, glaring at me in the weird half-shadows the lantern cast and looking very much like the devil he was.

"Not until I take a pound of flesh for every year I rotted away in that cell. Not before I take a life for every year Theresa's been gone. Then I'll hand you over to Ace, let him take his piece of you too. You'll be begging for death by the time we're both through with you."

I fought the immediate, visceral fear that tried to choke me at his words. Instead, I raised a brow and said, "Revenge has made you stupid."

This time, when he hit me, I reached out and swiped the key from his sweatshirt, tucking it into my palm.

He grabbed my chin, scowling down at me. "Defiant little shit. Maybe I'll enjoy breaking you before I hand you over to Ace. Maybe I'll call your daddy and make him listen while I take you. Maybe hearing you scream will make him show up faster."

"He's in Australia, fuckhead. It's not like he's in Vegas. He can't bend time to get here."

Dad would if he could. Hadn't we joked about him being a superhero and turning back time?

This time, when he hit me, it was a punch to the stomach,

and the pain that soared through me was followed by a brand-new fear I wasn't quick enough to hide. My baby. The little human Parker had already claimed as his.

Ike laughed. "There's the fear." He yanked my hair and pulled my face close to his. "Now shut the fuck up before I do cut that pretty little pinky off."

He dropped me and stepped back.

"How do you think you'll get out of here without being caught?" I demanded.

"I'm not as stupid as you think, bitch. I'm not telling you my escape plan. But I will take every ounce of revenge I can before I disappear. I already killed that bastard who shot my sister. He was easy pickings tucked away in jail. After I've had my fun with you and give you to Ace to gut, I'll finish Daddy off. Then, I'll take out that slutty trophy wife of his, followed by your siblings and your mother. The only thing left of the Marquess, Harrington, and Hurly families will be an ugly memory. Maybe, just for some added fun, I'll take out your boyfriend and his little kid too."

While he'd run on, he'd missed what I'd noticed. He'd missed the masculine, earthy scent of hope that had wafted to me in the dark.

I raised my chin, looked him in the eye, and said, "Husband."

"What?"

"He's my husband. And you forgot one important thing about him."

"Yeah?" he asked scornfully. "Like what?"

"Like I'm a fucking Navy SEAL trained to hunt and kill." Parker rose from the shadows behind him.

Before Ike could even lift his gun, Parker had slammed it out of his hands. Ike recovered quickly, kicking out at him. Parker grabbed his foot, twisted and tossed Ike to the ground. Ike snarled, pulling the second gun from his back. I screamed Parker's name, but Parker was already aiming his own weapon. Two shots rang out, echoing across the stone walls. Ike's body jerked. Blood bloomed on his chest and forehead.

Relief flooded my veins as Parker sprinted across the cave and slid to his knees in front of me.

The damn tears I'd been holding back threatened again.

God. Was it really over? Just like that?

All I knew was Parker was safe. Theo and my family were safe.

But what about my baby? Please, let the baby be okay.

A click from the dark behind us drew my gaze over Parker's shoulder just as a female voice full of as much hate and anger as Ike's said, "Freeze, asshole."

Parker's eyes locked on mine.

"Celia. You don't want to do this," I said.

Parker started to move, and she fired the weapon. I felt it in the air as it blew past me and landed with a crack in the rock to the right of me.

"That was just a warning. I do know how to use a gun. Turn around and scoot back against the wall," she said to Parker.

He swiveled on his toes but didn't sit.

"Put the gun down," Parker said. "And you might get out of here alive."

Celia laughed. "Alive? My life ended two years ago. This is how I get it back. I promised Ace I'd make sure the bitch died. I promised I'd make her suffer and I wouldn't let Ike fuck it up in his desperate attempt to get to her daddy. We don't care about Rafe Marquess. It's Fallon who destroyed everything for us! Making her lose everything, her reputation, her fucking inheritance, was only the start. I had it all in motion. I'd set her up perfectly with the altered video footage, the strand of hair on her sweatshirt, and her fingerprints. But Ike had to go and get impatient. He'd already waited years, so why the hell couldn't he wait a few more days?!"

Her voice had gone up with each word until it had become a brittle, sharp scream. She kicked Ike's dead body. "Fucking moron."

"You don't know anything about SEALs, do you?" Parker said quietly.

"What?" Her eyes jerked back to his face. "I don't fucking care who you are or what you do. It's just too bad for you that you came for her. Now, you'll die too."

As if she hadn't spoken, Parker continued, "You should care, Celia. Because, you see, SEALs don't work alone. They're part of a unit. A team."

Her eyes flickered for half a second before the muzzle of a gun landed on the back of her head. "Drop the weapon."

Sweeney shifted into the weird light of the tunnel. Celia screamed in fury, and she raised her gun, finger squeezing the trigger, but Sweeney reacted first. Her head jerked as the bullet blew through her. Her body swayed, and she hit the ground.

Dead eyes found me. The same dead, soulless, evil eyes that poured from Ike. The same ones I'd seen in Tennessee when Theresa Puzo had hit the ground.

My body quivered and shook.

Parker twisted around, scanning me. His eyes lingered on the slice on my arm still dribbling blood and the bruised flesh on my wrists from where I'd been trying to bust the zip ties. Then, he was kissing me. It was fierce and desperate and dark. I felt his fear and rage and relief in it, tasted the metallic of the blood from the cut on my lip.

And yet, it was the best kiss of my life.

Because we were all alive. We'd made it. The bad guy had lost, and we'd won.

Parker drew back and pulled his knife from his pocket. He sliced the ties and then eyed the manacle on my ankle.

"Fuck. Sweeney, we need a blowtorch," he said, looking back over his shoulder at his teammate.

"No, we don't," I breathed out. Parker turned as I opened my clutched hand to show him the key.

Surprise coated his face. "How the hell did you get that?"

"Used my expert antagonization skills."

His eyes narrowed on my swollen cheek and mouth. "And paid the price, damnit."

He unlocked the metal and then pulled me from the ground and into his arms. His warmth seeped into me, the love I felt covering the fear that still lingered in the air around us.

"They're asking for a sitrep," Sweeney said behind us.

Without letting go of me, Parker pressed a finger to his comms unit. "Ducky secure. Repeat. Ducky secure. Targets neutralized."

From beyond us in the dark of the caverns, a "Hooyah" sounded.

And that was what broke me. A sob escaped, tears flooded me, and the shaking took over in full force. Parker looked down into my face, his own turning squinty. "Damn it. Don't cry."

"I wasn't afraid, P-Parker. He was mad because I wasn't afraid, but I knew you'd come. I knew I wasn't alone."

Before he could respond, more bodies filled the cave opening, shifting in the shadow and light.

The rest of his team. My team.

Our family.

♪ ♪ ♪

In the quiet of my kitchen, I slowly pulled out the ingredients for the churro waffles that were one of Parker's favorite morning dishes. I was sore. Bruised and cut and tired. We both were, but our wounds would heal. We were alive, and the baby was okay. Those were the only things that mattered.

When we'd gone to the ER, and I'd told the doctor I'd been punched in the stomach, I thought Parker was going to lose his shit all over again. But the doctor had performed an ultrasound and said the baby appeared to be just fine. When we'd heard the heartbeat, the look Parker got on his face—the complete and indescribable love—had me falling for him all over again. He was madly in love with not only me but a baby that might not be his by DNA, and who he'd already claimed as his.

She was ours and no one else's.

While the ultrasound hadn't been able to reveal the gender of the baby, for some reason, we'd both taken to calling the baby *her*. It had to mean something, didn't it? Some kind of universal parent intuition? Regardless of its gender, the baby would be accepted and cherished. It wouldn't be an obligation to raise her. It would be an honor.

After finally unburying the waffle maker from the far recesses of the cabinet, I stood up too fast and banged my head on a cabinet I'd left open.

I swore silently just as the machine was ripped from my hands and tossed onto the counter beside me.

"What the hell is wrong with you? Rest! You need rest, goddamnit. For at least a week. No more bangs to the head or cuts or kidnappings. You will do nothing but lay around and heal. You'll take care of yourself and that little one inside you, or I'll tie you to the bed myself."

I rubbed my head and glared. "I wanted to make my *husband* breakfast."

His eyes flared. That word, that single word, got him every time, and my heart leaped with joy. I was going to like using it on him for the rest of our lives.

I fisted his T-shirt, rose on my toes, and kissed him before murmuring against his lips, "But I kind of like the idea of being tied up in bed as long as you're in it with me."

He snorted out a laugh. "That wouldn't be rest."

"How about if I promise not to move even an inch. Not even a finger. You can do all the work."

Stormy eyes met mine. "We might be able to arrange something like that, Wife."

My heart tripped at the matching word he was going to enjoy using on me just as much as I'd enjoy using *husband* on him.

I raised a brow. "Yeah? Then, when the doctor clears me, I'll tie you to the bed and return the favor."

"Fuck. Our parents are ten minutes from here, and I'm hard as a rock."

"Our parents?!" I scrambled to put distance between us. "Why didn't you tell me? Why are they coming?"

He looked at me as if I'd lost my mind. "Ducky, our plane crashed, and you were kidnapped. I think our parents want to see that we're all okay with their own eyes."

"Is Theo coming with your parents?"

He nodded, and that soft look returned to his face. Love.

No remainder of the furious Navy SEAL I'd witnessed yesterday was on his face today. But I knew it existed inside him. I'd seen it in action firsthand in a way I never wanted to see again. It was a piece of him he'd honed and developed and that he was giving up to be here with Theo, me, and the baby.

"Stop," he said.

"I want to hate when you do that."

"What?"

"Read my thoughts. But I can't find it in me to actually hate it, because it means you know me better than anyone. It means you love me."

Even as I said it, I knew it for the truth it was. He really did love me exactly as I'd always dreamed he would.

"You're right, Wife. I do."

He kissed me slowly and thoroughly in a way that made me hope our families would be a bit longer than ten minutes. But just as my knees went weak, a clatter of footsteps on the porch had him pushing me behind him.

At some point in my life, I might have been frustrated by those protective instincts, but instead, it filled my chest with warmth. I'd never be alone. I'd never be without protection, because I had someone who would always put me and our children first.

The lock clicked open, and Mom rushed through the door on two feet. Her moves were awkward and stilted, but she was upright on a prosthetic limb hidden below her yoga pants. Joy at seeing her standing had me rushing over to her, prepared to swoop her into my arms, but I didn't get a chance. She hugged me to her first, holding on so tight I thought we'd both topple to the ground.

"I'm sorry," she cried. "God, I'm so sorry I wasn't here."

I squeezed her back. "I'm sorry you were hurt before they came for me."

Then, Dad was there, striding into the house behind her and pulling us both into strong arms. For a moment, it brought back pained memories I'd tried hard to forget—us sharing this same kind of desperate and relieved hug after Sadie and I had been taken by Adam and Theresa.

When we eased back, Sadie was there, taking her turn squeezing me.

"You saved yourself again," she said, emotions choking her.

I pulled back to wipe at the tears on her face. "No. This time, Parker saved me."

"You left the clues for Sweeney and me to follow, Ducky," Parker said, easing in next to me. "You had the key to that goddamn shackle before I'd even gotten to you. I'd say you were well on your way to saving yourself."

Dad and Mom watched with narrowed eyes as Parker drew me to him so my back was to his chest and his arm banded my waist.

Before they could comment, I asked, "Where are Spencey and Caro?"

"We sent them on to Tennessee with the jet," Sadie said. "We weren't sure what we'd find when we got here."

Her eyes were cloudy, and I hated that what had happened was making her relive her own traumas—not only the time with Adam but the things that had happened to her long before I'd ever come into her life. But maybe it was those shared traumas that had bonded my stepmom and me more than I'd ever felt bonded to my mother.

When I looked over at Mom, she looked sad, as if she was once again on the outskirts of my life. Some of that had been her doing. Some of it had been mine. But I could fix it. I could jump the gap and pull her close. I could do my best to make sure she didn't feel alone any more than I did.

I moved away from Parker and clasped her hand. "I love you, Mom." Her eyes turned wide. I looked down at her prosthetic. "And I'm so proud of you. For your bravery and resilience. You know I learned that from you, don't you?"

She sobbed and leaned into me.

A car engine drew our gaze to the yard. The dark SUV had

barely stopped before the vehicle's back door opened, and Theo jumped out.

As he raced up the steps, Parker bent low, and the little boy flew into his arms.

"Missed you, bud." Parker's voice was thick and heavy with emotion. He extended a hand toward me, and I went to them, surrounding them with my arms and my love.

Theo was the first to pull back, looking from Parker to me. "Grandpa said the bad guy is all gone. Did you rescue Fallon from a tower like in that princess movie?"

I smiled, and Parker laughed. "A cave. And Fallon is a warrior princess who was already beating the bad guy at his own game before I got there."

"And you helped me," I told Theo.

He looked at me wide-eyed, pointing to his chest. "Me?"

I nodded. "You were right. The bracelet you gave me worked like a charm. I used it to leave clues for Parker to find me."

Theo flushed happily.

"We'll replace it," Parker said solemnly. "Then, you'll always have protection."

And in the rosy hue of sunrise that filled the house, my life felt miraculously whole. Not just because of this family Parker and I were forging but because of the people who'd stood by me my entire life, waiting for me to realize I'd never been alone and never would be again.

Chapter Thirty-nine
Parker

MAKING MEMORIES OF US
Performed by Keith Urban

PRESENT DAY

> HIM: *When is everyone leaving?*
>
> HER: *What's got you so growly, Husband?*
>
> HIM: *You promised I could tie you to the bed. It's been hard to concentrate on anything else since then.*

Fallon's house was packed to the brim yet again as dinner wrapped up. Our families, the ranch's staff, and our friends had been in and out all day. The mood had been celebratory. Evil had been banished. Love had won. But it still had come at a cost. A price had been paid in lives and trust and nightmares that would haunt us.

My new goal was to make so many good memories that the dark ones would be lost in the shadows.

Watching Fallon smile with her family and seeing her light shining brightly once more was a start to the happily ever after I wanted more than anything. How had I denied myself these moments tucked up next to her for so long? Not simply as her friend but as her lover, her bae, her husband. All I wanted to do was shower her with love and kisses.

I wanted everyone gone so I could do just that.

Theo's giggle drew my gaze from the text I'd just sent her.

He was teasing my dad about something he'd drawn. The kid was an artist. I'd have to find a way to encourage those skills…no, *we'd* figure it out. Fallon and I together.

That thought twisted happily in my chest.

Fallon and I had each tried to shoulder our lives alone for too long. But there was a beauty to shouldering it with another person, in sharing both life's burdens and joys.

"Time for bed, bud," I said. Theo groaned, but didn't put up a fight.

"Let me help you move the cot into my room," Fallon said, starting to rise, but Lauren stopped her.

"Keep him in my room. I'm only here for a day or two before I go back to the rehabilitation center to finish my therapy. I'll stay at the hotel."

"Mom—"

"I'm sure, Fallon. Don't argue with me on this one thing."

Fallon and I exchanged a look, and she shrugged. So I had Theo say his goodnights and helped him get ready for bed. He fell asleep before I even finished a book again, and I sat looking down at him for a long moment, wishing Will was here to see how much he'd already changed in just a month. How much he flourished tonight under the attention of a room full of adults.

Emotions were weighing heavy on me—love and regret and hope—as I came out of the bedroom to find everyone but our parents had left. In the place of friends and staff was the sheriff, and Fallon was watching him with a wary look on her face that made her seem paler than she'd been all day.

I strode over to the couch and slid in beside her, pulling her hand into mine just as he started talking.

"I wanted to give you all a final update before I headed home for the night. Lorenzo Puzo called the Las Vegas PD and pointed them in the direction of a cousin he thought might have helped Ike," Wylee said. "Bruno Manziniti has done demolition work for Lorenzo in the past and was one of Ike's best friends growing up. They caught Bruno on video leaving your hangar in Vegas the night before last. While he was being interrogated, a warrant was executed on his house, and they found two more bombs and timing devices similar to the one used here at the cabin and on the Cessna. We're still unclear how Celia was able to get Fallon's fingerprints on some of it." When both Rafe and I made annoyed noises of disapproval, Wylee cleared his throat and continued, "But we all agree that it doesn't matter at this time."

"I'd like to do something for the families of the men who died at the airport," Fallon said. "They were trying to help us, right? When the plane crashed. He killed them because they ran out of the tower?"

I heard the agony in her voice, the frustration that someone else had been hurt in this war that had been waged against her family. I hadn't checked the plane myself before we'd taken off from Vegas. That was on me. I'd failed. My head had not been on the mission. My love for her and my desire to find Ike had me rushing off instead of assessing all the possibilities.

It wasn't the only time I'd lost focus. If Sweeney and Cranky hadn't been here to help remind me of my training when I'd arrived at the ranch, I might have done something stupid. I might have gotten myself or Fallon hurt rushing in without a plan. While Sweeney and I had followed the beads Fallon had left behind, he'd talked sense into me. He'd centered me on the mission.

Get in, get the job done, and get out.

But those moments over the last two days proved I was doing the right thing by resigning my commission. I'd never be able to focus on the job when I had Fallon and Theo waiting for me here. I'd always be wondering and worrying about what was happening with them. My head would be on returning home instead of on the job.

"We're not sure exactly the order of events at the airport, and we'll never know for sure, as Ike is not alive for us to question him," Wylee said, sending me a dark look. But I didn't give a shit. I'd done what I had to do, and I'd do it again. If I had any regrets, it was not making him hurt before I'd killed him. But it hadn't been worth the risk. It was cleaner and easier to end him before anyone else got hurt.

"We'll pay for the funerals and put together a trust fund

for their families," Rafe offered, regret in his voice before it hardened again. "What's happening with Ace Turner?"

"Detective Harris scooped him up just as he was packing his car to leave. They had a look at his phone, and the last message was from Celia, telling him Ike had Fallon. Our best bet is that he was on his way here. He'll go back to jail for aiding and abetting and won't be out any time soon."

"And JJ?" I asked, his name burning my tongue.

"He seemed legitimately surprised Ace was involved in any of it. He hadn't seen Celia in months. JJ will do time for the charges already stacked up against him, but we can't tie him to any of this."

It burned inside me, knowing he'd be out before too long. But I'd have a nice little chat with him to ensure he knew if he ever came near my wife or her family again, no one would ever find his body.

The sheriff smacked his notepad shut and looked around at all the faces in the room. "I think that closes up everything."

But it didn't. An elephant still existed in the room that no one had mentioned today, even though his absence had been felt.

"You're forgetting Teddy," I said, purposefully keeping my voice calm and steady, even though every time I'd thought of him, his betrayal infuriated me. "What role did he have in any of this?"

Fallon's eyes snapped to Lauren's face. Her mom looked pale and shaky.

"If it's okay"—Wylee stood, making his way to the door—"I'd like him to be able to explain it for himself. He's waiting outside."

I wanted to say no. I wanted Teddy far away from Fallon, Theo, and Lauren, where he couldn't hurt them emotionally or physically. But Fallon squeezed my hand and said softly, "He deserves a chance to defend himself."

The sheriff left, patting Teddy on the shoulder as he passed him in the doorway. Fallon's body stiffened and tension returned to the room that had drifted away throughout most of the day.

Teddy's shoulders were sloped, and he spun his hat around in his hands while taking everyone in with eyes so sad I wondered if I'd jumped to the wrong conclusion. Maybe Lorenzo Puzo had thrown us in the wrong direction simply because he liked pulling strings and watching people jump. Or maybe he'd wanted time to ferret out the bad seeds in his nest before the cops started looking too closely at his organization.

When Teddy's gaze settled on Lauren, the look in his eyes was pure love. Adoration. Not a hint of animosity or anger existed. He was the same friendly man I'd always known, who Fallon had grown up caring about.

"I appreciate you all seeing me tonight," he said. "I realize I've got some explaining to do."

"Damn straight you do," Rafe said, stepping toward the man. Sadie grabbed his hand and held him back in much the way Fallon held me.

Teddy shifted, ran a hand through his hair, and then looked again at Lauren. "You didn't know what you would do when Fallon came home from college. You didn't want to crowd her—not at the resort and not here." He waved his hand around the house. "You said it was time for you to step back, but you didn't know where to go or what you'd do next."

Lauren blinked rapidly as she nodded, and Fallon's fingers tightened around my hand.

"Then, you got hurt..." Teddy's voice cracked. "And I knew, even with your prosthetic, there'd be days you'd be in a wheelchair. You needed a home with accommodations. A place with a ramp and bathrooms that would be safe for you to maneuver in."

Fallon looked from her mom to her dad and then back to Teddy. Her voice was choked with emotions when she said, "We didn't... God, we didn't think. Mom?"

Lauren shook her head as if to shake off the apology that coated her daughter's words. But she directed her response toward the farmhand nervously twirling a hat by the door. "Oh, Teddy. What did you do?"

"You'd talked about restoring the old Hurly place. No one has taken care of it since Adam went to jail, but it was yours. Your family's. It needed work to be habitable again and even more to accommodate your needs. I talked to a few banks, but no one would loan me the money, seeing as the house wasn't mine."

"So, Lorenzo gave you one," Rafe said, frustration in his tone. "How the hell did he find out?"

Teddy shrugged. "I'm not sure. You know he still has ties here in Rivers. I'm assuming one of the loan officers told him something. All I know is he offered to loan me the money. No exorbitant interest rate or anything."

"But there was still a price?" Rafe's voice was gruff.

"He just wanted to be kept abreast of how things were going here, said he felt responsible after what his kin had done to y'all. He said he just wanted to help if you ever needed it."

"You told him about the attacks on Fallon and the ranch." It wasn't a question when I said it, but he nodded anyway.

"I'd been sending him weekly reports since April, but once things started happening, he asked me to report to him daily."

It suddenly hit me. Lorenzo had sent someone to help. "The man who was wearing our security uniform and saved that guest at the beach. He was working for Lorenzo."

"Puzo said it was a safety measure, that someone here had to have been helping whoever was attacking Fallon, and that his guy could protect her," Teddy acknowledged.

Lorenzo Puzo was an unsolved riddle, threatening on one hand and protecting on the other. He enjoyed having all the power and holding all the cards, and information gave him that control. Maybe it was nothing more than that. Maybe Puzo simply wanted to prove he could find out anything he wanted and insert himself in whenever and wherever necessary.

Maybe he really did care about what happened to Fallon and her family.

When no one responded, Teddy shifted uncomfortably and looked up at me. "Anyway, that's why some of the cameras were off around the old Hurly residence and along the fire road leading to it. I didn't want anyone to see the work crews I had coming in and out of there."

"You've already started the renovation?" Lauren asked breathlessly.

He nodded and then smiled shyly. "They actually finished earlier this week. I used that drawing you made—the one with the garden blooming out back and the porch extending all the way around the house."

Tears streamed down Lauren's face, and she rose awkwardly, shifting on her mechanical leg and heading straight to him. She pulled his face into her hands and kissed him, sweet and slow and long enough that Fallon and I raised our brows at each other.

"Thank you," Lauren said softly, "for thinking of me."

"He didn't need to," Rafe said gruffly. "Fallon and I would have handled it if you'd told us what you wanted."

Lauren twisted around and glared at him. "I don't want you doing more for me than you already have. I'm not your responsibility. I haven't been for a long time. I have my own money—more than enough, seeing as you and Fallon ensured I received a cut of the resort's profits." She turned back to Teddy. "You didn't need to take out a loan."

He flushed. "You were so sad at that rehab center, darling. I just thought, if you had something to come home to, something that was just yours, it would help."

Lauren patted his cheek. "Why don't you take me home, Teddy? Show me what you did."

His face lit up.

Fallon was up and out of her chair before I could stop her. She hugged her mom. "You don't need to leave because of me, Mom. Not here or the resort. It takes a community to keep this place running, and you are an integral part of it. I *want* you to be a part of it."

Lauren brushed her hand over her daughter's hair, tugging at the braid. "Honestly, Fallon, I'm tired. I've been struggling and fighting for this place for too long. All of the Hurlys have. It's time to let go. It's your legacy now. You watch over it and see that it continues to flourish."

It took another round of hugs and quiet words before Teddy was able to draw Lauren's hand into his, help her down the steps, and take her away in his truck. Fallon watched from the porch while they drove off.

I was grateful when our parents followed their lead, stepping out of the house to say their goodnights. They promised to check in on us in the morning.

"Or you could just leave us to enjoy our honeymoon," I offered, keeping my tone light but also landing the point I'd wanted to make.

Rafe glowered, but my mother laughed.

"You have a four-year-old in the bedroom across from you, so I'm not sure how much of a honeymoon you'll actually have."

"Theo is right where he belongs," Fallon insisted. And I felt it all the way to the bottom of my soul. She'd claimed him just like I had. Just like I'd claimed the baby as mine.

In the quiet that was left behind as their vehicles drove away, I turned Fallon around and searched her tired face. "You've done too much again, Wife."

She put her arms around my neck and smiled. It was tired but full of that glow that was the essence of her, the light I'd seen most of my life, the one that had flickered briefly and was back with an extra force.

"Maybe you should swoop me into your arms and haul me to our room. You threatened to tie me to the bed, didn't you?"

I didn't even bat an eye. I simply did just that, striding down the hall with renewed purpose.

She laughed the whole way, and I promised myself I'd make her laugh every single day for the rest of our lives. I promised there would always be more joy than sorrow, more pleasure than pain, and more love than hate in her life. In *our* lives.

When I set her on the bed and tried to step back, she latched on like a monkey. The unexpectedness caught me off guard, and I toppled onto the mattress. I barely had time to brace myself and prevent my full weight from landing on her.

Her mouth found mine. Greedy. Hungry. Full of all the same pent-up longing I'd felt all day.

Clothes disappeared, and skin glided against skin. Mouths and hands caressed and cherished and teased. I watched in awe and fascination as she started to slip over the edge, chanting my new favorite word, before I slid home, planting myself deep inside her with a satisfied groan. Her hips thrust into me, and I settled my hands on them, holding her down.

"No activity from you, Wife," I growled, mouth brushing against hers.

"It feels too good."

"Don't make me stop," I said, meeting her gaze with mine. It was supposed to be a command, but it came out more like a beg.

Her smile was stunning and beautiful. Her fingers traveled over my lips.

"I waited a lifetime for you to say that, to beg just like that. *Never* wasn't quite as long as either of us expected, was it?" Mischief lit up those amber eyes along with lust and love and relief.

It wasn't the goddamn tease that did me in but the grateful knowledge that *never* hadn't been the end of us. I'd finally torn down the boundaries I'd put up and fallen right where I'd always wanted to be. With her. Completely and utterly twined with her in body, heart, and soul.

We went over the swell together.

The way I promised we'd do everything from here on out.

Chapter Forty
Fallon

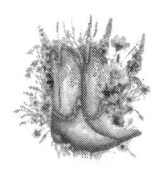

LIVING IN THE MOMENT
Performed by Ty Herndon

PRESENT DAY

> HIM: *Did you change my alarm tone, Wife?*
>
> HER: *I can't wake up to that metal racket again, Husband.*
>
> HIM: *But did you have to choose that country song? Do you want my nuts to shrivel up every morning?*
>
> HER: *If that's all it takes to shrivel your nuts, we have bigger problems.*

My thoughts were conflicted. Part of me itched to escape the house where I'd been all but locked up for the last few days, and part of me never wanted to leave it again. I'd shared tantalizing dream-like moments in the quiet with Parker and teasing laughter-filled moments with him and Theo. And in between, our family and friends had drifted in and out, bringing food and information.

But today, I couldn't stay tucked away in our little hideaway again. It was a big day for the resort, and I was determined to be a part of it. While the Fourth of July could be a problematic holiday, the Harrington Ranch had done its best to make it a community-building event, something that brought us together instead of tearing us apart. I was overjoyed that Andie and the mayor had been able to restore the festivities to the ranch in such a short time.

My injuries would limit me this year—I wouldn't ride Daisy in a show—but I'd spend the day with Parker and Theo. We'd visit the game booths, stuff our faces with junk food, and root on our favorites in the various competitions. We'd end up lakeside, enjoying a huge barbecue dinner we served for free to the entire town, and watch as folks danced to the live band we'd finagled into showing up last minute.

It was actually Parker's dad who'd pulled some strings and found us a replacement. The wife of Jim's old SEAL buddy had previously worked for the one and only Brady O'Neil, and once the country artist had learned about our troubles, he'd packed up his wife and hoodwinked his daughters into flying here and helping out. So our evening would end with his performance and a spectacular fireworks display over the lake.

We were just finishing up slathering ourselves with sunscreen and donning hats when my mom arrived with Teddy. They brought the masked puppy Teddy had given to Theo, and from the moment they arrived, the yard was chaos. Mom and I watched from the porch as the men chased the dog through flowerbeds and brush, trying to put a leash on it, while the little boy squealed with delight.

"Love looks good on you," Mom said softly, nudging my shoulder.

I turned to take her in. Her cheeks were flushed, but it wasn't from drugs. Her eyes were clear and sparkling. Her lips were tilted upward. My heart hurt for all she'd been through, but somehow, she'd finally found her feet again.

I nudged her back. "Looks good on you too."

She blushed to her roots and looked out at Teddy. "I loved Spencer and your dad both so fiercely. But looking back, sometimes I'm not sure if it wasn't tainted with that Hurly desperation, that need to reclaim what once was ours. Adam went about it by hurting people. I think I went about it by trying to make them love me." She was quiet for a long moment. "With Teddy, it's just about us. Him and me. Nothing else. No past lives hanging on us. No expectations. I feel…wooed." She laughed. "Such an old-fashioned word, but it fits."

Teddy glanced our way, and the sweetness of the look he sent my mom proved her point. Teddy was an old-fashioned kind of guy. I hated that, for a few moments, I'd thought the worst of him. I wasn't crazy he'd been sending reports to Lorenzo on me and the ranch, but I could appreciate why he'd done it. I could even love that he'd had Mom's best interest at heart when I'm not sure anyone—not even me—had thought of her first in years. Maybe ever. She deserved that sort of affection and dedication as much as I did.

"When I come home from the rehabilitation center," she said. "I won't be stepping back into my role at the resort." I started to reply, and she cut me off. "No, I mean it, Fallon. I want something easier. I want to get back up on a horse with my new leg and take long, aimless rides through the hills with Teddy at my side." She shifted on her mechanical foot. "And I want to help him grow his dog-breeding business. I want him to have something that's his after all he's done for me."

I swallowed hard. "I guess I'll be hiring two new people."

She smiled, wrapping her arm through mine and then resting her head on my shoulder. A squirrel appeared on a tree branch, chattering angrily down at the ruckus the puppy and the men were making. The puppy headed straight for it, and Parker had to use his long legs and agility to catch him before the dog disappeared into the brush.

Mom laughed. "You're going to have your hands full. You sure you're up for it? Taking the ranch on and becoming a wife and a mother in one fell swoop?"

For a moment, I was startled, thinking she meant the baby, but then I saw her eyes on Theo and relaxed. For the first time in more years than I could remember, I wanted to tell my mom my secret. She'd keep it. She was good at keeping secrets. But then I watched as the smile spread over her face when Teddy tipped his hat in her direction, and I bit my tongue.

It could wait. For now, she needed more joy than worry.

We all did.

"I love you, Mom. I wish…" I shook my head. I didn't know what I wished. That I'd been more forgiving as a teen? More understanding? That she'd reached out instead of pulling away? I didn't know.

She tugged my braid. "No regrets, Fallon." She waved to the yard and the men and the ranch. "Somehow, we all ended up where we were supposed to be."

Goosebumps covered my skin, not in fear or dread, but at the sheer enormity of her words. The sheer truth.

"Teddy, take me home. My leg is ready for a break," she shouted, and he instantly jogged over to the porch and held out a hand to help her down the steps.

"You're not going down to the resort?" I asked. I couldn't remember the last time Mom hadn't been a part of the Fourth of July activities.

"We have better things to do," she said with a wink.

"Um. No. Just no. I don't want to know or think or even hear about it," I said.

She laughed, and just that sound eased something in my chest. She was free. Maybe we had been cursed, but if we had, it was gone now. Mom would be happy. The ranch would thrive. And I'd have Parker and the life I'd once dreamed about.

As Teddy's truck left, kicking up a cloud of dirt, Parker strode toward the porch with a wiggling puppy wrapped in his arms, the leash attached to its collar dangling in the dirt, and Theo running after them. They were already dusty and rumpled, and our day hadn't even really begun. But I loved it. Loved the joy and pleasure that it signified.

"Ready to go celebrate, Husband?" I asked and was rewarded with that stormy look returning to Parker's eyes. The look that was all mine and usually ended with us twined skin on skin.

"You don't play fair, Wife. I have to wait hours to reward you for using that word."

"Don't worry, I'll keep track, and I'll make sure I get what's coming to me."

"Theo, grab Bandit's leash," he said.

Parker had barely handed off the leash before he was dragging me to him. With a hand on the back of my head, Parker slanted his mouth over mine, claiming me and lighting me up.

Every nerve ending burst into flames.

I was just thinking maybe we didn't need to go down and celebrate with our family, my staff, and the whole damn town, that maybe we'd stay home just like Mom and Teddy, when Parker broke our kiss and grinned at me.

"Now you'll be as hungry as me."

"I'm hungry too!" Theo said, lifting the hand with the leash up in the air. The dog escaped, Parker chased after him, and my heart nearly exploded with love and hope and joy.

Epilogue
Parker

(I'VE HAD) THE TIME OF MY LIFE
Performed by Bill Medley and Jennifer Warnes

EIGHT MONTHS LATER

>*HER: Do you know what time it is, Husband?*
>
>*HIM: Time for me to come home and reward you for using my favorite word.*
>
>*HER: As much as I'd love that, it's time for you to meet me at the hospital.*

"*Hurry the fuck up,*" *I told* Sweeney, "or pull over and let me drive."

"I'd like to make it into town in one piece, thank you," Sweeney groused.

"I knew I shouldn't have gone up today," I growled, hitting my fist on the dash.

Our baby girl had helped us out by holding on to her mama and being two and a half weeks past her real due date. It meant no one would think twice when Fallon went into labor a couple of weeks earlier than when we'd told everyone she was due. But I'd been sweating it out every day.

And this morning, when Fallon had felt more uncomfortable than usual, I'd almost cancelled the flight planned for the ROTC kids. But she'd insisted I go, insisted my fledgling business needed to honor its commitments. "How will it look to kids you're trying to teach about duty and honor if you don't show up?"

I'd hated that she'd been right. But for the first time since Sweeney and I had started the flight school, I hadn't looked forward to going to it.

Sweeney and I had resigned our commissions in September and spent five months getting the school up and running. We were training the high school kids pro bono. It served as both charity and advertisement, making us look good to the community and the government bigwigs who still had to approve our contract for the military training we had planned.

We'd barely hit the ground after the jump with the teens, repacked the parachutes, and started a debrief when my phone had started jangling.

Lauren hadn't sounded frantic. She'd been perfectly calm, but knowing Fallon had been in the far field, checking on the goddamn cows, when her water broke was enough to make me more agitated than I'd ever been.

"I told her to stay close to the resort today, but did she listen?" I asked.

Sweeney grinned at me. "Did you really expect her to?"

No. I loved her for that independent, defiant nature. For the endless energy that meant she could work hard all day and then spend hours tangled with me in the sheets at night.

Back in July, when I'd made Fallon mine, I hadn't thought I could love her more, hadn't thought I could love anyone more, but I'd been wrong. Every day, the love I felt for her, Theo, and the little girl inside Fallon seemed to expand until it was spinning out endlessly, until I'd finally realized it would never stop growing. I'd always love them more today than I had the day before. More with this very breath than I had the last.

Sweeney turned the corner, and the hospital finally came into view.

The truck hadn't even stopped before I leaped out, running at full speed for the entrance. I knew the way to the maternity ward like the back of my hand. I'd done enough reconnaissance missions to make sure I could get us here in record time.

At the outer doors of the ward, I pushed the intercom and tried to keep my voice calm as I asked to be let in. The nurse at the desk directed me to a room, and I jogged in just as a gasp of pain escaped my wife.

She was in a hospital gown, brows furrowed, sweat beading on her forehead, braids askew, cheeks flushed, and she'd never looked more beautiful—another thing that seemed to grow every second of every day.

"What's wrong?" I demanded, all but pushing Maisey aside to take Fallon's hand.

Maisey chuckled, noting something down on her tablet. "Nothing, idiot. She's in labor."

I turned to see Lauren in the corner of the room, pacing. Her stride was smooth these days. If you didn't know she had one mechanical leg, you'd never be able to tell by how she moved. She did everything with the same powerful movements as her daughter.

A moment later, Fallon relaxed, the anguish disappearing from her face, and a small grin took hold. "So. How did the flight go?"

I chuckled. "Damnit, Ducky. Don't make small talk. I'm mad at you."

"I knew you would be," she said. "Everything is fine. She's fine. I'm fine. You're here. That's all that matters."

"Where's Theo?"

"With Teddy."

"Why were you in the goddamn far field with the cows?" I demanded.

"Because she's the most stubborn person I've ever known," Lauren said, approaching the bed. "More stubborn than even her father—and that's saying something."

"Oh God, here we go again," Fallon said, hunching over, pain coating her face, and grabbing my hand and strangling it.

"Has the doctor been in? What happened to the epidural?" I snapped.

"The doctor's been in and out, and she's had an epidural," Maisey said calmly.

"And she's still in this much pain?" I croaked. Fallon had an enormously high pain tolerance. I'd seen it firsthand. Broken fingers. Cracked heads. Emotional distress. She rarely even blinked through half of it.

"If you can't stay calm, you'll be asked to leave," Maisey said with a wink.

"Like hell am I leaving." I focused on Fallon, watched her breathe through the worst of the contraction, and then my entire being eased as her face relaxed again.

"Ducky," my voice broke. I hated seeing her this way, hated there was nothing I could do to ease it or make it go faster or to skip time till the worst was over.

But she wasn't alone. I'd promised her never again, and I'd keep that promise today just as I did every single day of our lives.

♪ ♪ ♪

Hours later, I was still in awe of Fallon, women in general, and the sweet little girl wrapped up in my arms as I sat on the bed next to my wife. When the nurse had come in with the baby, she'd given her to me instead of waking up Fallon, who was asleep with her head on my shoulder.

Lila was fussing, wiggling, and almost ready to cry. I placed a gentle kiss on her forehead, and she scrunched her face. I wanted to laugh because the expression was just like Fallon's had been when she'd been a little girl and hadn't gotten what she wanted from Rafe.

I ran a finger along her cheek as words I never thought I'd sing came quietly pouring out of me. "I've had the time of my life… And I owe it all to you…"

"I wish I was recording this," Fallon teased, shifting next to me. "I bet I'd get good money selling it to Sweeney and the gang."

I ignored her and kept singing to my daughter until Lila's little lashes drooped, and her fussing stopped.

All I could do was stare in wonder at the beauty of her.

Fallon trailed a finger along the baby's downy hair. Fine and thin but light, like her mama's. "She looks like me, don't you think?"

I heard the worry in her voice, the fear that somehow the little girl would end up looking more like JJ than her. That someone would question who the father was.

I shifted, putting Lila in her arms and then pulling them both against my chest. "I know they say babies look like nothing, like little impressionable blobs, but I don't agree. She does look like you. Even your mom said so."

Fallon stared into Lila's face with a fierce look, one full of love and determination—one I'd seen Fallon give me and Theo and all the people she cared about. But somehow, this time, it was different, as if she was daring the universe to try to take the baby from her.

I'd sworn I wouldn't bring up his name today, wouldn't even give him a thought, but he was in the room with us anyway. He was bringing fear to a day that should have been nothing but joy.

In the months since he'd been arrested, JJ had reached out to Fallon twice. The first time, she'd gotten a letter. The second time, it had been a message left with the front desk at the hotel. Both times had sent her into a tailspin of worry.

On one of my trips down south to meet with my former commander about the training facility Sweeney and I were building, I'd stopped by the prison where JJ was doing his time. I'd pulled some strings, so I'd been able to walk right into his cell instead of meeting with him in an interview room. The message had been crystal clear—it would be easy for me to get in and finish him off if he ever contacted her again. And it would be even easier to get to him once he'd done his time and was out on parole. If he wanted to live to see his forties, he'd forget he ever knew someone named Fallon.

Prison had already beaten him by the time I got to him. He'd already been skittish and wide-eyed. My threat had landed on perfectly persuadable ears.

I hadn't kept the visit from Fallon. I'd simply told her after the fact. I wanted her to know he'd be stupid to even come near her, to even lift a finger in her or Lila's direction. But the truth was, she'd always have a teeny-tiny fear I wouldn't be able to completely wash away without ending JJ's life. But she wouldn't let me. She didn't want me to have that on my conscience. I didn't care about mine, but I did care about hers, and she'd carry the weight of the loser's death if I killed him.

So I didn't. But I would, without hesitating, if I ever sensed he'd become a real threat.

"She's you," I told Fallon, "from the top of her head to her little tiny toes, and all the way into that fierce heart." I kissed Fallon's forehead before placing a similar one on Lila's. Our daughter's lashes fluttered back open to stare at us with as much wonder as we were staring at her. "But you see that look in her eyes? That's all Steele. She's mine."

I was surprised to see a tear land on the baby's cheek. Fallon quickly wiped it away, and I pulled her chin up, watching helplessly as more tears fell from her eyes. "What's wrong, Ducky?"

She leaned in and kissed me…with love and passion and hope.

"It's the stupid hormones. I'm happy, Parker. So happy. Thank you for choosing her. For claiming her just like you claimed me and Theo. For agreeing to my stupid proposal and making us a family. Thank you for loving us enough to give up your dreams and be here with us every day."

"I haven't given up my dreams," I insisted once again. I'd told her this a hundred times over the last eight months, but I'd just keep telling her until she finally believed it. "I didn't ring a bell, Ducky. I didn't give up or give in or choose something lesser. I simply signed up for something greater, with much better rewards. Thank you for showing me it was possible. For giving me a better life than I'd ever imagined for myself."

I kissed her, trying to infuse every ounce of love I had for her, our children, and our life into it so she would finally accept the truth—this was the only dream worth living.

♫ ♫ ♫

Thank you for reading Fallon and Parker's heart-stopping spin-off of my Hatley Family series. I hope you loved it as much as I loved writing it. If you're not ready to let Fallon and Parker go quite yet, you can **download a bonus epilogue** to see what happens when Parker finds out Fallon is pregnant again. **You'll also get a hint of what's coming next to the town of Rivers with Maisey and Beckett's second-chance story.**

Free with newsletter subscription

And if you're looking for **more single-dad, small-town, grumpy-cowboy, romantic suspense** and haven't read the original Hatley Family series, you can get all three books now in Kindle Unlimited. Check out this sample:

SAMPLE
THE LAST ONE YOU LOVED
Prologue - Maddox

AIN'T ALWAYS THE COWBOY
Performed by Jon Pardi

The lake shimmered in the moonlight. The warm breeze stirred up tiny waves, sending white sprinkles shifting across the surface as it drifted toward the shore where we were parked.

We were on the tailgate of my beat-up Bronco with our hands and limbs joined. McKenna's jean-clad legs were flung over my lap, and her head rested on my shoulder. Her cowboy boots were off, lost somewhere behind me in the chaos of blankets and food wrappers. I ran the fingers of my free hand over the gentle arch of her foot, and she jerked it away, laughing.

"Don't you dare tickle me unless you want to end up with a busted nose," she teased, her soft voice washing over me.

It wasn't like I hadn't known she'd pull away. Ten years of knowing her meant I knew just how ticklish her feet were, but I'd done it anyway in an attempt to lighten the mood. But the sound and scent and feel of her made it almost impossible to feel anything but sorrow. It might be the last time I would hold her like this, and my heart screamed as if it could change what was happening by merely twisting inside my chest.

"Wanna go for a swim?" I asked.

It was still humid outside, even though the sun had set hours ago. Long enough that the twilight sounds of the bugs and wild animals had almost disappeared. Instead, a quiet had taken over the space, a preview of what would happen once she drove down the road tomorrow and my life was forever changed.

In answer to my question, she slid off of me and started discarding clothes. She was wearing a string bikini under her jeans and floaty blouse, as if she'd known I'd ask for this—us in the water. I swallowed hard at the gentle curves I'd spent years getting to know as well as my own. I glanced down at my sinewy body toughened from years of working on the ranch. She'd always said my muscles were the very best kind—built from hard work. Would anyone else ever care about them the way she had?

I hadn't been as prepared as she'd been for a swim, so my boxer briefs were going to have to do. Once I'd stripped down, I recaptured her hand, determined to touch her for as long as possible, and led us toward the water, picking our way through the twigs and rocks as we went.

As soon as we hit the cool water, I shivered. It was a soothing relief to the heat and heaviness of the day. If only it could lift the weight inside me as easily as it chilled my skin.

We swam toward the makeshift dock someone had fastened to the middle of the lake decades ago. We didn't pull ourselves up on top. Instead, we hid in the shadows. She wrapped her long limbs around my waist, and I looped an arm through one of the ropes hanging off the wooden slats to hold us steady while my hands continued to touch her.

She kissed me. Wet and wild. Slow and torturous. Love and goodbyes blended into the movements as we rejoined our bodies in the way we'd been doing over the last couple of months. Like a flame on the wick of a firecracker, burning, burning, burning until it finally ignited into a shower of light and sound.

Until it became nothing but us.

She moaned into my mouth when my fingers slid under her bikini, touching pieces of her that were aching for me. I wanted to cry out as well, but with a different ache. I wanted to let my tears wash into the lake.

But it would be selfish because I wouldn't be crying for her. I'd only be crying for me, and that didn't seem fair. McKenna deserved the future she was heading toward—her dream of becoming a doctor finally starting. But her desire to escape this town and her mother hurt because it meant she was escaping me and my family as well—the people who'd loved and sheltered her.

Knowing it was coming hadn't eased the pain of its arrival. As much as I wanted to follow her, I couldn't. My life was here with my family, and the ranch, and my own dreams of serving my community. Even if everything at home had been perfectly fine, I wasn't sure I'd want to leave our small town for a place where you couldn't see the stars. Here, they were so bright it seemed like you could grab them, put them in your pocket, and take them with you. If I was forced to live in a city, I'd burn out just like those faraway suns. If you forced her to stay, she'd wither like the roses I'd given her last week. Dust into dust.

We loved each other more than I'd ever thought was possible, especially considering we were just two kids, barely legal. I knew her smiles and looks and moods better than she knew them herself, and vice versa. But this was where the road we were on finally divided after a decade of running side by side. A bitter taste rose inside me because I wasn't sure our roads would ever cross again.

"I'll come visit," I told her, breaking my mouth from hers. "Thanksgiving or spring break. Whichever works."

Could I get through to spring without seeing her? Touching her? Loving her? How would I even come up with the money for the trip?

She rested her forehead on my shoulder, placed a gentle kiss there, and then looked up at me with sad, tormented eyes.

"Maddox…between college, medical school, and a residency, it'll be at least eleven years before I'm done. I'll always be your friend. I'll always love you…but…I just…" A choked sob broke free from her, and my throat bobbed, eyes watering.

"You want to break up. You don't even want to try?" I asked, that bitterness coating my tongue and my mouth growing. She had choices. She could have applied to Tennessee State. She could have kept us closer, but even as I said it, I knew she couldn't. McKenna needed to put her childhood behind her…even if that meant giving me up along with it.

She put her hands on my cheeks, cupping them and kissing my lips sweetly.

"You're my favorite thing. My favorite memory. My favorite gift. My favorite person," she said quietly.

I could no longer hold the tears back. I didn't know how to let her go. But I'd have to because it wasn't always the cowboy who ran away.

Sometimes, it was the golden-haloed woman with a future so bright the gods had to be jealous.

That was my McKenna.

And tomorrow, she'd be gone.

No longer mine, but the world's instead.

Maddox

TEN YEARS LATER

The Moments You Were Mine

I pulled back just in time, letting the fist barely graze my chin. The movement was enough to send my Stetson flying, landing amongst the straw where it was going to get trampled. It was the sight of my hat on the ground that pissed me off more than the fist or Willy Tate's drunken, angry snarl as he lunged for me again.

I ducked the second shot and shoved my shoulder into his gut, taking him down to the ground with me. The music had stopped, the customers in the bar quiet as they watched two burly men wrestle. Several chairs were tipped over, tables were bumped, and drinks were spilled as we rolled around. It took me one too many moves before I finally had him pinned facedown with his hands behind his back and my knee holding him in place.

"Damn it, Willy, you owe me a new hat!" I growled.

Clapping filled the air along with hoots and hollers that made my eyes roll.

"Thanks for the show!" someone in the back yelled as someone else shouted out, "Brings me back to my sheep-tying days!"

"Thanks for the help, y'all," I said sarcastically, eyeing my brother sitting calmly on a stool at the bar with a crooked grin.

"Why, Sheriff Maddox, no one would ever presume to think you needed help." Ryder's grin grew, and then he had the audacity to wink at me as he raised a beer in my direction. I barely resisted flipping him the bird as laughter erupted from him, causing his blue eyes that matched mine to crinkle at the corners. He brushed a hand over his perfectly tousled dark-brown hair that should have been smashed flat after wearing a hat all day but instead looked like he'd stepped off the page of a damn magazine.

I was not anywhere near picture-perfect. My dark-blond hair was standing up in places, and the stubble on my chin—a day past trendy—was dripping and sticky from the whiskey Willy had thrown at me. The alcohol had stained my tan shirt, and our scuffle had snagged the ends of my olive-green tie, almost ripping it from my neck.

"She left me, Maddox. For a goddamn suit from Knoxville." Willy was crying now, and it almost looked ridiculous on the six-foot-three mechanic with the hair and beard of someone who'd been lost in the wild for one too many years.

"Taking it out on everyone here isn't going to make the pain go away, shithead," I grumbled. "You gonna start swinging again if I get up?"

Willy shook his head. I stood and then helped the man to his feet. His sad, puppy-dog eyes were full of tears that tumbled down his cheeks.

"You going to arrest him for hitting a lawman?" Gemma asked, trying not to giggle. My sister was sitting next to Ryder at the bar. Her long hair was the same color as mine, but her hazel eyes were full of our brother's laughter. Ryder tapped her elbow with his in appreciation of the taunt she'd thrown my way.

Willy hunched his enormous shoulders. "Fuck. I forgot you're the sheriff now."

"I've been an officer of the law for damn near six years, Willy. Hitting me before or after I'd been elected wouldn't change a damn thing." I leaned down and picked up my hat, brushing it against my thigh and shoving him toward the door of McFlannigan's. It was the only bar in town and normally looked as Irish as my uncle who owned the place, but on Thursdays, they had two-dollar beers, line dancing, and a live band. Uncle Phil brought hay in from the ranch to make it more *Tennessee barnyard* than *Dublin dive*.

I'd told him more than once the hay was a hazard, but as he was friends with the county health inspector, who just happened to be in one of the booths tonight with his wife, my uncle clearly didn't have to worry about being fined. That was the way everything in this town worked, and while I'd been able to turn a blind eye to some of it as a deputy, since I'd been elected, it had been harder to do.

The people of Winter County had put their trust in me. Maybe it was because Sheriff Haskett had thrown his hat in my direction when he'd stepped down, or maybe it was because the

Hatley family had been in Willow Creek since its inception. Regardless, they'd taken a chance on a green twenty-seven-year-old last year, and I'd spent twelve months proving to them it had been the right choice.

Willy and I were at the door when Ryder called out, "Going to come back and have a beer with us after you get him home?"

I shook my head.

"Come on, Maddox, one drink!" Gemma called.

I had no desire to sit at the bar, shooting the shit with my siblings, after the long day I'd had. If the bar hadn't been mere blocks from my house when the call had come in as I walked out the station door, I would've let one of my deputies handle the call. Now that I'd done my civic duty for the night, I had only one goal, and that was getting home to my girl.

I directed Willy into the passenger seat of my ancient green and rust-covered Bronco, wishing I'd driven my sheriff truck instead. But the Bronco had called to me this morning—the date dragging at me as it did every year.

The date I tried to ignore and failed miserably to do.

I got Willy tucked into the small apartment above the garage his family had owned almost as long as mine had owned the ranch and then headed to my 1950s-style bungalow two streets over. After three years of hard work, the house was pretty much how I wanted it. The wood siding had a fresh coat of pale-yellow paint, new black shutters edged the multi-paned windows, and a burnt-orange custom door invited you in, just like the swing tucked in the corner of the front porch.

An antique lamp on the hall table cast a gentle light onto the dark plank floors as I let myself in, and the murmur of the television in the open-space living area greeted me. Rianne looked up from the cushy, leather couch I'd spent a small fortune on as I hung my destroyed hat on the rack by the door.

Her bright-red lips curved upward in greeting, and her dark-brown face was just starting to show signs of wrinkles even though she was as old as my grandparents. Her black-and-white corkscrew hair was tucked beneath a vivid-blue scarf littered with pictures of baby ducks. She had so many head wraps I thought she could wear a different one every day of the year and still have more.

"How is she?" I asked.

"Like always. Pretending to sleep but really waiting for you," she said, turning off the TV and rising. She was wearing soft jeans and a long tunic top, looking far more casual than she ever had as my third-grade teacher. When I'd been a rowdy eight-year-old, I'd adored her, and now that she'd turned in her teacher badge and taken on helping me, I loved her almost as much as I loved my mama.

"You smell like a liquor cabinet." Rianne's nose squished up, but there was a smile on her lips.

I sighed, ran my hand over my half-assed, alcohol-soaked beard, and grimaced.

"Had to pull Willy out of McFlannigan's before he tore it apart."

Rianne's face fell. "Aw, he's taking the loss of his woman pretty hard."

I nodded. It was why I'd tucked him at home instead of locking him up in a cell at the station. I knew what it felt like to watch your woman drive away. The agony I'd felt didn't make me want to bleed out on the floor anymore, but the reminder on this day, more than any other, made the hurt tumble through me as if it had happened yesterday instead of a decade ago.

Rianne gathered her things, and I walked her to the door.

"Try to get some rest tomorrow, and I'll see you on Sunday," she said before leaving.

I was technically off the clock for a whole day, but that never meant much when you were one of only twelve people holding down the only law enforcement agency in the county. We didn't have a lot of crime in Willow Creek, but we did have a lot of work. On any given day, I might be helping round up stray chickens one moment and taking beer from underage kids at the lake the next. The biggest pain in my ass was the motorcycle club, The West Gears, who used their headquarters up in the mountains right at the county line to deal drugs and store stolen merchandise. The Gears were the reason I was dead on my feet tonight after a day of hunting them down.

I headed down the hall, feet stalling as I passed Mila's door. She'd expect me to crawl into bed with her, and I didn't want to do that smelling like whiskey, so I continued on to the one room I hadn't let Mama or my sisters help decorate. Instead, the main bedroom reflected me like almost no other part of the house. It was full of dark woods, navy linens, and black-and-white photographs of the lake and the ranch.

I locked my weapon away in the gun safe, showered in the bathroom filled with teak woods and blue linens, and then changed into sweats and a long-sleeve T-shirt before padding on bare feet back to Mila's room. I turned the knob as quietly as possible in a vain hope that she might actually be asleep but chuckled to myself when I saw her dart her head under the covers.

Her room looked like a rainbow had thrown up in it. She was obsessed with them. She'd even convinced me to paint her white headboard in rainbow stripes. Between that, her four pastel-colored nightlights, and the pile of stuffed unicorns that filled an armchair in the corner, it felt like walking into a cartoon world. I crossed the faux-fur white rug and stood looking down at the rainbow comforter that shed glitter like it was a cat changing seasons.

"Oh good, Mila is asleep. I don't have to read *The Day the Unicorns Saved the World* for the one-thousandth time," I said softly.

The covers were thrown back, and beautiful wheat-colored eyes stared at me under thick brows that were almost black and contrasted with the honey-blonde hair spiraling in waves around her round face. "I'm not sleeping, Daddy! You *have* to read it, or I'll be up all night."

There was a little whine to her sweet voice and a pout to her lips that made my mouth twitch. I sighed dramatically, looked up at the ceiling, and pretended to contemplate the fate of my life before pulling the book from her nightstand.

"Scootch over," I said as if this wasn't our nightly routine.

She pulled back her covers and moved to the side as I slid in with her. Her tiny, five-year-old body curled up against me, and I put one arm around her, holding her tight. She smelled like the berry shampoo Mama had bought for her birthday, and she had on a pair of fuzzy, pink-striped pajamas that had been from my sister. Her body was warm and her tiny hand soft as she placed it on my arm. My heart filled to near bursting just by having her there.

"How was your day?" I asked.

"I learned that the letter L says *lllll* like in lion, and that five and two more is seven. Seven is my birthday number, so Mrs. Randall let me use the butterfly pointer and lead the class in the alphabet song."

Kindergarten. My baby had started kindergarten at the end of August. I hadn't expected it to be as hard as it had been to drop her off at school and walk away. I mean, I'd been leaving her every day for the four years of her life that she'd been mine. But there was something different about leaving her with Rianne versus taking her into a classroom full of kids who I couldn't guarantee would be nice and adults who were strangers. I'd run the name of the principal and every teacher at the school to make sure there weren't any scumbags hiding in the system, even when I knew the state wouldn't have given certificates to criminals. I'd sort of gone off my rocker for a day or two. The only thing that made it easier was knowing Mila liked being there.

"That sounds like a really good day," I told her.

"Yeah. But Missy wouldn't give me a turn with the hula hoop." She pouted, and every vein in my body tightened. The need to protect her, even from other five-year-olds, was a strange sensation. There was a time in my life when I hadn't wanted to be a dad, when I'd promised another blonde-haired girl that we wouldn't have kids because she was adamantly opposed to having them.

"I'll buy you your own damn hula hoop tomorrow," I told her, voice gruff with emotions. She giggled.

"You cussed again, Daddy. You owe me another dollar for the cuss jar."

I smiled with my lips against her hair. She'd have enough money in that jar to go to college if I wasn't careful. The thought of her being grown up and going away to college threatened to rip some more at the scars that had already cracked open today.

I pushed the pain away, opened the book, and started reading as my girl snuggled deeper into my chest. My heart expanded until it was quadruple the size it should have been. This was perfect. I didn't need anything else in my life but this.

KEEP READING *THE LAST ONE YOU LOVED* FREE IN KINDLE UNLIMITED

Keep tabs on the next **RIVERS SERIES** book with Maisey and Beckett by subscribing to my newsletter.

Or following me in any of these locations:

@ljevansbooks

About the Book

Just a few quick notes to clarify things in this book.

The crash of Fallon's Cessna Skylane took a bit of creative license. It's doubtful it would have happened in quite that fashion, but it was much more fun this way. I hope that scene had your heart pounding like I'd intended.

When I was looking into ways for prisoners to escape, I came across a story from just this year where a prisoner had gotten out by pretending to be another prisoner who was being released. I was surprised that in our age of technology, facial recognition, and DNA testing that it could still happen, but apparently, it does. Enjoy going down the same rabbit hole as I did looking it all up. 😊

And yes, just like the town of Rivers is made up, the Silver One Squadron SEAL team and the Laguna Heights National Park in San Diego are both made up as well. Thank goodness for creative license and fictional worlds.

If you're interested in the Easter eggs I dropped about Jim Steele's SEAL buddy Nash and the legendary country artist Brady O'Neil, check out my *Anchor Novels*.

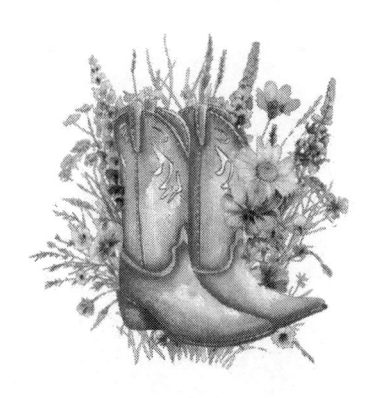

Acknowledgements

I'm so very grateful for every single person who has helped me on this book journey. If you're reading these words, you are one of those people. I wouldn't be an author if people like you didn't decide to read the stories I crafted, so THANK YOU!

In addition to my lovely readers, I need to acknowledge these people:

My husband, who never ever lets me give up on myself, even when the battles seem endless. Your sacrifice, your strength, your laughter is what gets me through the dark, guiding me home. Thanks for pushing me to take the next big gamble!

Our child, Evyn, owner of Lycanthrope Media, who remains my harshest and kindest critic. Thank you for helping me create my stories and driving me to be a better human. Love you, kiddo.

My parents, sister, and in-laws who listen to me gripe about publishing and then cheer me on as if I'm the greatest writer on earth. Thank you for making me feel loved and valid every single day.

My talented author friend, Aly Stiles, who read the beginning of this story and told me exactly what was missing. Fallon and Parker's beginning wouldn't be the same without you, thank you for your honesty and friendship.

My beautiful author friends, including my daily hype friends Stephanie Rose and Kathryn Nolan along with Erika Kelly, Lucy Score, Hannah Blake, Maria Luis, Annie Dyer, Alexandra Hale, and AM Johnson, thank you for proving to me over and over that my worth can't be found in a series of algorithmic numbers.

Katelyn and Kala at Calli, whose enthusiasm actually made me excited for a book launch for the first time in years, you were truly a gift this summer.

Jenn at Jenn Lockwood Editing Services, Karen Hrdlicka of Barren Acres Editing, and Stephanie Feissner, who have been on this journey with me since nearly the beginning and continue to have faith in me no matter how ridiculous my mistakes become. Your edits and proofs are always the perfect polish that my words need.

The entire group of beautiful humans in LJ's Music & Stories who love and support me. I can't say enough how deeply grateful I am for each and every one of you. Thanks for celebrating Taylor Swift, National Days, and books with me.

To the host of bloggers who have shared my stories, become dear friends, and continue to make me feel like a rock star every day, especially

Michelle at Brayzen Bookwrym and Lindsey at romance_book_affair who go over and above to share my stories almost every single day. Thank you, thank you, thank you!

All my ARC readers, who have become sweet friends and true supporters, thank you for knowing just what to say to scare away my writer insecurities.

Leisa C., Rachel R., and Stephanie F. Thank you beyond words for being the biggest cheerleaders, partners, and friends I could ever hope to have on this wild ride called life.

I love you all!

About the Author

Award-winning author LJ Evans lives in Northern California with her husband, child, and the three terrors called cats. She's written compulsively since she was a little girl, often getting derailed from what she should be doing by a song lyric that sends her scrambling to jot a scene down.

A former first-grade teacher, she now spends her days deep in the pages of romance and mystery with a bit of the otherworldly thrown in. Her favorite characters are those who live resiliently—stubbornly and triumphantly getting through this wild ride called life with hope, love, and found families guiding the way.

Her novels have won multiple industry awards, including ***CHARMING AND THE CHERRY BLOSSOM,*** which was Writer's Digest's Self-Published E-book Romance of the Year.

For more information about LJ, check out any of these sites:

www.ljevansbooks.com

Facebook Group: LJ's Music & Stories
LJ Evans on Amazon, Bookbub, and Goodreads
@ljevansbooks on Facebook, Instagram, TikTok, and Pinterest

Books by LJ

Standalone

After All the Wreckage — Rory & Gage
A single-dad, small-town, romantic suspense
He's a broody bar owner raising his siblings. She's a scrappy PI who loved him when they were teens. When his brother disappears, she faces deadly family secrets to help him.

Charming and the Cherry Blossom — Elle & Hudson
A small-town, he-falls-first, contemporary romance
Today was a fairy tale…I inherited a fortune from a dad I never knew, and a thoroughly charming guy asked me out. But like all fairy tales, mine has a dark side…and my happily ever after may disappear with the truth.

Lost in the Moonlight — Lincoln & Willow
A grumpy-sunshine, small-town, romantic suspense
My new neighbor is all too enticing, but I have one job—to stay hidden—and the media's fascination with Lincoln can destroy my safe haven. So why can't I stay away?

The Moments You Were Mine — Fallon & Parker
A single-dad, bodyguard, small-town, romantic suspense
When the woman I grew up loving is threatened, I'll do anything to keep her safe, even break the oath I made to never make her mine.

The Hatley Family Standalones

The Last One You Loved — Maddox & McKenna
A single-dad, grumpy-sheriff, romantic suspense
He's a small-town sheriff with a secret that can unravel their worlds. She's an ER resident running from a costly mistake. Coming home will only mean heartache…unless they let forgiveness heal them both.

The Last Promise You Made — Ryder & Gia

A single-dad, grumpy-cowboy, romantic suspense

He's a grumpy rancher who swore off all relationships. She's a spitfire undercover agent who brings danger to his life. Desire is an inconvenience. Falling in love is absolutely out of the question...

The Last Dance You Saved — Sadie & Rafe

A single-dad, grumpy-cowboy, romantic suspense

Sadie's world is disrupted by a grumpy cowboy who thought he'd left the ranch and relationships behind for good. When danger finds them and he tries to send her away, she proves that with love at stake, she's willing to risk it all.

Perfectly Fine — Gemma & Rex

A fish-out-of-water, celebrity romance

He's a charming, A-list actor at the top of his game. She's a determined, small-town screenwriter hoping for a deal. They form an unexpected connection until heartbreak ruins their future. Available on Amazon and also FREE with newsletter subscription.

The Anchor Novels

Guarded Dreams — Eli & Ava

A grumpy-sunshine, forced-proximity, military romance

He's a grumpy Coast Guard focused on a life of service. She's a feisty musician searching for stardom. Nothing about them fits, and yet attraction burns when fate lands them in the same house for the summer.

Forged by Sacrifice — Mac & Georgie

A roommates-to-lovers, second-chance, military romance

He's a driven military man zeroed in on a new goal. She's a struggling law student running from her family's mistakes. Nothing about them fits until one unforgettable kiss threatens their roommate status and their plans along with it.

Avenged by Love — Truck & Jersey

A fake-marriage, forced-proximity, military romance

When a broody military man and a quiet bookstore clerk share a house, more than attraction flares. Watching her suffer in silence has him extending her the only help he can—a marriage of convenience to give her the insurance she needs.

Damaged Desires — Dani & Nash

A frenemy, bodyguard, military romance

Reeling from losing his team, a growly Navy SEAL battles an attraction for his best friend's fiery sister, until a stalker puts her in his sights. Now he'll do anything to protect her, even take her to the one place he swore he'd never go—home.

Branded by a Song — Brady & Tristan

A single-mom, small-town, rock-star romance

He's a country rock legend searching for inspiration. She's a Navy SEAL's widow determined to honor his memory. Neither believes the attraction tugging at them can lead to more until her grandmother's will twines their futures.

Tripped by Love – Cassidy & Marco

A bodyguard, single-mom, small-town romance

She's a busy single mom with a restaurant to run, and he's her brother's bodyguard with a checkered past. They're just friends until a little white lie changes everything.

The Anchor Novels: The Military Bros Box Set

The 1st three books + an exclusive novella

Guarded Dreams, Forged by Sacrifice, and *Avenged by Love* plus the novella, *The Hurricane*! Heartfelt military romance with love, sacrifice, and found families. The perfect book-boyfriend binge-read.

The Anchor Suspense Novels

Unmasked Dreams — Violet & Dawson

A friends-to-lovers, forced-proximity romantic suspense

As teens, they had a sizzling attraction they denied. Years later, they're stuck in the same house and discover nothing has changed—except the lab she's built in the garage and the secrets he's keeping. When she stumbles into his covert op, Dawson breaks old promises to keep her safe. But once he's touched her, will he be able to let her go?

Crossed by the Stars — Jada & Dax

A frenemies-to-lovers, forced-proximity romantic suspense

Family secrets meant Dax and Jada's teenage romance was an impossibility. A decade later, the scars still prevent them from acknowledging their tantalizing chemistry. But when a shadow creeps out of Jada's past, it's Dax who shows up to protect her. And suddenly, it's hard to remember exactly why they don't belong.

Disguised as Love — Cruz & Raisa

An enemies-to-lovers, forced-proximity romantic suspense

Cruz Malone is determined to bring down the Leskov clan for good. If he has to arrest—or bed—the sexy blonde scientist of the family to make it happen, so be it. But there's no way Raisa is just going to sit back and let the infuriating agent dismantle her world…or her heart.

The Painted Daisies

Interconnected series with an all-female rock band, the alpha heroes who steal their hearts, and suspense that will leave you breathless. Each story has its own HEA.

Swan River — *The Painted Daisies* Prequel

A rock-star, small-town, romantic suspense cliffhanger

The Painted Daisies are more than a band. They're a beloved family. With their star on the rise, life seems perfect until darkness strikes. When the group's trouble points to the band members' various secrets, it'll take strength and perseverance to unravel the mystery. Available on Amazon and also FREE with newsletter subscription.

Sweet Memory — Paisley & Jonas

An opposing-worlds, friends-to-lovers romance

The world's sweetest rock star falls for a troubled music producer whose past comes back to haunt them.

Green Jewel — Fiadh & Asher

An enemies-to-lovers, single-dad romance

Snowed in with the enemy is the perfect time to prove he was behind her friend's murder. She'll just have to ignore her body's reaction to him to do it.

Cherry Brandy — Leya & Holden
A forced-proximity, bodyguard romance

Being on the run with only one bed is no excuse to touch her…until touching is the only choice.

Blue Marguerite — Adria & Ronan
A celebrity, second-chance, frenemy romance

She vowed to never forgive him! But when he offers answers her family desperately seeks and protects her from the latest threat to the band, her resolve starts to crumble.

Royal Haze — Nikki & D'Angelo
A bodyguard, on-the-run romance with a morally gray hero

He was ready to torture, steal, and kill to defend the world he believed in. What he wasn't prepared for…was her.

My Life as an Album Series

My Life as a Country Album — Cam's Story
A boy-next-door, small-town romance

A first-love heartbreaker. What happens when you've pined your whole life for the football hero next door, and he finally, finally notices you? You vow to love him forever until fate comes calling and threatens to take it all away.

My Life as a Pop Album — Mia & Derek
A rock-star, road-trip romance

Bookworm Mia attempts to put behind years of guilt by taking a chance on a once-in-a-lifetime, road-trip adventure with a soulful musician. But what will happen to the heart Derek steals when their time together is over?

My Life as a Rock Album — Seth & PJ
A second-chance, antihero romance

Trash artist Seth Carmen knows he deserves to be alone. But when he finds and loses the love of his life, he still can't help sending her love letters to try to win her back. Can he prove to her they can make broken beautiful?

My Life as a Mixtape — Lonnie & Wynn

A single-dad, small-town, rock-star romance

Lonnie has always seen relationships as a burden instead of a gift, and picking up the pieces his sister leaves behind is just one of the reasons. When Wynn offers him friendship and help in caring for his young niece, he never expects love to bloom or the second chance at life they're all given.

My Life as a Holiday Album – 2nd Generation

A small-town romance

Come home for the holidays with this heartwarming, full-length standalone full of hidden secrets, true love, and the real meaning of family. Perfect for lovers of *Love Actually* and Hallmark movies, this steamy story intertwines the lives of six couples as they find their way to their happily ever afters with the help of family and friends.

My Life as an Album Series Box Set

The 1st four Album series stories plus an exclusive novella

In *This Life with Cam*, Blake Abbott writes to Cam about what it was like to grow up in the shadow of her relationship with Jake and just when he first fell for the little girl with the popsicle-stained lips. Can he prove to Cam that she isn't broken?

Free Stories

Get these novellas, flash fiction stories, + bonus epilogues for **FREE with a newsletter subscription at:**

https://geni.us/AJFree

Perfectly Fine — A fish-out-of-water, celebrity romance

He's a charming, A-list actor at the top of his game. She's a determined, small-town screenwriter hoping for a deal. They form an unexpected connection until heartbreak ruins their future. Also available on Amazon.

Swan River — A rock star, romantic suspense *prequel*

The Painted Daisies are more than a band. They're a beloved family. With their star on the rise, life seems perfect until darkness strikes. When the group's trouble points to the band members' various secrets, it'll take strength and perseverance to unravel the mystery. Also available on Amazon.

Rumor — A small-town, rock-star romance

There's only one thing rock star Chase Legend needs to ring in the new year, and that's to know what Reyna Rossi tastes like. After ten years, there's no way he's letting her escape the night without their souls touching. Reyna has other plans. After all, she doesn't need the entire town wagging their tongues about her any more than they already do.

Love Ain't — A friends-to-lovers, cowboy romance

Reese knows her best friend and rodeo king, Dalton Abbott, is never going to fall in love, get married, and have kids. He's left so many broken hearts behind that there's gotta be a museum full of them somewhere. So when he gives her a look from under the brim of his hat, promising both jagged relief and pain, she knows better than to give in.

The Long Con — A sexy, antihero romance

Adler is after one thing: the next big payday. Then, Brielle sways into his world with her own game in play, and those aquamarine-colored eyes almost make him forget his number-one rule. But she'll learn—love isn't a con he's interested in.

The Light Princess — An old-fashioned fairy tale

A princess who glows with a magical light, a kingdom at war, and a kiss that changes the world. This is an extended version of the fairy tale twined through the pages of *Charming and the Cherry Blossom*.

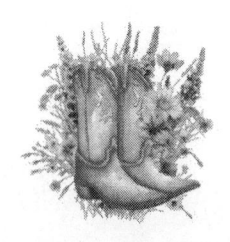